PRAISE FOR *IGNORING GRAVITY*:

"This contemporary tale of sisterhood and identity is immediately engrossing. Sandra Danby writes with great empathy and wit." Shelley Weiner, author of *The Audacious Mendacity of Lily Green*

"What really sets this novel apart is the author's descriptive skill. By tackling the ever popular themes of adoption and infertility, Sandra Danby's *Ignoring Gravity* is mining a rich vein in women's fiction and is bound to appeal. But her take on these painful subjects is somewhat original and her story has an unexpected twist in the tail." Jane Cable, author of *The Cheesemaker's House*

"Drama? Check. Suspense? Check. Romance? Check. Will-they-won't-they? Check. Great twists? Check, check, check! I am pleased to say this story has them all and then some." Kerry Burnett, *Kerry's Reviews Blog*

"Did I like *Ignoring Gravity*? I loved it!" Michelle Clements James, *Book Chat*

IGNORING GRAVITY

Sandra Danby

b

ISBN-13: 978-0-9931134-1-3

First published in the UK by Beulah Press 2014

This novel is entirely a work of fiction and, except in the case of historical fact, any resemblance to actual persons, living or dead, events or localities, is entirely coincidental.

For Mum and Dad, always

1 PROLOGUE 1968

There was a sharp slap followed by a cry. The sound of an animal echoed in my ears and my soul and my empty womb and didn't fade.

'4lb 3oz. Girl. Write it in the Statement Book, then take it away.'

2 THIRTY-FIVE YEARS LATER: ROSE

Someone took her by the arm, forcing her to sit down. Breath warmed her cheek. She was icy all over. She could see nothing, nothing except one word written in the diary.

Adopt.

Suddenly pain, starting at her cheek and spreading through her head. Again, and again. Each slap beat that word deeper into her unconscious.

Adopt.

Rose Haldane fell off the edge of the world.

Three days earlier, it was 10 a.m. on Thursday morning and Rose was sitting on a sofa the size of a generous double bed. Black, low, leather, polished steel feet, it was positioned on one side of a glass coffee table bigger than her kitchen. Opposite was a black-leather swivel chair that screamed 'executive.' She sat on the sofa gingerly, lowering her bottom until, just as she expected to hit the floor, she sank into the sumptuous cushions.

'He'll be at least ten or fifteen minutes,' his PA

Amanda had said when she showed Rose into the room, using the tone that meant, 'he's very important and you're not.'

The room was silent, the air still, no movement except for her chest, which she realised was heaving up and down as if she'd run up the thirty flights of stairs instead of taking the glass-and-steel bullet lift. This had happened only once before, at a big interview. Nerves. She touched her cheeks. Burning.

Do something, she told herself. *Yoga.*

She lay backwards on the sofa as if it were a bed, her head touching the wall behind her, her legs stretched out in front. Ignoring her pulse, she breathed deeply.

In, out. In, out.

She focussed on the questions she was going to ask, her eyes closing as she concentrated…

3 NICK

Nick Maddox, managing director of Biocare Beauty, was sitting at his desk, thinking about face cream. In particular, the failure of the bottling machinery at the Scottish factory that manufactured his best-selling Natura-Refresha Night Flower serum. Should he shift production to Devon? Or cross his fingers that the machines would be fixed in time to fulfil his export order to France next week?

At that thought, he leant back in his chair and allowed himself a small smile of achievement. *Me, exporting face creams to France. It's like selling an English striker to a Brazilian football club.*

Having decided to trust the Scots, his mind shifted to the press interview with a financial journalist that was due to start – he glanced at his watch – five minutes ago. He sighed. It was the last in a schedule of PR interviews about his management buyout of the company. This was his least favourite part of the job, talking City talk with business journalists wearing expensive suits and carrying all the latest techie gadgets while examining his desk for similar gadgets, and who were sure they knew more about face creams than he did.

4 ROSE

'Miss Haldane?'

Rose sat bolt upright and stopped breathing. Her notepad and pens scattered across the smooth grey slate floor, coming to a stop beside a pair of well-polished black shoes.

She looked up. A neat man with cropped pale-blonde hair stood in the open doorway. His lips twitched, Rose was unsure whether with disdain or amusement. Neither was the response she wanted to provoke.

'Sorry to keep you waiting. I'm Nick Maddox.' He bent down to retrieve her stationery, placed it on the coffee table in front of her, then sat down in the Mastermind-style chair and looked at her.

She sat up straighter and tugged at what she now realised, given the depth of the sofa, was an unsuitably short skirt. Her mother would have disapproved.

'I'm Rose Haldane, from the *Herald*, but of course you know that. Thanks for the opportunity to interview you, it's…' she couldn't think of the right adjective, '…good of you.'

He looked at her, one eyebrow slightly raised.

She tried to shuffle her bottom into a more comfortable position without seeming to fidget or nudging the hem of her skirt even higher.

'So, so... shall we start? Tell me... what's it like being your own boss?' *Rubbish, Rose. What a predictable opening question to ask an MD who liked the company so much he bought it.* To gain a little time, and to avoid looking at him, she opened her shorthand notepad.

When he didn't answer, she looked up. He was staring at her like a university professor waiting for her to provide an answer he knew she didn't know.

'You know, being in control of your own destiny? Making your own history?' *Shut up, Rose.* Journalism rule number one: don't put words into his mouth.

'Destiny?' He leant back in the swivel chair. 'That's an interesting word.'

Boy, is he confident. Arrogant. She hated arrogant men.

'I wouldn't say I'm in charge, the bank is. I just have a new boss.' His voice was strong, as if he were answering questions he expected to be asked. Every now and then he glanced down at a paper in the folder he'd laid open on the coffee table. A briefing paper supplied by his PR, she guessed, a list of predictable questions and answers. His smile just about reached the edges of his mouth but fell short of his eyes.

Politeness guarantees boring copy. Journalism rule number two: if in danger of boredom, use shock tactics. 'You're very modest for a man who's just completed a £50 million MBO. You've upped your salary and bonus to seven figures. What will you do with the cash? Buy a yacht?'

Too much. She waited, wondering if she'd blown it.

When he spoke, he was so quiet she had to lean forward to catch his words.

'You shouldn't believe all you read in the papers.' His smile tightened.

Ooh, he's hiding something. 'I don't, that was in the disclosure documents provided by your merchant bank.' This was one of the things she'd read online before leaving the office. She was subbing for a sick reporter so there'd been no time for proper preparation, no time to buy a pot of Biocare Beauty's top-selling face cream and try it at home.

'Right.'

Rose watched the displeasure tighten across his cheeks. *Perhaps now he'll stop treating me like some unqualified reporter on* Back-of-Beyond-Gazette. True, her first job was for the *Littlethorpe Mercury,* but she'd worked her way up to the *London Herald* and had interviewed people far more intimidating than Mr Nick Maddox. So she held eye contact as he studied her, determined not to flinch. Most people she interviewed wouldn't look her in the eye.

Journalism rule number three: think, say, feel, do. Was Maddox saying one thing and thinking another? Many people did, the trick was to unlock the puzzle.

His eyes narrowed slightly, then he smiled without warning. It lit up his face, and she forgot to wonder what he was thinking. 'You have done your homework. That's refreshing. I'm tired of journalists who research online and think they're instant experts on my company. It's insulting.'

Why is he being nice?

He turned in his chair. 'Look at them.' He pointed to the people sitting at desks in the open-plan

9

area on the other side of the tinted glass partition. 'They made it happen, not me...'

While he talked, Rose noticed his hands. Light golden skin with long fingers suited to playing piano octaves. She found herself wondering how it would feel to be touched by those hands, and was horrified to realise she hadn't heard a word of what he'd just said. She nodded and stared down at her pad, her face hot. Carefully, she wrote the shorthand symbol for 'Maddox'.

'...banks are only interested in cash flow, covenants and the bottom line, they want their repayments. The bank doesn't care if I make face creams or screwdrivers.'

'So, now you can enjoy running your company.' Her eyes were still fixed on her notes. *Wrong again, Rose.* Journalism rule number four: statements are not questions.

'I've always enjoyed it, and it's not strictly speaking *my* company. The MBO is the beginning, not the end. You wouldn't believe...' His sentence ground to a halt and he slowly took a sip of water. 'No, I shouldn't tell you that. You're a journalist,' he spoke softly, as if to himself.

Hell yes, I am a journalist. Irritating man. Why did he start a sentence that sounded juicy, only to stop halfway through? She'd expected him to be media-savvy but things weren't going well. First, his PA refused to admit her because she wasn't Alan Smart, the slick, sick journo she was subbing for. Anyone less than Alan Smart, who regularly featured on *BBC Business News*, would be a waste of her boss's time, the PA implied with a glance down her aquiline nose. Then, there was the lying down on the sofa thing. Her cheeks had only just cooled from that blush when she caught Maddox trying to read her shorthand notes upside down. She offered the notepad to him, but he refused without a flush of shame. The chemistry hadn't recovered.

She put down her pen. 'Look, if you want to tell me something that's off the record, that's fine.' She adjusted her face into a no-compromise look. 'It's fine as long as you say so now, before you start talking. I won't quote you until you say it's okay. We can go back on the record later. But you can't decide after the interview that some bits are on the record and other bits are off. I don't work like that.'

She held her breath.

He swivelled in his chair, his eyes fixed on her. 'Sounds fair.'

She exhaled and smoothed her hands over her skirt to hide their trembling.

He called for more coffee. Rose watched Amanda's procedure with cups, milk, sugar, and chocolate digestives without a word. *She loves him, maybe not romantically, but she'd throw me out of the window if she had to. What is it about him that inspires such loyalty? Perhaps Amanda likes his golden hands too.*

He talked for half an hour without pause, at the end of which she could see glimmers of the real man sitting in the black leather chair.

Ask him something personal now. The barriers are down, ask him…

But his mobile rang and he excused himself to answer it. Rose glanced at her watch. Jim, the photographer, was due in five minutes.

'I'm sorry, that was a call I had to take. Shall we continue?' Maddox was playing with a black fountain pen and studying her legs.

She sat up straight with her knees pressed together. She wished her mother could have seen her ladylike posture.

Maddox didn't hurry his appraisal of her legs, and when his eyes rose to meet hers, they showed no embarrassment at being caught out. *Damn him.* To her dismay, Rose felt her cheeks grow hot again. She wasn't ashamed or embarrassed or angry. *It's just a bodily reaction beyond my conscious control.* That was how her father had explained it to her when she was five and blushed every five minutes. 'The blood vessels in your skin get bigger to let the hot blood reach the surface so your body temperature is balanced,' he'd said.

Where is Jim, for God's sake?

Maddox poured water into two glasses, watching her discomfort with obvious amusement. Rose clenched her teeth and stuck her tongue in her cheek to prevent it forming the words that her mouth wanted to unleash. Arrogant, pompous, self-important... *I didn't say that aloud, did I?*

'Are we finished here?'

'Almost. We just need to take the photograph.'

'Right.' He was looking at her knees again.

What a creep. When would she stop being attracted to the same type: gift-of-the-gab salesmen who sold themselves as energetically as they flogged advertising space and houses and... face creams? *Does he give all his female employees this treatment? Shut up before you say something you'll regret.* She stuck her tongue back in her cheek again. *Come on, Jim.*

'Did you know that the phrase 'cheeky' means tongue-in-cheek?'

What? Can he see inside my mouth now?

'Er, no.' Her face grew hotter.

'The Victorians thought it was rude to show your cheek in this way. They were the first people to tell children off for being cheeky.'

'Really?' *How does he know stuff like that? He must be making it up.*

She tweaked her blouse, which was clinging to her breasts, then sensed him watching her. Instantly, her nipples hardened. *Oh shit!* She took a deep breath and folded her arms over her breasts. *Take control. Say something, quickly. Before he does.*

'So, how long have you been at the *Herald*? Do you enjoy it?'

Too late. Now he's making polite conversation.

'I love it.' *Liar, that sounds so insincere. It is insincere.*

He raised his left eyebrow. 'Really?'

He said 'really' as if she'd said she'd always wanted to be an exotic dancer. Feeling the flush building again, her eyes dropped to her hands and she babbled about university, work experience, and the farming magazine she'd worked on before breaking into local newspapers. The school nativities, council meetings, obituaries, police briefings. Then the job at the *Herald* and her flat in Wimbledon and–

At last... Jim shuffled into the office, laden with camera gear.

Rose stifled a sigh of relief and ran a hand over her brow. Her face was burning.

Thirty minutes later, Maddox shook her hand.

His grasp was firm, his palm cool and dry, his fingernails neatly clipped and filed.

'Anything you need to ask, facts you need to check, just email me or give me a call. Amanda will put you straight through.'

You bet she will. 'Thanks.' Rose's eyes were magnetically attracted to the philtrum connecting his nose and upper lip in a line like a dot-to-dot picture. It was deep and dark, with a hint of afternoon stubble, and she wanted to run her finger along it.

'Here's my mobile number.'

She took his business card without touching his fingers, and shoved it in her pocket. *Did he see me staring?*

He held the door open for her. 'I'll be glad to help, anytime.' His voice dropped low on the last word. Then he turned into his office and the door closed. Amanda didn't get up from her desk but simply pointed towards the lift in the lobby. Rose smiled at her graciously. It was always worth keeping the secretaries on-side, but she'd need a blow torch to thaw this one.

Outside, she lingered on the pavement and looked up at the top floor of the glass-and-steel building, trying to work out which was Maddox's office. A shadow flitted across one panoramic window. She ducked behind the bus shelter. After waiting for what seemed like ages, she sneaked another look.

The shadow was still there, an arm lifted in a wave.

Oh. My. God.

Rose tucked her chin to her chest and walked away very fast.

5 NICK

He stood with his nose pressed to the window, his breath misting the glass, watching her disappear. Knowing he would never see her again, knowing he shouldn't want to see her again.

'Can you sign these?'

Amanda's words made him jump. She had entered his office silently and was standing close behind him. Too close. Sometimes he suspected her of creeping. He took the folder and signed the documents without reading them, like he had a million times before.

He waited until the door closed, then went to the window again. She'd gone. What was it about her that drew him to her? She was a journalist, a type he avoided on principle, but... there was a vulnerability beneath the efficiency which attracted him. And her eyes, blue... almost aquamarine.

A knock at the door and he jumped again, startled from his reverie by a line of people filing into his office. The finance team. Within moments, he was absorbed in packaging costs, and forgot all about Rose Haldane.

6 ROSE

Until she started her training as a journalist, Rose
Haldane hadn't realised one of the key skills required
was the ability to bullshit.

If you knew nothing about your subject matter,
you just had to do it. Hopeless at bullshitting and
equally terrified of writing nonsense, Rose faced each
new assignment as if preparing to appear on *The Money
Programme*. Consequently, she bungee-jumped off a
crane tied to the mayor of Littlethorpe to publicise
Public Safety in Kent Week, then wrote about whiplash
while wearing a neck collar. For two weeks, she lived on
maple syrup and water, supplemented by copious
amounts of disallowed toast, and illustrated the finished
feature with before-and-after photos demonstrating the
reduction in the size of her bottom. This feature attracted
quite a few letters to the editor, and one blind date,
which had been disastrous.

Many years later, she joined the *London Herald*
as a health reporter. She worked in a skyscraper at
Canary Wharf, not a grey warehouse on a shabby
industrial estate in the flat, grey world of North Kent.
But she felt stuck.

Since the first-ever story of hers ever published
– about a dog that had been run over – she'd scored each
article out of ten. She was still waiting for that elusive

Tenner – the ten out of ten feature she was convinced would change her life. She knew pretty much what the score of each feature would be before she typed 'end'. She needed a Tenner to get away from the *Herald*.

She worked on her Maddox notes for two hours, then wrote him a quick email asking a few extra questions. She debated how to sign off the message – best wishes, regards, kind regards. She eventually settled on, 'Thanks, Rose'. She sent it, logged off for the night, and reached for the tiny blue bottle of soothing eye drops that someone had sent in for a feature. Her head was tipped back against her chair, one hand pulling her lower eyelid down, the other trying to aim the bottle in the right direction.

'Rosie, love.'

She jumped as if electrocuted. Sam was leaning over her shoulder, breathing evidence of his mid-afternoon cheddar-and-onion sandwich into her face and making her gag. She made a creditable attempt at covering up the retching as a coughing fit, her hands over her mouth, pinching her nostrils.

'There you go, Rosie, clear out your pipes.' He patted her on the back.

She flinched at the bastardisation of her name. There were hundreds of varieties of roses and some days Rose certainly didn't feel like she merited the association, though she preferred the name to Rosemary. 'I'm a flower, not a herb,' had been her standard retort as a child.

Sam called her every derivative, every bastardisation, including Roz, Rosa, and once even Rosalind, Shakespeare's heroine. This insulted Rose the most; she preferred Beatrice's wit. 'Rosalind,' she'd once written in a sixth-form essay, 'was rather wet.' Her teacher had scrawled across the bottom in green ink: 'Subjective. Prove it. Facts, not assumption.'

That was the day Rose became obsessed with facts. That was why she was so hopeless at bullshitting. And though she would deny having anything in common with Sam, her dedication to facts placed her firmly alongside him in the old-school journalism camp. Fleet Street hackism, not Canary Wharf soundbite-journalism. Sam was a builder's tea journalist, not an espresso one. He hated adjectives, and he hated working in Docklands. The arse of London, he called it. He used the word 'arse' a lot. 'Get your arse in gear and do what you're told. Work your arse off and you and me'll get on just fine,' he said to Rose on her first day. Only the thought of the mortgage on her lovely flat stopped her shouting back at him, that and the sensible voice in her head, which told her to be a sponge and soak it up. Working in London fattened her CV.

'Rosie, love. Fertility. Eight hundred words. I want it straight after you've finished that eye-strain feature.' Sam dropped a briefing paper on her desk on top of her half-eaten banana.

Rose, who believed children should be served lightly grilled with a green salad, did not feel fertility was her natural territory.

'Please Sam, can't someone else write it? Someone who…'

'No.'

'…likes children.'

'No.'

'Someone who can empathise...'

'No.'

'... with their pain at being childless.'

'You're a journalist, Rosa, aren't you? Your job is to empathise when necessary, disassociate when necessary. Get your arse in gear, be an instant expert.' He prodded a sticky finger at the briefing paper. 'Male fertility. There's a new report that says infertility is more the bloke's problem than the woman's now.'

Rose shut her mouth, unable to object to writing a story about male fertility.

'Lead is a problem, so plumbers and painters need to be careful. Generally, the theme is that as the biological clock ticks, sperm motility drops.'

Frank, the features writer who sat at the next desk, winked at her over the top of the dividing screen.

'Then a list of the obvious, you know, boxers versus Y-fronts, smoking, drugs.'

'Right,' said Rose. 'Boxer shorts. Plumbers and painters.' She tried to make her eyes twinkle, she couldn't tell if it worked, but the corners of his mouth twitched.

She logged back on and considered fertility. Early crocuses peeping through grass. The call of the first cuckoo quickly followed by the thud of tiny chicks being tossed out of their nest. Tins of baked beans on the altar at Harvest Festival. Season of mists and mellow fruitfulness, leaves on the line.

The telephone rang.

'Oh, Rose.' It was her younger sister, Lily.

'I ate a piece of toast with marmalade and Marmite for breakfast this morning.'

'Er, why?'

'Because if I'm pregnant it would have tasted great, everyone knows that's the litmus test.'

'Do they?'

'Oh Rose, you don't know anything.' Lily sighed. 'I'm never going to get pregnant, am I?'

The day she married William more than three years ago, Lily announced she was going to have a baby straight away. After that, she phoned their mother on the first day of every period in tears as her dream of seeing the smudge of her foetus on a scan drifted further out of reach. This was Lily's sixth similar call to Rose since their mother died of breast cancer. Rose was still at a loss how to help; she was good at practical support, action, doing things, but hopeless at heart-on-the-sleeve stuff.

'Marmite really is disgusting. I was sure I'd love it because William does.'

Rose smiled despite herself. Lily had never known what she liked or wanted, except that every day it was something different. Rose remembered clearly the day at primary school when Lily declared she was French. She insisted on being called 'Marie-Claire' until a boy in her class made her cry at playtime by shouting 'wee wee' at her. Rose, fifth recorder in the school band and good at football, kicked the boy's ankle, and then played *Sur La Pont d'Avignon* on their way home in an effort to cheer her up. Lily sung along in what she thought was a French accent, getting every other word wrong. She infuriated Rose so much that, in the end, she dared Lily to prove she really was French. Lily went to the fridge, took out the jar of Dijon mustard which their father liked on a ham sandwich, and swallowed a whole tablespoon of the thick yellow goo. She was sick three times and Rose howled with laughter before being smacked on the backside by her mother and sent to bed without supper.

'Just relax and let it happen, Lil. There's loads of time. I'm older than you and my biological clock hasn't even started ticking yet.'

'That's because your battery's flat.'

After five minutes of Lily going on about babies, Rose finally put the phone down.

She's wrong. My battery's not flat, it's disconnected.

7 LILY

Lily put the jars of marmalade and Marmite back in the fridge, then swallowed her daily folic acid and zinc tablets with the last mouthful of lemon and ginger tea, rinsed the mug, and set it to drain. It was her favourite mug, bone china with the Japanese *kanji* for 'peace' picked out in chains of daisies, lupins, bluebells, and buttercups. Not as traditionally Japanese as peonies or chrysanthemums, but she loved it all the same. William gave it to her soon after they met. The only reason she knew what the *kanji* meant was because it was explained on the price ticket, which William had forgotten to remove.

They had sat next to each other on the first night of 'An Introduction to Japanese' at the local adult education college and soon her only motivation for going to class was William. She'd originally enrolled because she'd seen repeats of *Shogun* on television. William's motivation for enrolment, he announced during student introductions at the first class, was promotion at work.

William, tall and earnest, his neck a little turkey-like in the too-large collar of his neatly ironed white shirt; William with the kind eyes, who wrote the answer in her notepad when the tutor picked on her with an impossible grammar question; William, who did something she didn't understand in the City; William, who nine months into the class had inexplicably asked her to marry him. She still couldn't believe her luck.

She sat in the rocking chair by the tall kitchen window, hugging her favourite cushion to her aching tummy, wishing her mother were here to talk to. Rose was wrong, they were both running out of baby time.

Wednesday was Lily's day off. For years, she'd had a Wednesday shopping date with Mum, they'd window shop and have tea and cake somewhere nice. Now Lily stayed home alone. She rocked back and forth and thought about seeing a doctor, then once again smoothed out the crumpled cutting from *Stars* magazine about how Sylvie Watson from *The Superiors* was adopting because she had early menopause and IVF had failed.

But she's years younger than me.

She pressed two paracetamol from their foil sleeve and swallowed them carefully with two gulps of sparkling mineral water. Then she popped the wheatie pad into the microwave and waited for it to heat up. She propped the lily cushion, embroidered by Mum for her eighteenth birthday, behind her head and leant back for a moment, rocking gently, eyes closed. Aah, that was better. Perhaps there was something in what Rose said about relaxing. That was easier said than done, usually the case with the advice Rose dispensed unasked.

The first time she read about Sylvie Watson inspired Lily to see a naturopath. She didn't like the idea of IVF. Ugh, all that prodding around and injections. The thought made her stomach ache even more. She'd come away from the naturopath with a bag full of vitamins and minerals and a dark-brown glass bottle of liquid herbs. She kept them in the bottom drawer of her wardrobe, next to the Predictor box and the ovulation test kit. The herbs tasted so disgusting she couldn't find the words to describe them, although Rose-the-walking-thesaurus would no doubt immediately think of five appropriate adjectives.

Lily only told Grandma Bizzie about the naturopath. Bizzie had been a nurse and was good at keeping secrets. When she was eight, Lily had written to the Prime Minister with Bizzie's help asking to dance *Swan Lake* with the Royal Ballet, and Rose still didn't know.

Lily had swigged the naturopath's herbs for a month and nothing changed except pictures in *Stars* of Sylvie Watson holding a Vietnamese baby. She looked so happy and so... needed.

Perhaps it was time to have a Chat. To show William her ovulation chart, make sure he really understood how important a baby was for their future. Directors always had a silver-framed photo of their wife and children on their desks, and William was almost a director. That was why he was working so hard, doing his Japanese exams – so he'd get promoted. She'd given him a silver-framed photo of herself for their first wedding anniversary, but it was still in the in-tray on his desk upstairs, wrapped in gift paper.

She checked her diary again. William had a late meeting tonight, tomorrow night was his Japanese lesson, and on Friday the new neighbours from Number 43, the biggest house in the street, were coming to dinner. William always wanted her to cook something from Nigella or Nigel or Skye. The cookbooks were piled by his bedside because he liked to read them in bed, but it was always Lily who cooked. He'd requested wild sea bass and beetroot for Friday. Lily had only ever eaten beetroot pickled with cold cuts for Christmas Day tea at Grandma Bizzie's.

She ran her finger down the page of her diary and wondered idly if beetroot improved fertility as well as turning your wee pink.

She looked at the diary again. Early on Saturday morning was her first opportunity to start the Chat Plan.

She wrote a tiny 'W' next to Saturday's date.

8 ROSE

'Isn't anyone here?' The voice sounded weary.

Rose peered around her computer screen. It was 6 p.m. and after an afternoon testing various eye care products and writing 1,000 words on 'Eye strain and how to avoid it', Rose longed to be at home, cheese on toast, Brad, perhaps a glass of wine. Instead she looked straight at May Magdalene, the *Herald*'s managing editor and definitely someone to be avoided if you wanted to get away before midnight. May was revolving on the spot as she looked around the sea of empty desks.

Rose ducked and immediately felt nine years old again, attempting to avoid the attention of Duckie the maths teacher – Mr Duckworth, who did look rather like a duck – when he wanted an answer to 1,783 divided by twenty-one.

'Ah, Rose. I suppose the rest have sneaked off early. Well,' May looked down at Rose, 'you'll do. Read these, will you?' Rose sat up straight, clenching her lips together to trap the 'No!' that crunched between her tongue and her teeth. Damn, the new series of *ER* started tonight. One hand reached for the pile of page proofs May was shoving at her, while in her other fist she concealed a tiny bottle of eye drops.

Why am I hiding this? Because I don't want May to shout at me like she shouted at that travel journalist yesterday, that's why. The poor guy had gone to lie down in the sick room for an hour with a migraine, only for May to drag him out shouting, 'Don't be so weak! You can work with a headache.'

'Sure, May, no problem.' The large type of the headlines swum in front of her eyes. She put down the bottle and rubbed her eyes. *Why can't May proof pages on pdf like everyone else?*

'Not tired, I hope? When I was your age, I'd be interviewing all day and writing all night. Typewriters mind you, no cut and paste, no spellcheck. Had nothing but fags and whisky to keep us going.' She turned quickly, wobbled slightly on her four-inch heels, then turned back. 'I'll have those, if you're finished with them.' She gestured towards the tiny blue bottle. 'Please.'

Rose handed them over. When May was out of sight she fished out of the bin the scrunched-up eye pads she'd tested two hours earlier. Perhaps they might work better if she dampened them with water.

By 8 p.m. she'd read four of the ten proofs when the phone rang. It was an external ringtone so she ignored it. May had already walked past her desk twice and huffed that she was a slow reader. Rose tried again to concentrate on the diagrams of DNA, which were twisting in and out of focus. She had to get this right or May would shout 'Weak!' at her too.

'The human genome has around 3,000 genes,' she read. Her mobile rang. She ignored it, waiting for the beep from 121. She clenched the phone between her jaw and left shoulder, and continued writing as she waited for the voicemail service to dance its jig and play the message.

'This is Nick Maddox.'

Rose's pen stopped in mid-air.

'I've received your email. You don't say how urgent this is, so I'm assuming you need it straight away. I'll get my PR to draft the answers.'

That's right, thought Rose. *Fob me off.*

'I'll be in Brussels tomorrow, ring me. Anytime.' His voice dipped low on the last word. He left his number and rang off.

Anytime?

Rose bought the first-floor one-bedroom flat in Monument Road, Wimbledon, near the All England Lawn Tennis Club, when she got her first byline.

Ten years later, she still lived a happy solo existence. It was a million miles from Lily and William's five-bedroom house (master bedroom, guest bedroom and one for each planned child), fifty-foot garden (ready for a tree house) and attic (big enough for a train set).

Lily's neighbours were chief executives, doctors, and lawyers. Rose's neighbours were Australians in flip-flops and Reggie the *Big Issue* seller, whom she suspected lived in the alleyway between the tube station and the fish-and-chip shop.

In the beginning, both mortgage and flat had been unknown quantities for Rose, huge and intimidating. Now the square footage of the flat had shrunk out of proportion to her increasing possessions. She longed for a spare bedroom, allocated parking, a back door with a cat-flap for Brad, and a garden for him to patrol.

The flat downstairs was silent. The previous

occupant was a rock fan with a very good quality sound system. Rose breathed in the quiet. In her tiny hallway, the red eye of her answerphone blinked. It was Lily, apologising for getting upset earlier.

She put a Robbie Williams CD on repeat play, poured a glass of wine, and settled back on the soft velvet sofa. Just as she closed her eyes and rested her cheek against the cherry-red cushion (inner-thigh material, her ex called it), the doorbell rang.

And there he stood. The Ex. James. His face stared back at her from the entry phone downstairs. Still unmarried at forty-five, which with hindsight should have been a warning. He hadn't changed in the three weeks since she'd chucked him out. Still too good-looking for his own good. Rose pressed the buzzer and heard the downstairs door open with a click.

And then he was standing in front of her. James bent to kiss her but hit her cheek instead as she ducked away. She heard Brad mewl in the kitchen, asking to be let out of the window: Brad never hung around when James arrived.

'Haven't you grown tired of this disco stuff yet?' James pushed past her through the door and turned off Robbie. 'Really, Rose, still listening to CDs? A girl like you, you should get an iPod dock like mine.' He always had the latest gadget, always assumed his taste in music was unassailable.

Rose switched the music back on and turned up the volume.

'What do you want?' She watched him flick through her CD collection.

He shoved Alanis Morissette next to U2 where there wasn't space for it, and turned to look at her.

Rose's fingers itched to put Alanis back in her rightful place after Madonna, but she didn't want to give him that small victory. 'What do you want?'

'Just my stuff. Some magazines and a jumper, the red one you used to wear, the one you shrunk in the wash, remember? You know, the one that makes your tits look like melons.'

Rose crossed her arms across her chest. She hated that James could still get to her like this. 'You can keep the jumper if you like, as long as I can watch you take it off.' He reached out and brushed his fingers along her arm.

The hairs on her arm stood to attention. She took a step back. 'Don't touch me.'

'You always liked it...'

'Well, I don't now.'

She walked straight to the hall cupboard and took out the cardboard box in which she had crammed his stuff. An insidious creep of his possessions had threatened to take over her flat and she'd emptied a shelf in her bookcase for him. It was as if he'd decided to move into her place CD by CD, tube of toothpaste by bottle of shampoo, but Rose had quickly wised up to this tactic, having tried it herself years previously on a boyfriend she'd thought she loved.

But it wasn't James's things messing up her neat flat which finally swung her decision to end it, it was something much worse. His 'nasty habit'. She thought back to when they first met and she couldn't remember him doing it then. Maybe love had been blind; maybe she'd just got more observant.

It had certainly taken the edge off his sexiness. In fact, she could pinpoint the decrease of her libido to the first time she saw him do it: re-adjusting his balls; shoving his right hand deep into his pocket and, well, arranging them. He did it everywhere, in restaurants, on the Tube, and once, unbelievably, at tea at Grandma Bizzie's. It wasn't a simple matter of realigning underwear. It was almost self-fondling.

Now she gave him the box and held the door open, one arm pointing down the stairs to the street, the white skin of the knuckles of her right hand stretched as tightly as her grimace. He smiled at her, blinked and blinked again, and she wondered, not for the first time, whether he used mascara.

His eyes were a strong point. Memories of Sunday mornings came flooding back and her face flushed with heat. *Damn it, don't think about sex now.* Her legs were getting hotter, the muscles on her face softened into a smile… and then he put his hand in his pocket and adjusted his bits.

'You've got everything. That's it, James, go, please.' She made her voice sound authoritative, like May, and waved her arm towards the stairs.

At the bottom he stopped and turned. 'You know, Rose, you shouldn't be such a cold bitch.'

After the bottom door clicked shut behind him, she breathed again.

No more estate agents for me. In fact, no men who are remotely involved in selling as a job, they're always the ones with the chat-up lines.

She closed the door and re-positioned the doormat, squared and centred in the doorway. Then she took a cream cotton blanket out of the linen cupboard and threw it over the red velvet sofa.

Next morning, the door to the empty downstairs flat was propped open by a pile of packing cases that listed severely to the right. A bicycle with a child seat attached was propped against the wall; beside it was a toy fire engine with three wheels.

As Rose squeezed past the handlebars, there was a loud crash from inside the flat, like china hitting a laminated floor, followed by a child's cry. Well, at least a baby wouldn't listen to Iron Maiden at 2 a.m.

At 9 a.m. the *Herald*'s features team gathered in Ivy, the fifth-floor meeting room with the blue-and-yellow Hockney swimming pool print *A Bigger Splash*. Rose usually passed the time in Sam's editorial meetings by considering Hockney's fascination with water. Her usual policy was to keep quiet until spoken to, but today was the day she was going to be noticed. Having done the Maddox interview, she wanted to do more and needed a pay rise to afford a bigger flat. Avoiding Sam was not going to achieve that, so, to raised eyebrows from the rest of the team, she suggested three feature ideas.

Sam, tapping his pen on the desk as if striking a drum, rejected them one by one as boring and predictable. 'No, no, Rosa, that won't do.'

She seethed silently through the next ten minutes while Frank suggested a survey of the sexual habits of single women, tying it to a giveaway of Desmond Morris's book, *The Naked Ape*. A girl, so quiet and pale in complexion and dress that Rose hadn't noticed her before, passed a piece of paper to Frank from which he quoted at length. It was all predictable stuff. She waited for Sam to reject it as predictable too.

33

'Old Desmond knew how to hit the right button, as they say. Eh, Rosie?' Sam winked at her. 'The poor old male ape has a hard time, he only gets his oats one week out of every four. At least single women are up for it all the time, eh? That's what we need to show in the results, Frank. Make sure you write the questions to get the answers we want. This could make the front page, maybe a picture of Cara or Keira. Or Hermione.'

Frank caught Rose's eye and winked, but she didn't wink back.

Yeah, right Sam, she thought. *The Naked Ape has some good stuff in it, hasn't it? If memory serves me right, it also charts the droopage rate of a man's penis as he gets older. So let's see, Sam, you must be in your early sixties, so that means you can only manage an erection for about five minutes. So if your wife's up for it all the time, as you claim all women are, where's she going to get her oats?*

She stifled a giggle.

'Is there something amusing you'd like to share with us, Miss Haldane?'

For one horrible moment, Rose thought she'd said all the drooping penis stuff out loud.

'Or are you considering the benefits of getting a boob job? If you do, let us know. We could make you a case study. Before-and-after pictures. From melons to fried eggs.' He sniggered.

Rose stood up. 'Perhaps instead of worrying about the size and shape of my chest, you should read what Desmond Morris has to say about the diminishing sexual performance of men of your age, Sammie.'

The blood rushed to Sam's face and leached from everyone else's. Frank's eyes burned into the notebook on his lap.

She couldn't stop the words from coming. 'And by the way, my name is Rose. Not Rosie or Rosa or Roz. Rose, like the flower.'

Silence hung in the air. She sat down again and invited eye contact, deliberately seeking it out, but no one looked at her. *At least I didn't say 'penis' out loud. Did I?*

'Miss Haldane. My office. Now.' He didn't look at her.

Frank shrugged at her sympathetically as everyone else trailed out of the meeting room behind Sam. Rose hesitated, alone amongst a sea of scattered chairs, paper snowballs, and abandoned coffee cups. She glanced towards the ceiling and was thankful her mother was not around to hear her language. She would have been appalled. Then she would have asked Rose why she was still working at the *Herald* if she hated it so much.

She heard raised voices coming from Sam's office. He was toe-to-toe with May, who looked down on him from her superior height. He shuffled backwards as if he didn't dare turn his back. You'd have thought it was May's office, not his. When he spun around and saw Rose standing outside the door, his face blazed as if doused in Shiraz.

'Rosie, I said now and I meant now. Get your arse in here.'

Rose put her hands in her pockets, dug her nails into her palms, and walked towards him, trying not to gag on the stench of stale cigarette smoke emanating from his misshapen green tweed jacket. She passed May on her way out.

He shut the door and didn't offer Rose a chair.

She stood there, wishing she'd never read
Desmond Morris.

'Your behaviour just now was completely
unacceptable. Completely unacceptable. If it was up to
me, you'd never write a feature again. But… there are
procedures to be followed and I can't just kick you out.
But be in no doubt, Rosie, if I could, I would.' He tapped
a cigarette out of the packet on his desk, then put it back
in again. 'Bloody "no smoking" do-gooders.'

Rose watched him.

'But… May thinks… May likes your writing
style… humph, "good at making something out of
nothing" is what she said. Never mind what she said, she
wants…' he looked at the folder in his hand, '… 3,000
words. Early menopause. You've got three weeks to
write it. Here.' He thrust the folder at her.

Rose stepped forward to take it from him. His
hand was shaking. So was hers.

'Case studies, expert witnesses, graphs, charts,
everything. The facts, the emotions, the tears.' He shook
another cigarette out of the packet and lit it.

Rose tried to breath through her mouth, hoping
the smoke alarm would go off. It didn't. He'd probably
disconnected it.

'This doesn't mean you're off the hook, Rosa.
Mess this up and your arse'll be out of here quicker than
I can fart.'

'Fart' was his second favourite word.

'As of now, you're under performance review.
You know the disciplinary routine. One more mistake,
you're out.'

Rose didn't know the disciplinary routine, had
never been in trouble, and was mortified at Sam's

assumption that she had. How exactly would Sam phrase her insult on the review form?

'*She used foul language and questioned my ability to satisfy my wife.*'

'*She challenged my authority and ridiculed me in front of my entire editorial team.*'

'*She insulted my capability as a man.*'

'*She said... penis.*'

But I didn't, she almost said aloud. No, she'd just have to wait to read the form to find out. And that's when she realised this would be on her personnel file forever. Inappropriate language. Insulting her manager. Things you shouldn't do, things Rose never imagined she would do. People who didn't know her might read it and make judgements based on these accusations. She felt ashamed, ashamed at being bullied and not fighting back, and frightened, yes frightened she might lose her job.

No matter how foul Sam was, no matter how much she was tempted, she must never insult him again. Even if it meant lying to his face.

'What are you still standing here for? You'll get an e-mail with a date for the disciplinary review. Get out.'

Rose got out.

'And case studies, Rosemary,' Sam shouted at her back. 'I want case studies. Excellent ones.'

She went out into the empty corridor and leant against the wall. She had to make this right, and quickly. This menopause feature had better be a Tenner. But case studies? Only three kinds of people wanted to be featured in case studies: self-promoters, liars, and madmen. Where was she going to find them?

Oh. My. God.

What a mess, what a chance. She was going to write her best feature ever. Sam's folder was stuffed with medical reports and newspaper cuttings. She picked out Sam's briefing sheet.

Premature Ovarian Failure.

Women who postpone having babies until their forties are finding out their biological clock stopped ticking in their twenties and they're prematurely infertile.

The punters'll love it. Don't make it too graphic, no need to go into gynaecological details. And for God's sake, call it 'early menopause', Premature Ovarian Failure sounds like something wrong with my car.

She read everything once. Then she read them again, this time writing notes. The more she read, the more her stomach twisted. One sufferer described could be Lily. Rose gazed into the distance, concentrating on how it must feel to want a child so much but be denied it by your body. *Is this how Lily feels?* For the second time that day, Rose missed their mother.

Well Mum's not here, so now it's my job to protect Lily.

Rose read an NHS leaflet which said the condition was inherited down the female line. The first step was to ask your female relatives about their experience of menopause.

Rose picked up the phone. There was only one person alive she could ask about the medical history of the women in her family. Rose let the phone ring and ring, expecting Grandma Bizzie to be in the garden, pruning roses or spraying her soft fruit with a soapsuds mixture to deter bugs.

'Hello?' Her grandmother's voice drifted up an octave on the 'o'.

'Gran? It's Rose. I need to ask you about The Change.'

9 LILY

Lily planned to wake before William on Saturday morning, stroke him gently till his eyes opened in that crinkly way she loved, then make love to him the way he liked best but which she hated. She hated it because she couldn't see his face. But afterwards, when he was relaxed and loving her for her unselfishness, she would introduce the subject of babies.

Instead, she awoke to the sound of William swearing in the en-suite because brown water was coming out of the taps and he couldn't have a shower before setting off for the rugby game. The alarm clock hadn't gone off and somehow it was her fault. It wasn't a good start. Following him into the kitchen, she hovered as he stood in front of the fridge.

He turned round and bumped straight into her. 'Jesus, Lily. Don't creep up on me.'

'I'm not.' She flicked the switch of the kettle and danced around him to the mug tree. 'Want one, darling? And some toast?' She kept her voice light, determined not to let his grumpiness drag her down. She loved him dearly, but he was a bear in the morning. She sank into the rocking chair, patted her lily cushion and made a wish. Her usual wish.

He shook his head as he rummaged through the fridge. 'I haven't got time to drink it, I'm very late.

Damn it.' Bottles and packets fell to the floor. Glass smashed, tins rolled and William's feet became islands in a sea of olives, gherkins, orange juice and smashed egg yolks.

Lily knelt down to gather up the tins of ice tea, peach-flavoured spring water, cranberry juice, echinacea and lemon spritz. Last out were William's purchases last night: something called La Fargé Fromage de Fruinet in a gold foil packet, boutique blue eggs, and unsalted butter from a Norfolk farm. All things William had slipped into the basket at the deli last night, the deli around the corner that was so tempting and expensive they could never manage to buy a bottle of milk there without buying other treats, the deli so expensive they'd nicknamed it 'The £10 Shop'. She needed her morning tea before she could face this mess, and picked her way to the kettle to grab her drink.

William stepped around the gold foil packet and missed squishing it by millimetres.

'Surely it's not that difficult to make sure the fridge has bottles of ordinary still water.' He snatched a bottle of peach water and turned from the fridge, again colliding with Lily, who was now standing at his elbow holding two mugs.

'Goddamnit Lily, I said I don't want tea.'

She took a quick step back as if bitten. 'Don't shout. I know you're late but I'm only trying to help.' The toaster pinged and two pieces of wholemeal shot into the air and fell onto the worktop in front of them. Both of them stared at the toast.

He tipped his head to one side and looked at her. 'I'm sorry. It's just that I promised Freddie I'd be there before kick-off.'

'And you always keep your promises.' Lily smiled at him and was gratified when he smiled back. *Now,* she thought, *do it now.* 'I got my period yesterday.' She waited for a response.

William was flicking through the unopened post. 'William?'

'What? Oh, sorry, sweetie, does your tummy hurt?' He put down a brown envelope and patted her on the arm. He'd never patted her on the arm like that before, the way you pat the arm of an aged aunt when she tells you the same thing for the eighth time.

Make eye contact, she thought, *like the self-help books say you should do when your husband's grumpy. Reward him for being thoughtful.* She forced a smile. 'So I think the time has come for us to have a serious talk. About a baby.'

'We will, sweetie,' he checked his watch again, then picked up his jacket. 'Just not now. I'm late and, well, there's obviously no urgency to do anything about it today, is there?' He nodded at her stomach.

Lily's hand instinctively went to her tummy. 'There are lots of things we... you don't have to do anything... I'll do it all.' The nearer he moved to the door the quicker her words were coming out. 'I've got a list...'

'I'm sure you have.' He picked up his keys and then turned back to peck her on the cheek. 'You start doing your stuff.' And he was gone.

10 ROSE

At Sunday lunch, Rose had to try hard not to think about her mum. She didn't want to. Not when she sat at the table next to her mother's empty chair, not when Lily grilled only three lamb chops instead of four, nor when she added a sprig of rosemary to the roasting potatoes as their mother had always done.

After Mum died six months ago, Lily suggested they cook a proper Sunday lunch every week for Dad so it wouldn't matter if he ate fish and chips every day of the week. And that's what they did.

'Right, if we're going to sort out Mum's cupboards, we'd better make a start.' Rose had been trying to drag lunch out to avoid reaching this point; a second helping of crumble, a mug of coffee rather than a cup, all the time dreading this invasion of her mother's privacy. A necessary invasion, so their father could move on. But she hated the idea of anyone searching through her own things. 'Come on,' she said to Lily.

They were searching the kitchen cupboards for bin bags when their dad stuck his head around the door.

'Just popping to the allotment. I promised Ron I'd help paint his shed. It's a messy job but it'll dry nicely on a fine afternoon like this. You'll get on quicker without me here. Here you are, pumpkin.' He pushed a piece of paper towards Rose. 'This is your mother's list, what she wanted doing with everything. No need to keep anything for me, I've taken some things already to... to remind me of her. Her watch, and her rings. Anyway, see you later.' He was gone, leaving an invisible mist of embarrassment in the kitchen.

Rose stared at the closed door. 'What's his rush?'

'Poor Dad,' said Lily. 'It must be awful having Mum's things in the wardrobe next to his, seeing them each time he hangs up his jacket. We should have done this straight after the funeral.'

'I know, I know.' Rose tried to think of how he must feel, smelling Youth Dew on her mother's dresses and jumpers every day, and the sadness bubbled up inside her. But then a bigger thought spoke in a sneaky voice deep in her head, that her father's hasty exit smacked more of avoidance than grief. If being widowed had added another layer of life experience, it had added a layer of fat too. His face betrayed a mid-afternoon love for sugar-dusted doughnuts and fish and chips for tea. Not for the first time, she wished her father had a brother or sister to help him grieve, as she and Lily had helped each other.

Rose looked at her mother's list, then shoved it in her pocket. *Mum's been dead for six months now, and she's still telling us what to do.* Then she felt horrible for even thinking that. There were things she wished she'd said to her mother, and some she wished she hadn't. *Perhaps if she'd been a bit more forgiving, a bit less prone to judge, we might have been better friends.* Like mothers and daughters should be. Rose sighed. How different her childhood would have been if she'd been friends with her mum.

She remembered their last Christmas all together.

They sat in front of the cosy fire, a rare moment of oneness, while Rose explained her photo theory. She hesitated, she had never shared it with anyone else.

'Each life experience adds a layer to your identity,' she said, 'like the layers of separated colour film that make up photos. Or like the dye used to screenprint the floral pattern on your blouse,' and she pointed at her mother's favourite turquoise Liberty-print cotton blouse. 'Each colour is applied separately, and only when the last one is finished can the real pattern be seen. Your full personality, your complete self, is revealed only when you look through the scars and shadows and rainbows left by the experiences of life.'

Her mother had smiled. 'But identity is much simpler than that, dear. Every woman is incomplete until she has a baby.'

Mum's clothes hung in the wardrobe, organised by colour. Rose took the turquoise Liberty-print blouse off its hanger and sniffed deeply. It smelled faintly of mothballs. She was surprised at the sudden swell of tears in her eyes. Lily patted her on the back.

Rose admired her mother's strong conviction about what colours suited her and wished she had that discipline: nothing red, brown, or orange was given rail space. On top of the wardrobe three old-fashioned hatboxes balanced on top of a heavy tan suitcase; how typical of their mother to use hatboxes.

Lily held up a pale pink sandal with a chunky crêpe sole.

'I hate throwing them out. Mum liked them so, and there's nothing wrong with them. Perhaps we should keep them.'

'Why? They're awful and they won't fit us.'

'Comfortable' was the first adjective that came to Rose's mind, and the pink was salmon.

'I know,' replied Lily, 'but still.' Her hand wavered for an instant, then she put the pink sandals beside her.

'They're Mum's.'

They continued sorting in silence. Rose watched a silent tear slide down Lily's cheek and wondered why she wasn't crying too.

Getting upset won't bring Mum back, she thought. *I can help Dad by being practical and this is a job that needs doing. Someone has to be strong.* She took a deep breath. Her mother had always been so organised, so practical, and now it was up to Rose to follow her example to steer them all through this trough.

They continued sorting. Lily put aside a blue-striped holdall.

Rose stiffened and reached out towards the holdall.

'Are you keeping that, too?'

Lily rubbed the back of her hand across her red nose, then looked up. 'Yes. I can use it for work and it'll remind me of Mum. You don't want it, do you?'

'I might. It was her favourite. You could have asked me first if I minded you having it.'

'I didn't think it was your style; it's a bit battered. But if you want it... here.' She passed the bag to Rose as if it were made of porcelain, not cotton.

Rose put it beside her. She only wanted it because Lily had taken possession of it as if by right. But all the same... She ran her hand over the cotton stripes, glad to have a piece of her mother.

An hour later, they looked up at the top shelf of the wardrobe, which was crammed with bulging plastic bags and cardboard boxes.

'Shall we have a break before we do the next bit?'

Perhaps now I'll get a chance to talk with Lily about early menopause.

Downstairs, Rose pushed their father's Sunday newspapers aside and sank gratefully onto the burgundy tweed sofa.

'Makes you think, doesn't it,' said Lily, as she poured the tea. 'Who'll do this for us when we die?'

Rose raised an eyebrow.

'You know.' Lily's arm gestured vaguely upstairs. 'Sort our stuff when we're gone. That's one of the nice things about having children, isn't it? You know there's someone to follow you, to continue the family line, to look after you when you're old.'

Rose hadn't given a moment's thought to being old or dying. 'Well, if you die before me, I'll sort out your rubbish, and you can sort out mine. But that's hardly a good reason to have children, surely? You make it sound like old age care provision.'

'No, don't be silly.' Lily frowned. 'But it has to be a part of every woman's life, doesn't it? Having a baby, I mean.' She stroked the scatter cushion at her elbow, then picked it up and hugged it to her tummy. 'I don't think you're really a proper woman until you've given birth.'

'It's not your womb that makes you a woman, Lily, it's your soul.'

'Yes, but you don't want a baby.' Lily sipped her tea. 'I do, I always have. As soon as William proposed, I decided to have loads.'

Rose hesitated. 'Does he want a baby too?'

'Of course. I'm afraid if I don't get pregnant soon, he'll get fed up with waiting.'

'And do what?' Rose had never seen William demonstrate the slightest sign of being a father-in-waiting, but then again, many husbands didn't, but liked a baby well enough once it arrived. 'You don't think you might be… overreacting just a bit?'

Lily banged her mug down on the floor so hard it made Rose jump. Peach and mango tea spilled over the Axminster carpet. Lily marched to the window where she stood looking out, twisting a strand of her pale blonde hair in a spiral around her finger.

'Overreacting? You know nothing about other people's relationships, Rose, you have no right to sit in judgement.'

'You're right, I'm sorry.' Rose mopped up the spillage with a paper napkin. 'It's just that I've… I've been worried this week. About you.'

Lily turned, her eyes oddly unfocussed.

'Whatever for?'

'I've been doing research for an article at work and it made me think of you… well, it might have nothing to do with your situation… not being pregnant yet.' She hesitated, this wasn't coming out right. 'Some women get their menopause early, that's all, their periods continue, but a bit haphazardly so they don't notice any big difference. But their ovaries stop producing eggs and so their fertility level drops. Like beginning the menopause. It reminded me of…' Rose hesitated again before saying 'you'. But she never got the chance to say it.

'… Sylvie Watson.' Lily finished Rose's sentence, reached for a dining chair, and sat down heavily.

Who? Does Lily actually know someone who has early menopause?

'I don't know who Sylvie Watson is, but…'

'Ohh myy Godd, Rose! You don't know who Sylvie Watson is? Call yourself a journalist?'

That got Rose's goat, but she stuck her tongue in her cheek. Which brought back the memory of Nick Maddox, and her cheeks warmed.

'Sylvie Watson is beautiful, and she's talented, she plays Megan Macanella.' Lily looked at Rose, whose face was blank. 'In *The Superiors*.' Blank again. '*The Superiors*, every Thursday night. Don't you watch TV?'

'Yes, but…'

'She's married to Joe Sherezade.' Rose shrugged. 'The film director. They got married barefoot on a beach in Baja, California, very hippy, and they were going to have lots of beautiful babies but she's still not pregnant and…'

'And,' Rose tried again, this time drowning out Lily's words, 'if she's got early menopause, it means she can't get pregnant. There won't be any beautiful babies. It's caused by a number of things, but it can be inherited, so I talked to Gran about it yesterday. She got her menopause in her fifties and she thinks Mum was starting it when she got ill, so that's normal. Great Aunt Bonnie though, she tried but couldn't get pregnant and… that made me think of you.'

Rose pulled up a chair next to Lily, sat down, and took her hand. It was rather cool. 'You should talk to your doctor.'

They sat there for a moment; the only sound in the room was the tip-tapping of the blind toggle against the open window.

'Just for some tests,' said Rose, getting up to shut the window. The clock on the mantelpiece ticked.

Lily stood up. 'No way. I don't need tests. I'd know if I'd got it. You're always talking about evidence and facts; well, Mum had us when she was in her twenties, didn't she, so there's the evidence that she didn't have it.'

'That's the point, Lil, your fertility reduces at an age when it never occurs to you that there's a problem. And you know nothing about it."

'We're not ill, Rose.'

Rose heard the 'we' but chose to ignore it. Lily's expression was strangely blank, and Rose regretted putting that look on her face. So she did what she always did for Lily and softened the blow. 'Look, maybe Sylvie Watson hasn't got it, maybe she just needs time.'

'She hasn't got time.' A single muscle flickered in Lily's cheek.

Rose hadn't expected denial. She'd expected the usual Lily tears and drama. Denial wasn't good. Denial was worse than tears.

Back upstairs, they sat on the floor, surrounded by the detritus of their mother's married life. Lily sat cross-legged, her skirt arranged neatly around her knees, not speaking, twisting her hair again. To give her a little space, Rose concentrated on the striped handbag. She emptied it out onto the carpet: bus tickets, tissues, purse, lipstick. Rose doubted her father had opened the bag since it was returned by the hospice. Men of his age had a thing about handbags, as if they were full of mysterious Women's Things. She sniffed the blue leather purse, hoping for a whiff of Youth Dew, but smelled only dust and worn leather and the metallic tang of coins.

Lily looked up. 'Do you really not know Sylvie Watson?'

Rose shook her head.

'Don't you read the gossip pages of your own newspaper?'

'Hardly.' Rose sneaked a glance at Lily, whose head was again bent over a box. 'Lil, do you really think William will leave you if you don't have a baby?'

Lily sighed. 'Yes. No. Not really… but he does get irritated with me. And when we do it, I can't seem to think about anything else but babies. Afterwards, I lie in bed with my legs on the top of the headboard and try not to move. Half an hour is best.'

Rose, in an effort not to appear judgemental, almost giggled the next words. 'And that's meant to help?'

'It gives his semen the best chance, you see… to find an egg,' Lily rushed on. 'I read it in a book. Apparently, that's why women always want to sleep after sex, its nature's way of increasing the conception odds.'

'Oh please, spare me the details. You should talk to William and go to see the doctor.'

'All right, all right. I'll do it. Stop nagging.'

'Okay.' With a sigh of relief, Rose picked up a photo album from the top of a pile and handed it to Lily. Lily flicked through the pages, falling on some photographs with a laugh and others with a groan.

'I did my first business interview this week. A managing director…' Rose hesitated, wondering how to describe Nick Maddox.

'And you like him.' Lily studied Rose. 'Your eyes have gone all soft.'

Rose immediately scowled. 'As if. No, he was arrogant, so full of his own ego. You know the type?'

Lily nodded. 'But he got to you, didn't he? Admit it.'

'Oh all right, yes he did, though I don't know why. And then he rang to thank me for the interview.'

'That's it? Just to say thank you? He didn't ask you out?'

'No.'

'What are you going to do about it?'

'I can't chase him, Lily, I interviewed him. It's not proper journalistic etiquette.'

'I didn't know journalists had etiquette.'

'Oh ha-ha.'

'Oh Rose, look at this.' She pointed to a black and white photograph of their mother and Aunt Kate. The sisters stood side by side at a barbecue. Rose recognised the style of dress her mother was wearing as typical of the garments hanging in the wardrobe: a round-neck, knee-length, pale-coloured shift. Rose would have laid bets that it was lilac. Kate's long wavy dark hair was plaited with beads and she wore a paisley crinkly skirt with tiny bells sewn along the hem. Rose could almost hear them.

'I wish Mum was here.'

'Me too.' Rose knelt beside her sister and hugged her as they both sniffed, overcome by the feeling of loss. There seemed no easy position in which to hold Lily comfortably, so she sat as she was, ignoring the tearing pain in her cramped muscles.

Eventually, Lily pulled away. 'I always get emotional when it's that time of the month. I'm okay.' She picked up a bundle of correspondence tied with blue ribbon. 'Do you think we should give these to Dad to read?'

'It's okay to read postcards. Every postman does.'

Lily read out the message on the first postcard. It was from their dad.

Ashmolean Garden Hotel, Oxford
12 August 1967
Dear Diana,
Sales conference started last night. V boring. Getting a lift back with Clive Finch on Friday.
John.

The postmark on the next card was smudged, but it looked like December 1967. The picture showed the inside of a church.

'I'm sure Mum would have preferred a postcard of a garden,' said Lily.

Rose thought it was the sort of postcard sold only in newsagents.

Cathedral Close, Canterbury
15 December 1967
Dear Diana,
Fixed up more appointments so won't be home on Thursday. Kate's here doing panto but I probably won't have time to meet her.
John.

'Aunt Kate must have travelled such a lot, acting,' said Lily.

Rose shrugged her shoulders. She remembered the photograph, the beads in her aunt's hair, the bells on her skirt – then looked at the heap of her mother's clothes. *What did Mum and Aunt Kate have in common?*

'No "love you", or "miss you",' said Lily, 'that's what married life does for you. William tells this joke: the quickest way to turn a woman off sex is to marry her.' Her laugh was hollow, her head bent over the postcard.

Rose thought it was a mean joke. She sneaked a glance at her watch. It was getting late. She watched as Lily wrestled with the next suitcase and extracted a pile of multicoloured school exercise books.

'Wow, diaries? Bags I read the one where she was dating Dad and they had sex for the first time.'

Rose shuddered. 'I can't imagine Mum doing it at all.'

'Everyone thinks their parents never did it, but we exist, so they must have done. At least twice.' Lily handed a yellow exercise book to Rose, then opened a red one and started reading.

Rose held the book for a moment before opening it at the first page. The handwriting was easy to read: tiny, italicised script, every letter carefully formed, every serif perfectly angled in relation to the full shape of the letter. A very neat version of the script familiar from every birthday card her mother had ever given her. Each diary entry was headed by a date, underlined precisely with a ruler, written in blue ink.

31 December 1964

It will be so romantic if John proposes tomorrow. A New Year's proposal. I'll drop a hint to encourage him, he sometimes needs a little nudge. I saw him smiling at Abigail Allen in the newsagent's yesterday, and I saw the way she fluttered her eyelashes at him. She's a cheap little flirt and she's not going to get him. I'll even do IT, if I have to.

If the handwriting in the diary wasn't so clearly in her mother's, Rose would never have imagined her oh-so-correct mother being so, so, girly.

1 January 1965

ENGAGED!!!!!! John proposed. On one knee too, except he didn't do it right the first time and I had to ask him to kneel down again and start over. But I wish he wasn't always trying to get inside my blouse (the baby blue one with mother-of-pearl buttons). But tonight was special, so I let him touch my bussies. At last I'm going to be a 'wife'. Mrs Haldane. Mrs Diana Haldane. Mr and Mrs John Haldane. Mr and Mrs Haldane and family.

4 January 1965

We've set the date. John's agreed to 5 April. I wonder where we'll go on honeymoon. Rome, Venice, Paris.

10 March 1965

My dress has a sweetheart neckline and pretty sleeves gathered in tiny puffs on the shoulders. We'll have five babies and live in a house in the country with a big garden and a tree house for the children; two of each, two boys and two girls, the fifth one can be pot luck. Mummy and Daddy gave us some pale-blue bed linen tonight, embroidered with our initials. Mummy's done

*two sets, one for me and one for K, for our bottom
drawers. K's set is lemon. I would have preferred a
cheque.*

Bottom drawer? Rose could imagine her mother
folding things carefully away in tissue paper, household
things ready for her marriage. Rose's bottom drawer was
stuffed with running gear she hadn't worn for ages.

Lily looked up from her book. 'There's no talk of
boys here, or Dad, just what she did every day. What
does yours say?'

'Stuff about how she let Dad touch her bussies the
night they got engaged.'

'Bussies?' Lily snickered.

Rose felt uncomfortable. She flicked idly past the
wedding gossip. The honeymoon had been a weekend at
a hotel in Rye. So much for Paris.

2 August 1966
*Why isn't it happening? We don't use a thingy.
Maureen's pregnant already and she got married two
months after we did.*

Rose looked at Lily. Was history repeating
itself?

3 September 1966
*Dr F said to give it time, relax, and it'll happen
naturally. I asked Mummy and she agreed, and she is a
nurse after all. I do try, but it's difficult to relax when
John wants to... Maureen showed me her book about
childbirth today, the diagrams were rather frightening.
I'd rather not know the details, thank you very much.*

Six months later and the neat handwriting was more of a scrawl.

5 March 1967

John says we can't afford a baby yet, but that's rubbish. Breastfeeding is free. He saw me counting the days on my calendar last night and ripped it up, and this morning he left without breakfast. It's the first time we've argued and not made up before we went to bed. It's our second wedding anniversary soon and I'm still not pregnant, it's never going to happen.

Rose flicked forwards, skipping entries, promising herself she would go back and read them later, and then a word leapt off the page and shouted at her, like spelling mistakes did when she was reading page proofs at work.

17 April 1968

Father's funeral this morning. More awful than I could have imagined. Then the answer to my prayers arrived. Amen. I'm going to adopt her baby when he is born. It'll be my precious secret. The baby is due at the end of August. I'll call him David.

Adopt.

Rose could hear the blood buzzing through her veins, flushing her skin bright red.

She tried to focus on the page, to read it again, but the words of her mother... her mother's handwriting... the words didn't make sense... and yet somehow, they did. There was no David Haldane. Only

Rose and Lily.

Rose Haldane, who was born on 29 August 1968.

Someone took her by the arm, forcing her to sit down. Breath warmed her cheek. She was ice all over. She could see nothing, nothing except one word written in the diary.

Adopt.

Suddenly pain, starting at her cheek and spreading through her head. Again, and again. Each slap beat that word deeper into her unconsciousness.

Adopt.

Rose Haldane fell off the edge of the world.

Her senses were turning on one by one. *I must exist, mustn't I?* The weight of her eyelids stopped her eyes from opening. The gooseflesh. This was what it must feel like to be buried by an avalanche.

Then arms were around her, hugging her, the warmth of another body, arms that settled her gently against something as soft as snow. 'You're okay, Rose, you're okay. Stay here. I'll make some tea. Breathe deeply.'

Rose felt her head nod. It was disconnected from her body. Nothing was connected. She breathed in and out, not knowing how long a second lasted. Then warm lips were brushing her cheek, a hand stroked her hair, and something hot touched her hand. She struggled to open her eyes. Lily, pale with worry, was gently pushing a hot mug against her hand.

Breathe in, breathe out. One thing at a time.

The yellow exercise book lay open at Lily's

60

side, and the pain etched across her face told Rose that she too had read that diary entry and come to the same conclusion. She knew the sorrow in Lily's eyes was a reflection of that in her own. She focussed on moving her hand to hold the mug.

Breathe in, breathe out.

The tea was half-gone before she realised it contained more granulated than Darjeeling. She grimaced.

'You're in shock, Rose, and Mum always said sweet tea is good for shock. Drink up, drink up.'

There was a pause as they both sipped.

'Perhaps… perhaps Mum was pregnant with you and went a bit la-la. It says in my baby book that your brain dissolves in the first few months of pregnancy.'

Rose raised a heavy eyebrow.

Lily rushed on. 'Or it was a short story, or homework for that memoir-writing class she went to, the one at the Cancer Therapy Centre.'

Rose sighed heavily and put down her mug. The tea was disgusting. 'I wish you were right, but the evidence disagrees. One: it's Mum's handwriting and the book is old, the ink is faded. Two: the dates tally with my birthday. Three: it fits with something Grandma Bizzie said, that Mum was desperate for Dad to love her. Desperation can make you do odd things.'

'Four…' She ticked the points off on her fingers. 'I can't think of a fourth.'

'So –' Lily's words were cut short by a dry sob. She swallowed. 'Mum and Dad aren't your parents and we're not sisters. I can't bear it, Rose.'

'Hey, come here.' Rose leant forward to hug her sister in a cushion of reassurance, as she always had. 'Of course we're sisters. We grew up together. We endured piano lessons with Miss Gofton. We embroidered daisies on handkerchiefs for that terrifying teacher at Youth Club, Mrs... Thing. This is just a stupid diary.' She could think of more appropriate words than 'stupid'; ripe words, satisfying words to say, to shout in anger.

'The daisies were pretty.'

'Yes.' Rose thought life was too short to embroider anything. 'That doesn't matter now. The fact is, we don't know what's true and what's not.'

'Dad'll know.'

'Yes, well, Dad's not here right now, is he?'

'What about your birth certificate? That's proof, isn't it?'

'I don't know where she kept it. Was it with our school things?' As she spoke, Rose knew she should have her own birth certificate. She was thirty-five, had a mortgage, a cat, and a pension. Well, that was easily solved; she'd ring Somerset House and get a copy.

Lily was still talking. 'But you must have it, you need it to get a passport.'

'I haven't got one.'

'Ah.' There was a pause. 'So you still get...'

'Yep, every day. Car-sick, boat-sick, train-sick, bike-sick.' She'd even got sick riding the red tricycle she got from her parents for her fourth birthday. Tablets dulled it a bit, and as for tests, she'd had them all; no inner ear infection. So she had learned to live with it, to work around it.

'And they don't mind at work?'

'Are you mad? I haven't told them.' Why haven't I, she wondered, her mind swirling as she wondered what was true, what she'd done and what she'd only considered, how many lies she'd told, white lies, grey lies, black lies…

'But what if they send you abroad? You know, the Cannes Film Festival, Paris Fashion Week…'

Rose laughed and noted with interest that she was still able to. 'It's not that sort of job.' Just the thought of getting on a plane made her flush from top to toe.

Now the small girl inside Rose wondered if she'd always known, deep down, that her identity was something she had to face up to before she could truly be an adult.

They took the mugs downstairs and sat down. Gradually Rose's heart rate slowed to its regular rhythm.

She put the yellow diary on the dining table. Both women looked at it out of the corners of their eyes, not wanting to pick it up, longing for their father to come home from the allotment and tell them it was rubbish, to make them laugh about their dramatics. The carriage clock on the mantelpiece donged like Big Ben and made them both jump. Six o'clock. He would certainly be back soon.

'We are so stupid,' said Lily. 'Your birth certificate must be here somewhere. Mum always kept things safe.'

They found school portraits, a green first-prize rosette Rose won for running thirty yards, fabric swimming badges fraying round the edges, old school reports, and exercise books full of essays. No birth certificate, no adoption papers, no more diaries.

Another pot of tea.

'Do you want to know?' asked Lily.

Rose had just asked herself the same question

and answered slowly yet truthfully, 'I don't know.' She might have had a different name. Did that matter? 'I am who I am, I don't need a birth certificate to tell me that.' Was that the Pointer Sisters, or Gloria Gaynor? Again, a feeling of wonder that she could make a joke. She picked up the yellow diary. Why would parents give a new baby away?

'Don't, Rose. Leave it now.'

But Rose didn't want to leave it. She read the page again. The words were the same as before. She turned the page – there were no more entries. No more clues. How could her mother stop writing there, why didn't she explain?

'Mum can't be writing about me.' She wanted to curl into a ball and disappear. 'Not me.' The sides of the armchair wrapped around her, holding her upright. The words stabbed her, each one a tiny knife cutting away the memories of her childhood into shards at her feet.

Rose looked at the carpet as if she'd never seen it before, hadn't learned to waltz with her father there, didn't recognise the patch by the front window where the carpet fibres were impregnated by decades of pine needles from the real Christmas trees her mother had insisted were more stylish than the shiny silver tinsel tree Rose longed for.

Lily stood up. 'This is ridiculous. Where's Dad? I'm going to ring him.' She disappeared into the kitchen. Rose focussed on the carriage clock. The weights moved round like a merry-go-round; circular, predictable, unstoppable, just like time, and time didn't lie. Her mind swung in time with the dancing pendulum, wanting to be alone but not wanting Lily to go. The thing was, Rose knew what the diary said was true. She felt it. Her eyes searched the room where she'd done her homework with the television turned down to a whisper, the room where Lily and William had stood in front of the mantelpiece and announced they were engaged, the room where she'd hugged her father before they left for Mum's funeral six months ago. A pair of figurines flanked the mantelpiece, left and right, each with an arm raised in a salute towards the ceiling – except the one on the right had only half an arm. It had been like that since Rose was ten and a failed attempt at keepie-uppie had amputated it at the shoulder. Her mother had heard the bang and seen the shards on the floor, and banned football.

Lily returned. 'His mobile's turned off. He must be on his way home.'

Rose stood up too. 'Let's walk round to meet him.'

She put the diaries in the boot of her car, and they walked to the allotment. The gates were padlocked. It was getting dark.

'Hello?' called Lily. 'Dad?'

Rose called too. All quiet.

They walked home again, checking their watches every few minutes.

'Something's happened to him,' said Lily, her breath coming out in sharp gasps, 'it must have done. Why wouldn't he just come straight home?'

'He'll be fine, chatting to someone probably.'

'No, he's had an accident, he's stabbed himself with his shears…'

Uh-oh, thought Rose, *next she'll be saying he's been run over.*

'… he's been run over. We have to go, Rose.

65

Come on!'

So they did the most obvious things. They got in Rose's Mini and drove around, calling his mobile every ten minutes. Nothing. They went back to the allotment, then to each of the nearby pubs asking, 'Has anyone seen John Haldane?' Nothing. They even drove to A&E at Kingston Hospital. Nothing there, either. Finally, they waited twenty minutes at Petersham police station while a very slow desk sergeant checked his database of incidents. Nothing.

Rose suddenly felt exhausted, every thought was an effort and Lily's panic was making her sink deeper.

'I tell you what we should do.' She put her arms around Lily and tried to soothe her, her mind still active enough to register a selfish need to be soothed herself. 'We should go home and get a good night's sleep. Dad's a grown-up, he can look after himself. It can wait till tomorrow.'

'We should at least report him missing.'

'You heard the sergeant, it's too soon. We can't do anything for forty-eight hours. The sergeant's got our details. But Dad's fine, I know he is. He'll turn up. He's healthy and not exactly old. He wouldn't thank us for sending out a search party or anything.'

Lily huffed.

They drove to Barnes in silence. Rose declined Lily's offer of tea and sympathy, just wanting to be home, quiet, and alone. She started to feel numb again and pulled over into a lay-by halfway to Wimbledon.

She sat and thought of her mother and father; her mother's face as the pain of cancer overwhelmed her, her father's empty eyes as he stood at the graveside. Car horns hooted and lights flashed as she did a U-turn and drove back to Richmond. Only one person could tell her the truth.

She was not provisioned for a stake-out. When they left their father's house earlier, they'd been in a rush and Lily pulled the door closed behind them, not expecting to return, not thinking of a key to get back in. So when Rose saw The Weavings still in darkness, she resigned herself to sitting in the Mini. She knocked at the front door and the back door, and rang the bell, cursing that last year after the burglary when new locks were fitted she hadn't insisted on having a key. She went back to her car, moved the seat back, and wriggled to get comfortable.

She had thought she was like everyone else: mother, father, sister, nice home, okay life, family history absorbed haphazardly over the years from stories and gossip and photo albums. Inheritance by osmosis. She had always accepted her dark brown eyes were inherited from her father's side of the family, but now her mother's words in the yellow book made all of this a lie. Her mother, who had owned up to taking a shop-bought cake for the primary school fete's homemade cake stall and saved her Monopoly money rather than buy hotels, was the same mother who had lied for forty years?

She sat up in her seat and pulled it forwards into the driving position. She'd had enough; her bed was warm and waiting for her in Wimbledon. Her father would be somewhere safe. Hadn't he been going to paint someone's shed? That was it; he'd be at this bloke's house having a thank-you drink. The clock on the dashboard showed 00.00 as Rose reached for the ignition.

She opened her front door, the pile of diaries and striped holdall clutched to her breast. In the dark kitchen, Brad mewed as he weaved round her ankles in a figure of eight. Rose opened a tin of tuna and looked down at the one definite thing in her life.

Sleep evaded her. She sat up and put on the light, and then did what her mother always did in a time of crisis. She made tea and sat at the kitchen table in the dark. The shadows of her mother's handwriting seemed embossed on her retinas, projecting like theatre lights onto the blank kitchen wall in exactly the spot where her father had never quite got around to fixing a bookshelf.

Rose looked at the window blind, the fridge door, the calendar – and the handwriting followed her gaze, marking the plain surfaces of fabric, enamel, paper and plaster with their message. *I'm going to adopt her baby when he is born.*

The faces of her mother and father floated in front of her, their empty words mute in the night, beseeching, explaining, excusing, apologising, their fleshy faces dissolving into skulls; empty skulls and empty words.

Shut your eyes and concentrate, Rose told herself, *think positive*. She needed a happy memory. Her mother bending over the pram, stroking her hair, shooing away the cat. Cheek-to-cheek with her father, looking out of a train window, stretching on tiptoe to see the green fields rushing by outside, the black blur of cows and brown blur of horses, his strong hand at her back, guiding her as he had guided her all her life.

But that strong hand didn't belong to my real father after all.

She sat through that long night on the sofa, a cold cup of tea in one hand, her eyes open, her mind closed but seeing the handwriting that followed her movement into the sitting room. She remembered the time she was sent to bed without tea for repeating a word she heard one windy day in the school playground and hadn't understood.

Bastard.

Then, finally, a memory that stemmed the tears. Rose, aged five, was collected from school one afternoon by Grandma Bizzie. Given the choice, Rose would have lived at Grandma Bizzie's house. She loved the sycamore, its five-pronged leaves which looked like a green giant's fingers, the delicate yellow-green flowers that dangled like earrings in the spring and the winged seeds which fluttered in spirals to the ground in the autumn. One day she was sitting on the first branch, wishing Lily liked climbing trees, when Bizzie brought out a glass of squash and a piece of homemade lemon cake with runny icing on top.

Rose patted the air next to her. 'Never mind, it'll stop bleeding soon.' Her friend Wanda, she told Gran solemnly, had slipped down three branches and had a long scratch on her leg.

'Poor Wanda,' Bizzie smiled at the vacant space on the branch next to Rose. 'Perhaps a piece of cake will make her feel better?'

Of course it did. Climbing trees was hungry work and from that day on, Rose often climbed the tree with Wanda and ate two pieces of cake each time.

Now, as she sat on the sofa, Rose licked her lips.

She could taste the lemon still. She opened her eyes. The sun had erased her mother's words off the wall and the room was her lounge once again. But the seat next to her was empty. Wanda was long gone.

The next morning, six-and-a-half hours after she'd left it, Rose stood outside her father's house again.

All was quiet, and the open curtains revealed an inner emptiness. Lily had closed the kitchen curtains before they'd left last night. He'd been home, then. It felt like spying. Her father's favourite mug, yellow with a bumblebee and 'To Bee or Not to Bee' written on it, was draining by the kitchen sink.

He's not dead. Her stomach gave a little twirl of relief, which felt almost like hunger. She rang Lily's mobile but there was no answer, Rose knew the phone would be buried deep in Lily's handbag in her locker at work. She tapped out a quick text - Dad's okay, don't worry - and pressed send. Then she ran to the allotment, tapping the lamp post on the corner twice as she went.

When she was little, she'd discovered that if she tapped a lamp post on her way home from school, or a tree, or the gatepost by the garage, it meant her father would be in a good mood that night and might play footie with her after tea. She climbed onto the bottom rung of the padlocked allotment gate, squinted into the bright sun, and cursed her lack of sunglasses. Her father liked to do a bit of early-morning weeding before work. Not today.

The receptionist at Woodbright Engineering's Welcome Desk was polite but firm. Yes, Mr Haldane was here today but he was in a meeting all day and not available without a prior appointment. Rose recognised the blocking technique. It was nothing the *Herald* wouldn't do if a woman with mad hair and what looked suspiciously like pyjamas underneath her raincoat rushed into reception making demands about an employee.

By the time Rose got back into the car, the morning rush hour was passing. Her head ached and her arms were covered in the stubborn sort of gooseflesh that refused to shift no matter how intense the rubbing. She needed a hug. She needed her father to tell her everything was a misunderstanding. She needed to crawl into the womb of her family and be fed toasted crumpets and strawberry jam.

When she got home, the red light of the answerphone was blinking, but again there was no message. Stupid machine. She picked it up, tore its plug out of the socket and threw it in the kitchen bin. The post was on the doormat. She opened a letter about her critical illness policy and slowly the fact sunk in that she'd lied on every application form she'd ever filled out. She sat at the kitchen table and put her head in her hands. This kind of form always asked for your mother's maiden name and your family's medical history. Would all her policies be void now? The critical illness policy joined the answerphone.

Rose had three hot showers throughout the course of the afternoon, but the gooseflesh was stubborn and she continued to shiver. It was less than twenty-four hours since she'd read the yellow diary and every time she thought about it, she ate something. The kitchen bin overflowed with empty tins of Ambrosia creamed rice, screwed-up Milky Bar wrappers, half-eaten slices of toast and strawberry jam, and damp tissues.

The diary sat on the coffee table, its corners

curling and grubby. The certainty with which she'd called herself Rose Haldane had evaporated. Her mother was not really her mother. Her father was not her father. Lily was not her sister. Bizzie wasn't her grandma. And that was only her mum's side, as her father had no living relatives. Her relationship with everyone was false. Her real parents could be dead or they could be criminals.

She picked up the soggy tub of ice cream and stirred the half-melted mess inside. One more mouthful and she really would be sick, but that would at least make good the lie she'd told at 8.45 a.m. She'd felt such a fraud – as of course she was, not Rose Haldane at all – in the past, whenever she'd phoned in sick, she had actually been ill.

'Flu?' May's assistant had said. 'Poor you. I hope someone's looking after you. Spoiling is the best cure for flu.'

Rose had put the phone down rather quickly as tears pricked her eyes. She desperately needed her mother's traditional sick cure of poached eggs on toast.

She was a mess; a few kind words from someone she didn't really know and she was in tears. There was no one else to poach eggs or hug her. Brad did a creditable job of nudging her wet cheeks with his head. She wanted a hug from her dad. She rung his mobile again, no answer. She retrieved the answerphone from the kitchen bin, plugged it back in.

Another trick learned from her mother was 'keep busy, do not succumb to self-pity', so she filed the critical illness policy in the blue ring binder where she kept all her statements and flicked through the different sections. Car insurance. Rates. Gas bills. Credit card bills. Bank statements. Her name leapt off every page.

Dear Miss Haldane, Re. renewal of car insurance, we enclose....

Dear Miss Haldane, Further to your letter of...

Dear Miss Haldane, Thank you for sending the cheque for £33.22 in payment of...

It was like a slap in the face.

I may not know my surname any more, I may not be a Haldane, but I am a journalist and a real journalist would not sit here crying.

A journalist investigated, dug deep to find truth, so that's what she would do. If in doubt about her subject, Rose liked to start with background colour, hints, and hearsay. Once she'd done that, the facts usually became a little clearer.

She reached for her mother's striped blue holdall, and took out the purse. It looked exactly as it had yesterday. Yesterday, when she'd been sure that Diana was her mother; yesterday, when she had been so certain that whatever your differences with your mother, she would always be irreplaceable. Today, that sentiment felt naive.

She unzipped the purse and tipped it upside down. Out fell the same bits and pieces that had fallen out yesterday. But there was something she'd missed: a tiny compartment, barely big enough to slip in two postage stamps, too narrow for a finger. Rose could feel the slightest bump of something inside. With tweezers, she pulled out a faded black-and-white photograph, folded in two. She gently smoothed out the crease. She had never seen this picture before.

A baby.

On the back was some writing in smudged pencil: 'Al... born 29th ...gust 1968.'

But 29th August 1968 is my birthday.

The baby's nose looked like every baby's nose, the rosebud mouth could belong to any newborn. Rose wasn't even sure it was a girl. Lily would know. She had a natural way of admiring babies and new hats and new haircuts, saying the right thing at the right time, masking doubt or giggles. The social graces were in Lily's genes.

Rose disliked social dissembling and found it hard to tell lies of the 'oh, isn't your baby beautiful' type when the child was clearly a relative of Winston Churchill's bulldog.

The handwriting on the back of the photo was unfamiliar too. Not her mother's exact script.

'Al… born 29th …gust 1968.'

The doorbell rang, but Rose didn't move.

Al… What names began with Al? She couldn't think of one.

Now someone was knocking at the door. It was the fourth time today. First, an eager young Polish guy keen to do her decorating; second, a pushy, podgy man who wanted her to change mobile phone networks; third, a delivery for next door. This time, she didn't even bother to raise her eyes to look at the caller's portrait on the entryphone. The phone rang but Rose let the answerphone take it. It was the library, chasing a book a month overdue.

Al what? Alexandra. Alison. Alice. Rose held the photo closer to the reading lamp, willing the baby to tell her its secrets.

'Who *are* you?' She spoke aloud but no one heard her.

11 LILY

Lily's first thought when she awoke on Monday morning was Rose, her second was about her Dad. Monday was a Good Times day, Good Times being the gift shop where Lily worked part-time in Chiswick. Usually it was her favourite workday of the week, the day for re-designing the window display, but today it was the last thing she wanted to do. She called Rose at 6.30 a.m., then her father, but both phones rang out. No answer from their mobiles either.

Bad, she thought, *I want to talk to her. But good too, because Rose is okay and at work, interviewing some captain of industry as usual. Typical, nothing gets her down. Well if she's strong enough to go to work today, so am I.*

Then Rose texted to say Dad was okay and at work. She knew it had been stupid to go to the police last night. Dad would be so embarrassed if he knew, he hated what he called 'flapping' but Lily couldn't help it. Mum was gone and she wanted to hold tight onto Dad. She wanted to talk to Rose too but didn't know quite what to say or how to say it, she rang again but just got Rose's automated message. Really, she just wanted to hug Rose and reassure her that they were still sisters.

Standing in the large shop window, something she still felt self-conscious doing, she looked critically at the half-finished display. Stretching out her right arm, she balanced a biscuit tin decorated with botanical flower illustrations on top of a pile of new books called *Flowering Shrubs for Lovers*.

It's not uncommon for Rose to ignore her phone, Lily tried to reassure herself; *she's often in meetings and interviews and goodness knows what. Worrying never helps anything,* she continued lecturing herself as she stretched a millimetre further to straighten the books and wobbled violently, knocking the biscuit tin to the floor.

She put the tin back in its place and heard the rustling of broken biscuits inside. Perhaps she could buy the tin at a discount so some poor unsuspecting customer wasn't disappointed by the shattered shortbread inside.

She experimented with the display, adding a new Scented Roses apron she'd just unpacked that morning. It worked, except that the pink roses reminded her of her mother just like the sandals, and this time sniffing wasn't enough, her eyes filled with tears. Suddenly it was yesterday again, yesterday, when her trust that her mother always told the truth was shattered.

Did Mum really adopt Rose and keep it secret for decades? No, Lily was sure her mum couldn't have done that. A secret like that would destroy you. Then Lily remembered William and the things she hadn't admitted to anyone else and she knew that every family had its secrets.

At midday, Lily faked a migraine and left work. She took three different buses to get to Wimbledon. *Rose had better be in when I get there,* she thought as the bus turned the corner near the brewery at Mortlake. *William will say it's a waste of time setting out without knowing Rose is at home. When someone doesn't answer*

their phone it doesn't mean they're dead or in trouble,
he'll say, *it simply means they're not in or don't want to
talk.*

Lily got off the bus outside the library and
looked up at the windows of Rose's flat opposite. The
curtains were open. She rang the bell, no answer. The
communal front door was ajar an inch, so she pushed it
wider and gently called, 'Hello?' Upstairs, she knocked
on Rose's door. Nothing. So went back down the stairs
and knocked on the door of Flat 1. There was a crash and
a bang and a young woman appeared, her reddish-blonde
hair tied up in a red-and-white chequered cotton scarf
looking for all the world as if she'd just been milking
cows on a Devon farm for a butter advertisement.

'Can I help you?' The woman stood with her
hands on her hips in what Lily took to be an accusatory
pose.

'The front door was open, so I came in.'

'Right?'

Lily felt like a trespasser, standing in this dull
hallway with a lingering smell of tomato soup. 'I'm
looking for my sister, who lives upstairs. Rose Haldane.
Have you seen her today?'

The woman's face softened and Lily suddenly
realised she was pretty, just tired. 'No, sorry. We've
been out.'

'I'm probably just being silly, but she's not
answering her phone.'

The woman pulled a face. 'Well, the phone lines
were down for hours yesterday.'

'Oh, right,' said Lily, grateful for the
sympathetic expression in the woman's eyes and she
knew at once this was what William would say too. It

77

was obvious. The phone lines were being repaired and Rose was being Rose and was probably interviewing some captain of industry.

'Yes, you're right, sorry to trouble you.'

'No trouble.' The woman turned away quickly, but not so quickly that Lily didn't notice the splodges of baked bean and egg yolk flattened across her left shoulder.

12 ROSE

When the phone rang, Rose was watching a tea-time
sitcom about a group of twenty-somethings living in a
cul-de-sac in a Welsh ex-mining village. It was Pick of
the Day in the newspaper, but she couldn't get a fix on
the plot. The answerphone invited the caller to leave a
message.

It was Lily, sounding like she'd been sipping
helium from a balloon.

'Rose, are you there? Rose? If you're not there,
you must be at work, so I hope you're okay. I got your
text about Dad, thanks. I wish we hadn't gone to the
police. Anyway, can't undo that now I suppose... I came
round earlier but you weren't in...'

Lily chattered on, something about an apron and
roses and their mother. Rose's mind blanked out, she
had hardly enough energy for herself. She longed for
silence.

But Lily's voice was small now, very young.
Rose sighed, and picked up the phone. 'I'm here,
Lil. Sorry, I was in the shower and didn't hear it
ring.' Oh, what a shameful lie.

'Oh hi! Hi! I was leaving you a message. I
wanted to ask what happened to Dad.'

'Don't know. I went to his office this morning
and they said he was in a meeting all day.' Rose didn't

have the energy right now to be angry about her Dad's night-time jaunt. 'So he's not lost or anything.' She felt stupid now for jumping to conclusions last night, for letting herself become infected by Lily's flair for drama.

'Well that's alright then. And you're alright, so, I wanted to tell you that I've done what you said. I've got an appointment with the doctor. I'm worried that…'

What about me, Rose wanted to shout at her. *Aren't you worried about me? Don't you get it? I've been surrounded by lies all my life, who can you trust if your parents lie to you?*

'… there's something medically wrong with me.'

Of course, Lily was worried about herself. 'Seeing a doctor is the best thing,' Rose said, a little coldly, 'well done. And it's good that William's taking time off work.'

'Oh no, he's not coming with me. He doesn't… I haven't… he's so busy working for promotion, did I tell you about that? So, well… I'll get myself checked out first.'

'Don't you think he'll want to share it with you?' asked Rose, more gentle now.

'Oh no, not really, I don't think so. William's not good at health things, the body and such, you know. He avoids going to the doctor at all costs. When he has a headache, he pretends the pain doesn't exist.'

'Whatever. I think you should talk to him tonight and get him to go with you,' she said firmly. 'After all, it affects both of you. Just remember, Mum and Dad told us lies for years. Do you really want to have secrets that serious from William?'

Silence, then a small, 'No.' Then more silence.

Eventually, 'Mum did lie, didn't she, about where you came from.'

'Yes, she did. Secrets are poison, Lily. Don't do it.'

'Yes, maybe.'

They were silent for a moment.

'Where were you today? I phoned but your mobile went to messages and your answerphone at the flat was on. I was so worried I came round.'

'I was here. I took the day off.'

'Well I rang the doorbell for ages. And I knocked.' Her voice sounded petulant now.

Oh God, thought Rose, feeling the particular kind of guilt that only Lily could produce. 'I must have been asleep. I was awake half the night, so I've been dozing on and off this afternoon. Earplugs.'

More silence. If Lily said that to her, she wouldn't have been convinced either. Rose rushed to fill the guilty gap. 'I looked at Mum's other diaries but there's nothing about my adoption in them. Just years of lists and recipes and housewife stuff.'

'Does she... does she write about her menopause?'

Rose was going to say no, then realised she didn't actually know. She'd only skipped through them searching for things about her adoption. 'I don't think so but you should read them yourself.'

Lily said hurriedly that of course she wasn't worried about the early menopause thing, it couldn't apply to her, after all, she was too young, had never been ill in her life, not since she had chickenpox as a baby, et cetera.

The word 'baby' reminded Rose of the photo.

'Remember Mum's purse that I took yesterday?'

'Yes.'

'There was a photo hidden inside. A baby. I think it's me.'

'Or it might be me.' There was a slightly sulky tone in Lily's voice now, Rose recognised it as the Younger-Sister-Not-Wanting-To-Be-Left-Out syndrome.

'No, the baby's got dark hair. Anyway, there's a name written on the back. It's in pencil and some of it's rubbed away. It says 'Al... born 29th ...gust... 1968.' It's not Mum's handwriting.' She couldn't keep saying 'Mum', it didn't sound right any more. But, Mum was still Mum.

'That's your birthday.'

'I know.'

'Al? Al what? Maybe Alberta, like Queen Victoria's daughter...'

How did Lily know the name of Queen Victoria's daughter? Rose had always won at Trivial Pursuit and Mastermind and Top of the Form. 'Lily, I was not called Alberta.'

'... or Alice, Alice in Wonderland. Or Alexis the queen bitch in *Dynasty*....'

'I sincerely hope not.'

'... Allegra would be nice, that means "cheerful" according to my baby names book.'

'Allegra?' Rose couldn't think of an answer to that.

They said goodnight. Determined to relax, Rose turned her mobile off, put in earplugs and lay flat on the bedroom floor, her arms and legs lolling outwards as she did in her yoga class, and tried to drift off. She remembered being wrapped in a blanket. There was a warm smell that she couldn't identify and had never smelled again. It wasn't her mother, who always smelled of Youth Dew.

Forget it, she chided herself. *Relax.*

But then the rain started to hammer on the window as only summer rain can, and the real world rushed in. Loathing herself, she poured wine into a tumbler and checked her messages. There were two.

The first was a rather sharp one from her best friend Maggie saying, 'Where the hell are you? It's seven-thirty and I've been waiting an hour.' Rose groaned. She'd forgotten the leaving party for Maggie's features editor at a fancy bar in Hackney. She called Maggie's mobile, but it was turned off, so she left a suitably grovelling apology.

The second message was from Frank at work. 'Oh go on, Rose, let me come round with a takeaway, I'll make you forget your flu. Feed a cold, starve a fever, my mum always says. So it's your call. Chinese, pizza, fish and chips, whatever you fancy. You won't regret it.' 'Yes, I will,' Rose muttered as she pushed the delete button.

Suddenly, she wanted to speak to someone who wasn't family, someone who hadn't been party to the lie. She scrolled through the numbers in her mobile's memory, no option except the one she said would never dial again.

She took a big gulp of wine as the phone rang. 'Hello, James, it's Rose. I –'

She held the phone away from her ear at his barking reply.

'Please don't be like that, I've had a real shock and I want to –'

Barking laughter this time.

'– talk.'

'You chucked me out, remember?'

'James, please I –'

He snorted. 'This is so typical of you. You only ever wanted to see me when there was something in it for you. I'm sorry your road is rocky, Rose, but love is a two-way street.' James always spoke in clichés.

'Please…' She was saying 'please' too much but couldn't think of a way to shut him up.

'I've met someone who wants to see me all the time, not just when it's convenient for her.'

'I didn't –'

'Ellie is fully committed to me, she wants to spend all her time with me.'

Me, Me, Me, thought Rose, *James always says 'Me', and always in capital letters.*

'But you, even the Valentine's card you gave me wasn't fully committed. It was a hologram with…'

What?

'… hearts that faded in and out of focus. It summed you up perfectly.' As he laughed sarcastically, Rose wondered how she could ever have fancied him.

'Rose is a rose is a rose is a rose, you know, Rose. They're ten for £5 at every set of traffic lights.' And he put the phone down.

Rose took a deep breath. Whoa. She hadn't needed that. Tears filled her eyes again.

Why am I doing this to myself, she thought. *It's ridiculous, unhealthy, and self-indulgent. I'm acting more like Lily than myself.*

Brad nudged her arm and rubbed his head against her chin, his fur damp with her tears. She'd always been proud of living alone, she'd banged on to anyone who'd listen that alone didn't mean lonely, that she would never rely on others for her happiness. She was proud to be self-supporting, self-motivated, self-fulfilled. Until this moment, Rose hadn't known what lonely really felt like. She needed tea. Her mother's prescription for all ills. But the teabag tin was empty and the milk smelled off.

She grabbed her purse and headed out. Thank God the rain had stopped. Head down, sunglasses on, she dodged steaming puddles as she crossed the road to Maya's corner shop opposite the tube station. She would be home again in two minutes. She gathered teabags, milk, bread, eggs, and baked beans, paid and turned, banging straight into a cyclist who appeared from nowhere in the shop door, huffing and puffing, radiating heat in fluorescent orange Lycra and smelling of sweat. The food bag fell at her feet.

'Watch where you're going.' She knelt and tried to scoop the food back into the thin plastic bag.

'Sorry, sorry,' said the man. 'My fault, I was thinking about something else. Here, let me help.' He crouched to pick up a tin and Rose noticed he had rather bony ankles. Her head whirled again, so she grabbed everything in one sideways sweep and turned towards home.

'Rose?'

Him? How could it be? Not here, not now, especially not now. Run!

She ran across the road. If she didn't look at him, he wouldn't see her, she would be invisible. Somehow she dodged a taxi, something silver, something red. A motorbike swerved to avoid her. Rose kept going. Almost there. Around the corner and safely out of sight, at last she reached the front door. She stabbed at the lock with her key, cursing until it opened. All was quiet behind her. She ran up the stairs to her own door, steadied her hand and opened this lock more quickly. She slammed the door behind her, dumped the stuff on the kitchen table, and curled up on the sofa, heart pounding.

She was safe. She sniffed and wiped her nose with her fist. She should have bought tissues. Imagining the look on her mother's face, Rose felt the beginnings of a smile. She took a deep breath and struggled up into a sitting position. Brad jumped on her lap and purred and Rose stroked him, feeling a little calmer.

The doorbell rang. Clutching Brad to her chest, Rose didn't move. Whoever it was would go away in a minute.

The doorbell rang and rang.

Keep quiet, quiet as a mouse, she thought. *But what if it's Dad?* Knowing she was being irrational, she tiptoed across the squeaky wooden floor to look at the hazy picture on the entryphone and couldn't believe her eyes.

Why now? Why tonight? Why me? She wailed silently. Standing on the doormat was Nick Maddox holding... holding... something she couldn't make out.

'Hello, Rose? Are you okay?' His voice came over the loudspeaker. 'It was me who bumped into you just now, in the shop. I wanted to say sorry but you ran away. I was worried, you looked a bit... odd... ill. So I followed you.' He shifted from foot to foot in the tiny screen, his face filling every square centimetre of space, his nose looming large at the camera lens. Not flattering.

'I've brought these, you left them behind.' He held up a box. Her teabags. 'I got your email on Friday with the questions and I've left messages for you. Did you get them? Your office said you were out. I thought you might be working from home, but obviously you're ill.'

Rose felt as if she would never work again, never be able to string two sentences together.

'Rose? Please let me in.' His voice was firm now, it was a command.

She pressed the button to open the downstairs door, then immediately regretted it. Why was she doing what he told her? The answer was easy: because she was tired, because she didn't know what to do any more, because it was a relief to let someone else take charge. But somewhere deep inside, the journalistic impulse stirred. No way was she going to let him read her article before publication, if that was what he was after. She started to scoop up the debris surrounding her – dirty dressing gown, *OK, Stars,* and *Heat* magazines which she had bought in an effort to understand Lily's thing about Sylvie Watson, ice-cream carton, damp tissues. The footsteps on the stairs grew louder and her bones transformed to fluid, so she pushed everything on the floor into one heap and kicked it under the dining table. There was a knock at the door. She opened it a crack, left the chain on. 'How did you know where I live?'

'I said, I followed you. Here.' His hand appeared through the gap, pushing the box towards her. 'Are you okay? You look awful.'

She passed a hand over her hair and touched a paper clip. She tried to pull it out without him seeing. 'Thanks. For the teabags.'

'Summer flu is nasty, I thought you might need stuff from the pharmacy, so…'

She'd meant to get some herbal sleeping tablets but in her flight after the collision she'd forgotten to go to the pharmacy. She desperately wanted to sleep.

'No, thanks. I don't need anything. I think you should go now.'

From behind his back, he produced a plastic carrier bag and showed her a bottle of Lucozade, paracetamol, box of tissues, peppermint teabags, bottle of eucalyptus oil, and herbal sleeping tablets.

She let him in.

He seemed to assess the situation with one glance and told her to get into bed. She did, fully clothed. She pulled the sheet to her chin and lay shivering, listening to him banging around in the kitchen. He was there ages. What was he doing? She remembered the debris of plates, mugs, and Brad's dirty bowls with something close to shame. She never normally left dirty dishes in the sink.

He had in fact been making peppermint tea. 'Drink this.' He handed her a steaming mug, and two tablets. 'Take these, then go to sleep.' He watched her from six feet away, sitting in the chair beside her wardrobe, his hands in his lap. She tried not to think about the fact he was sitting on Sunday's abandoned clothes, her skinny jeans, favourite cream bra and knickers, the blue-and-white striped cotton shirt her father had once told her suited her eyes. All now creased by the weight of his sweaty body. She tried not to look directly at the orange Lycra. It was very bright. He didn't ask one question. He didn't mention the article. He just watched her. She blew on the tea until it was cool enough to drink, then took the paracetamol, trying not to look at his hands, not to wonder how they would feel on her. It was all very disconcerting. She closed her eyes, but her eyelids weren't heavy any more. Where had sleep gone? Why didn't he say something?

'My head, it's going round in circles, I'll never sleep.'

'Try.'

'I'm not really ill, I've had some bad news and, you see, I don't...'

'Not now. Sleep.' He took the mug from her hands, closed the curtains and turned out the light, then sat down on top of the duvet at the very edge of the bed. He was almost a foot away from her, but his weight pulled the duvet tighter around her body and the mattress tipped her ever so slightly towards him.

Actually, Rose thought, his sweat smelled quite sweet. She looked at his face and wondered if he had his father's eyes or his mother's.

'Erm, Nick?' It didn't feel right calling him 'Nick', he was a client; professional integrity and all that. But then, he was sitting on her bed.

'Mmm?'

'Where do you think your identity comes from?'

'Rose, close your eyes and go to sleep.'

She closed her eyes. His concerned face was the last thing she saw; no words on the walls, no skulls, no Wanda.

She woke with a start at 2 a.m., took a deep breath, and eased the stiffness in her right shoulder. The flat was still. Her dehydrated tongue had swollen to the proportions of a bath sponge and was pressing uncomfortably against her teeth. She lay for a while, watching the luminous numbers of the clock radio, and feeling increasingly hot thanks to the fact she was still wearing her white velour Jennifer Lopez tracksuit bottoms and purple ABBA T-shirt. Oh God, almost as bad as orange Lycra.

In the kitchen, she fumbled for a bottle of water in the fridge and wondered if she'd dreamed him. But the kitchen was tidy; pots were draining by the sink, and in the middle of the table, propped up against a tin of tuna Whiskas, was a note.

'Hope you feel better. Take two paracetamol every four hours and drink as much water as you can. Nick.'

He really does think I have flu, she thought. For just a moment, she forgot she wasn't Rose Haldane any more, she was just a girl trying to decipher the workings of a man's mind. But try as she might to keep his face in her mind, the horror flooded back in a relentless tide: the words, the diary, the skulls, the life-that-might-have-been, the history stolen from her.

Are none of my memories true?

The laughter while playing Scrabble with Mum and Lily and winning; Grandma Bizzie pointing out the difference between the great tits and blue tits on the bird table by her kitchen window; dancing with Dad to *Sing Something Simple* on the radio, her red sandals on top of his suede brogues, swaying around the sitting room together and singing made-up nonsense songs...

'You are my little Rosie, Rosie...
And I am your Daddy-o...'

13 ROSE

When she woke again, it was morning and she didn't feel like a dishrag, which was amazing, as one glance in the bathroom mirror told her she looked like one. She showered, put on some mascara, and went out to buy a newspaper. It was 6 a.m. Not her usual time. Time to catch up on the *Herald* and its rivals, try to return to some sense of normality.

Newspapers tucked under her arm, she let herself in to find the stairs up to her flat blocked. A small dark head sat hunched forward over the carpeted bottom step, shoulders quivering like a newly set jelly turned out of a rabbit mould, the same shape as the once-white lop-eared bunny discarded on the entrance hall floor.

'Hello, can I get by?'

The face that turned to look at her was stained with tears and something beige that might have been Weetabix or paint or snot. His red-blotched cheeks clashed violently with his strawberry-blonde hair and orange-and-green striped T-shirt. He opened his mouth, hiccupped, and burst into tears. Rose thought fleetingly about patting him on the head but was thankfully rescued by a voice from the doorway on the right.

'Oh, I'm sorry.' A woman appeared from the downstairs flat. She had to be his mother, they had matching warm blonde hair. 'He's been a naughty boy, haven't you, Lewis? So he's sitting on the naughty step.' Rose thought about pointing out that the stairs was a communal area, but Lewis was scooped into his mother's arms and the obstruction went away. 'But five minutes on the naughty step is enough, isn't it Lewis?' He nodded solemnly and flung his arms around his mother's neck.

'Come on then, let the lady get upstairs. Shall we have toast with strawberry jam for breakfast?' She stopped at the hall table and leafed through the junk mail that Rose had been meaning to throw in the recycling box.

Rose stopped halfway up the stairs and turned. Lewis was peeping over his mother's shoulder at her. He waved. For a moment she hesitated, not wanting to encourage his attention. But then she remembered her mother making her stand on the front-door step one winter's day for an hour. She'd been playing tag in the garden with Lily who had tripped over a tree root and skinned her knee. It was only a scratch, but Lily cried and screamed as if her leg had been chopped off. Rose had told her to shut up.

It had been very cold on that step.

So she waved back at Lewis.

She spread the newspapers on the kitchen table and that's when she saw it again. The note.
'Hope you feel better. Take two paracetamol every four hours and drink as much water as you can. Nick.'
He hadn't been a dream then.

14 ROSE

On Tuesday, yesterday's lie was feasibly extendable. It took her a fraction of a second to decide. She extended it.

In Richmond, her father's car, a ten-year-old VW with a dent on the driver's door and a crack in the front number plate, was parked in the drive. She walked up the path, tapping the gatepost twice as she passed. This was a safe place; she'd grown up in this house. The door was unlocked. She stepped into the kitchen, wishing she could hear her mum's 'yoo hoo' call of greeting, missing the blue pottery jug that for years had sat in the middle of the kitchen table filled with a hotchpotch of flowers and glistening green leaves from the garden. The jug was sitting atop the fridge stuffed with seed packets. Nothing physical in the room had changed since Sunday, but the emptiness seemed deeper.

'Hello?' she called. Nothing. 'Hello?'

'Down in a minute,' a faint voice drifted from upstairs.

As it was Tuesday, she knew he would be holed up in his den in the loft, a human island amidst a sea of gardening magazines and seed catalogues. He worked from home one day a week, supposedly to do his admin. Rose tried to think positively. He was here then, not at the allotment, collapsed amongst his runner beans, not dead of a heart attack.

'Put the kettle on, will you?'

The kitchen table was piled high with stuff. Piles of alphabetically arranged files of Kalamazoo index cards, the brown cardboard curling and torn, which he used for his client records; a new laptop in its cellophane-wrapped box; an old box for a mobile phone, empty. What was that about? Her father didn't do technology. His company insisted on sending him on computer courses but he stuck with his creased and grease-stained record cards, which featured comments such as WOS (waste of space) and WKR (wanker) and SOB (short of a bob). Rose had figured out the abbreviations years ago, she doubted her mother had ever understood.

While the kettle rasped into life, Rose stood at the mantelpiece and looked at her parents' wedding picture. It stood in the same place it had all of Rose's life. Usually it made her smile, but now she felt betrayed. She laid the photo on its face.

As she turned away, her father walked into the kitchen. He looked as if he had a hangover, flu, and a migraine all at once. A faint smell of camphor, stale beer, and unwashed male followed him into the room.

'Sorry love, I was on the phone.' He scuffed his feet along the floor in his twenty-year-old moccasin slippers. 'This is a surprise, pumpkin.' His smile didn't fit his mouth.

She heard his casual words with disbelief. Her voice, when it came, didn't sound like her voice at all. She spoke with a desperation she hadn't owned up to before, not even to herself.

'Dad, I've been trying to speak to you since

Sunday. Didn't you get my messages?' She was frightened by how cold her heart felt.

The kettle boiled and he turned to pour the water into the teapot.

'You never came home. We waited, we even went to the allotment.'

'Blimey, Rose, since when did you turn into your mother? I'm not ten years old. I went to The Bull with Ron Fosdyke, all right? He bought me a pint for helping him paint his shed.'

'Until midnight?'

'All right, it was more than one. I slept on his sofa, if you must know. I am over twenty-one, you don't have to wait up until I come home.' He turned towards her with an empty mug in his hand and a smile, which faded as soon as he saw Rose's eyes scanning the detritus on the kitchen table, now seeing a letter marked 'private and confidential'. A Sorry-to-see-you-go card. 'Dad?'

Rose had seen her father cry only once. Seeing it again, seeing him so vulnerable, made her feel old.

'They haven't…'

'Yes.' He passed her a mug. 'I got called into a meeting yesterday. I'd been expecting it. They took my mobile away, gave me an hour to clear my desk. As if I was guilty of something. I was supposed to meet some of the lads last night for a drink, but I couldn't face it. After all those years, just brushed aside like a piece of cotton thread.'

'But why?'

He took a swig of tea. 'Failure to meet sales targets, failure to maintain margin, failure to use the central computer database, failure to keep up with the times, failure to – to do any of the things I was told to do when they warned me three months ago that if I didn't do them, I'd be out. So here I am, out.' Another swig of tea.

She didn't know what to say, so she took a sip of tea as well. It was the same strong Darjeeling with too much sugar in it that Lily had given her on Sunday after finding the diary. The memory made her retch and she pushed the mug away. She looked at her father. He'd known for three months that he might be sacked, been worrying about it, not sleeping, drinking more, eating Sunday lunch with her and Lily… and she hadn't noticed anything was wrong. Rose felt ashamed. Since her mother's death, he'd gobbled indigestion tablets like they were Smarties and there was an angry patch of eczema on his neck that wouldn't heal. But Rose had put all this down to grief, symptoms that would pass with time.

'Can't you appeal?' But as she asked the question, she knew it was futile. If a company wanted to get rid of someone, it was easy to make it happen and there was little an employee could do to counter without the battle of industrial tribunal. Rose wondered if Lily knew about Dad's sacking and felt a frisson of triumph that she knew something about their father before Lily did. Lily would take over now, nurse their father's emotional strength, encourage him to get a part-time job, perhaps doing garden maintenance for her rich neighbours in Barnes. Actually, he would probably like that.

He shook his head and turned to the teapot, topping it up with hot water from the kettle and adding another teabag. 'I'll survive, worse things can happen.

I've got my health, that's what counts. But you didn't come to see me on a Tuesday morning to talk about me.

'What is it, love? You haven't been sacked too, have you?' His smile wobbled around the edges.

'No, no, it's not work.' Rose's fingers held the creased baby photograph tightly in her pocket. Should she say something now? Maybe not. He looked like shit; he must be feeling like shit. But… she felt like shit too. And he had lied to her all her life.

'Did you know Mum kept a diary?'

His shoulders sagged slightly, like an airbed with a slow leak. He slowly stirred the tea in the pot and shook his head.

'We found a stack of them, in a box, at the back of her wardrobe.'

'Ah.'

'In one of them, she writes about how she couldn't get pregnant and so she adopted a baby.'

Silence. He was looking down into the teapot as if searching for answers, but he was leaning so far forwards Rose thought he would fall in. She walked around the table and took the spoon out of his hand. His loose fingers gave it up without protest. She pushed him down into Lily's old chair and swept a clear space on the table. She sat opposite him in her usual chair, the table dividing them.

'Dad, I'm not blaming you or Mum, but I do need to know the truth.'

'What,' he spoke so quietly she had to lean in to hear, 'does it say?'

'That she can't get pregnant, that she finds a girl who is pregnant and can't keep the baby. They do a deal… a deal about the baby.'

His dark brown eyes bored down into the table.

'Am I that baby?' Her heart was pounding so loudly, she thought he must hear it.

He stroked the dents made by Lily with a dinner knife when she was six. Rose looked at the tiny heart she'd tattooed in ink next to her place. Now she stretched across the table and stilled his arm, then pulled the tiny photo out of her pocket.

'Dad, is this me?'

He took a deep breath, so deep she could hear his lungs expand. His eyes were fixed on the photo.

'Yes. You were… pretty, very special, we both thought you were very special.' Very Special. Two words pronounced as if they should be in quote marks or have capital letters, two words straight out of a book for parents on what to say when your daughter asks you if she was adopted.

'If I was so special, why have you never told me?'

Her father was whispering now. 'Special.'

'Sp…special?' Rose's voice rose uncomfortably close to shrill, her words sputtering out like water from an air-blocked tap. 'I can't believe you never told me. Were you going to let me die an old woman having lived a lie?'

'No, of course not. It's just… I never… we never found the right time.'

'Well, you could have tried.'

They sat, looking in opposite directions.

'Was everyone in on the secret?'

He was rocking slightly now, shaking his head.

'You must have known Mum kept a diary?'

'No… no, I didn't… why would she write it

98

down?'

Thank God she did, thought Rose. *If she hadn't, I would still be living a lie.*

'What about Grandma?'

He looked up, his eyes glazed. 'I don't know if Bizzie keeps a diary.'

'No. Did she know about me?' *Not Grandma Bizzie, please, no.*

'Rose, not now. I can't deal with this now.'

A grey shadow fell across his face, the same shadow as when he stepped forward to throw a handful of earth on top of her mother's coffin. Rose tried to push that memory aside.

'Where did I come from? I mean, am I English?'

'Yes, of course you are.' He was starting to sound a little exasperated.

'But how do you know? Did you meet my parents? What were they like? Do I look like them?'

'Rose. Slow down. You're firing questions at me like a machine gun.' There was a tiny flicker underneath his right eye now. 'It's – it's come as a bit of a shock.'

'A shock. Well, how do you think I feel?' Any higher and Rose's voice would shatter the sherry glasses.

Her father hung his head. 'This is all too – much. And I've got to…' His eyes drifted to the boxes of Kalamazoo cards. 'I've got to return stuff to the office, files, record cards… They even want the original box for my mobile. Don't know why. Just being pedantic, I think.'

'Okay, fine.' Rose stood up and pushed the chair away with such a jerk it clattered against the fridge. 'I've got important things to do too.'

She couldn't get out of the house quickly

enough. Trembling with adrenalin, her eyes wouldn't focus and her fingers wouldn't work. She tripped over the kerb, then dropped her car keys twice before she managed to open the door. She didn't bother with the dropper on the Rescue Remedy dropper, she just swigged it. She drove so fast she scared herself, unable to control her foot, which was a brick on the accelerator pedal. She was flashed and hooted at for what seemed like miles until she swerved left and stopped in an empty corner of a DIY superstore car park.

He didn't deny it. I haven't misunderstood the diary. I'm not being hysterical. I was adopted.

It was fact and she knew what to do with facts. You checked them and researched them and they led you to the next fact and the next and the next.

15 ROSE

Bizzie was baking jammy oat slices. They were Rose's favourites; she'd eaten them a thousand times and knew Bizzie's method by heart. First she lined a Swiss roll tin with shortcrust pastry and brushed it with jam. Any sort would do as long as it was red, but homemade strawberry was best. Then she mixed rolled oats with golden syrup and piled the mixture onto the pastry. They came out of the oven twenty minutes later, glorious and sticky. Rose had eaten them since before she could remember. Now she hesitated by the window, watching her grandmother bend to put the tray in the oven, wondering how to break the news to her.

'I know, Grandma.'

'Know what, love?'

'That I'm adopted.'

Moving in slow motion, Bizzie wiped her hands on her pink floral apron, reached behind her for the kitchen chair, and sat down. Rose waited. There was a long silence, broken by Bizzie, who rubbed her eyes.

'I told Diana it would hurt you more if they didn't tell you when you were young, but she wouldn't listen to me. And Howard,' she twisted her gold wedding band, worn almost as thin as wire, 'your grandfather had passed by then. Diana never would listen to me.'

Rose had been holding her breath and now felt a silent sigh escape.

'So, you knew?' If Bizzie said it was true, it must be. She never lied.

'Oh yes, love, I'm ashamed to say it is. Secrets only bring hurt. But you never want to fall out with your own children and you were such a lovely baby. Then Lily came along and I suppose it was easier to forget about it than to upset things. I'm sorry, love. I suppose if anyone was going to take her to task, it should have been me. Maybe if Howard had been alive…' Her voice was beseeching, full of hope for forgiveness, for understanding about how children continue to run your life until you die. Bizzie reached out, stretching her hand across the table.

Rose sat down and took her grandmother's hand, sticky with jam. Her lovely, soft, comforting grandmother, who had always been there to kiss her scrapes and make them better, had lied to her too.

'Is this why you were asking about The Change last week?'

Change? What change? Oh, early menopause. 'No, that's just an article I'm writing at work. You know, Gran, the more I think about being adopted, the more things start to make sense.' Rose reached into her tight jeans pocket and pulled out the photograph.

'I found this in Mum's old purse.'

Bizzie reached for her glasses, then took the photo and smoothed out the creases with her thumb. She studied the baby then read the pencilled words on the back. She shook her head a little. 'I haven't seen this before, but it is your birthday.'

Rose put the photo back in her pocket. Bizzie

stood up, switched on the kettle, and started putting teabags into the pot. The smell of strong tea made Rose think of her father.

'Can I have a coffee instead, Gran?'

Rose sat at the table, an icicle in the warmth of Bizzie's kitchen. Her grandmother took the jammy oat slices out of the oven, cut them up and laid them on the rack to cool, and slowly the repetitive familiarity of the scene started to melt the ice inside her. She looked at the familiar china cup and saucer, green with an ivy pattern, which Bizzie placed in front of her, the silver teaspoon with its delicate scalloped edging, and the jammy oat slice on a matching side plate. It smelled wonderful. It smelled of childhood. Rose wasn't sure what she wanted at all, except that this quiet should go on and on and make everything all right.

'You've spoken to your father?'

'Yes. I asked him who my real parents are, but he wouldn't tell me.'

'I doubt he knew, dear. I don't. Adoptions were done confidentially then. To protect everyone.'

It doesn't protect me, thought Rose. 'Can you remember anything? Please?'

Bizzie rubbed her temples. 'It was so long ago.'

Try! Rose wanted to shout.

'Let me see, one day out of the blue, your mum said she was adopting a baby and the next day she came home with you. My first grandchild. You were so beautiful. I was very sad that your grandfather never saw you.' Bizzie glanced up at her wedding photo, a framed black-and-white print of her standing on the church steps next to an elegant yet severe man with a wave of black hair.

103

'But I'm not your granddaughter, Gran. That's the point.' As soon as she'd said the words, Rose wished she could take them back. Bizzie's cheeks slumped to her jawline.

'Oh Gran, I'm sorry, you're being really sweet and I'm upsetting you. But I just don't get it. Why did they adopt me in the first place, and why didn't they tell me the truth?'

Bizzie's powdered face was pale and she looked older than her seventy-nine years. 'Perhaps they were waiting for the right time but it never came, and the longer they waited, the harder it got. "Roses all the way, so so." I told your mum you had a right to know and that it wasn't fair on me to have to tell lies. But Diana always did as she wanted and everyone else, well, we had to like it or lump it. The only ones who stood up to her were your grandfather and Kate.'

She paused. 'Your mother did love you, Rose.'

At that moment, Rose was finding it difficult to locate love for either parent. 'I can't believe Dad didn't tell me.' A sniff turned into a deep snort.

'Now, now, he's just not good at talking, that's all. Remember that he loves you, we all do. He finds it difficult to talk about private things.' Bizzie handed her a tissue. 'Blow.'

Rose felt five years old.

Bizzie watched her wipe her eyes and nose. 'You look just like your Granddad when you do that. He used to pull that face when he had to do something he didn't want to, usually when I asked him to do the drying up.'

Rose smiled. She knew the strands of her DNA and Granddad Howard's didn't match up. And everyone pulled faces.

'Don't worry yourself about your dad at the moment. He's missing your mum, that's all, it's natural. He said last week he can't sleep, hates the empty house, he goes down to the allotment at night when he can't sleep. I'm worried he'll get muggled.'

'You mean "mugged", Gran.' At that moment, Rose didn't care if he was digging up potatoes at two in the morning. 'Didn't people think it was strange when Mum turned up one day with a baby?'

'People were too polite to ask and Diana carried on as if it was perfectly normal. I wasn't proud of her, I'll admit it now. Looking back, I think your dad let her make all the decisions just for a quiet life. That's no way to run a marriage. But she was so desperate for a baby. She told me once that... no.' Bizzie gave her head a small shake.

'Go on, please. I want to know.' It couldn't get any worse.

'She said if she couldn't have a baby, she would be a failure. She was worried your father would leave her and start a family with another woman. I don't know where she got that from; it was Diana who was obsessed with babies, not John. She got more and more obsessed about it.'

Rose tried to imagine her parents in their twenties, newly married, trying to make a baby. She saw nothing. She saw Lily.

'She was right, wasn't she? They had two babies and were still married when she died. Dad stayed.'

'That's a cynical comment and very unattractive, Rose.'

A howl threatened to uncurl in Rose's stomach.

'It's difficult not to be cynical, Gran.' She took a deep breath and made the howl wind up into a ball. A few more deep breaths and she was able to speak. 'And then Mum fell pregnant with Lily so soon after adopting me.'

'Well, sometimes when you stop worrying, it happens naturally.'

'Perhaps.' Rose tried not to sound bitter. Bizzie looked very weary, very old, and Rose hated herself for hurting her grandmother but there were some things she needed to say aloud. 'I could have had a different life. If Mum had waited to get pregnant, if she hadn't adopted me, my real mother might have kept me. Or I might have been adopted by a different family.'

'Try not to be so hard on her, love.'

But Rose's imagination was on a roll. It was so easy to picture it. Growing up in the country in an old stone house with an orchard and a paddock where she kept a black pony. Two brothers, one older, one younger, her father a farmer, her mother a farmer's wife who baked cakes and warmed newborn lambs in the bottom drawer of the Rayburn. Freezing winters; tobogganing with rosy cheeks, a snowman with a carrot for a nose. Summer; tadpoles and picnics and paddling in the stream.

'You know, Gran, I spent my whole childhood wanting Mum to be pleased with me, but she never was. Every time she looked at me she must have seen nothing of herself to love.'

'She always loved you.' Bizzie's voice was very quiet.

'Yeah, right.' Rose moved to the kitchen window and looked out. Bizzie came to stand beside her, their shoulders brushing. Outside, a great tit and a blue tit were at the bird table, squabbling over some peanuts. Rose's eyes felt hot. Bizzie's shoulder burned through Rose's jumper, Bizzie, who had always been taller than Rose; Bizzie, whose back was now bent with the years. Rose turned to her grandmother and hugged her, relaxing into those oh-so-familiar arms, giving and receiving comfort and warmth.

Rose's eyes prickled. 'I have to find them, Gran, my other parents,' she spoke into the soft woolly shoulder. 'Until I do, I don't know where I belong.'

'You belong here, you always have done. Whether you like it or not, we are your family.'

When Rose got home, the light on the answerphone was flashing '2'. Was it her father? Was it... Nick Maddox?

'Rose, it's May. Where are you? If you're sick, you should be at home, and if you're not sick, you should be here working. Two days is quite sufficient for a journalist to recover from infection. You've had four...'

I haven't, thought Rose angrily.

'... including the weekend. I want you at your desk before nine tomorrow morning.'

She pressed 'next'.

'Hello, Miss. This is Sergeant Wilcox at Petersham Police Station. With regards to your reporting a Mr...' there was a pause, '... Mr John Haldane missing on Sunday June first, I can confirm that we have received no reports of an incident regarding this gentleman. If you wish to submit a Missing Person Report, please call me on 0208......'

I will go back to work, she told Brad firmly as he

washed his face with his paws, his purring sounding like the distant rumble of traffic. *Because words are my thing. They never let me down, words don't lie to me. I'll start now, I'll write down how I feel about what happened.*

She took her mug to the computer and started to write. But every other keystroke was 'delete', so when the phone rang she answered it with a sense of escape. Nick?

It was Maggie. 'I got your message. What's wrong?'

Rose precised the events of the last three days.

There was a long silence on the other end of the line. 'I don't know what to say, Rose. I'm so sorry I haven't been around.'

'It's okay.' Rose liked the sympathy but wondered idly why everyone automatically assumed it was bad news to hear you'd been adopted. Could it ever be good news?

'I'm coming round. You shouldn't be on your own.'

'No, not today. Maybe in a couple of days, okay? I'm fine, really I am.'

'Well... just ring me if you need me.'

Rose needed to think clearly. *What I need to do is stop thinking about Nick Maddox.*

Nick, who hadn't rung to see if she felt better.

A week ago, Rose would have been intimidated at the thought of having strange parents, let alone strangers – possibly with criminal records. Now, she just wanted to find them. She logged on and searched for 'adoption' – 0.07 seconds later it produced 4,380,000 results. Nonsense. In her inbox was an email from Maggie listing six adoption websites. 'Try these,' said her message.

Rose rang the helpline at the top of the list, ARAP, the Association for the Reunion of Adoptees and Parents, and spoke to a very matter-of-fact lady who was obviously accustomed to dealing with emotional wrecks. 'Well, as you don't know your birth name, the first thing you have to do is apply to access your birth records,' advised the lady, who introduced herself as Bella. 'You can download the form from the Direct Gov website and post it. Then you see an adoption advisor for a disclosure interview, where you'll be given the information you need to apply online for your full adoption certificate. That's the document used for all legal and administrative purposes, just like an original birth certificate is.'

Rose wished she were writing this down, she'd never remember it all. 'Why can't I just apply online?'

'It doesn't work like that.' Rose could hear the patience in Bella's voice, the warm weariness from explaining this incomprehensible procedure hundreds of times to confused people. 'You were adopted prior to 1975. You see, before that date, many parents were led to believe the child they gave up for adoption would never be able to find them. So it'd be a bit of a shock, you turning up on their doorstep. There is a fixed procedure to follow.'

'But it's urgent.' Yet a reasonable voice in her head said, *Don't shout at this lady, she's trying to help.* Journalism rule number five: polite apology followed by an appeal to the offended person's expertise.

Rose apologised.

'Remember, your birth mother may be terrified

you'll hate her and will want to punish her,' Bella warned. 'Or perhaps she's worried her family will judge her. She might have told no one about you and done everything to avoid seeing you. Ever. Take it slowly, Rose. I'll send you an information pack to get you started. Let me know how you get on.'

Rose knew she would ring again, just to hear Bella's calm voice. She always found it soothing to plan, so that's what she did now. She started a 'Things to Do' list. It was already in her head, but seeing it in blue ink on paper made it real.

One. Download and fill in Application for Access to Birth Records form

Two. See an adoption advisor

Three. Get my adoption certificate

Four. Find my birth parents

She did Item 1 then read the list again. There was a lot to do. Should she get help? Lily? Maggie? No. She wanted to ask the questions and hear the answers first, then work out what she thought before telling anyone else.

Sleep was elusive that night. Rose tried thinking of the work piling up in the office, the deadlines she'd missed, but Nick's face hovered in the margins, smiling, saying he knew the name of her birth mother, knew where she lived. Rose lay in the dark for an hour, before getting up to make a cup of tea.

Her dirty trainers lay on the backdoor mat.

She looked in the telephone directory and found what she was looking for. Easy.

Half an hour later she was driving furtively through Battersea towards the Thames, looking from the

bleak concrete tower blocks on the right to the red-brick
Victorian giants on the left. She pulled over, turned on
the interior light and looked at her notes.

*Nicholas Derek Maddox, 23 River Reach, River Drive,
Battersea.*

She got out and looked around but couldn't see a
River Reach. She started to jog in the general direction
of the power station. She'd never run at night before, but
once she got over the initial fear that someone was
lurking behind each tree with the sole intent of jumping
out at her, she started to enjoy it. The cool, the quiet, the
empty pavements and roads were pleasant, so different
from jostling elbows with pedestrians during daylight
hours. No jogging on the spot waiting for green lights
before crossing a road. Up ahead she could see a church,
an alleyway at its side. She turned and yes – there it was.
The Thames, moving with a slow inevitability
downstream like a band of dark blue oil leaching into the
black night. She ran along the riverside path, praying she
wasn't stepping in any dog mess but trusting her nose to
warn her of danger, and then she saw it. A black gate set
into a high white wall. A small sign; brushed metal lit by
a single downlighter. Clean and polished.
    'Access for River Reach residents only'.
    Rose looked up at the glass-and-steel building
looming above her. Nine, no ten storeys high, tall for
this part of London excepting Chelsea Harbour opposite.
A couple of windows were asleep behind pulled
curtains, some were bright and awake and staring at her
rudeness, more blinked at her with half-pulled blinds as
if saying, 'Hello there, I am cool aren't I? Fancy coming

111

up for a cocktail?'

Wow. Did Nick live here? Rose tried to remember Nick's CV. What had he done before Biocare Beauty? Was there family money? He didn't seem the type. Or had he exited his previous company with a golden handshake? Possibly. He looked the type of command the sort of contract that included a huge payout, even if he got sacked. Rose jogged on the spot, wondering idly how one went about getting a contract like that.

A light went on in a second-floor flat, the door slid open, and a figure appeared on the balcony. Rose looked around for a bush. Nowhere to hide. She stood back-to-back with the white wall, trusting to the shadows, pulling in her chest and ignoring the sharp edges of the painted concrete sticking through her thin T-shirt. There was a click of a cigarette lighter and Rose breathed deeply, unaware she'd actually been holding her breath. Nick didn't smoke, or at least he didn't smell like a smoker. The smoke drifted down and her mood passed. She could go home now.

The return drive took ten minutes. By 1.30, she was sitting up in bed, nursing a mug of peppermint tea and feeling sneaky. She couldn't believe she'd actually done what she'd done. If someone had spied on her like that, she would never want to see them again. She got out of bed and went to her desk. The note with Nick's address on it lay beside her mobile. The paper seemed whiter than white, its words written very large in extra bold type, as if shouting their inappropriateness. She picked up the paper and stuck it in the shredder, watching it chew up the evidence of her sneakiness.

Then she got back into bed and waited for sleep.

Her muscles ached comfortably, the warm ache of self-righteousness you get after exercising, though in truth she hadn't jogged more than half a mile. Just putting on her trainers was sufficient to make her feel athletically virtuous these days. As she waited for her cheeks to cool, her mind ebbed and flickered and flowed, wondering about the nature of truth. Was it always better to know the truth, to know that Mum wasn't her genetic mother? Would Nick want to know she had stalked him or would he be happier in ignorance? Would she be happier now if she were still unaware she was adopted? She was in no doubt that Mum would be horrified to know Rose had discovered her adoption secret, just as she, Rose would be horrified if Nick knew what she'd done. She'd closed the circle and was back to her sneakiness.

Rose lay with her eyes closed until she felt the early morning light warm the pillow beneath her cheek, so warm, so familiar, just like the afternoon sun in those endless school holidays in Richmond. She could smell Bizzie's lemon cake and hear Wanda's giggle as they sat on the branch high in the sycamore tree. The aroma of trees and leaves and dust calmed her. It never rained in her memories.

At last, Rose dreamed of a voice humming her to sleep, whispering Tennyson...
She is coming, my dove, my dear;
She is coming, my life, my fate;
The red rose cries, 'She is near, she is near';
And the white rose weeps, 'She is late'.
The larkspur listens, 'I hear, I hear';
And the lily whispers, 'I wait'.
And, at last, she slept.

16 LILY

Lily was peeling potatoes for dinner. Colcannon with pan-fried salmon fillets. She didn't particularly like colcannon, but it was William's choice. She left the potatoes soaking in a pan of cold water, and then trimmed a Savoy cabbage, aiming the thick outer leaves at the compost bucket but missing more often than not.

Should she force William to talk to her somehow? How? Why didn't he want to listen to her? He used to. She rinsed the cabbage in so much cold water that she rinsed the sink and worktop too. As she mopped the floor, she wondered again how she'd got it so wrong last night.

William had returned home yesterday from Geneva a day early and in an ugly mood. She felt like she'd won a chance to talk to him, so she conjured up his favourite fish stew with a tin of tomatoes and tuna (oily fish, good for everything, and sustainably caught), with organic broccoli (folic acid, essential for a healthy foetus) on the side, followed by banana cake (yet more folic acid, what he didn't know he couldn't object to). She hadn't once mentioned the words 'sex', 'pregnancy', or 'baby' while they ate dinner and was proud of this because, after the discovery of the diary and Rose's hints about early menopause, they were the only three words in her head. It took an enormous effort to behave

115

normally. But when she'd stroked his arm as they lay in bed and said 'I missed you,' he didn't even put down his book.

'I'm really tired,' he'd said, and turned onto his side away from her. *Not too tired to watch the ten o'clock news though, not too tired to read,* she'd wanted to say, hating herself for not confronting him.
Why is it always me who has to do what he wants?

She skinned the salmon fillet and left it to marinade in olive oil and lemon juice. That was William's second-favourite dinner prepared. Next, the laundry. Except she didn't feel like ironing William's shirts just now. She didn't feel like doing anything for him. With her heart lightening at the thought of escape, she picked up her jacket and bag. She would talk to the one person who loved her unconditionally.

She headed to the allotment. Her father was tying up canes. It was a pretty typical scene, one that had occurred throughout Lily's childhood. She remembered the first time he'd trusted her to plant his baby cabbages, patting down the soil and watering them in with her own red watering can. She was good at this. And everything felt familiar now except for the silence. It took her a moment to work out what was missing: he wasn't whistling. He always whistled, show tunes mostly and songs from films. 'Moon River' was a favourite, 'I Talk to the Trees', and 'June Is Bustin' Out All Over' which Lily had thought was about a lady with a large chest. But he hadn't whistled since the funeral; it was as if he'd forgotten how.

'Now then.' He didn't raise his head but seemed to know she was there, and this made her feel warm inside. He was tying up the spaghetti-thin green shoots of runner beans, training them upwards towards the sun. But when he looked up, Lily was shocked to see his face so pale, grey even, and she was immediately furious with Rose. She must have confronted him about the adoption.

Typical Rose, she never stops to think that poor Dad is still grieving.

He straightened up and staggered slightly. Lily took his arm. 'Are you all right?'

'I'm fine,' he said, reaching into his pocket and bringing out a foil strip of indigestion tablets. 'I just stood up too quickly.' He popped out two tablets and chewed.

'Well, I think you should go for a check-up, it could be your blood pressure.'

'I'm fine, I tell you. Stop fussing.'

'Dad, please go to the doctor. For me?'

His head jerked in what Lily took to be a small nod of agreement. They sat on the narrow wooden bench outside his shed. His hand shook as he opened his flask and poured tea, first into the lid, then into the white plastic cup nestled inside. The tea steamed – the air was chilly despite the warmth of the sun. This was the moment to ask him, she thought.

He took a gulp of tea, rubbed his mouth with the back of his hand, and sat back.

'Aah.'

How did you raise such a thing with your father, she wondered, about the mechanics of getting pregnant? About sex? How would Rose ask?

He asked, 'When did you last see Rose?'
The sigh was out of Lily's mouth before she could stop it. So he was more interested in Rose than in her. Lily

hated tea from a flask, it tasted plasticky, but she hadn't wanted to offend by refusing and now she took her time swallowing. Did he know? If so, what did he know? Should she tell him, or was it best coming from Rose? She decided not to mention the diaries at all.

'I talked with her on the phone on Monday evening.'

'Monday?' Colour was creeping back into his ashen cheeks.

'Have you seen her then?'

He took another big swallow. He never waited for drinks to cool, preferring them straight from the kettle. 'Yes. She came to see me yesterday, said you two found a diary in Mum's wardrobe.'

Oh, thank goodness, he knows. 'Diaries, yes, we did. Dad, did Mum always write a diary?' She waited, willing him to answer, but hearing only silence.

He tossed the dregs of tea over the weeds at his feet and stood up. 'Lily, I don't really want to talk now.' He screwed the lid back on to the flask. 'I've got three rows to sow with lettuce seed, and the compost needs turning.'

'I'll help,' she said, jumping up. She picked up the seed packet and rake. 'Where do you want them?' She smiled, but her mind was somersaulting. She wasn't going to leave empty-handed. Her father must have more diaries and Lily knew there would be some sort of record in the diaries, because her mother had taught her to do it when she was eleven. 'Be discreet,' Mum had counselled as she gave her a pink diary with a golden lock. 'You only need a tiny question mark in the margin to show the date you're due, and a ring around the date of each day you're on. It's a little code. No one else

118

needs to know what it means.' If she could see the codes in her mother's diaries, it would prove that her mother had regular periods.

She jumped up and followed him along the path beside a long thin strip of freshly turned soil. Halfway along, he stopped suddenly and they collided. Off-balance, Lily stepped aside on to the fresh earth but he looked fixedly at her footprint so she swiftly stepped back onto the grassy path.

'So, how was Rose?' she asked.

He took a dibber from his pocket and sank to his knees at the beginning of the row.

She knelt beside him. It felt a bit like they were praying.

'Angry,' he said at last. He pushed the dibber into the soil with force, then gestured to her to put a seed in each hole.

Lily thought the holes were too deep for lettuce; she sowed her lettuce seeds in shallow drills in her back garden, but she did as he said, as she always had.

'Well, it was a shock, of course she's angry. But Rose is strong, she'll get over it. After all, she's not the only one with problems.' That was her big hint. *Ask me now, please, Dad.*

He continued dibbing.

Just when she was wondering if he would ever speak again, he did, and he sounded so wistful her mouth went dry.

'It's not the same without your mother. She made things nice, she knew how to make me forget work in the evenings. Now I can't forget anything.' He shuffled sideways on his knees and dibbed again. 'Even gardening doesn't help.'

Lily had a sudden impulse to hug him but his body was all angles and elbows and it didn't work. 'Oh Dad, when you feel low you must come and spend some time with us. William would love to see you.' She bit her lip at the lie.

More seeds were planted in silence, a more companionable silence this time. Lily so wanted to ask her father what to do about William, but that tight expression was back on his face, so she concentrated on the lettuce seeds, knocking a little soil back into the hole before dropping in a seed and covering it with earth. Just being next to him was a comfort of sorts.

17 ROSE

Over the next few days, Rose's routine didn't vary. Each morning and lunchtime she rang her father, and each time there was no answer. She understood his avoidance technique, she didn't particularly want to talk either, but it had to be done or she would never find out the truth.

So every night after work she drove to Richmond. Each night her father's car was in the drive but The Weavings was empty. Slight changes suggested the house was occupied at some point during the day – on Wednesday night empty milk bottles appeared on the doorstep that hadn't been there in the morning, the rubbish bin was at the kerbside awaiting collection – so she could only conclude that he was still alive and getting on with his life. Rose decided to follow his example.

On Friday night, she didn't get home until after 10 p.m. She gobbled beans on toast, sprinkling extra cheddar on top because she couldn't resist the smell of melted cheese, and almost instantly fell asleep on the sofa in front of the TV. Her dream was vivid. There was a babushka doll, hand-painted in tiny brushstrokes.

Every time Rose opened a doll she found a miniature inside, each one getting smaller and smaller. Every face was blank; even the tiniest, the size of a thimble. Then with a pop the featureless face disappeared and Rose woke with a start. It was midnight; there were cheers from the TV, a women's basketball match, smiling faces, scowling faces, angry faces. Not one face on TV was expressionless.

She locked up, went to bed, and slept like the dead.

Saturday morning dawned wet. Every night this week, she'd stayed late in the office to catch up, no spare time for adoption research. So as soon as the library opposite opened at 9 a.m., she was in there. She took three books off the shelf: *A Little Blessing; Adoption and Fostering 1950-1970: the Richer Report;* and *A History of Adoption*. She stood in line at the 'Books Out' desk behind a smart elderly gentleman holding a weighty biography of Churchill and a whey-faced teenager clutching the equally weighty *Women's Health Questions Answered* under her arm. As she waited, Rose flicked through the books on the 'Favourite Books' table and added *Harry Potter and the Philosopher's Stone* to her pile.

She walked home via the corner shop to pay her paper bill and picked up a six-pack of Coke, a bunch of bananas, and an 'affordable classic' copy of *Great Expectations* from the bargain shelf. She must stop acquiring random books. Her shelves were heaving and, despite using the cupboard space vacated by James's possessions, her new books were stacking up on the floor.

At home a pile of post was waiting on the doormat, including a large brown envelope marked 'ARAP'. She slit it open and out fell a booklet, the colour of Dijon mustard, entitled *Searching for Your*

Birth Family.

At 10.30, she started reading the booklet. Adoptions in the 1960s could be done in all sorts of ways and the booklet made a major assumption: that you knew how yours was done. Rose had no idea. Once again, she wished she could talk to her mum. She read on. In a survey conducted by ARAP in 1972, only half of adoption placements were made by voluntary agencies or local authorities, the rest were made privately. Rose stroked Brad as she tried to apply the statistics to herself. She knew local authorities, she'd reported on council meetings and interviewed mayors and officials and councillors; local authorities were run by civil servants. They were anal about records. But for them to talk to her, she needed to know her birth name and where she was born. Hopefully the adoption advisor could give her the facts. She'd got a cancellation for Monday evening.

Next she picked up *A Little Blessing*. A thin A5-sized paperback with a picture of a baby on the front, a halo over its blonde smiling face. It was the book her mother and father should have read before telling her the truth when she was five.

Why didn't they? Didn't they have to, by law?

'No,' said Bella on ARAP's helpline. 'At the beginning of the twentieth century, it was accepted that the best thing for the adopted child was a clean break with no contact with their birth parents, and no rights to search for them when the child was grown up. Then in 1953 a government report recommended that adopted children be told they were adopted or chosen.'

'But only recommended?' interrupted Rose.

'Yes. The report said that if the child wasn't

told, quote: "At best there is a serious risk of totally destroying the child's trust and confidence in the adults who have been deceiving him/her about his/her parentage…"'

Yes, thought Rose, *my trust has been destroyed.* She forced herself to concentrate on what Bella was saying.

'… to us that sounds really cold. But it recommended that adoptive parents be forced to tell their child of its origins, but no law was passed and telling was left to the whim of the adopters.'

'But if a law had been passed, Mum and Dad would legally have had to tell me and I wouldn't be sitting here now wondering if my real parents were acrobats or journalists or bricklayers. I would know whose genes I inherited.' *And whose medical history, whose skills, whose nose and smile and toes.*

'Yes,' said Bella. 'Nature or nurture.'

'Nurture explains modern success. People aren't born with skills, they learn them. I know I have, I studied and trained for enough years to become a journalist. It's taken me years to get to where I am now.'

'You sound very analytical, Rose. Most people I speak to are in pieces.'

I am in pieces, thought Rose, *just because I don't weep and wail doesn't mean I'm not feeling it.*

'Just remember it's okay to allow yourself time to get upset about what has happened to you.'

'I do get upset, I *am* upset.' No, that sounded too sharp. 'Sorry Bella, that didn't come out right. I didn't mean to snap, you've been great. Thanks.'

'Anytime.'

Rose settled down with *Adoption and Fostering*

124

1950-1970: the Richer Report. It was dry reading. By 4 p.m., her temples were tight and she felt more like a thorn than a rose. She reached for the remote. Tennis of course, *Brief Encounter*, horse racing, quiz show, horse jumping, cricket chat, *Wizard of Oz*, previews of tomorrow's tennis, highlights of yesterday's one-day international cricket from India, exclusive interview with England's retired cricket captain, live county cricket. Rose didn't like cricket.

'Toto, we're not in Kansas any more. We must be over the rainbow.'

Rose watched Dorothy find her way home to her family then went to the bedroom and fished her red stilettos out of the wardrobe. She'd bought them to go to a New Year's Eve party with James and only worn them once. Although they made her legs seem five feet long, they had rubbed her heels raw and her feet had slipped down to the toes and jammed into the leather like a test crash car hitting a wall. James said that didn't matter, that the shoes would only be on her feet for seconds when they got home. James would choose sex and blisters over comfortable shoes any day, as long as he got the sex and she got the blisters. But then again… the red slippers had worked for Dorothy.

So Rose sat on the sofa wearing the red stilettos, cut-off denim shorts, and a white cotton vest, with Brad purring beside her, and felt the best she'd felt for a week.

18 LILY

Lily had Saturday all planned out. They'd have a leisurely breakfast and read the papers outside at the teak table on the decking, soaking up the sun's vitamin D.

New research proved that babies conceived in the spring and born in the late summer were taller and stronger because their mummies soaked up the sun's goodness. Lily thought it must be good to get in early, like folic acid, and build up a credit balance. Then she'd booked an outside table for lunch at a place in Ham which William had read about in the Sunday paper and mentioned at least three times since that he'd like to try. The cult food and lovely garden surroundings would lull him into that lazy sensual mood she loved about him, so that when they came home she could talk to him about babies, they'd make plans and make love and hopefully make a baby, with lots of cuddling afterwards. Then for their supper she'd ordered a delivery of sashimi, sushi and sake, because he loved everything Japanese. She was going to wear the new lemon kimono-style dress she'd bought at Kiko's in Barnes Village, which she thought would nicely underline the Japanese theme.

She carried the breakfast tray outside. The first thing wrong was the tea. She had emptied his bag of favourite Arabica coffee beans onto the compost heap because caffeine decreases fertility but is excellent for composting, and instead made a pot of green tea, which is packed with antioxidants and anti-cancer stuff and generally very good for the immune system. And the Japanese drank it all the time.

William didn't even pick up the cup. 'I'm not drinking this crap.' He lifted the teapot lid and peered in. 'Ugh, looks like lawn clippings.' He pushed his cup towards Lily. 'You have mine. I'll make a quick espresso.'

Lily watched him stalk across the terrace and into the kitchen. She pictured him walking around the distressed oak table, past the cherry-red Kitchen Aid mixer, past the six-burner hob to where there was a large space between the microwave and the stainless steel toaster. She wished she'd patted her lily cushion for luck. She had ditched the coffee beans and machine without visualising his reaction.

'Where the fuck has my espresso machine gone?'

It sounded to Lily as if he'd said 'my' in capital letters, which she objected to as she had bought and paid for said espresso machine. Yes, she'd given it to him for his birthday, but really he should have said 'our'. This was what got to her: he assumed everything in the house was his.

You can't afford to think like this, she warned herself. Today was meant to be a calm, positive day, so she breathed deeply in and out and waited for him to come back so she could tell him about their lunch plans.

His breakfast lay untouched on the teak table. A lazy wasp was taking an interest in it. Lily shooed it away with her hand, but it was persistent. She shooed it again. His bowl contained organic fair trade muesli with

128

honey and extra-chopped Brazil nuts (selenium for protection against cancer and heart disease; she was determined that William would not have a heart attack like Granddad Howard), soya milk (low cholesterol), and chopped apple from Kent followed by plain bio-yogurt from Dorset cows. Where was he? Really, the wasp was showing more interest in breakfast than William.

She went to the kitchen door, the room was empty. 'Darling,' she called, 'a wasp is circling your breakfast. You'd better come and eat it.'

He appeared suddenly at the door and made her jump. He could move silently for such a tall man, his nearly six-foot-frame almost filling the doorway. 'Freddie's just called, he needs me at rugby. I haven't got time to eat.' He disappeared again.

Rugby needs him?

'But you have to eat, darling,' she called, 'just sit down for ten minutes and eat your muesli. Or I can make something for you to take with you.' A hard-boiled egg (free-range), she wondered, with sliced bread and butter (seedy low GI bread, unsalted butter) and Marmite. William never refused Marmite. She bustled around, assembling the ingredients, loving working in her kitchen, loving doing something for William.

'The captain's injured and Freddie's taking over.' He was back quicker than she expected, buttoning his shirt, the blue checked lumberjack shirt she'd bought for him on impulse last week and for which he hadn't said thank you. Thank you it's my favourite colour, thank you darling for thinking about me.

Lily stood, the egg box in hand. 'What?'

'It's a key game. If we beat South Linton Swifts,

we go to the top of the league. Above Bridingham Bees.'
He looked at her as if he expected a reaction.

'Oh,' she said. *But you can't go out*, she wanted
to shout. *Don't shout*, she almost shouted aloud to
herself. *Say nothing.* 'But I wanted to talk about having a
baby.' She ignored the way his eyebrows raised; she'd
started so she might as well say it all. 'I went to the
doctor yesterday to ask why it hasn't happened and he
said the first thing is not to panic.'

William stared at her, his fingers still on the
bottom button of his shirt. 'We're not panicking.' His
voice had changed. 'Lily, we can't talk about this now,
Freddie needs me, kick-off is at eleven and it'll take me
an hour to get there.'

And he turned and was out the door before Lily
could say, 'But I booked a table at Ham Hock for lunch.'

It was nine-thirty, plenty of time to get to Ealing.
Quite how William could help Freddie from the side of
the pitch, Lily did not know. He seemed to need a lot of
help and support though, and for a fleeting moment she
wondered if Freddie was gay.

Lily spent the rest of the day devising Sunday's
lunch: 'Plan Chocolate'. She liked to give her lists a
memorable name. She went to the bottom freezer drawer
and checked her notebook, hidden where William never
looked because the drawer was full of leftovers she
bagged and froze to eat as single meals when he was
away. William wouldn't eat leftovers, not knowingly,
anyway.

'Plan Sushi' was the Japanese dinner tonight.
Inviting William's dad as well as her own for Sunday
lunch was the only guaranteed way of keeping William

in the house all day. She leafed through the lists until she found the ones she wanted: vitamins and supplements; daily pre-pregnancy, pregnancy, and post-pregnancy exercises; things to do while pregnant, like get her teeth fixed for free on the NHS; list of good foods for William to eat; list of good foods for Lily to eat.

She checked 'Plan Chocolate' again. They would sit in the garden and drink a bottle of red wine from William's stainless steel wine rack on the wall of the utility room (full of procyanidins, if she'd pronounced it right, good for the heart) and chat nicely, then everyone would snooze in deckchairs after lunch. William liked his father. Sometimes Lily thought he was the only person William did like. Now she'd be able to serve freshly picked spinach too (lots of iron and fibre, so good for digestion).

William was always in a good mood after seeing his father. The three men would talk about the stock market and equity and bonds and all that sort of stuff, then Charles and Dad would go home, leaving William mellower than he'd been all week.

Then Lily would talk to him about babies.

19 ROSE

Twenty-four hours and two frozen pizzas later, Rose put
down the last library book. She rubbed her temples.
Reading *Harry Potter* made two things clear. First, don't
believe everything people tell you about your parents.
Second, never trust your initial assumptions.

Why must she always think the worst? It might
be a happy story, or at least, not an unhappy one.

*Because they might have died of a heroin
overdose,* said that sharp cynical voice in her head.

*It's better to know the truth, whatever it is, than not to
know,* said Strong Rose's calmer voice. *Even if they're
dead.*

Cynical Rose: *Of course they're dead. It's the
only thing that makes sense.*

Rose thought it made sense too.

Harry Potter made a third thing clear, she
thought suddenly. Everyone who met Harry told him he
had his mother's eyes.

Whose eyes did she have?

When Rose arrived at Café Blanc on Monday
lunchtime, there was no sign of Maggie. She bought a
bottle of mineral water and bagged a table outside. She
loved this place, it smelled so good. Coffee but with
something sweet, vanilla perhaps, vanilla syrup, and

onions from the toasted paninis. Freshly made, not wrapped in plastic with a use-by date. Rose's stomach rumbled; she hoped Maggie wouldn't be long. She couldn't afford to be one minute over the hour or Sam would add it to his list of complaints at the impending disciplinary review next Monday.

This lunch was a tradition, interviews allowing. Rose pulled *Great Expectations* out of her Mulberry tote. She'd started reading it in bed last night and though she'd read it for O Level she'd forgotten it, forgotten that Pip was an orphan brought up by Mrs Joe, forgotten that Pip knew what happened to his birth family. He'd looked at their gravestones. She made a mental note to take flowers to Mum's grave; she hadn't been for weeks and felt the tug of duty. But there was a corresponding tug, the one that said 'she lied'.

She hadn't got to the bit yet about Miss Havisham. When she'd read the book as a teenager, this example of rejected love had made her scoff. No woman should be so reliant on the love of one man, she'd told her damp-eyed classmates.

'Great book.' Rose looked up to see Frank standing in front of her, rucksack in one hand, tray in the other. At the unmistakeable smell of roasted onion and toasted Emmental panini, Rose's stomach rumbled again.

'May I?' he gestured towards the empty seat.

'Just for a moment, I'm waiting for my friend to arrive.' Though they sat next to each other at work, they had never socialised and Rose realised she knew little about him.

He shrugged and gestured towards her paperback. 'Dickens was a journalist too, you know.

Started at sixteen as a court reporter, taught himself shorthand from a book. He was a parliamentary correspondent, wrote travel articles, plays, you name it.' He tapped the cover of Rose's book. 'This is good, *Bleak House* is better.'

Frank's eyes were deep liquid black, like Guinness, and they were looking straight at her. *Does he know I'm thinking about his eyes, not about Dickens?* He was waiting for her to speak.

'I'm waiting for Maggie, my friend, she works at *Xtra*.' *Why am I gabbling?*
She smiled but then realised she was flirting so stopped. Frank wasn't her sort of man.

'Ehm…' *Why can't I say something more intelligent than that? He must think I'm a real dork.* He smiled, turned and went inside.

Out of the corner of her eye, Rose watched him join a table of the *Herald*'s sales reps. There was some loud laughter, then Frank looked back at her and smiled to reveal a row of brilliant white teeth. Pavé slabs of white enamel. Teeth ran in families; she'd bet his parents had strong teeth too, and wondered about the incisors and molars of her parents. Were they full of amalgam like hers? Tonight the adoption advisor would tell her the names of her parents and maybe she could find out what sort of teeth they had.

'Oh, I thought I was never going to get here.' Maggie sank into the spare chair. Her attempt at dressing in 'creative Fleet Street journalist' style had collapsed and she looked more like fashion student doing wacky. She dumped a pink leopard-print rucksack at Rose's feet. 'What a morning. I'm doing a vox-pop on Oxford Street. I hate that. Asking strangers how many people they had sex with this weekend. It's demeaning, but oh boy, do they boast. I am better than this, I know I am. Why do they always give me the shittiest jobs?'

Rose opened her mouth and shut it again quickly. Best not to answer that one.

'Someone up there doesn't like me,' said Maggie, 'not after last night. I went out with some girls from work and ended up going to bed with our art editor's flatmate. Bad news. He seemed okay in the pub but he fucked like a baboon, in and out in seven seconds, maximum fifteen pelvic thrusts and then he was gone. I have got to get my sex life sorted out. It's not a sex life, it's sex moments.' She paused for breath.

Rose always felt as if she'd been hit by a whirlwind whenever Maggie first arrived.

'You need to get a new job, Mags. You're even speaking like an *Xtra* article now.'

Maggie started dragging an orange sweatshirt out of her rucksack, followed by a pair of black court shoes, popsocks, a dotty blue-and-white chiffon blouse, and a green baseball cap.

'And I just know it's going to rain this afternoon, look at those clouds. I'm going to get drenched.' She put the cap on her head.

Rose smiled, the overall effect had now changed to trainee plumber/wacky. She waited while Maggie crammed everything back into the rucksack.

'A cholesterol-laden lunch will make you feel better. What do you want?'

Both agreed they were ravenous and could eat a pig. So they chose prawn triple-decker sandwiches bulging with mayonnaise, buttercream-filled buns for that essential afternoon sugar boost, and a large pot of proper tea. For a few minutes, they ate without speaking. It was companionable. Rose chewed and tried not to think about tonight's meeting with Mrs Greenaway, whose name reminded her of her first primary school teacher. Greenland, was it, or Greenlove. Green-something, anyway. She swallowed the last mouthful of cake and felt sick again.

Maggie chewed, a blob of buttercream hovering on the tip of her nose. 'Sorry I didn't ring you back last weekend. My cousin got married on Saturday in Scotland, I never want to drink whisky again, and my shift started at five yesterday. I had such a hangover. For God's sake, don't read any of my articles this week, if I wrote them yesterday they're rubbish. They always are when I work on a Sunday night.'

'I know the feeling. I don't want my byline on that farmer's lung feature I wrote on Thursday.'

'I am not even going to ask what farmer's lung is.' Maggie laughed, but the laugh dried in her throat and she reached across the table to take her friend's hand. 'So, how are you now?'

At last, it was Rose's turn to talk. But she wasn't quick enough.

'Heh, there's a guy at a table over there who keeps looking at you.' Maggie pointed. 'He's quite cute.'

Rose pushed her friend's hand below the table. 'Sssh, keep your voice down. And it's rude to point.' *Oh God*, she thought, *I sound more like Mum every day*. 'That's Frank, from work.'

'Ooh, so that's Frank.'

'Mags, don't stare.'

Maggie chuckled. 'He could be worth

cultivating.'

Rose knew she was enjoying teasing. 'No, not unless you like arrogant, macho, groin-emphasising, smarmy gits.'

'Ooh, so you do like him.'

'I thought you wanted to know how I am.'

'I do, I do.'

Rose didn't waste time wondering what kind of friend Maggie was to talk about herself for the first twenty minutes and then tease her so excruciatingly. She just felt relieved to finally have someone independent to talk to. 'I had an adopt-fest weekend.'

'A what?'

'An adopt-fest. I read about adoption, watched films about adoption, dreamt about adoption. I watched *The Wizard of Oz* on Saturday....'

'*The Wizard of Oz*? In God's name, why?'

'Dorothy had no parents. She was brought up by her aunt and uncle. But I tell you something, I'd forgotten the scary bits. The Wicked Witch of the West. I actually dreamt last night that she was my real mother. I woke up at two, my heart thrumming like a train the Wicked Witch sent me to work on a weekly newspaper in the Outer Hebrides. Well, you can imagine how that went, can't you? Train-sick, bus-sick, boat-sick. So it was the middle of the night and I was wide awake, feeling sick.

'Bed-sick? Even you can't get motion sickness in bed, surely?'

'Believe me, the bed was spinning.'

'So?' prompted Maggie. 'What did you do? Read another adoption book?'

'No, I channel-hopped. I found *Peter Pan* on a

138

children's satellite channel.'

'In the middle of the night?'

'It was some tribute to black and white films. Oh Mags, I don't remember it being so sad. I cried when Peter told Wendy no one sent him any letters because he didn't have a mother. I cried when he went back to his bedroom window but it was shut and another little boy was asleep in his bed. And I cried when the lost children, the pirates, and Captain Hook all wanted Wendy to be their mother.'

Maggie swallowed a large lump of cake and stared. 'That's a lot of tears for someone I've never seen cry. Not cry properly, I mean, ignoring that time you hit your thumb with a hammer putting up the blind in your bathroom. Is it still wonky or did you straighten it?' Rose stuck out her tongue.

'Oh nice,' Maggie pulled a face. 'Best make a mental note not to stick your tongue out when you've just eaten a bun filled with buttercream.' She took another bite. 'I thought you didn't like children, Rosie Posie, so why are you crying over them? You're not identifying with children, are you?'

'Nooo, just the wrong time of the month, I guess.' Rose leant forwards and wiped buttercream off Maggie's nose with a paper napkin.

'Damn, isn't it always?'

They laughed and Rose felt a stretch in her under-used smiling muscles. It felt good. She drank the last of her tea. 'I tried all last week to talk to Dad, I rang three times yesterday, but he's never there. He's always done this vanishing thing, it used to drive Mum mad. I even followed him once, years ago. He went to the corner shop and bought a Party Seven, then took it to the allotment and drank it in his shed. Mum wouldn't let him have beer at home, she said it was unrefined. I'd imagined he was a spy. So finding out about the Party Seven was a bit of a letdown.' She held on to her mug, letting the last dregs of warmth leach into her fingers. Suddenly she felt cold inside. 'He got the sack last week.'

'At his age, that's really difficult. Look, you should go to him. He needs you. Just go and sit on his doorstep till he comes home.'

'I don't want another argument.'

'You just need to be there.' Maggie looked at Rose in that knowing way, which Rose knew meant she was reading the meaning behind her verbiage. She'd been looked at that way by Maggie many times before. 'You don't want to talk to him at all, do you?'

'Of course I do.'

Maggie balanced on the back legs of her chair and studied her.

Rose watched her rocking to and fro. If Rose had done that, her mother would've told her off for damaging the chair.

'You've always avoided confrontation. That's why you put up with Sam pissing you around at work. That's why you make yourself unavailable to boyfriends just before they finish with you. That's why you avoid their calls and delete their emails. Confrontation, Rose, sometimes it has to be done.'

Rose huffed. So calling Sam impotent was non-confrontational, was it?

Maggie sighed and leant forwards on the table. 'Just go and see your dad, all right? Tell him you love him. That's my last word on the subject.'

Rose wasn't sure she did love him right now, but she nodded anyway. She couldn't remember the last time she'd told someone she loved them.

'Okay, but not tonight.'

'And why not?'

'Tonight,' Rose said so loudly that a woman with frizzy hair at the next table turned round. 'Tonight, I get counselled.'

'Why?'

'To find out where I was born, my original name, my birth parents' names. Hopefully there'll be files on me, records.'

Maggie reached a hand across the table and covered Rose's fist. It felt warm. 'Do you want me to come with you?'

Rose shook her head. This was doing research, she could do this bit.

Maggie hesitated. 'Have you thought your mother might have been a – a – bit of a goer, a regular Ceres, a fertility queen. It was the Sixties. You might have brothers and sisters, nieces and nephews. A huge new family. Auntie Rose.'

Auntie Rose. Lily's face swam into view. Rose blinked, hard. 'Oh, believe me, I've thought of every type of relation it's possible to have.'

Maggie pursed her lips. 'I feel awful for being away this weekend when you needed me. Ring me, okay, any time. Even if it's just to cry.'

'I'll be okay.' Rose glanced at her watch. She was due back at her desk in ten minutes. She smiled at her friend. 'So what about you, what did you do last week apart from bonking?'

'Nothing, really,' said Maggie, who suddenly

started picking at a fingernail.

Maggie kept her nails immaculate. Today they were coral with white tips. Rose raised her eyebrows and waited.

'Well, I wasn't going to say anything…' She was picking her thumbnail now. A fleck of coral drifted onto the table. 'It's not as if families are your favourite subject right now.'

'Spit it out.'

Maggie's words rushed out of her mouth. 'I talked to my gran at the wedding and she told me some interesting stories, family stories. Family history. You can even get special software to do all the family tree charts. No fiddling around with Word or Excel. So, I'm going to get it.'

Rose felt cynical but tried not to sound it. Not all families were as fucked up as hers. 'That's… great.'

'Yeah, anyway it's got me thinking about the past and I wondered… what do you think about organising a uni reunion?'

Wow, I didn't see that one coming. 'Isn't the whole Friends Reunited thing a bit passé?'

'Come on, it'd be fun, catching up with Smelly Mel.'

'No, thanks.' Rose reached beneath the table for her bag. She had to write 1,000 words about wheat intolerance by 4 p.m. and it wouldn't write itself.

'Oh look,' Maggie pointed at Rose's cup. 'Oh, I know what this is. A mushroom in your tea leaves means an unexpected event, maybe a new relationship. You're going to find a new man, Rosie Posie. You must have someone lined up.'

Rose picked up the cup, poured the slops into

the saucer, and the mushroom disappeared.

'You've just written a feature about reading tea leaves, haven't you? You do know it's all a load of rubbish?'

'Aah, come on, Rose. It's just a bit of fun.' And they laughed as they gathered their bags and walked the three blocks to Maggie's bus stop. Rose tried to forget about the 'tea-au-fate' and focussed on wheat. Pasta... Weetabix... cakes... biscuits... bread...

'Oh, my bus, gotta go.' Maggie ran and jumped on the Oxford Street-bound Number 53 just before the doors closed. The bus pulled out into traffic and disappeared, just as the sky emitted the most enormous throaty roar of thunder.

Rose didn't see the bus go. She was looking at a display in a bookshop window. *When We Were Orphans* by Kazuo Ishiguro. *Orphan,* she thought, *I'm an orphan, aren't I?* And her legs suddenly felt as if she'd run ten miles.

Five minutes later she left the shop, book in hand. The shelf that James had vacated in her flat was filling up fast.

After twenty minutes of pinning down the differences between gluten allergy and wheat intolerance, Rose wrote the first paragraph of today's feature.

'The number of people self-diagnosing themselves as being wheat intolerant is growing and can lead to more harm than good, according to new nutritional research. Wheat aversion, a psychological condition, is also on the increase. Are the two trends connected?'

It was true, but she pressed the delete button and

watched her words disappear. Sam would never approve it; all the space sold for this feature advertised wheat-free biscuits and free-from bread. She stared at the empty white page.

'Anyone wanting to avoid wheat in their diet today is going to have a hard time finding wheat-free and free-from products that don't taste like sawdust.'

Noooo… he wouldn't approve that either. She pressed the delete button again. She knew the signs, she needed a breather, she needed a fresh start to the feature, she needed coffee.

'Crap coffee?' she asked Frank, who nodded without a pause in his typing. He was on a tight deadline too, Sam had already shouted at him twice since lunch. Rose wandered towards the coffee machine, enjoying stretching her legs.

'Coffee break already, Rosie?' A waft of smoke followed Sam down the corridor and around the corner. This was beginning to feel like persecution. Couldn't she even get a drink now? Did Sam have her tagged by GPS or something?

She carried two cups of brown liquid back to her desk. Frank exchanged his cup for a note.

2.15. Nick Maddox called.

'He sounded verrry disappointed that you weren't here, said he'd ring back in five.' Frank studied Rose, his eyebrows furrowed.

The heat rose in Rose's cheeks and she sat down behind her computer screen to hide her face. Frank promptly stood up and peered at her over the top. He waited, eyebrow raised.

'I just emailed him some queries. I'm surprised he didn't get his assistant to call me though, you'd think someone like him would be too busy.' *I'm babbling*, Rose thought as she watched a smile spread over Frank's face. Her phone rang. With relief she grabbed it. Frank's face didn't disappear.

It was Nick Maddox. A bubble of excitement rose in her throat.

They both spoke at once. 'Sorry, you first,' she said, feeling a fool.

'I hope you're feeling better?'

'Yes. Thanks.' She was mortified. Why couldn't he be a gentleman and not mention last week? She'd tried many times to forget how he'd put her to bed, and now her cheeks blazed. Thank goodness for the telephone. But she was uncomfortably aware that Frank could hear everything she said.

'Rose?'

She'd forgotten Nick. How could she forget Nick? *Say something!* 'Thanks.' No, she'd already said that. *Say something intelligent.* 'Er...'

'Good. Any news yet when my interview will be published?'

So that was why he'd rung. Her cheeks quickly cooled. 'I think it's scheduled for a couple of weeks' time, but it could be put back. Nothing is written in stone. Features get pulled all the time to make way for breaking news – war, riot, someone dying.' She recited the standard *Herald* policy.

There was a slight pause. 'I see.' His voice had cooled.

Oh no, she thought, *here we go*. His pause said it all, he was a complainer. She was disappointed and it made her snap more than she should.

'Well, there's no guarantee, you know, that

145

anything's going to be published at all.'

'At all? That would be disappointing.'

Rose listened to his evenly spaced breathing. She wasn't
going to apologise for the paper's policy; she didn't
make it. She played the silent tactic; be unapologetic, let
him speak first.

Silence.

Rose's heart pounded in her throat. And then she
sneezed, a real snorter, right into the phone. Rose didn't
have a tissue so there was nothing for it. She sniffed. Her
mother would have been mortified.

'Bless you.'

More silence as Rose contemplated wiping her
nose on her sleeve.

'Rose, can I assume by your silence that you
think I'm mad at you because you don't know when the
feature will be published?'

'Mmm.' She took the tissue Frank was waving
at her from the other side of the partition.

'I admit I am disappointed… disappointed
because I won't have an excuse to ring you for weeks, to
say thank you when it's finally in print.'

What? Is he flirting with me?

'But really, there's no need to wait that long, is
there? Would you like to go to dinner? Think of it as a
pre-publication thank you.'

Rose had never had a pre- or post-publication
dinner invitation from a client. She wondered vaguely if
Sam had a rule about it.

'Rose?'

'Yes please.'

'Tonight?'

Her heart sank. 'Sorry, not tonight.' He was

bound to be one of those sorts of businessmen with no 'windows' in his diary. That was it, she'd blown it.

'Tomorrow?'

'Yes.' She really must try and say words with more than a single syllable. He'd think she was vocabulary-challenged. *Vocabularily-challenged?* She smiled. 'Yes, please.'

'Eight. Nobu.'

'Great.' She'd never been to Nobu. 'I'll see you there.'

20 ROSE

Rose crossed and uncrossed her legs, and then crossed them again, snaking her feet around her ankles, the toes of her tan gladiator sandals squeaking slightly as they rubbed together. Then her mother's firm voice rang in her head, 'You'll get varicose veins if you sit with your legs crossed; sit like a lady.' Rose uncrossed them and pressed her knees tightly together. Her inner thigh muscles began to ache.

She'd been sitting up straight for ten minutes in this corridor; a tunnel of wood-panelled walls, darkened with years of polish and dirty fingerprints. She started to cross her legs again but remembered in time and forced her knees back together. This was more efficient at muscle toning than that horrible machine at the gym, the one where you sat with your knees wide apart and tried to push them together against the weights. Her mother would certainly have disapproved about the legs wide apart bit.

Footsteps approached from the left.

'You must be Rose. Can I call you Rose?'

Rose nodded.

The social worker was a large lady wearing a tailored jacket and pussybow blouse, a brown wool skirt stretched across her ample bottom. Rose hadn't seen clothes like that since Mrs Thatcher.

'Come through."

Rose followed her into a meeting room which was as brown as the corridor.

'I'm Mrs Greenaway. I'll start by asking you a few questions, Rose, and then I'll answer yours. Is that okay?'

Rose nodded. She recognised the method of buying-in from her teamwork seminar: frequent reaffirmation that everyone was on board, reaffirmation of the team's ongoing commitment to the project, reaffirmation that no one could do a runner. She'd seen the technique work at the *Herald.*

'How long have you wanted to find your birth mother, Rose?'

'I've only just found out I'm adopted. It was a bit of a shock. I… well, I had no idea.' *Stop jabbering like an idiot and speak clearly*, she told herself, and smiled, realising as she did it that the smile was too wide.

But Mrs Greenaway didn't seem to notice anything odd, she simply nodded and leaned forwards to peer at Rose's file. Rose folded her hands in her lap and tried not to be irritated that the woman hadn't bothered to read the file before the meeting. The folder only seemed to contain two pieces of paper.

'I want to find my birth parents.' She hadn't meant to shout. 'If they're still alive, of course, to see if we're alike. I've always felt a bit different from my –,' she hesitated, not sure how to make it clear which family she was talking about, but Mrs Greenaway was still nodding, so Rose ploughed on, '– my family, but never known why. So I'd like to find my birth family because my differences might be like theirs, so at last I'll belong to a family where I fit.' The last words came out in a bit of a rush and she realised she'd said 'family' a lot.

Mrs Greenaway nodded again, her hands folded on the desk in front of her.

Rose took the nod as signal to continue. 'I want to understand why my mother, my birth mother, why she gave me away and why no one stopped her, and if she was eventually happy or... or not.' On her way here, she'd thought carefully about what she wanted to say, but now it was coming out all twisted. 'I just want to know the truth.'

'Have you asked your adoptive mother any of this?'

'She died six months ago. I found out after she...' Rose closed her eyes and was standing beside the grave again, watching as Mum's coffin was lowered into the hole. There was a polite cough. Rose opened her eyes to see Mrs Greenaway offering her a box of tissues. She shook her head.

'All right to go on?'

Rose nodded.

'All right then. You talk a lot about your birth mother, Rose, and hardly mention your birth father. Why is that? You seem to be blaming both your mothers, without paying much attention to your fathers. Do you blame your adoptive mother for taking you away from your birth mother?'

Yes. Yes. The words screamed inside Rose's head. She hadn't thought of it like that. She viewed Mrs Greenaway more cautiously now.

'I guess I do blame her, yes, because I found out I was adopted by reading her diary. Not a diary my father wrote. And the most basic connection is between mother and child, isn't it? So I feel betrayed.'

Mrs Greenaway nodded encouragingly. 'Well the search won't be easy, Rose. The older you are when you start, the harder it is, and you're not guaranteed to find out anything additional to what I can tell you today. Searching takes a lot of time and energy and money. It will help if you try to involve your adoptive family in what you're doing. Show them papers and photos. But some of your relatives and friends may be unhappy with what you're doing. How is your adoptive family taking the revelation?'

'My dad doesn't want to talk to me about it at the moment.' Mrs Greenaway raised an eyebrow, so Rose rushed on, 'But I'm persevering with him. My sister is supportive, though she has her own... her own issues at the moment.'

'And is your sister adopted too?'

'No.' *Why didn't I think of that? But Lily is so much like Mum they must be blood relations. Is that why Lily keeps asking for the diaries?*

'Well, keep talking to them.' Mrs Greenaway took a quick glance at her watch. 'Right.' She shuffled the papers.

Rose wished she had X-ray vision. 'So, who were my birth parents?'

'There are some things we need to cover first. Finding your birth parents is not a solution to problems you may have now with your adoptive family. In fact, it can cause more problems. You should be prepared for an emotional time.'

Talk about stating the obvious. Rose bit her lip and forced herself to nod. With all the nodding going on, she felt like the basset hound noddy-dog her father replaced on the parcel shelf of their dark blue Austin Maxi every time Mum moved it to the glove compartment.

I need this woman's help. Is it too much to nod and smile at the same time? She tried it. Mrs Greenaway nodded and smiled back.

'Look, I do know all of this. I know I'm older than average for making this sort of discovery. I don't blame myself for whatever it was that made my birth parents give me away, they had their reasons. I just want to understand. I'm not seeking to blame them for inadequacies in my own life.'

She glanced out of the window. The view was a red brick wall, the glass speckled with raindrops. She could feel Mrs Greenaway's eyes focussed on her left ear.

'I have had a fantasy since I was a child that I had a friend, a friend who was fun to play with, a friend who understood me.' She swallowed. 'Since I found out I was adopted, I've wondered if she might be my lost sister, if she was some residual memory from when I was a baby, that I have a real elder sister.' Wanda's face swam into focus.

'But the sister you grew up with, err...' Mrs Greenaway looked down at the file again.

'Lily.'

'Yes, Lily. She is still your sister. You grew up together, you share a common history. No one can take that away from you.'

Rose looked Mrs Greenaway straight in the eye. 'No, they can't. But I'm tired of wondering. I want to know if I have a lost sister or not, so can we just get on with it?'

'Sometimes the birth mother may be dead or…'

'Or a criminal, or worse. Yes, I know. I have thought about these things.' *And I'm trying to be positive*, Rose reprimanded herself. *My mother could be a businesswoman, an actress, an opera singer, an author. A journalist, like me.*

Mrs Greenaway straightened her shoulders as if she had made a decision.

Rose leant forwards. *Is this it?*

'You have a legal right to the following information.' Mrs Greenaway's voice sounded as if she were quoting from an official handbook. 'Here is Form CA5.' She pushed a sheet of paper across the desk towards Rose, text side down. 'It gives you the information on your original birth certificate: your name at birth, the names of your birth parents, and the district of your birth. I'll give you a moment to read it.' And she left the room, shutting the door quietly behind her like a doctor leaving a grieving relative.

Rose looked at the paper for a moment, savouring what was to come, triumphant that she had come so far so fast.

Her own name was in the top right-hand corner of the form:

Adoptive Forename and Surname: Rose Haldane.

Forenames at Birth: Alanna Jane.

Rose stopped reading. Alanna, it was beautiful, it sounded Gaelic.

'Alanna,' she tried to say it aloud, but all that came out was a whisper. 'Alanna.'

Did she feel like an Alanna? No, she was Rose. The name was difficult to say, alien to her tongue. She tried again. 'Alanna.' Her voice was louder this time, and her tongue clicked flat against the roof of her mouth on the first syllable.

Alanna. Not Alberta or Alison or Alice. The baby in the photo was Alanna. *My real mother called me Alanna.* There it was, a connection to that sad, lonely woman who had known she would never see her baby again but still named her. And such a beautiful name. Alanna was an unknown quantity except, Rose realised, she wasn't, she had seen Alanna's face already in the creased photo hidden in the purse.

For a moment, Rose wanted to tear up Form CA5, tear up Alanna's name and go back to being just Rose. But her eyes were drawn like gravity to the page again.

Birth Mother (if known) …

Next to it was a name Rose knew. She read it three times before she admitted to herself that she recognised it.

Katherine Ingram.

Katherine Ingram? Aunt Kate? Mum's sister, Bizzie and Howard's youngest daughter. Hippy Aunt Kate who'd died in the Sixties. The actress. How could Aunt Kate be her mother? *She's dead.*

It wasn't supposed to be like this. She re-read the form, words swimming.

Birth Father: unknown.

Kate must have known. Where was he when her birth was registered, didn't he have to sign the register too? Was this document legal?

District of birth registration: Enfield.

Enfield. She'd been born in Enfield? She'd never even been to Enfield.

Birth date: 29 August 1968.

Yes, it's me.

Instead of being Rose Haldane, Virgo, born 29 August 1968 in Richmond, she was Alanna Jane Ingram, Virgo, born 29 August 1968 in Enfield. What did Alanna Ingram look like? Alanna sounded blonde, but Rose was dark. She sounded tall and soft and willowy, but Rose was small and wiry. Alanna was a girly name, a giggly name. Rose knew Alanna hugged her friends a lot. Oh, how Rose longed to be hugged right now. Her hands fell to her lap and the form slipped to the floor. Her breath faltered.

There was a gentle knock at the door; it was Mrs Greenaway. For such a large lady, she moved lightly on her feet and Rose was grateful for her delicacy.

'All right?' She held out a plastic cup.
Rose took it and sipped the lukewarm metallic-tasting water from a machine, waiting for it to lubricate her dry throat.

'Yes,' she croaked, and sipped again. 'She's dead.'

'You won't know that until you look for her,' reassured Mrs Greenaway, showing a chink of the warm human beneath the professional veneer.

'Yes, she is. She's dead. The name of my birth mother on this form is the name of my aunt who died when I was four months old.'

'Oh my dear. Well, perhaps that's why you were adopted. Perhaps she had a serious illness.'

'I don't think so. At least, no one in the family has ever mentioned that.' But Rose realised she had no idea how Aunt Kate had died. Cancer? Car crash? Why didn't she know? Why were there so many secrets in her family?

'Are there other files on me?'

Mrs Greenaway turned back to the file. 'Here's a copy of your short adoption certificate. You mentioned you hadn't found it amongst your adoptive mother's property.'

Rose took the piece of paper: a small document for a small child. She'd expected something bigger. It looked like a normal birth certificate; nowhere did the word 'adoption' appear. She scanned it quickly: date and place of birth, sex, adoptive name. Nothing new, then. 'But this is insufficient for legal purposes, to confirm your identity or apply for a passport, for example. For that, you need your full adoption certificate, which is like a replacement birth certificate.'

That's where my father's name will be registered. 'How do I get that?'

'You can download a form online then post it. Now let me see if there's anything else to give you.' Mrs Greenaway passed over another paper. 'Here's the court information sheet which names the court where your adoption was processed.' One more search of the folder. 'No, there's nothing else here that I can add. Your next step…'

Disconnected words floated around Rose as she held the official pieces of paper. A world she did not know surrounded her, even the air smelled different. *Aunt Kate?* Rose passed her hand in front of her face; she could see it move, it looked normal, but nothing would ever be the same again.

Mrs Greenaway was still talking, smiling

reassuringly at her, but Rose was struggling to match the sentences to her moving lips.

'… so my best guess is that your adoption was arranged privately. The highest-ever number of adoptions took place in 1968, but pre-computer, I'm afraid that many files contain nothing. I'm sorry I can't be more positive.'

Ah, she got that sentence. Mrs Greenaway was sorry. Rose forced herself to speak through the churning water surrounding her. 'I'm a journalist, I'm used to finding things.'

'Very well. There is one more place I can ask. In the case of a privately arranged adoption, a file may be held by the social services department in the area of the court where the adoption order was made. There might be nothing, but it might contain information about your birth and your first few days. Would you like me to ask on your behalf?'

'Yes, please.' Rose was on automatic pilot but Mrs Greenaway was looking at her, waiting, so she must have asked another question. Rose shook her head. She didn't know who might answer the question; somebody else was inside her head now. Could she be Rose and Alanna at the same time? How were they split? Fifty/fifty? Twenty/eighty? One/ninety-nine? Mostly Rose, with a touch of Alanna?

Without remembering how she did it, she was standing up, shaking hands with Mrs Greenaway, and walking out of the office.

21 ROSE

Darkness was falling by the time she got to the allotment. She stumbled on the uneven path, cursing herself for not keeping a torch in the car as her mother had instructed her. She found her father's patch: empty. For the first time in a long while she felt kinship with her mother, who had often pursed her lips at Dad's ability to disappear at moments important to her – parents' evenings, Christmas drinks with the neighbours, choosing curtains.

A light was flickering in the far corner of the field, like a light bulb with dodgy wiring. He had to be where that light was. Everything else turned black and she stumbled over the knobbly earth, not caring if she scuffed up sacred lettuce or radish seedlings. Lily would be able to tell the difference, but she couldn't, not even in daylight. Now she could see the outline of a shed, a neater one than her father's, painted bright blue. The tang of fresh paint and something yeasty hung in the air. It was Ron Fosdyke's shed. His name was on the door, burned roughly out of a lump of wood with a hot poker and nailed to the front. The sign was blue too, it tilted slightly to the right.

The door was propped open by a breeze block and the voices inside spilled out into the cooling night air. The deeper of the two baritones belonged to a stranger.

'So I told him, I said, I wasn't having it, see, I
told him – I did.'

'Of course you did… I can imagine.'

'Asking for it he was… Nasty little… he was.'

'Chin up, mate. Cheers.'

Bottles clinked, and there was the sound of
glugging, then a dull thud as glass hit earth, followed by
the swish of a bottle top being twisted off. More
glugging. The metal disc flew out the door and hit Rose
on the arm.

'Beer won't bring Mum back, Dad, or get you a
new job.' She hadn't meant to speak and wished her
words hadn't come out as a whisper, which drifted away
into in the emptiness of the night. She cleared her throat.

'What the? There's someone outside.' A bulky
shadow loomed in the doorway. 'Oi, you, get out of it.
This is private property.'

'Leave it, Ron mate. Don't make a fussh.' Her
father's voice again.

Rose realised they couldn't see her and took a
step forwards into the pool of light.

'Oh Christ.' Someone burped. It didn't sound
like Ron.

One more step and Rose was in the shed. 'I think
you've had enough, Dad.'

She planned to take the bottle off him but hadn't
bargained on Ron, whose considerable physical bulk
moved between her and her father.

'Now then, love, don't be so hard on him. A
little home brew's not going to hurt.'

'Ron. This is nothing to do with you. I need to
talk with my father. It's not about the beer.' She stared

up at him, he was at least a foot taller and a foot wider than her. 'Please.'

At a nod from John, Ron shrugged and strode into the darkness. For a moment, Rose felt alone with her father, then she heard Ron's breathing, thick from fifty years of cigarettes, and the sound of rustling leaves. He was standing guard. The stool in the shed where Ron had sat was surrounded by a stash of empty beer bottles, a half-drunk litre bottle of whisky, and a rusty biscuit tin, which stank of fag ash.

'Hello pumpkin, my lovely Rosie. Come and sit here.' He gestured towards Ron's stool. 'Have a whisky.'

'You knew all the time who my real mother was, didn't you, Dad?' She almost spat out the last word. 'Aunt Kate. I've got it in black and white, Aunt Kate was my mother.'

She waited, but he grinned at her like a clown on acid. She wanted to slap him hard so shoved her hands deep into her pockets. 'Mum and Aunt Kate had an arrangement. It's in the diary in Mum's handwriting. Do you expect me to believe you knew nothing? You've lied to me all my life, and now…' she looked at her father, who was tipped back on his stool, leaning against a shelf piled high with empty plastic plant pots, '…now when I need you, you're a mess.'

Her father and the plant pots slid slightly to the right.

'You've lost your job, that's all. You're not ill. You're not homeless. Pull yourself together.'

'Have a heart, love,' said Ron's voice from the shed door. 'He's lost your mam.'

She shook her head. 'She wasn't my mother,

Ron, that's the point. And please don't attempt to comment on something you know nothing about.'

'Lost Diana, I've lost her,' her dad whispered. 'She's somewhere around here, I know she is.' And as he bent to look under his chair he retched and the pile of plant pots collapsed on his head.

She drove straight to Kingston. Bizzie's house was alight with electricity, curtains thrown back. From the front gate, Rose could see her grandmother sitting in an armchair doing a crossword in the newspaper. She leant against the gate, the lichen slightly dew-damp under her elbows, knowing she was delaying, fearing what she might see in her gran's eyes. She took a deep breath and walked up the path she had walked up a thousand times before, but now for the first time she was frightened. She sat in the chair opposite Bizzie, looked her straight in the eye, and told her about Mrs Greenaway. It was a five-minute monologue, the sixth minute was silent.

'Kate?'

'Yes.'

Bizzie's eyes were full of sadness and they didn't lie. She hadn't known of her daughters' secret. 'You're sure?'

'Positive.' Rose understood the need to disbelieve. 'Here.' She handed over the form given to her by Mrs Greenaway, the form from hell. 'You never knew?'

Bizzie shook her head. She took off her reading glasses, polished them with the yellow felt cloth from inside her glasses case, and settled them back into the pink grooves on either side of her nose. She read the form slowly once, then again. She didn't look up.

'Oh, Kate.' Her head bent and tears started to fall onto her skirt, a silent rainfall of dots on dark-green tweed. Rose knelt at the side of her grandmother's chair and leant her head against her shoulder, rubbing her cheek against the tickly pink wool of Bizzie's cardigan, wishing she could rub away the words on the form, wishing she could take the paper back, wishing she'd never found that damned diary. Anything to stop her gran from crying.

After a while, Bizzie sat up a little straighter. 'I never knew Kate had a baby and to think... that baby was you.' She looked at Rose over the rim of her glasses, smiling a wobbly smile.

'Tell me about her.'

'Well now, you have to understand that Kate was a mystery, even when she was little. So mischievous, always in trouble. She slapped a girl in the playground once, an older girl. That was all manageable, the headmistress said she was spirited and that was a valuable quality, which sounds all well and good for a ten-year-old but is different at fifteen when she should be more ladylike, more restrained. Turns out she'd started going to demonstrations, said she was an activist. We only found out when she came home smelling of cigarettes. So we were pleased when she started acting professionally, thought it would settle her a bit, get her into a different circle of friends. And it did. But after *Fields of Gold* we hardly saw her at all, she was always rehearsing, performing, in such demand. We didn't want to stand in her way. It upset me not to see her, but she did love acting so.'

Rose didn't understand half of what Bizzie was

saying, but she didn't want to interrupt. Bizzie's eyes kept drifting to the adoption form as if hoping the printed words had morphed into something else, a council tax bill, a bank statement.

'So this is why we didn't see her at the end, when she died.' She dropped her head and spoke into her hands. 'We thought she was ashamed of us.'

Rose patted the pink fluffy shoulder. 'Oh Gran, no one could be ashamed of you.' She reached out to prise the form from Bizzie's hand, wanting to take it all back, wanting this to end now, wishing she had never come.

But Bizzie's fingers were clenched so tightly, the paper was as creased and crumpled as her face. She shook her head vigorously. 'Oh but Rose, you don't know. She led such a wild life. Your granddad and I were too old-fashioned for her. She'd telephone every now and then from some new town.' Bizzie pointed at the form. 'Enfield. What was she doing in Enfield?'

'I thought you might know.'

'She lived in so many places, dear, but I never knew she lived in Enfield. Sometimes she lived in North London, sometimes she was on tour, acting at different theatres, Bournemouth one week, Carlisle the next. She was like a gypsy. In London, she shared a house with lots of people – actors, students. Diana said they were hippies. She…'

'Hippies? Did Mum go there, did she see them?'

'Oh I don't think she ever went there, dear, but she spoke to some of them on the phone. Your mum said it was an illegal squat full of dirty hippies and that they had no right to be there.'

Typical of Mum, thought Rose fiercely,

condemning a place she'd never seen, people she'd never met. 'What did Kate say to that?'

'She would shrug and make a joke, put on a voice. Diana hated that, she was always telling Kate to talk properly, that it was like trying to have a conversation with an alien. She was good at doing accents. "I don't know if I'm talking to you or some part you're playing", Diana used to say, but Kate would just laugh and call her a snob. She had a lovely laugh, did Kate. A lot like yours, now I come to think of it.' Bizzie took off her glasses again and dabbed at her eyes with a tissue. 'I wish we'd seen more of her, but wishing never makes anything happen. She did call in here one day out of the blue and fell asleep on our bed in the afternoon. A few months before your grandfather passed... I wonder if she was pregnant then.'

'Why?'

'Oh, her face had fattened up, and when you're newly pregnant you're tired all the time. I was.'

'You didn't ask her?'

'Oh no. She had quite a temper, you see, the shouting, well you wouldn't believe it. It was such a treat for her to visit us that I didn't want to spoil it by starting a row. But I shouldn't have left it.' More dabbing, then a sniff, then a weak smile at Rose. 'So so.' And Bizzie clapped her hands together in time to a rhythm only she could hear, catching the words from her memories. 'So so.'

Rose forced herself to stay silent, to wait for Bizzie to remember.

'You'll find when you have children, Rose, that they come to you for two things. Advice and money. They always take the money, seldom the advice. Kate

got a bit too big for her boots. Yes, she did, Rose,'
Bizzie said quietly, as Rose shook her head, 'she thought
the world owed her a living. I wanted to visit her at the
hippy house but your granddad wouldn't have it. "If you
don't want to hear the answer, Bizzie, don't ask the
question," he said. And then he died. Now I wish...
When they found her body they took it away. The doctor
said she died because she drank too much vodka and
then took pills and that her face was badly misshapen.
The coffin had to be closed. Your grandfather thought it
would be too upsetting for me to see her, and I wanted to
remember her as my pretty girl. Your mum and dad went
together to identify her but Diana fainted, she couldn't
go in. So John did it on his own. He never talked about it
after.'

Kate died of an overdose? Rose hadn't thought
her head could reel with the unexpected again tonight.
She tried to focus on Bizzie who, Rose realised with a
shock, had lost her husband and youngest daughter
within a year. Rose wondered how she didn't know this
fact, had never once thought to ask her grandmother. It
made her dislike the ignorance of her youth, the lack of
thought, the selfish rush to live her own life and not find
out about her family.

'But Kate hated taking medicine, even for a
headache. She made such a fuss over taking a pill,
putting it on the back of her tongue and then drinking a
whole glass of water to make it go down.' Bizzie mimed
the action as she talked, throwing her head back sharply
and gulping.

'I do that.' Rose's head moved backwards too,
knocking back an invisible paracetamol, trying to
swallow non-existent saliva. 'Gran,' she hesitated,

knowing she had to ask, unsure how to do it, 'the adoption advisor suggested that Kate might have given me up for adoption because she knew she was really ill, because... she was going to die.' *Or, because she was suicidal?*

Bizzie shook her head firmly. 'What a lot of poppycock. She'd have told us if she was sick, I know she would, surely she'd have asked for help.'

But she didn't tell you she was pregnant, thought Rose sadly. She so wanted to picture the smiling Kate in Bizzie's photograph, not a dead Kate surrounded by empty bottles of pills and vodka.

Bizzie sniffed, pulled a white cotton handkerchief from her sleeve and dabbed at her nose. 'After all these years, I still don't understand. She and Diana had their fights, but they always helped each other.'

Rose almost laughed out loud at that. Patently, they didn't.

'No, it was an accident fair and square.' Bizzie blew her nose, hard.

Was it though? Rose added a mental note to find out if there'd been a post-mortem. Then Lily's voice broke into Rose's thoughts, berating her for making Bizzie cry, so she turned back to her grandmother who had stopped crying but was looking as pale as her treasured collection of Royal Worcester porcelain in the display cabinet behind the sofa.

'I'm sorry I've upset you again, Gran, it's the last thing I wanted to do.'

'Nonsense, dear. I'm sorry too. I wasn't brave enough to tell you that you were adopted. I never dreamt Kate had a baby... I don't know what to think of it.'

Neither did Rose.

Bizzie smiled shakily and held out her trembling arms and Rose leant her cheek against the soft pink shoulder again, inhaling that familiar scent of Camay. Bizzie stroked her hair and Rose could feel her breath warm on her scalp.

Her grandmother's voice was soft in her ear, the same tone she'd used to soothe away little Rose's tears. 'Well, we know one thing at least. You are an Ingram. I am your real grandmother. We are your family.'

'Yes.' And Rose suddenly realised that her adopted family was her birth family after all. Well, half of it anyway. 'Yes, you are.' And they hugged, tighter than Rose could remember every hugging anyone. She closed her eyes, breathed deeply and was five again, safe for the moment in her grandmother's aura.

'And that is worthy of celebration.' Bizzie stood up a little shakily. 'Get the glasses from the cupboard, dear,' and she pointed to the oak dresser. 'I'll get the sherry.'

'Tell me about Kate,' Rose asked for the second time, waiting as Bizzie studied her face for a moment. She wished she could plug straight into her Gran's memories of Kate, her face, her smile, her talents. They both took another sip. Rose's sherry was almost gone, Bizzie's glass half full.

'I don't think anyone understood her.'

'Not even Mum?'

'Diana least of all. Like chalk and cheese they were. If I hadn't given birth to both of them in the bed upstairs, I wouldn't believe they were sisters.'

Rose put down her empty glass. 'Mum never

talked about Kate. Of course we knew she existed, but we didn't know anything about her.'

'Diana was a very proper little girl, an indoors girl. Kate loved the outdoors. Kate loved singing and dancing, she seemed to fill whichever room she was in. Diana would struggle to find a quiet corner to read or crayon. Things changed when Kate started acting in the drama group at school, she was out more, at rehearsals. Diana seemed happier then, as if she'd reclaimed the house as hers. They were together every day but I don't think they talked much, really talked, I mean.'

Bizzie was staring into nothing, her eyes glazed with the effort of remembering. 'Then Kate went on tour. They kept such impossible hours and moved so often, we never really knew where she was. She was always phoning from a different town. Really, Maureen spoke with her the most.'

'Maureen?' It had never occurred to Rose that Maureen might have information about Kate. Maureen, her mum's best friend, the girl next door, the bridesmaid at her parents' wedding. Maureen, who had married a dentist and still lived in Richmond.

Bizzie hadn't noticed Rose's distraction. 'Kate was such a free spirit. Your grandfather said we should let her have her wings and fly away, that she would discover the world and fly back home again like a homing pigeon. It terrified me, she was so young... oh dear.' Her voice faded as her eyes misted with tears.

Rose wasn't convinced about her granddad's pigeon theory.

'Diana thought we were silly, letting Kate go touring like that in *Hair*. Perhaps we were...'

Kate was in *Hair*? Naked on stage? Rose didn't

know whether to feel admiration for Kate's bravery or sympathy with her mum's prudery.

'…reckless. But she wasn't a child.'

'Right,' said Rose. A new picture of Kate had sprung into her head, daring, adventurous, and yes, brave.

'Ask Maureen, she'll tell you what it was like.'

'Would she…' Rose could hardly get the words out, '… would she know about Kate's boyfriends?'

Bizzie sighed again. She was sighing a lot, and with each sigh, a piece of Rose's heart wilted. 'Asking won't hurt, I suppose the girls must have talked. It's clear now that they didn't tell me everything, although I thought at the time they did.' She laughed and Rose detected a hint of sadness. 'I'm not sure about anything any more, Rose. I don't think I knew either of my daughters very well. Here I am, and they're both dead. That shouldn't happen.'

Rose took Bizzie's cool hand in hers and smoothed the knotted blue veins and wrinkled knuckles as her grandmother talked on.

'I always thought Diana was the sensible one, but then she got it into her head that your dad would leave her if she didn't have a baby and she wouldn't listen. Not to anyone. And then she announced they were adopting a baby and she came home with you. She said… she said she'd adopted you from…'
Rose held her breath.

'…from a poor girl in a home in Lewisham.'

'Lewisham?' Why Lewisham? And who was the girl? How young was she?

Bizzie shook her head. 'I simply don't know what to think any more, Rose, but I am sure of one thing.

170

Diana did her best for you. She gave you a proper upbringing. You're a lovely young woman, Rose, and I'm proud of you. Diana was too.'

Rose swallowed hard, and clutched her grandmother's hand. She wished her mother had told her that, just the once.

Thanks to Bizzie, Rose now had a photo of Kate on her own. Bizzie thought it had been taken the last time Kate called at the house in Richmond, en route between *The Importance of Being Earnest* in Watford and *A Taste of Honey* in Portsmouth. She was sitting on the back doorstep, a striped scarf knotted around her neck. She was smiling. Her knees bent beneath her chin, her hands clutching a floral mug, her long, dark wavy hair parted in the centre and pulled back behind her ears, a bit like a young Ali McGraw. She looked happy. For Rose, it was like looking at her own reflection in the mirror.

Me, but not quite me. Like a non-identical twin.

She could trace the line of Kate's nose in her own. Cut her mother's hair short and let the natural curls bounce unchecked, and the two of them could be carbon copies. If Bizzie was right – Rose did a few rough calculations – it meant the photo had been taken almost three months after Kate fell pregnant. Within a year, she was dead.

Tears rolled silently down Rose's cheeks. She longed to tell Kate she was sorry. Sorry they had never met, sorry for all the unhappiness.

22 ROSE

The first thing Rose looked at when she awoke early the next morning was Kate's photo.

Hello Mum, she thought. *Mother. Mummy.*

She strode lightly from bedroom to bathroom to kitchen, flicked the switch on the kettle, then logged on and searched for Kate Ingram. Loads of entries, but different Kate Ingrams. A town councillor in Ayrshire banned for dangerous driving. A footballer who had scored the winning goal in Dewsbury Ladies' 3–2 win over the Doncaster Darlings. A four-year-old victim of a hit-and-run driver at a zebra crossing.

Kate died almost thirty years before the Internet was in general use; she didn't have a Facebook page or an entry in Equity's online directory. The waking urge to talk to her, to know more, became a fully conscious need, like the need to eat or pee or sleep. With a wave of shame, Rose realised she didn't know where Kate was buried.

Bizzie would know.

'St Agnes's in Kingston.' Rose could hear the smile in her Gran's voice. 'Where your mum and granddad are. Comfortable benches. I go to see them all once a week. So so.'

This made Rose, who hadn't been to the cemetery since standing beside her mother's grave six months ago, feel even more guilty.

Just as the church clock struck seven, Rose was walking through a wooden gate and along a grass path fringed by weeds and wildflowers, past gravestones, past rambling brambles and ivy. Some graves were neatly kept; grass clipped, headstones scrubbed. She stopped for a moment beside the graves of her mother and grandfather lying shoulder to shoulder in the early morning sunshine. Howard Ingram and Diana Haldane lay with their heads against a south-facing brick wall, sheltered from inclement weather, beneath an old rambling rose. Her grandfather's grave was comfortably messy, like an old squashy sofa, lived-in and loved, and with space on the granite headstone for Bizzie's name when her time came. Rose thought of Bizzie last night looking at Howard's photograph, and knew he was missed every day. In contrast, her mother's grave was a wound in the earth. There was a thin sprinkling of new grass covering the turned soil, and a small wooden peg marked '363'.

Rose stood for a moment, looking at the earth that covered her mother. She wanted to ask so much, but it didn't feel right standing here now, as if she'd crept up and caught her at a disadvantage. She resented her mother's lies, but didn't hate her, though she had expected to.

She looked at the next plot, expecting to see Kate's name. 'Albert Querry' said the words on the headstone. Where was Kate? She walked slowly along the winding path under the archway of a tall yew hedge, this section of the graveyard still in early morning shadow, to a shady area where brambles, buddleia, and bergenias thrived. Dusty green grass sprouted at the base of one pink marble headstone, the stone cross of another leant to the right as if its occupant had had one too many.

Then, past a large oak tree on the left, there it was.

"In Loving Memory
Katherine Ingram 20th February 1947 – 1st January 1969
Much loved daughter and sister"

And mother, thought Rose. *My mother. They left that out.*

'They even lied on her headstone,' she said aloud into the empty morning air, shocked at how her loud voice echoed in the stillness. Why was Kate alone? Why did one sister get to be with their father but not the other? Who made these decisions?

Kate's gravestone was hard and unchangeable, like the facts she'd discovered. Rose knew she had to accept the truth, accept that some questions would remain unanswered. If she didn't, she would turn into a bitter woman.

Blinking away tears, she pulled up the long grass at the foot of the white marble slab, emptied the sad twigs and brown slime out of the marmalade jar left by someone else and rinsed it under a nearby tap. Then she filled it with the yellow freesias she'd bought at the 24/7 garage en route from Wimbledon.

She knelt beside the grave. 'I'm sorry, Kate, for everything that happened to you,' she whispered. 'I don't know the full story, and I can't claim to understand why you gave me away, but I know you must have had your reasons. I'm much older than you were then and I can't begin to think how I'd cope with what happened to you.' Her voice grew stronger. 'I'm glad I know about you and I'm proud to be your daughter.'

Unable to decide what to say or think or do next, she knelt in silence for a moment. Then, feeling the damp seeping through the knees of her jeans, she sat on a bench nearby. She'd never enjoyed silence before. She was a city girl, busy streets, traffic, talk, noise, but when she felt the first vibration through the soles of her sandals, then heard footsteps crunching on the gravel path that led from the vicarage through a moss-covered wooden gate in the wall, she felt sad.

A shadow fell over the grass path by her feet. A vicar stood three yards away with two Yorkshire terriers, pulling on long retractable leads, their top-knots tied with tartan ribbon dancing and nodding as they sniffed Rose's shoes.

'Lovely morning, isn't it?'

She nodded, rising to her feet. She wasn't keen on dogs but it didn't seem appropriate to shoo them away so she contented herself with taking a step back.

'I don't think I recognise you from my congregation.' He smiled, waving her back towards the bench. 'Everyone's welcome. Sunday, ten thirty.'

She sat. 'Thank you. I'm just here to see my mother's grave.' She waved towards the yellow freesias.

'Ah, well. I'll leave you to your thoughts.' He let the Yorkies loose and threw a stick along the path for them to chase. But he didn't follow them.

'I've just found her, you see.' The words popped out of her mouth without forethought. It felt good to say it aloud. 'I didn't know she was my mother.' She pointed at Kate's grave again.

'Ah?' He waited, examining his shoes. The bigger Yorkie ran back to examine them too.

'I found out a little over a week ago that I'm adopted, and last night I found out that Kate is my birth mother. I've been sitting here talking to her.'

'It must be difficult, to want to find someone so much, only to find that they are gone.' He spoke in the sing-song rhythm Rose associated with church services. 'You must miss her very much.'

'Yes, I do. Even though I never knew her.' He sat beside her, his elbow comfortably warm against hers.

'How are your parents coping with the news?'

'There's only my father now. It's been… difficult. I –' she stopped, not knowing what to say next. The vicar patted her lightly on the arm and Rose felt encouraged to continue.

'I don't want to upset him, but I do need to ask him questions, find out what happened, what…' Her words trailed into nothingness. Seldom did words let her down. But the vicar was smiling at her and Rose felt reassured that he understood the unspoken.

'I could do a blessing for you, when you think the time is right. I have a short family service which welcomes an adopted child.'

'But I'm an adult.'

'Your age doesn't matter, child. We're all children in the eyes of God, and our parents, until we die. The service includes a prayer for your natural parents and for your adoptive parents. It's a way of coming to terms with change and embracing unity. It helps everyone to look forward with hope.'

'Could it take place here, by her grave?'

'I've never been asked that before.' He rubbed his chin. There was a tiny piece of tissue stuck to his jaw, bloody from a shaving nick. It made him seem vulnerable, ordinary. Then he smiled at Rose. 'I don't see why not.'

It felt right to accept Kate as her mother here, at her resting place, with her father, Bizzie, and Lily at her side and her mother and Granddad Howard a stone's throw away.

But the blessing would have to wait. She wanted her birth father to be there too.

Five hours later, Rose stood on the steps of Way Forward PR in Chiswick where she'd just left a breakfast press briefing about the New You range of slimming products. *New You: The All-Natural, Organic Way to Detox and Not Go Hungry*. In her hand was a carrier bag containing the press kit. Product samples (sachet of powdered milk shake, energy bar, and vacuum pack of dried savoury rice), press pack, scented candle to help her feel positive about her body image, notepad and ballpoint pen stamped with the New You logo. Standard press reception fodder – Rose would take the bag back to work and it would go into the goodie drawer. When the drawer was full, Sam's secretary would fill up carrier bags and hand them out to the features team. This would be followed by a frantic trading session as the men swapped the lipsticks in their bags for the disposable razors in the women's bags. It was one of the perks of working on the features desk. Rose hadn't bought soap, or pens, since she'd worked at the *Herald*.

Now, bag in hand, she stood on a street corner and looked around to get her bearings. Cars queued at traffic lights by Turnham Green church. Turn right for Chiswick High Road and she was minutes from where Lily worked. Rose desperately needed to talk to her, to tell her about Kate face-to-face, so she dug out her mobile.

'Lunch? Great,' said Lily. 'I finish at one, so we'll have time for a lovely long talk.'

Rose wasn't sure that 'lovely' was the right adjective.

'You've finished with the diaries then,' added Lily, just as Rose thought the conversation was ended.

'Yes, I have.' Rose kept her voice neutral. She'd totally forgotten she'd promised to give the diaries to Lily.

A quick glance at her watch told her there was just time to go home and get back. In fact, she was back in Chiswick with half an hour to spare, so she walked around the small green sandwiched between the church and the corner with the traffic lights, and sat on her second religious bench of the day. She sent Lily a text saying where she was, then let her mind wander to the morning's graveyard conversation.

Her attraction to the idea of an adoption blessing was nothing to do with religion. It was about being surrounded by her family, her real family who accepted her as she was and didn't want to her to be something else. She started to flick through Diana's diaries. A faded blue hardback book looked the oldest but was fastened by a metal lock that she couldn't open, so she flicked through the others, the breeze turning the pages for her, random mentions of her name catching her eye.

Wedding anniversary. 8.30, Aldo's. The lasagne was

lovely but I could have it made it at home a lot cheaper. Got a babysitter. But argued with John about having a conservatory put on the back of the house.

There was still no conservatory at The Weavings.

Took the girls to see The Nutcracker *at Kingston Arts Centre. Lily loved it and is begging for ballet classes. Rose was silent throughout. At least she didn't complain.*

Rose still disliked ballet.

Doctor Waters says it'll take six months to recover from the hysterectomy and recommends I go back to work part-time. John and I agreed I should resign from British Water. Perhaps I'll get a job at the Oxfam shop on Welbeck Rise. Rose buys books there so it must be well run if she likes it.

Rose still bought second-hand books from Oxfam, but had never known that Mum valued her judgement. She wondered what else her mother had felt but never said.

Car horns blew, brakes screeched, shouts and whistles.

'Oi, look where you're going!'

'Get your eyes tested!'

'Bastard!' A truck driver stopped at the traffic lights gesticulated out of his window, his middle finger pointing to the sky.

Bastard. Rose had used the word enough times but had never once thought about its real meaning:

baseborn, illegitimate, misbegotten, unwanted. She was a bastard. Never again would she use that word. For the first time, she felt a label was stuck to her forehead and she couldn't change it. Not a scarlet letter A for 'adopted', but a red letter B.

Don't think about it.

The traffic moved on. The sun was hot, and she closed her eyes. She jumped when her mobile rang. It was Bella from ARAP, wanting an update on the counsellor meeting.

'Oh my goodness,' she said, after listening to Rose's summary. 'Perhaps you'll never really know the full story. And that's okay, Rose, it's okay to not know.'

'But I want to know.' There was a pause while Rose reflected on how childish that had sounded. 'I'm going to order my full adoption certificate next, so I can find my father.'

'We-e-ll... not necessarily. Those forms aren't always conclusive when it comes to the father's identity.'

'Why not?'

'Because it was customary to automatically put down the husband's name as Birth Father. Unless the mother was unmarried and didn't know the father's name. If that was the case she could put Father Unknown.'

But Kate must have written my real father's name on the form, thought Rose. *She wouldn't lie about something so important.*

She'd see what Lily thought about it.

'Good luck telling your sister. And Rose, be gentle. It'll be a big shock for her.'

The church bells rang out, a peal of ascending

and descending notes, an inevitable rising and falling of the scales. Rose squinted against the sun to look at the bell tower. The jumble of bells and sun and traffic made her head ache. Nearby, a gardener pushed trimmings into the mouth of a large yellow machine. The whining monster chewed up the living wood and spat it out in neat chips ready to mulch perfect gardens like Lily's. Rose's head pounded. Her history had been chipped and spat out too. She took an ibuprofen with a large swig of water from her bottle, closed her eyes, and waited for the pounding to stop.

'What lovely marigolds. I've planted some by my tomatoes so they repel the greenfly.'

Lily was standing beside her, holding a parcel wrapped in tissue paper the colour of a Granny Smith apple. 'Here, this is for you. It was damaged when we unpacked the boxes, so I bought it for £1.' She was always giving Rose damaged goods or sale items. Inside the tissue paper was a notebook. On the cover was a picture of a two-headed goose with a human body.
'I thought you could use it for your notes, when you're interviewing someone.'

'Err… thanks.' Rose tried to picture the look on Nick Maddox's face if she'd produced this at the interview. But Lily had thought of her, so she smiled. 'A goose?'

'It's Hapy, the Egyptian fertility god of the Nile flood.'
Fertility god, right. Rose tucked it into the New You carrier bag. The last thing she needed to do right now was challenge Lily's obsession with fertility.

They chose a pizzeria and sat down at a table in the front window. Both ordered chilli pizza.

'I was glad you rang,' said Lily in that tone of voice Rose knew usually preceded a complaint. 'I really want to tell you about my new strategy to get pregnant.' Rose wondered what it could be. Visualising giving birth while having sex?

'I've started taking this special honey to improve my fertility. I want to give myself a boost... but... well, for maximum benefit, William should really take it too, but he... you know, I haven't found the right time to tell him about it yet. Perhaps I'll slip it into his food somehow.'

In Rose's experience, all men hated honey. James had steadfastly refused to eat anything that came out of a bee's bottom. Rose nodded in what she guessed were the right places and said 'really' in an encouraging way whenever Lily stopped for breath, which was rare. She had a way of talking that was difficult to interrupt politely, taking breaths in the middle of sentences, not at the end, so there was never a long enough pause for Rose to speak. Even Rose, with her training in interview techniques, found it difficult to manage conversations with her sister.

Finally, Lily took a long enough breath to get in a word.

'I rang you five times this morning.' Rose knew her voice had a Lily-like whine but was unable to stifle it. 'I saw the adoption counsellor last night.'

Lily swallowed her mouthful of chilli pizza quickly. 'Are you all right?'

'The diary is right.' Rose hesitated, remembering Bella's advice to take it gently. 'Mum didn't give birth to me.'

Lily stared. 'So who...'

'My real mother was Aunt Kate.' Maybe that wasn't gentle enough, maybe she should have gone round the houses a bit.

Lily's jaw dropped. 'Ohh myy Godd.'

This was the phrase they had adopted as teenagers as their favourite expression of shock. Rose enunciated each word clearly with capital initial letters and full stops for emphasis, more 'Oh. My. God', whereas Lily shrieked the three words as one high-pitched, continuous note. She was shrieking now.

'I know.'

'But,' Lily put down her knife and fork, 'it's great. It means we're cousins.' And she burst into tears. 'Ever since we read Mum's diary, I've thought we weren't related at all. This is brilliant news.'

A pile of damp tissues soon gathered in the centre of the table. Their pizzas abandoned, Rose talked soothingly while Lily calmed a little. Rose didn't normally cry. She thought tears were a sign of giving in and wasn't going to give in to anyone or anything, so to stop herself crying she focussed on comforting Lily, patting her arm.

'Every night since I found out... I've been dreaming,' Rose said. 'I'm about ten and I'm sitting up in bed at The Weavings, wearing my favourite nightie, you know, the pink brushed-nylon one with the embroidered roses on the yoke? Yours was –'

'Yellow with embroidered daffodils. You've had the same dream every night for nine nights?' Lily's voice sounded a little more normal and people had stopped staring and were eating their pizzas again.

'The door opens, someone comes in, and tucks me into bed. That's what changes, who it is. One night it's Mum. The next night it's someone famous.'

'Like who?'

'Quite often it's Ma from *Little House on the Prairie,* there's the smell of apple pie baking in the oven. But don't you see? It doesn't matter who it is. My subconscious is fantasising about my birth mother. It's because my memories are all wrong.'

'Oh Rose, your memories don't change about things that really happened.'

'You know, the best thing about confirming that I'm Kate's daughter is that now I know I'm an Ingram. You're not my sister but you are still my cousin, and Gran is still Gran.'

Lily's face was still pale. Rose hated seeing her little sister look so bereft. *Concentrate on the positive*, she thought. 'I know half my medical history now, so that's good. I've been worrying that I might have inherited a genetic disposition to cancer or something.'

'Well, thank goodness there's a happy ending.' Lily tidily arranged the knife and fork on her plate side-by-side, indicating she'd finished eating.

Happy ending? 'But this isn't the end. I've only found half my family.'

'Rose, be careful.' Lily took her napkin off her lap and started to fold it. 'I think you're getting obsessed with this whole thing. Of course everyone's upset for you, but this continual searching is damaging. Dad doesn't know what to say to you and when I spoke to Grandma earlier she was in tears. She wouldn't say why except that you were there late last night and phoned at dawn this morning. I think it's time to stop.'

'But it's only –' *Obsessed? Lily's calling me obsessed? Pots and kettles.*

'Lily, it's only ten days since I found out.'

'No, let me finish.' Lily twisted her napkin in her hands as if making some sort of free-form origami table arrangement. 'You've found your real family. Us. Aren't we real enough for you? You're healthy with a good job, a nice home, and a family that loves you. There's real pain out there. People alone, with no money, no family at all. If you knew what it felt like not being able to have a baby, you'd…'

Oh, I wondered how long it'd take to get around to babies, thought Rose wearily.

'No. It's not enough,' she said, scrunching her napkin into a ball and tossing it onto her plate, 'because it's only half the picture. I can't stop searching. I might as well try and ignore gravity. I've found half my family. Half, fifty per cent, not a hundred per cent. The Ingram half that I've found is great, it's all of you. But half my heart, my genes, my DNA is still missing and I have to find it. I'm sorry if I'm upsetting you, Lily, I don't mean to, but this is something I simply need to do. I didn't ask to be adopted, it happened to me. I'm the victim here.' She hadn't admitted that before, she didn't like the idea of being a victim; she was a fighter.

'You've already got a father. He's called John, he lives in Richmond and he's lonely. He's lost his wife and job and thinks he's going to lose you too.'

'He hasn't lost me.' *But he is a quitter,* she added to herself, *a drunk who runs away from reality, who's been drinking in his shed since my childhood.* She hated thinking this about her father, but it was true. Then she remembered she hadn't told Lily about the scene at the allotment last night. Now was not the time. 'Why do you think I'm so wrong to need my birth father?'

'I, I, I. Me, me, me. It's not just about you, Rose. You're wrecking our family!' Lily was shouting now, unconscious of the glares from other tables, waving her hands as if conducting Mozart's *Requiem*.

Rose took Lily's twisted napkin out of her hands and threw it on the table. 'I'm not trying to wreck anything. But, just think, I might have other sisters and brothers. I might be an aunt.' As soon as she said it, she knew it was a mistake. A big one.

Lily pushed her chair back as if to get up and leave, but didn't move. Her face was screwed up and red.

Rose suddenly felt very tired. The conversation wasn't supposed to go like this. She'd done it all wrong. 'Lily, I'm sorry I said that. I'm sorry you're not pregnant.' *Perhaps if your husband was at home more often, you'd have more sex.* For a horrible moment, Rose thought she'd said the last bit aloud. But she hadn't. It was the penis thing all over again.

'Look,' she reached across the table to take Lily's hand. 'The birth of a baby is a time of celebration, you of all people will appreciate that. How do you think it feels to know that my birth caused regret, conflict, arguments, guilt?'

Lily sniffed.

'I need to find out who I am and I'd like your support. But if not, I'll do it on my own.'

'Why? You're still Rose Haldane, aren't you?'

'Not really. I'm an Ingram, not a Haldane.' Rose tried to keep her voice calm. If Lily didn't understand this, would anyone? Her tongue was dry and her mind was empty and meanwhile Lily was standing up and shouting.

'And you just go off and do things that affect us without a word, but you expect us to understand why you're doing it. We're not telepathic.' And with that, Lily grabbed her bag and turned for the door.

'Don't forget these!' Rose called after her, and pushed the pile of diaries across the table.

Lily turned back, scooped up the diaries without a word, and left.

Rose sighed heavily. Well, that hadn't gone to plan.

23 LILY

She stormed along the street, not knowing if she'd turned left or right.

How dare Rose imply that my life's a mess? Of course I want to get pregnant, doesn't everyone? Poor Dad, poor, poor Dad. And poor Mum too, she wanted a baby so much, she must have been at the end of her tether, so lonely. No wonder she asked her sister for help. Well she was lucky she had Kate to turn to. I wish I had a sister like that.

That was a cruel thought, and Lily wasn't used to being cruel. But it was true.

Instantly she felt alone on the crowded pavement. Rose wasn't her sister any more. Being cousins wasn't the same at all. Suddenly Lily sensed she was being stared at. She was muttering to herself. She shut her mouth, took her sunglasses out of her bag, and put them on. She stopped to rearrange the pile of diaries better in her arms, but the blue one on top slithered to the pavement. Its metal lock burst open and loose pages spilled onto the hot pavement. Lily dropped to her knees to pick them up and the words flew off the open page straight into her heart.

Ovulation takes place twelve to sixteen days before a period and these two to five days are the only time it's possible to fall pregnant.

The handwriting, written in faded ink inside a bleached blue hardback book, echoed exactly the instructions on the ovulation test kit Lily had bought that morning.

'Oh Mum, it was the same for you.'

And then it hit her. *If Mum had early menopause, maybe she never got pregnant. I might be adopted too.* Two emotions swept over Lily, overwhelming her in their truth. For the first time in her life, she felt jealous of Rose for knowing the truth. Perhaps she shouldn't have been so harsh with her just now, but really, sometimes Rose made her feel like arguing for the sake of it. But now she understood how Rose must have felt when she first read the diary. Afraid. Not knowing was more painful than knowing the truth, whatever it might be. Realising she was still kneeling on the pavement, she started to gather her belongings. This wasn't just about Rose being adopted any more, it was about her too. She had to know.

Fumbling, she gathered everything together. She must read them now. Walking quickly, she pushed roughly past someone wearing red.

'Ow.'

Lily turned to apologise then stopped. It was a young mother with a buggy, face pale, eyes puffy, red sweatshirt full of uncontrollable boobs, short finger-dried hair fluffy in the afternoon sun.

But you have a baby, Lily wanted to shout at her. *You should be happy. If I had a baby, I'd never be unhappy again.*

She found a quiet cafe, away from the mothers

and their buggies and babies, and ordered a cappuccino. Then she looked at the cover of the bleached blue book and hesitated. Did she really want to know?

No.

Yes.

24 ROSE

I shouldn't have let her go without apologising, I should have run after her, but really, sometimes Lily...

An eastbound train pulled in and Rose found a seat by the window in a half-empty carriage. The train had just started moving when her mobile rang. Lily's name flashed up. Rose hesitated. It was a tiny hesitation and Rose hated herself for it.

'Sorry,' said Lily.

'I'm sorry, too.'

And there was a moment's silence.

'Sorry,' repeated Lily, 'I was so busy getting upset that I forgot how upset you must be. You don't always show your emotions, you know, and sometimes it's like you have no feelings.'

'I do have feelings, Lil, I'm not a robot.'

'I know, and I'm sorry for saying you're obsessed.'

'Well, I have been a bit obsessed. But no more...'

'No more than me trying to get pregnant,' Lily finished. 'I know. Sorry.'

'I think that's enough apologising.'

'Okay.'

That word floated in the air and Rose got the feeling Lily had something else to say. She waited.

'But there's more we need to talk about. When I left you I went to a cafe and started to read Mum's diaries and…'

'What?'

'No.' Lily spat out the word like a bullet. 'I can't possibly tell you over the phone.'

Oh for goodness' sake, thought Rose, and was immediately glad she hadn't said it aloud. It suddenly dawned on her that the diaries might say Lily was adopted too. *This is mega. I need to be there with her, not going in the opposite direction at 60mph.*

She deliberately calmed her voice and got ready to say soothing things about them being sisters of the soul and that blood wasn't all it was cracked up to be. 'Well, I can't come back, I'm late for this stupid press reception already.' She dropped her voice a tone and softened it, like she did when she was conducting sensitive interviews. 'Tell me, Lily. Is it news about me or about you?'

'Both of us. Mum definitely had me, I mean, she gave birth to me. It's all there in her handwriting in the blue diary. I had a horrible moment thinking she'd adopted me too, because in the first bit I read she writes about not conceiving. But then later on in the same book it's there, in her own handwriting, about my birth.'

Rose felt such a swooping joy for Lily that she almost whooped aloud. 'Oh Lily, that's fantastic, I'm so pleased you *are* my cousin. What a relief.' And it was. Rose hadn't realised until now exactly what it would mean if Lily were adopted too. She so regretted not sitting down with all those other diaries and reading them cover to cover nine days ago. It would have meant nine days' less pain for Lily. 'Hey,' she was almost laughing now, 'that

194

means you can get pregnant too.'

'Yes, it does.'

Lily sounded strangely muted. Rose wanted to shout it out loud to all the passengers. 'My sister *can* have a baby!'

'Rose,' Lily's voice repeated in her ear.
And suddenly Rose realised Lily wasn't celebrating with her, and an iron vice gripped her stomach. Was there something else?

'Rose, Mum wrote more about you. About when she'd just got you. She says...'

'What?' If Lily didn't want to say, it must be horrible.

'I...'

'Lily, just say it. We both need to understand what Mum was going through if we're ever going to get to the bottom of where we come from. And it is about both of us now, isn't it?'

'Yes, I know it is... but I want you to hear it from me... only from me...'

The hushed tone of Lily's voice, her hesitations, her heavy breathing, her sadness transmitted through the phone signal and made Rose float away from her seat, away from the rattling of the track and the tinny base beat of someone's iPod, so she was sitting in a bubble while the outside world rushed on normally around her. 'Go on, please.' She had to hear it. Life would stop until she'd heard whatever it was.

'There are a couple of mentions about how she couldn't rock you to sleep. She was worried you would never love her properly, like a real mother, and it seemed to bother her that you didn't look the slightest bit like her. And...' Lily stopped.

There's more? 'What? What?'

'…and that having you wasn't the same as having her own baby.'

Rose heard Lily's breathing, irregular little gasps.

'Oh it's so awful, Rose, I knew I shouldn't have told you on the phone.' Her tone was rising towards shriek level again. 'Maybe I read it wrong, maybe she wrote that entry after a really difficult day, maybe...'

'No, you read it right.' Rose's stomach dropped like lead and hit her feet. Of course her mother must have felt like that; there had been many difficult days throughout Rose's childhood. She remembered one day in the queue at the butcher's, she must have been about four and Lily three, a stranger patted Lily's blonde pigtails and said, 'Aren't you a cutie? You're a miniature of your mummy' and looked over the top of Rose's head as if she didn't exist. Their mother said nothing. That still hurt.

'Rose? I'm sure she didn't mean it.'

'It's okay. Well no, it's not okay, but it's not a surprise. No woman can expect to bond instantly with a tiny baby she hasn't given birth to.'

Rose felt her own breaths start to follow the same panicked rhythm as Lily's. She tried to be calm. *I am calm.* 'Lily, it's all right. Honestly.'

'No, it's not all right, it's really sad. I want to help you Rose, if there's anything I can do. But I'm sure you've got it all in hand, I mean –'

'Yes please. Thank you for asking. You can help.'

'Really? Ooh, I'll write a list.'

As soon as Rose heard the gratitude in Lily's

voice, she knew she shouldn't have cut Lily out. She should have asked her to help from the beginning. 'I didn't realise you wanted to help. I'm sorry I haven't asked you before. I don't know… it's like I had to do things on my own so I could deal with the enormity of it. There are lots of things to check out, I can't just follow one line of research at a time. That'd take forever.' Rose immediately thought of her lines of enquiry and what there still was to do. What could she give to Lily? 'There is one thing the counsellor suggested last night. It might be a bit of a wild goose chase…' Rose remembered Hapy, the goose fertility symbol on the front of the notebook. She opened her bag and looked at the book – the picture was silly but Lily obviously believed this sort of crap would help her get pregnant. A positive mental attitude, et cetera.

'I'll do it.'

Rose could picture Lily's face shining with eagerness. She had been holding her breath and now she let it go. Of course Lily didn't need Hapy now, or her thermometer or ovulation chart to get pregnant. An invisible boulder lifted off Rose's shoulders. 'My birth was registered in Enfield. My counsellor is finding out if the Social Services department there has a file on me. But we can try to get other information, the sort that's not in files. Can you ring Enfield Council and find out where they keep the records of former mother and baby homes in their area? It's so long ago, but you never know, there might be something. Maybe the library can help. The home was probably absorbed into a children's home or an old people's home. We might be able to find a nurse who remembers Kate, or a patient who was there when Kate was.'

'Okay, so what do I ask?'

'We're looking for the sort of information they don't put in the records. Anything. Everything. What the home was like, photos...' It was the longest of shots, but she had to try, if only to cross that avenue of enquiry off her list. 'Where the medical records are now, that sort of thing.'

'I'll do it. Just don't let's argue like that again. I couldn't bear it if we fell out like Mum and Kate did.'

'We won't.'

'Rose, why do you think they argued?'

'I don't know, but I wish every day that I'd asked Mum about Kate just once more before she died.' She'd asked many times as a child about their mysterious Aunt Kate, but received only a slap around the back of her legs for being rude and too inquisitive. When she was big enough not to be slapped, she should have asked again, but Aunt Kate's curiosity value had been superseded by how Maltesers were made and whether Marc Bolan's hair was real or a wig.

'You could ask Gran.'

'No,' said Rose vehemently, 'I'm not going to make Bizzie cry again.'

For a moment, they were silent.

'Rose, I promise never to argue with you like that.'

'I promise too.'

25 ROSE

Rose left the Pre-Tox Party Kit press reception two hours later with another PR goodie bag. At Waterloo she ran for it, but reached the barrier less than thirty seconds before departure. She watched the rear of the train disappear.

She rubbed her aching neck and looked up at the indicator board: twenty minutes before the next Wimbledon train. Her muscles and emotions were bound as tightly as a new ball of wool. She'd need some serious help to relax tonight. If she was quick, she could nip into her favourite shop on Waterloo Bridge Road. She seldom left Cool Beauty without a bottle.

So she nipped. As she stepped through the shop door, the unravelling experience began. She sniffed and sampled her way along the shelves through 'Refresh' and 'Revive' to 'Renew' and with each step her shoulders eased as a frayed end of wool teased its way loose. But she knew that only when she was lying up to her chin in fragranced bathwater tonight would the last strands of tight muscle unwind from her neck and down her spine, releasing each vertebra one at a time. Then she would rub Soothing Rose lotion into every square inch of her skin and allow the French rose petals to renew her.

The bath didn't happen. She spent an hour at her laptop fiddling with the Direct Gov website, trying to order her birth certificate, until finally the site crashed. 'Not responding' was the Windows message. Rose's brain wasn't responding either. And now she was late for her yoga class – inspired by Lily, she had signed up for a course of ten called 'Ultimate Relaxation'. She ran to the church hall, where she spent the next sixty minutes lying on the floor, hands at her side, palms upwards, feet splayed out, trying not to worry about not relaxing. A sore spot nagged her right shoulder blade where a bobble on her bra strap dug in deep; a blister on her left heel caught against the hard wooden floor, a lorry beeped as it reversed outside. She breathed deeply, her eyes closed.

Did Kate tell her boyfriend that she was pregnant, that the baby was his?

Rose wasn't sure what was worse, if he did know about the pregnancy and didn't help, or if Kate didn't tell him at all.

And if... no, not if... when... when I find him, will he love me?

Will. Breathe in.

He. Breathe out.

Love. Breathe in.

Me? Breathe out.

She stretched her legs, fingers, and arms in turn, feeling each muscle relax until she stretched out her left foot and inadvertently hit the blister. She opened her eyes, lifted her head a fraction, and looked around. Everyone's eyes were closed, so she lay flat again. There were so many questions to ask. She was good at that, working out her questions in advance, planning

200

interview tactics. A restaurant would be a good place for the reunion, or a hotel, somewhere busy, somewhere with lots of people where they wouldn't be on their own, somewhere with distractions to make polite conversation about.

She was good at making conversation, it was part of her job.

'Did you know Kate was pregnant?'

'Why didn't you ask her to marry you?'

'Did you lo…'

Suddenly her head was pressed back down to the floor with a firm pressure on her forehead that brooked no objection.

'Lie down, you'll never reach a true state of relaxation if you don't concentrate.' The yoga teacher's hand weighed a ton.

An hour later, Rose walked home feeling an inch taller. Tonight would be a night off from adoption, she decided, as the door shut behind her with a satisfying clunk that said 'peace', 'privacy', 'home'. Tonight would be about pampering, self-indulgence, calm. She poured a glass of wine and wandered from room to room, picking things up and replacing them in exactly the same spot, straightening the already straight cushions on the sofa. Moving Kate's photo from room to room with her. She turned on the TV and channel-hopped for a while. A preview of Wimbledon tennis … the Prime Minister at a primary school reading Dr Seuss to the reception class… puffins in Scotland…

She wandered to the window, threw it open and looked down on to Monument Road. A man in his sixties holding a beer can walked slowly along the pavement beneath her window, a younger man at his side. Father and son? The older man studied the footpath in front of him as if searching for coins. The younger man, a mirror copy of the elder, waited patiently at his side. Every now and then the elder would stumble and the young man took his elbow. Their words drifted up to Rose's windowsill. 'The game... kick-off... no ball control, that Billy... wide right... wanker... flatten 'em...' They crossed the road and disappeared from sight into the black hole that was the open door of The Eagle. 'European Football Live', said the sandwich board outside, 'Guinness Special.'

They looked like they shared genes.

They could be my father and brother, she thought. They were dark, like her. The younger man's hair curled around his ears, like hers did. They looked bonded and Rose realised she didn't know what that felt like. She wanted to go the pub, to ask them what it felt like to have that 100% bond of blood.

Tears came from nowhere and suddenly she felt very alone. She dialled ARAP, but Bella had gone home for the night.

'Stop crying,' she said aloud. Hearing the words somehow made her take more notice of them. She went into the kitchen and filled up her wine glass. 'Just forget all about this stuff for one night,' she said into the fridge. 'Just one night.' She paced around the kitchen table and Brad retreated, his back to the wall, his eyes wary. 'At least I'm not crying,' she said as she passed him for the fifteenth time.

The doorbell rang. It was Maggie with a bottle of plonk, a tube of Pringles, a chocolate orange, and, under her arm, a newspaper.

'Girls' night in,' she declared. 'I want to hear all

about the adoption advisor last night.'

'Oh Maggie,' said Rose, and fell forwards into her friend's arms. 'You are my friend, aren't you? You are, aren't you? Say you are.'

'Of course I am. Hey, come on, it's not like you to get emotional.'

'I know,' Rose said and made a noise that was part-sniff and part-snort. 'You're my only friend in the whole world that I know will tell me the truth.'

Maggie glanced around the room and took in the wine bottle and the puffins on TV. 'The truth? Okay. The truth is, you need a big glass of water.' She nudged Rose backwards onto the sofa, filled a tumbler with water, and sat down beside her.

'Tell…' her words dried up as she stood up again and examined the sofa. 'Hey, since when did you put a cotton throw on top of your wonderful velvet sofa? It's the nicest thing in this room.'

'I've gone off red,' said Rose, blushing at the memory of James and inner-thigh material.

Maggie sat down again. 'Fine, whatever, don't tell me then.' She tore the foil top off the Pringles in one sweep, and looked at Rose expectantly.

Rose passed her the form from hell. Maggie read it slowly, silently, as if proofreading a front-page story. Finally she looked up.

'Who is this?'

'My Aunt Kate, Mum's sister.'

'The hippy one?'

A nod.

'But I thought she died?'

Another nod.

'Oh, whoa. You've really unleashed the genie,

haven't you?'

A third nod.

'Didn't it occur to anyone that this little family secret was bound to come out in the end?'

Rose shrugged her shoulders.

'Let's get drunk,' said Maggie.

And so they did, horribly. So drunk they decided the best way to find out the truth was to ask Kate. Really ask her. Maggie thought the new Chinese destiny was the thing to do; Rose preferred the Ouija board. They were in Rose's flat, so she won. She rummaged around in a cupboard and retrieved the board from a box of Christmas decorations; it had been her Secret Santa present at work. She suspected it was Frank's purchase and had meant to throw it out.

They laid the board on the coffee table and sat hunched forwards, their hands on the glass. 'Kate, are you there? Who is my father?' Rose felt stupid, talking into space. Nothing happened. She repeated her question.

'It's not working. This is a stupid idea.'

'Sshh,' giggled Maggie, 'you've got to give it time. Kate may be a long way away.'

Rose slapped Maggie's fingers where they rested on the upturned tumbler. 'Hey, don't cheat. You're not allowed to push it.'

'I'm not pushing it, you are,' said Maggie as she leant forwards over the table.

'Are too.'

'Am not.'

Rose stood up, swayed slightly, and pointed her finger at Maggie. 'Are too.'

'Am not.'

Maggie stood up so they were nose-to-nose, swaying from side to side, scowling. And then they burst into laughter.

'Let's have another drink.'

'Okay.'

They topped up their glasses, sat down again, straightened their faces into a pose of mock seriousness, settled their fingers lightly on the tumbler and stared at each other with glassy eyes. Maggie's eyes dipped to the table.

'Look at me, look at me,' Rose repeated, 'you're not supposed to look at the glass. Don't force the answer, it has to come naturally.'

'I'm not forcing it.'

Rose reached out towards Maggie's chin, lifting it slightly so their eyes met. 'Yes, you are.'

'Am not,' Maggie mumbled.

Rose sighed. 'I'm not doing it if you don't take it seriously, Mags.'

Suddenly, Maggie gasped. 'Oooh.'
The glass started to move.

Rose gasped too. 'Look. V. I don't know anyone with a name starting with V. Do you?'

Maggie shook her head, her eyes focussed on the glass.

'Vince,' said Rose. 'Can't think of another name beginning with V. No, yes I can. Violet. Verity. Vernon.'

'Your father's got a man's name, idiot. Since when did you know a man called Violet? Or Verity?'

The glass stopped next beside the letter L. Then A. When the glass stopped moving it had spelt out:
VLADMB GORSBSYK.

'Oh God,' Rose jumping to her feet, 'my father's Russian.' She collapsed back onto the sofa. 'Smirnov, Molotov, Gorbachov, Anna Kournikova. My real name is Rose Gorsbsiyuk…'

Maggie shook her head. 'No, you're not Russian and that's not what it spelt anyway. It's not 'yuk'. This isn't working,' and she tossed the glass over her shoulder where it bounced off the back of the sofa and crashed against the skirting board, intact.

'Can't spell Russian,' said Rose. 'Can't speak Russian… never be able to understand him.'

'Forget it, Rose. You're not Russian. Can we try this now?' Maggie picked up her copy of *Xtra* and pointed to a headline on the cover: 'Find Your Destiny the Chinese Way'.

'Okay.'

Maggie read the instructions, then tore up some blank paper into scraps and wrote the numbers one to a hundred on them. Rose twisted them into balls. The pile grew like a heap of discarded sweet wrappers.

'Okay, we have to ask a question. Out loud.' Maggie closed her eyes and wrinkled her nose. 'I want to know… when will I meet my true love?'

'That's a bit slushy.'

'Nothing wrong with slushy.' Eyes still closed, Maggie stuck her hand into the pile of paper twists and pulled one out. '34.'

Rose ran her finger down the list. '"Cloudless Sky. Your heart is clear and the way is open". That's not true, it's your legs that are always….'

'Don't be filthy.'

Rose giggled before reading on: '"Be honourable and sincere. Do not plague yourself with doubts. Everything will go as you wish.""

'Yes.' Maggie's smile was like that of a ten-year-old eating a whole tub of chocolate ice cream. 'Chinese proverbs are cool.'

'Everything will go as you wish? And you believe this... this rubbish?' Rose tossed *Xtra* onto the floor. 'I've been saying this to you for months, stop looking for the right man and he'll turn up, but you never listen to me. Anyway, who are you so keen on?'

'No one, just hypothetical.'

'Yeah, right.' Rose wrenched the crumpled paper square from Maggie's fingers, re-twisted it, and replaced it in the pile. 'My turn now.'

'Oh,' Maggie pulled a face, 'it's not such a pile of rubbish after all then?'

Rose scowled and closed her eyes. 'I want to know... who is my real father?' Then she slid her hand to the bottom of the pile of paper twists, picked up a handful and scattered them through her fingers onto the sofa. '20.'

'Hmmm. 20.' Maggie read from the magazine. '"After the Rain. You have found the hidden treasure."'

'Hidden treasure? Well, he's definitely hidden because I haven't found him.' Rose drained her wine glass.

Maggie read on. 'It says, "Be happy, the nightmare wasn't real. Work hard for your dreams."'

'Well, the nightmare is real.' Rose swept the paper twists off the sofa into a heap on the floor. 'I want another drink.'

Maggie disappeared into the black hole that was Rose's hall cupboard and emerged with their third bottle of wine in one hand, *Harry Potter and the Philosopher's Stone* in the other, and a cushion under her arm. She settled back on the sofa, propping the cushion behind her head, and waved the book at Rose.

'What's this?'

'Hey, give that back.' Rose stood up and reached for the book.

'An English degree, a journalist on a national newspaper, and you're reading children's books now?'

'Adults read them, and he's adopted.' Suddenly Rose felt stupid. She hoped Maggie hadn't noticed the other adoption books in the cupboard, or looked too closely at the cushion. Mum had embroidered it for her eighteenth birthday. Rose thought the rose design was the naffest example of homemade sewing around.

'Well, at least your adoptive parents didn't lock you in a cupboard like Harry Potter's did.'

'Give it back.'

'You didn't have to hide cakes under a floorboard, did you?' Maggie's hand wavered as she poured the wine and Sauvignon Blanc splashed over the coffee table and the day's *Guardian*. 'They didn't abandon you at King's Cross with an owl and a trunk.' Rose's mind registered the spillage, the newspaper pages puckered and the wood veneer paled.

'Actually, as good as. When I went off to uni, they took me to the train station with all my bags and,' Rose could still picture it, she was opening the window as the Bristol-bound train pulled out of Paddington, eager to wave, only to see her parents' backs disappearing through the exit. She sniffed, 'and they didn't wait to wave goodbye. They left.'

Maggie stared at her. 'You've never told me

that, we've known each other, how long…' she counted on her fingers, '…I can't count any more.'

'It's not something I'm proud of, having emotionally cold parents.'

Maggie tossed the book into the air. It landed out of sight with a dull thud. 'That's a bit harsh, Rose. Admittedly, your mum was a bit challenging, but your dad's not bad, for a bloke.' She sank back onto the sofa. Rose wasn't sure she liked Maggie telling her the truth like that. 'Hugs are important. Everyone needs a hug.'

'You just need a man.'

'No I don't, I'm perfectly okay on my own, thanks.'

'Every woman needs a good man.'

'Oh. My. God. What are you, my sister? I never thought I'd hear Maggie, Queen of the One-Night-Fucks, needing a good man,' Rose sniggered. "So much for feminism."

Maggie's face was red now. 'I meant *you* need a good man, not that I do.'

'Well, maybe *you* should get one.'

Silence fell. Maggie emptied her wine glass and looked at the bottom.

Rose drained her glass in one swig and turned towards the kitchen. 'Do you want a mug of peppermint tea?'

A noise came out of Maggie's mouth that sounded like a snort. 'Since when do you drink peppermint tea?'

'Always.'

'Never, more like. We've been pissed hundreds of times and I've never seen you drink peppermint tea.'

'Nick made it for me,' Rose admitted in a small

209

voice, not wanting Maggie to know how much she liked him, but wanting to talk about him all the same. 'Nick Maddox. The beauty guy. He made me a cup, that time he came up when I was ill. Except I wasn't ill, not in the way he thought I was.'

'Ugh, dried-up leaves. Disgusting,' said Maggie, shaking her head as if it were a duster she was trying to rid of dust. 'You're not going to turn into one of those creepy women who adopts her boyfriend's likes and dislikes as her own, are you? If you're that keen on him, as you obviously are to even consider dead plants, why don't you just ring and ask him out for dinner? It's that easy, you know.'

'Oh. My. God.' Rose's hands flew to her mouth. She suddenly felt cold and very sober. 'Nobu.'

'What?'

'I forgot! Dinner. Nobu. Well, that's it. He'll never ask me again.'

'What?'

'I was supposed to have dinner with him tonight. I've got to call him.' She stumbled towards the phone, knocking the empty fruit bowl off the coffee table on her way.

'Rose, it's,' Maggie glanced at her watch, 'one o'clock. He's not going to be pleased if you wake him. I don't think that'll help, and anyway he hasn't called you, has he? Have some peppermint tea instead.'

'But I want to,' Rose dialled as she talked, 'I want to tell him... he has the cutest... ssssh... ssssh... his machine is talking to me.'

'Why are you whispering?'

'Dunno.'

Then just as his machine beeped to start

210

recording her message, Rose burped. Not a delicate ladylike burp, but a burp from the depths of her gut that smelled of last night's vegetable stir-fry. She slammed the phone down and the two girls rolled on the sofa, laughing, hiccupping and hugging.

26 ROSE

Ibuprofen, birth certificate, and an apology were Rose's three priorities when she woke too few hours later. The ibuprofen was easy, but the Direct Gov website was still 'undergoing a few problems which we hope to resolve soon so please visit us later' and every attempt to speak to Nick failed. Gatekeeper Amanda was polite when she took Rose's first message of the morning, but her voice grew more curt with each successive call.

By 11 a.m. she was nowhere near clearing the backlog. That was why she was working at home in the first place: peace, quiet, no interruptions, complete concentration, and so on. That was the theory. But the 500 words she managed to squeeze out about psoriasis were rubbish and would have to be rewritten from scratch, which meant she would miss her deadline. She longed for espresso, the really strong espresso that was only available from the Coffee Crema van round the corner from Southfields tube station.

As she stood in the queue, her mind wandered away from itchy skin to Nick. Nick, who preferred peppermint tea. Peppermint tea, the same taste as toothpaste, Polo mints, chewing gum, after-dinner mints. *Forget Nick. Think about your father instead.*

She pictured two hands putting her birth

certificate into a large brown envelope. Except they were Nick's hands. She pictured a pink tongue sealing the flap with a slick lick from left to right. Except it was Nick's tongue. She pictured fingers sticking the stamp in the top right-hand corner. Except they were Nick's fingers.

You won't hear from him again after last night's burp, she told herself sternly. *Focus on now.* A teenage girl, loaded down with Top Shop bags, bumped Rose's arm, spilling scalding espresso on Rose's right hand. Then Lily rang with no news, just to say she was trying. Rose scowled; didn't Lily know that the definition of news was something happening, not something not happening? The Direct Gov website working – that would be something. Nick ringing her back – that would be something. He was everywhere she looked, in the man jogging by, in the face creams displayed in a pharmacy window.

Go away, Nick. Not now. I can't afford to think of you now.

The fresh air was nice and her headache started to ease. She sat on a bench in a quiet corner of the library garden to drink her coffee, and stared at a war memorial she'd never noticed before. A grubby concrete statue of an angel holding a grey pigeon in each hand. She read the names of local men who'd died for their country. There must be 300 names, many surnames repeated, all old enough to be Granddad Howard or Granddad Haldane, both long dead, or her birth father's father. Three granddads.

The names of the soldiers swam in front of her eyes… Private John Worth, Private David Worth, Sergeant Christopher Worth… she saw a clear picture: her fingers opening the envelope, unfolding her certificate…

Then there was music somewhere distant, repetitive music, and the laughter of a mother and toddler sitting on the library steps sharing an ice-cream and reading *The Gruffalo,* repetitive laughter, and the realisation that it was her mobile ringing. The two pigeons flew away, leaving the angel to look kindly upon the fallen alone.

Please let this be Nick. Rose picked up a pretty pebble from the path and smoothed it in her hand. It felt lucky. She could do with some luck. She answered the phone.

27 LILY

It took Lily three phone calls, ten minutes of Beethoven, four of ABBA, and six separate explanations before she was put through to the right department, and then only ten seconds to confirm that Rose was right. There had been a mother and baby home in Enfield in 1968 but it had closed in 1969. A client services assistant at Enfield Council said the files – she called them statement books - – would have been passed on as a matter of protocol to the adoption agency concerned, AA Adoption Agency. Lily wrote it all down carefully. But AA Adoption Agency had merged with another agency and changed its name, said the client services assistant, and Lily was now waiting for someone from the council to ring her back with the new name. She was proud of what she'd discovered in such a short time just asking questions. Was this what Rose's job was like? For the first time, Lily thought she understood what Rose did every day. She normally thought of journalism as 'writing', she'd never considered how Rose knew what to write in the first place. Eager to tell Rose how useful it was to think of questions in advance and write them in a list before telephoning anyone, she picked up the phone to call Rose's mobile.

She put the phone down five minutes later. Rose

had been full of thanks, not a single sarcastic comment, and quick to say 'great', 'well done', 'thanks', 'you've been a great help'. And she sounded like she meant it. She'd even given Lily some information without being asked, something about a war memorial and grandfathers. Lily wondered if they'd get on better as cousins rather than sisters, more like real friends. Being cousins meant they could choose to like each other, rather than feeling obliged to be 'sisterly'. When Lily thought of the word, it was always in quote marks because she wasn't quite sure what sisterly meant. She'd only ever known one sister, Rose, but she knew other women who spoke to their sisters five times a day, lived a street apart and spent every spare moment together. There were so many types of sisters, stepsisters, half-sisters, adoptive sisters, no one seemed to have a simple family. She was the only one at Good Times not divorced, and the only one without children. At that thought, she clenched her fists so tightly, her fingernails left indentations in her palm.

She would marinate the leg of lamb and hope the council would call her back soon. It was a nice feeling, helping Rose, and it stopped her worrying about William, whose domestic demands and food requests were becoming time-consuming. It was almost as if he wanted to keep her busy. She pressed two garlic cloves on top of the small pile of grated root ginger already in the marble mortar, added a dash of lemon juice, a slug of dark green olive oil and some chopped rosemary, bashed it with a pestle and then poured the lot over the lamb. As she massaged the oil deep into the meat with her fingertips, she tried to remember the last time William had called her his beautiful girl. Their honeymoon…

then once after a night at the theatre… and… and… that was it. She remembered the play, two tortured couples unfaithful, deceitful, manipulative. She hadn't enjoyed it, but William had taken her by the hand as they left and said, 'That'll never happen to us, beautiful girl.'

She put the lamb in the fridge and looked around for something else to do, avoiding eye contact with the kitchen table. After William had left without breakfast that morning, she'd piled her mother's diaries in the middle of the table and circled around them for hours. But now there were no more chores left to do.

'Richard of York gave battle in vain,' she sang in her light voice as she organised the notebooks into the sequence of colours in a rainbow. Red. Orange. Yellow. Green. Blue. Indigo. Violet. Unsure of the exact shade of indigo, she did the best she could. She placed the bleached blue book with the lock, THE book, with its hints and medical facts about ovulation, second from the right next to violet. It made a pretty pile. She couldn't put it off any longer. She had to read her mother's words. After flicking through two diaries yesterday in the café, Lily wasn't at all sure whether she wanted to read more. *Diaries are personal*, she told herself, *full of secrets and confessions, locked with tiny shiny keys, hidden under mattresses and inside shoeboxes. I can't be angry with Rose for acting on what she read in Mum's diary if I read them too.* A part of her liked being angry with Rose, liked occupying the high ground.
I'm being silly. Mum didn't have early menopause and neither do I.

'If Rose is brave enough to face the truth,' she told the kitchen at large, 'so am I.'

So she turned off her mobile and turned on the

answerphone, took a deep breath, and opened the red book at the top of the pile. She wanted the one that was written in the nine months before her birthday. Red was 1971. Her birthday was 1 June 1969, so Lily put that one aside and opened the next. Another red: 1976. She worked her way down the pile. Second from the bottom was 1968. Orange. Rose had been born 29 August 1968. Lily was born the following year when their mother was twenty-three. Not like Sylvie Watson who couldn't have a baby at all, in fact Lily wasn't sure now if she'd got that story right.

She went to the study, logged on and searched. There were fifteen million results for the actress. Fifteen million! How did Rose use the Internet for research when there was so much to read? She clicked a photo and saw Sylvie with her Vietnamese baby. She imagined a silver-framed photograph on the mantelpiece, William standing under the oak tree in the back garden with one arm around her shoulders and the other cradling a tiny Vietnamese baby. Cute.

The 1969 diary was sky blue and full of notations about baby formulae, feeding routines, and weights. Lily's first smile. The handwriting was not as neat as in the preceding diaries and Lily imagined her mum as a young mother with two babies under a year old. She read on. First word. First step.

Dark green, 1970, was better. Rose's first haircut. Lily's first clearly decipherable word. Cat. Light green, 1971. Lily's favourite toy: tambourine. Rose's favourite toy: wooden building blocks.

Scarlet, 1972. A fancy dress party, Lily as a white crêpe-paper lily, Rose as a scarlet crêpe-paper rose with a crown.

Lily read, then scanned, then flicked until her eyes ached. How did Rose do all this reading and research for work? She'd been sitting at the kitchen table for three hours reading, and she was exhausted.

Magenta, 1975, was the one. Diana was twenty-nine, and the way she described it in her neat script was exactly how Lily thought of her own periods. *Haphazard.* Lily closed the magenta book with a bang. If her mother did have early menopause after all, it was no wonder Lily didn't have a little sister or brother, no wonder her mum had struggled to get pregnant with her. Anger rose up her breast and into her throat with a whoosh like flames up a staircase, followed quickly by fear. *If Mum had warned me. If only I could get my facts straight enough to explain to William, we might have tried earlier, he might have believed me.* If, if, might, might.

Rose keeps going on about not knowing where her genes come from, Lily thought, swallowing and swallowing, her parched throat burning. *Well, my genes might have given me early menopause. That's what genes do. It's not just about passing on good stuff, there's bad stuff too.*

She sat and waited for the tears to arrive. When they didn't, she took a sip of tea. It was cold. She boiled the kettle again, this time choosing a lemon and ginger teabag, and stood at the kitchen window watching the blue tits squabble over the nigella seeds she'd put on the bird table that morning. She was surprised she couldn't cry. Usually she cried at the drop of a hat; Rose was the dry-eyed one. 'Cry baby', Rose used to taunt her. But it was Rose who had warned her about early menopause, after all, and those words of warning drummed inside

221

her head now. She should have listened to Rose's warnings about early menopause. A magpie swooped to the bird table and the blue tits scattered.

She picked up the magenta book again, turning its pages, twisting the paper then smoothing out the wrinkles, putting it down and picking it up again. Rose was always talking about facts, and how you needed facts to prove a supposition – did she mean supposition or suspicion?

Unbidden, she saw William's unsmiling face. She thought of all the fear and suspicion and doubts she'd read in her mother's handwriting and saw the fear and suspicion and doubts in her own marriage. Things she'd been ignoring, denying, pushing deep into the dark corners of her mind now spun together in the washing machine of her brain on the Extra Intensive spin cycle, twisted and tangled in a knot. And mixed in, like a pair of red knickers in a whites-only wash, was Rose's voice saying 'get it checked out, Lily'.

She didn't know what truth meant any more.

28 ROSE

An envelope was waiting for Rose on the table in the communal hall when she got home from work the next day. A letter bearing the red-inked stamp: 'General Register Office'. So twenty-four hours after sitting on the bench beside the war memorial, Rose returned to the same place, seeking calm in her secret green corner behind the library after the day's madness of deadlines, proofreading, and caffeine overload. Squabbling sparrows were her only company.

She turned the envelope over in her hands, wanting to open it, not wanting to open it. *The name of my father is inside.* Her eyes drifted over the names on the obelisk... Worth... Thewlis... Clarkson... Smith... Brady... Out of a brown paper bag she emptied her hasty purchase from the limited alcohol shelf in Maya's corner shop: two mini-bottles of gin and fruit-flavoured alcopop. She drank a bottle straight down in one go, pursed her lips at the alien taste of saccharine, artificial colourings, and E numbers, then put the empty bottle back in the bag. She'd never been fond of gin, 'mother's ruin', her mother's drink for special occasions, to be mixed with bottled orange juice and sipped through pursed lips, but she needed the alcohol hit and it had been this or whisky in a plastic bottle.

Clutching the grey-and-white marbled pebble

she'd picked up yesterday for luck, she tore the envelope open. Two pieces of paper fell out. On the first, her father's name was missing. She scanned it quickly again, top to bottom. No, his name definitely wasn't there. 'Father Unknown'. Disappointment pinned her to the bench like gravity; disappointment that Kate didn't know whom she'd screwed or had forgotten his name while her thighs were still sticky, maybe never asked his name or just didn't want to say.

Permissive hippy chick. Indiscriminate, selfish, stupid bird.

Rose shook her head to get rid of the anger. Insulting Kate wouldn't help and it made her feel shitty. She looked at the certificate again, reading more slowly this time. There were two new things. Kate's address at the time of birth: 12 Child Street, London N1; and the place of birth, Westmead Home for Ladies, Enfield. Enfield had suddenly become a strong lead. Perhaps Lily's 'good news' would turn into 'Really Good News'. All she knew about Enfield was that it was at the end of the Northern Line, or was that Edgware?

The second piece of paper was Kate's death certificate. Seeing it in black-and-white made it final. Death by misadventure.

Rose read and re-read both certificates until their images were burned on her retina and she cried. 'Father Unknown'.

She threw the bag and bottles into a nearby bin, then fished her mobile out of her bag. She would telephone everyone, tell them she didn't have a father, would never have a father, and that it was okay because she'd done her best to find him.

Wednesday was Lily's day off, so Rose called

her. No answer, she left a message. 'Ring me, please – I've got my adoption certificate. Pleeease…' She didn't care that she was pleading.

Dad next. His new pay-as-you-go mobile went to the message service too. Damn it, Dad.

Maggie, she thought. Maggie will talk sense. But *Xtra*'s editorial secretary said Maggie was in a brainstorming meeting and would be tied up for what was left of the day.

Next, dare she? Her carefully prepared words of apology dried on her lips as the ringing didn't give way to Nick's voice or to Nick's answerphone, but to a recorded French woman talking at high speed. Rose's schoolgirl French didn't equip her to translate even one word of the official sounding announcement which presumably was French British Telecom saying something about lines being unavailable. It was clear Nick didn't want to talk to her. She took a deep breath to calm herself and a wide band tightened around her chest, as it had that time she'd had pneumonia.

Bizzie, bless her, answered on the fifteenth ring. 'Child Street? Yes, that's it. You are clever, Rose, a proper detective. Oh, hold on.' There was some mumbling in the background, then a rustling sound and someone else came on the line.

'Hello, Rose, it's Maureen. I remember the squat. Kate lived there with some other girls and a friend of hers. Sheila, I think she was called…'

Maureen? Of course, dammit, I should have talked to her when Bizzie first mentioned it. Stupid, stupid.

She was so busy cursing she'd lost track of what Maureen was saying. "Hang on a moment, Maureen, did

225

you say Sheila?"

'… or maybe it was Sarah. No, no, it was Susan.'

'Susan? Susan what?'

'Sorry, I don't know. To be honest, dear, I don't think I ever did know.'

Rose's heart leapt. She had another lead. A minute ago she'd never heard of Susan.

'I might have met her once though.'

Oh wow, Maureen, thank you. She fought her instinct to shout aloud and tried to keep calm. 'What was she like?'

'A pale, freckly thing… sorry, mind's gone blank.'

Rose almost laughed at the irony of it. Her next lead hadn't come from the birth certificate at all but from Maureen, whom she should have talked to days ago.

She was home in five minutes. When she opened her door, there was another envelope on the doormat, marked in the top left-hand corner 'by hand' in blue ballpoint. Nick. Had Nick written her a Dear John letter? Because of the burp? Rose's hands shook as she ripped it open.

There was a single sheet of paper, and a compliments slip with a scrawled signature in the same blue ballpoint that didn't say Nick Maddox but quite possibly might have said: 'E Greenaway'. The band around her heart tightened a little more.

At the top of the sheet of paper were the words 'Adoption Order' and an official red crest.

Child, Name at Birth: Alanna Jane Ingram.
Child, Adoptive Name: Rose Haldane.

226

Consenting Birth Mother: Katherine Jane Ingram.
Consenting Birth Father: Unknown.
Adoptive Mother: Diana Elizabeth Haldane.
Adoptive Father: John Frederick Haldane (in absentia).
Date of Adoption Order: 30 September 1968.
Name of Officiating Court: Enfield Magistrates Court.
Presiding Official: James Charlton Roscoff.

The Adoption Order was a photocopy, the print was blotchy and speckled like an old mirror, the handwriting old-fashioned and loopy, blotted with ink stains.

Father Unknown again.

Soon the photocopy was smudged too.

She stepped out of her steaming bath water later that night and picked up the bottle of Soothing Rose lotion she'd bought at Cool Beauty yesterday. *Mmm, roses*, she thought, *the heady scent of summer*. But the top wouldn't budge, not even when she tried to loosen it with her teeth. Shivering now, she wrapped herself in a towel. Somewhere, there was a pair of pliers. Leaving a trail of water across the floor, she checked in the hall cupboard, then the drawer in the dresser. She finally found them in her toolbox at the bottom of her wardrobe, squashed between her Dorothy stilettos and favourite tan cowboy boots. With one tug, the threads at the neck of the plastic bottle gave way and the top was released. Her stomach lurched at the overwhelming stink of artificial flowers; chemical copies, not real roses. Rose stoppered the bottle quickly. It had smelled all right in the shop, but perhaps everything had changed now she was Alanna Ingram.

Wrapped in her bathrobe, dozing uneasily in front of an ancient repeat of *ER*, dreaming of twin sisters who continually morphed in and out of each other's bodies, Rose was stirred by the sound of knocking. Her heart stopped for a moment as she thought of opening her door a week ago to Nick in orange Lycra. Rose still didn't understand how she could fancy a bloke who wore orange.

There was a knock again and with effort she refocussed her mind on the present. Someone was on the first-floor landing, outside her door, and she hadn't buzzed them up. Rose put on the chain and peered through the gap as she opened the door. Outside stood a familiar yet unfamiliar woman, her left hand wrapped in a red towel.

Rose opened the door all the way. 'Yes?' Blood dripped onto the hall carpet.

'I'm so sorry to trouble you. I've had an accident,' she held up her hand. Then she smiled at the look of miscomprehension on Rose's face. 'I'm Michelle. From downstairs.' She waved vaguely at the floor with the towel-wrapped hand and Rose watched a fleck of blood fly through the air in an arc and hit the banister.

'I've tried to stop the bleeding but it's getting worse...'

Like I hadn't noticed, thought Rose, instantly feeling bad for thinking something so awful. *For someone bleeding so much, she seems very calm*, thought Rose. Then she realised Michelle was looking at her expectantly.

'... so I think I'd better go to hospital. The only

thing is, I'd just put Lewis down before it happened…'

Ah.

'… and he went straight off to sleep. He's not been well this week, bit of a sniffle, so I don't really want to wake him and take him with me.' Her eyes appealed directly to Rose's. 'I wondered, would you mind sitting with him while I go for stitches? I've got a taxi waiting outside. Please? I won't be long.'

'Of course, I was only watching TV.' Rose nodded calmly at Michelle who was saying that Lewis was a good boy, never an ounce of bother. Rose pulled on a T-shirt and track bottoms and followed Michelle downstairs. Through an open door, Rose glimpsed a duvet bundled up on a child-sized bed in a dark room.

Oh. My. God. How am I going to do this? I've never spent one hour alone with any child.

Michelle hurriedly showed her into the kitchen, opened the fridge and pointed to a blue plastic drinks bottle decorated with spaceships. Rose swallowed and nodded as if babysitting was one of her regular activities.

Oh. My. God. It's not going to wake up is it?

She helped Michelle gather her handbag and phone and bundled her into the taxi.

Oh. My. God.

She fumbled with the unfamiliar TV, found *ER* and sat down on the sofa, trying to ignore something sticky on the arm which transferred to her elbow. She held her breath for a moment, then exhaled slowly. She'd been here five minutes and all was fine. Looking after children was not difficult: she had a degree, she worked a professional job, how hard could it be?

'Mama…?'

Rose's heart sank. She turned slowly.

'Mama...?'

'Hello, Lewis, remember me? I'm Rose, the lady from upstairs? Your mummy's had to go out for a while and so I'm staying here with you.' She was talking rather too loud and slow, and smiling too much, but couldn't stop herself.

Lewis stood in the doorway and looked at her, his right hand rubbing a dark grey rag against his cheek. He rocked slowly from left foot to right. Rose looked at the round blue face on the rag, which she saw now was a blanket. A tank engine with wide-open eyes stared at her solemnly. Thomas, she assumed.

'Would you like to take Thomas and go back to sleep?'

No answer. His thumb was in his mouth now.

'Shall we go and pop you back into bed?'

'Pop'. She never said 'pop', and she smiled as she realised she sounded just like Bizzie. She'd be saying 'so so' next.

Lewis simply stared at her. Hang on a minute, he wasn't looking at her, his eyes were focussed slightly to her left. She looked over her shoulder at the TV. Lewis was watching two people in white coats in the middle of a big snogging session. Damn, she'd missed the beginning of a new episode.

She looked back at Lewis. He was transfixed by the snogging. 'Come on, Lewis, let's get you a drink before you go back to bed.'

He nodded, slowly. She turned off the TV and took hold of the hand holding the blanket. The thumb seemed clamped in his mouth.

Fifteen minutes later, she was sitting at the kitchen table surrounded by full glasses, cartons, and bottles. Lewis hadn't liked the orange squash she'd poured into his plastic spaceship bottle, or the milk, or the tap water, or the apple juice, or the cola or lemonade. She was seriously contemplating trying him on Somerset cider next. Lewis sat opposite her. She still hadn't managed to make him speak. He just stared, his eyes wide and unblinking, as if he could read her thoughts. Time to take charge, she decided. No more options, he needed a command. 'Lewis, make up your mind which drink you want. Then it's definitely time for bed. Come on, young man.' She stood up to demonstrate movement. Taking charge didn't work. After a struggle which involved Lewis going rigid, arms and legs outstretched like a starburst, and Rose first scolding, then pulling, next pleading, and finally shouting, she left him sitting at the kitchen table and returned to the TV. *ER*'s credits were rolling; next up was a rerun of *Friends*. Ten minutes later, the sound of falling plastic bottles in the kitchen reminded her she wasn't at home. Lewis was sitting in the same chair, soaked in every single type of beverage, drawing pictures in the wet mess on the tabletop.

'Right, that's it.' Rose carried him squirming and wriggling into the bathroom, stripped off his sticky blue pyjamas, sponged him with a damp flannel, waved a towel over the slippery wet bits, then carried him to his bed, where she attempted to clothe him in a faded dinosaur T-shirt and red bottoms she found on what she guessed was the ironing pile in the hall.

'No.' He struggled as she tried to force his suddenly baseball bat-like limbs into the narrow arm and leg holes. How could he be so small and so strong? How did clothing manufacturers seriously expect a three-year-old's arm to fit in there? Wasn't there some sort of drug she could give him which would send him to sleep?

'Want Thomas,' he shouted.

'Oh no you don't, I'm not falling for that again, young man. I'm not getting all your T-shirts out of the drawer for you to try on and then change your mind. You can wear this one, it's perfectly clean.' At the precise point that Rose's tone of voice changed from frustration to anger, Lewis's lungs opened into full-on bawl. As he jumped up and down on his bed, she sank to the floor beside it and wondered how Michelle coped as a single mum. She must be shattered all the time. Logic didn't work, kindness didn't work, brute force didn't work.

After a final struggle, which resulted in Lewis wearing the dinosaur T-shirt back to front, she went to the fridge and found a wine box, skulking behind a huge tub of Postman Pat raspberry yoghurt. She filled a plastic Buzz Lightyear plastic tumbler to the top, and sat on the sofa. Lewis could scream, as far as she cared. She was only a temporary member of the mother's club and her membership would be rescinded indefinitely after this.

I screamed as a child and it didn't hurt me, did it?

She was halfway through her second Buzz Lightyear and feeling slightly calmer when Lewis appeared in the door again, this time with a book in hand. Rose wearily patted her knee and he climbed onto her lap and opened *Mr Sneezy*. From the first page, he had the better of her; he knew every word and corrected every mistake she made. It was endlessly repetitive. When she accidentally turned over two pages at once because Ross and Rachel were snogging, Lewis spotted

232

the gap in the story and made her go back. He shuffled his bottom into her lap and laid his head against her shoulder. Rose smiled and a punch of sadness hit her in the pit of the stomach. Kate had never got to hold her like this.

As she turned the pages, Lewis's eyes began to close. She sniffed his hair as his head grew heavy against her arm, expecting baby shampoo but getting apple juice. Ignoring her sticky nose, Rose shed tears for Kate and for herself. They had both lost something so huge, the removal of something valuable, followed by a great gaping hole every morning where a mother and daughter should have been. A hole that was still there.

Lewis snuffled in his sleep and as she shifted his heavy warmth slightly on her knees to relieve pins and needles, Rose surrendered to the feeling of companionship. Perhaps it was time to stop chasing an enigma.

29 ROSE

She was sitting at a bench on the wide pavement outside The Eagle, nursing a St Clements and watching the late commuters straggle out of the tube station when he arrived. A large folder was on the seat beside her. Something had shifted inside her last night and things had become clearer, one of the clearest was that she wanted to see Nick again. She'd called this morning and was put straight through by a secretary who wasn't Amanda. They arranged to meet after work.

'I haven't been exactly... truthful with you,' were the first words she spoke. 'I'm sorry I didn't come to Nobu and I'm sorry I didn't apologise properly.' He simply looked at her, waiting. She knew he was doing to her what she did in interviews when she wanted the other person to carry on talking. She'd always been hopeless at apologising, trying to avoid it where possible.

'Things happened that night and I completely forgot about Nobu. I was mortified when I realised I'd stood you up, though it can be argued that as I actually forgot about our date completely... if it was a date,' she could feel her cheeks glowing, '... I mean I didn't stand you up on purpose, I didn't make a conscious decision to... so really, I didn't stand you up at all.' She smiled, feeling verbally challenged again in front of him. *Damn him, if only he didn't affect me this way.*

He raised an eyebrow, and a shiver went down her spine.

'I'm behaving oddly, I know, but there is a reason why.' She took a deep breath.

Her staccato words regulated into andantino then andante as she showed Nick her birth certificates, baby picture, and Kate's photo. Feeling calmer by the minute, helped by the pressure of his arm against hers, she told him things she didn't even know she'd been thinking until the words were said.

He let her finish speaking. 'Hey.' His fingers reached out towards her, as if to stroke her hair.

Rose held her breath.

He withdrew his hand. 'That's the first time you've said all of that out loud, isn't it?'

She looked at Nick and wanted to fall into his eyes.

'I think what you're doing is very brave.' His voice was quiet.

Brave was the last thing she felt. *He thinks he knows me, but he doesn't have a clue.*

'You've got the courage to ask difficult questions that others have hidden or ignored since you were born. You're facing a brick wall of things you're afraid of. Other people would back off or try to find a way around it, but you're climbing it all on your own even though you know the answers will be hard to hear.'

Rose could hear the 'but' coming a long way off.

'But before you ask the questions you know will hurt you, and others, you need to think about what sort of answer you're expecting and if it's worth the pain.'

He was beginning to sound like Mrs Greenaway. 'I have thought about it, Nick. I'm not stupid.'

'Be honest, at least with yourself if not with me.'

Her response came out as a yawn. 'Oh, I'm so tired.' And suddenly, she was. Exhausted. She stifled a second instinctive grab by her brain for oxygen. 'But that's good, at least I'll sleep tonight. These days, I've got to be completely physically exhausted so that my mind stops spinning.' A third yawn. 'At least I won't have to go running tonight to tire myself out.' The last was a mutter, a thought verbalised.

He sat up straighter. 'I never put you down as a runner. How many miles do you do a week?'

Miles a week? What? And then Rose remembered the orange Lycra. 'Erm, I'm not really into record-keeping. But I run a fair distance once a week.'

'Oh,' he said, with a slight shrug of his shoulders, 'you're a jogger.' The tone of his voice said that jogging was something only unfit people did. 'You do stretch properly first, don't you? It's particularly important to stretch the hamstrings. This is the best prep.' And he was standing, squatting down and demonstrating the exercise. 'Push down and hold, here, count to ten, then the other leg. Whatever you do, don't jig up and down. That stresses the muscle too much.'

Rose nodded, never having stretched before exercise in her life but appreciating the way his jeans tightened around his bum during the demonstration. Perhaps she should stretch next time she jogged. The riverside path was becoming quite familiar now. Last night she'd stood for a while beside the white brick wall outside River Reach and watched the Thames, its water churning and spitting as upstream met downstream at the turn of the tide. Then she'd jogged 400 yards back round the corner to where she'd parked her car.

'It must be great, living by the riv–' she stopped, horrified at her gaffe, '… I mean, it's great, jogging by the river at night.' Now she was babbling and he was staring. 'There's no one about, no traffic. It gives me time to think.'

He stared at her like he was seeing her for the first time. 'You jog at night? Rose, that's a bad idea. A really bad idea. You don't know who else is out there...'

No one, thought Rose, *I never see anyone.*

'Burglars, muggers...'

Next he'll be saying 'druggies'.

'...druggies.' He leant towards her, concerned. 'Rose, when you can't sleep I want you to promise me you'll drink peppermint tea. If that doesn't work, ring me and I'll talk so long you'll fall asleep through boredom.'

Rose liked his concern, and the way his eyes smiled when he looked at her, but she didn't like being told what to do. On the other hand, she doubted he would ever bore her.

'Okay?' His eyes weren't smiling now.

'Okay.' He sat down again, their legs touching from hip to knee.

'So, let's examine the facts.'

Great, facts. Rose was comfortable with facts.

'We'll clarify your objectives and prioritise them. Is that all right?' He took her pen and pad and wrote 'Action Plan' at the top of a blank page.

Rose tried to ignore the combined heat generated by their legs, which was flooding up her body.

'I want to know about my real family. I've

always felt out of step with the Haldanes, always liked different things, had different ambitions. I want to know why my birth parents didn't keep me. I realise they didn't give me away because of something I did, I was too small, but were they in trouble, or just *too* young? I know bits about Kate but zero about my father. Who is he, where was he when Kate was pregnant? Did he know? Why didn't he marry her or at least help her? Where is he now?'

It was like a strategy meeting at work and the familiarity calmed Rose. Nick identified the tools and skills she had, time required, possible sources of help and information. Thirty minutes later, he'd written a one-page plan, the action points were initialled either R or N. Rose looked at the Ns and opened her mouth to say she could do it all. Then she shut it again.

'Is this what you did when you decided to do the management buyout at Biocare?' asked Rose, nodding at the action plan.

'Yes, it is actually.' As he bent to add a note to point eleven, his ear dipped towards her, just within reach. It was more a cockle than a mussel, definitely not a limpet. If she stretched just a little, she might be able to lick it.

Nick sat up and Rose drew back just in time. 'I use this approach with any problem I face.' His expression darkened for an instant, but the moment passed so quickly, Rose fancied she'd imagined it.

'Well, thanks for helping. You've made things a lot clearer.'

'You're welcome.' He leant down to straighten the papers.

It was now or never. Rose leant towards him and

kissed his left earlobe.

'Rose…'

'Ssshh.'

She kissed each corner of his mouth and then his lips. And just as she was losing herself in their soft warmth, just as she tasted beer on the tip of his tongue, he took her gently by the shoulders and pushed her away.

'Time for me to go. I've got an 8 a.m. meeting with the bank tomorrow and I have a presentation to prepare.' He stood up and was gone.

Rose sat back on the bench and felt suddenly alone, sitting amidst the crowd of summer evening drinkers.

I thought he wanted it too. I thought he liked me.

Nick. Nick. Nick.

For the first morning in a week, Rose's first waking thought was not about Kate. His name ticked and tocked in her brain. His warm words, his soft lips as they… didn't kiss her. Nick, who pulled away, rejected her, left without saying when – if – he would call.

Rose turned the water in the shower from hot to cold and yelled so loud that Michelle and Lewis downstairs must have heard.

Nick. Nick. Nick.

'Pull yourself together, girl.' Rose told her reflection in the glass of the shower door. 'He doesn't fancy you.' Rose had never known a man not kiss her back, harder and insistent. What had she done wrong? What had changed? He'd wanted to kiss her, hadn't he? Could she have misread the signs? He'd certainly led her to think he'd like it, wanted it. Perhaps she'd cried too much. She made a mental note to show Nick the Strong Rose in future, if there was one, the Rose she used to be before the adoption thing.

She was running late, no time for breakfast. She opened her bag and swept the pile from the table – today's paper, yesterday's unopened post, and her iPod – into it.

On the first tube train, she read the same paragraph of the *Herald* three times. While she waited for an eastbound train out of Earl's Court, she started a story about the NHS but stopped reading when the hospital spokesman quoted was called Nick... something. She licked her lips, but the taste of his mouth had long gone. The train swayed over the points outside Clapham Junction and she swallowed, feeling nauseous. She'd been in such a rush this morning that she'd forgotten her motion sickness treatment; a drop of peppermint oil on each wrist didn't make the sickness disappear but at least made it bearable. She focussed on her newspaper again, and turned the page to where a headline about squatters occupying the empty house claimed by a local MP as his second home caught her eye. In Battersea. Where Nick lived. It was a good story, but no byline. That was the sort of story she wanted to write, potentially an Eighter, maybe a Niner if the story was expanded. There was a photo of the house. She didn't know if it was Nick's part of Battersea or not.

She took his one-page action plan from her bag and read it for the fifth time since waking. Though she knew each word, her heart leapt at the sight of his handwriting, the long lazy looping g's and j's and y's which hinted at a looseness behind the businessman's mask. It was incredibly sexy. He'd written this for her.

She thought for a moment, forming words sufficiently relaxed to show him she was still interested but wasn't a stalker, then dialled his mobile. It was turned off. She left a polite message thanking him for his help last night, saying it'd be great to speak with him again. The tension in her throat made her voice sound formal; she spoken to him as if she were a journalist. Oh well, she'd already got it horribly wrong, she couldn't be any more embarrassed than she was now.

There were no seats on the next eastbound train, so she stood in a squash near the doors. The swaying was not good. Then a schoolgirl in a neat pale grey uniform with blue tie stood up and offered Rose her seat. Rose accepted gratefully, wondering if the schoolgirl thought she was pregnant. She did feel pale. She opened her newspaper again and read the Bank of England's economic forecast with commentary by a City expert, called Martin Meadows. She pushed the newspaper into her bag and pulled out the envelope marked 'Enfield Foster & Adoption Centre'. Her hopes weren't high. Bella had explained the tortuous process involved. Despite the Freedom of Information Act, the correct hoops had to be jumped through in order to protect everyone involved in the case.

'It's not worth getting annoyed about, Rose, believe me. Often the files which exist at these places contain no more than copies of the documents already in circulation.'

Rose prepared to read things she'd read before.

Dear Miss Haldane,
Further to a request by Mrs Eileen Greenaway of
Wimbledon Social Services, please find enclosed the

following documents:
Two birth certificates related to yourself (photocopies);
Letter to EFAC dated 26 September 1968 from the
Westmead Home for Ladies, Endeavour House, Church
Road, Enfield (photocopy).
Yours sincerely,
Emma Turner (Miss)

'The next station is Westminster,' said a computerised voice.

Papers in hand, and Rose got off the train just before the doors slid shut. She changed to the Jubilee Line, her pace slowed by the powder-blue kitten heels she'd slipped on as an impulse this morning because thinking of Nick every second had made her feel girly. So instead of walking down the escalator on the left as she usually did which made her feel fitter and therefore more healthy than those just standing, she stood to the right and didn't complain as her elbow was jostled by the virtuous ones.

She leafed through the 'Enfield Foster & Adoption Centre' papers. She'd got the birth certificates. The 1968 letter had a signature at the bottom, which she recognised. 'Received with thanks. Diana Haldane'.

Received with thanks? Was Alanna received with thanks? Was I received like a parcel?

The letter was a list of things that had been passed to Diana Haldane on 30 August 1968.

Alanna Jane Ingram
White cotton gown
12 hospital-issue terry napkins
White knitted bonnet

First she was a parcel, now she was an object on a list. She stumbled off the bottom of the escalator. The heat in the tiled tunnel was overpowering. A woman was walking towards her with a white-wrapped bundle strapped to her chest, and from it a tuft of hair reached for the sky as if styled by static. Suddenly, Rose was that small. She was Alanna, and Kate had just given her away. Rose stopped dead in her tracks and howled inside. It was a scream stored deep inside her all these years.

'Excuse me.'

'Watch where you're going.'

Irritated commuters flowed around her like cars driving round a roundabout, dancing about each other and missing collision by moments. Gulping warm air to stop herself from howling aloud, she saw the mother and infant rise to the top of the escalator and disappear from sight.

Later she had no memory of either the Jubilee line train or the DLR. She felt as if she'd been spun in a tumble drier. Her mobile got its signal back as the train rose above ground and beeped as it came to life. She took it out of her bag and dialled. There was one person who would be torn by the sight of an infant.

At the sound of Lily's voice, Rose opened her mouth to speak but the words would not come.

'I…' she gasped. Why was breathing so difficult?

'Rose, take deep breaths. Come on now, breathe, and again, that's better. Now speak slowly. What's happened? Where are you?'

The words spilled out. The letter, the list, the

baby.

'Ah,' said Lily. 'I guess you saw that baby and thought it was you?'

'How... how tiny I was, defenceless, innocent.'

'Yes, you were. It's horrible what happened to you, Rose, the lies, the secrecy. But it didn't ruin your life. It hasn't stop you doing things, becoming successful, growing into a wonderful young woman. And you are wonderful, you know.'

'I am?'

'You are.'

30 ROSE

By the time she knocked at Maureen's door at 7 p.m.,
Rose felt calmer. There was a knot in her stomach. She
wasn't sure if it was anticipation or hunger.

She wanted to ask about Susan as soon as her
foot was in the door, but hearing Diana's voice in her
head – 'be polite!' – Rose first devoured the dish of
pasta spirals in tomato and sardine sauce that Maureen
set in front of her.

'I didn't realise how hungry I was.' Rose wiped
her dish clean with a chunk of crusty bread. 'I love
tomatoes. Any sort of tomatoes, those little cherry ones
that are great in a salad or the big fat ones you have with
mozzarella, and tomato sandwiches in the summer with
a sprinkle of salt. Mmm, lovely.'

'Your… 'Maureen cleared her throat before
continuing, '…your mum loved tomatoes too.' She stood
to clear the saucepans from the hob.

'No she didn't, they upset her stomach. Too
acidic.'

'Not Diana. Kate.'

'Oh.' To hide her confusion, Rose laid her knife
and fork neatly side by side on the plate, imagining Kate
eating pasta spirals in tomato and sardine sauce. Kate
was Kate, not Mum.

'What was she like, Maureen?'

'Kate was mysterious. There were always people around her but I expect not many of us really knew her.' Maureen filled the teapot with hot water, covered it with a quilted tea cosy, and cut two slices of fruitcake. 'She had the most beautiful long, wavy dark hair you've ever seen. She would tie it back in a sort of loose plait that was so hippy. I envied her her hair.'

'I've got a photo where she has her hair braided in ribbons, she looks like a flower child.'

'Perhaps she was that day. The next day she'd be something else. I think she played lots of roles, depending on how she felt or whom she was with. She was always practising, changing accents, repeating lines. Diana said she was a class snob, trying to speak like a dockworker, trying to look like a socialist, denying her middle-class roots. But however she spoke, Kate turned heads, people wanted to talk to her, not because she was beautiful... I don't know, she had an aura about her.'

'So was she a hippy?'

'I'm not sure what that really means, but she was certainly the hippest person I knew. She was into crystals and meditation, she re-used the backs of envelopes as notepaper and made a rag rug for her bedroom. Way before her time, Kate was. She wanted to go to India but couldn't afford it so she burned incense sticks instead. Diana said she'd burn the house down one day.'

Rose laughed. She could imagine the look on her mother's face as she said that.

'You went to the squat, didn't you?'

'Once, yes, when she first moved there. The house wasn't up to much but it was no worse than my student digs in Brighton. Dirty mugs, bikes in the hall, weeds in the back garden, you know the sort of thing.' It sounded like Rose and Maggie's student flatshare in Bristol.

'What were her friends like?'

'Well, there was that one girl I told you about, Susan. She seemed nice enough, long blonde hair, braided like Kate's, maxiskirt to her ankles, bangles all the way to her elbow. I remember watching her walk up those narrow stairs and wondering how she managed not to get her feet tangled up in the hem.'

'You haven't remembered her surname then?'

'Sorry, love, I haven't.'

The knot in Rose's stomach released, leaving a vacuum. She hesitated before speaking again. It felt awkward, as if she was interviewing Maureen for an article.

'How are Kate and I alike? Or perhaps we aren't?'

Don't be so nervous, it's only Maureen; she won't get upset.

Maureen sat back in her chair and studied her. Rose felt as if her face was having a CAT scan. She wanted so much to hear that she looked like Kate.

'Your hair's the same, these crinkly waves,' Maureen reached across the table and touched a curl above Rose's left ear, exactly where Nick touched her yesterday. 'But your eyes are a different colour, hers were dark brown, not hazel like yours...'

Rose's hand went to her eye, stroked her eyebrow.

'... but when you smile you get the same crease there.' Maureen brushed Rose's cheek with her fingers.

Rose felt a wave of delight. 'I always thought

my likeness to Mum was slight.'

'Yes, you are more like Kate than Diana. Kate was much taller than you though, she was about five-ten, I think. But you're both skinny. Kate could eat like a horse and not put on a pound. I think that's another reason why Diana was irritated by her.'

'Mum was irritated by lots of things. It was hardly Kate's fault if Mum had a slow metabolism and couldn't lose weight.' Rose remembered her mother's rule about sugar. No Sugar Puffs. No Frosties. No Tony the Tiger. Only Ready Brek and Weetabix.

'No, but remember Diana settled down early to suburban family life while Kate gallivanted around the countryside.'

'Stuck at home with a baby, Kate's baby, me. Anyway, it cuts both ways, doesn't it?' Rose was thinking aloud. 'Kate was probably jealous that Mum was married and settled with a home.' Rose thought of Lily's home in Barnes, of the cool hall with its large mirror, the welcoming kitchen table with its carefully mismatched designer chairs, the garden full of shrubs and flowers, and wondered if Kate felt the same way about her sister's home, had yearned for more, for a different life.

'I once overheard Howard tell Kate she should try harder to be more like Diana. "Only the triers succeed," he said. It was an unkind thing to say and I felt so sorry for her, but she just carried on doing her own thing regardless. She –'

'But that's what Mum was always saying to me,' interrupted Rose, 'she wanted me to be more like Lily.' Rose knew she sounded like a grumpy ten-year-old, but she felt better knowing that Kate would have understood how she felt.

'Oh, Howard was just trying to encourage her, in his creaky sort of way. And your mum didn't want to change you into Lily, not really.'

In her heart, Rose knew Maureen was right, that Mum just wanted her to be neat and polite. 'I know she didn't,' she said quietly, 'but Lily and I are so different.'

'Diana and Kate were too. Not all sisters live in each other's pockets, you know. Kate's clothes were so eccentric,' continued Maureen. 'She'd wear things that Diana would have used as dusters.'

'Mum's style was really formal, wasn't it?'

'Yes, she liked to be smart. I remember going round for tea and Kate would be dancing to records while Diana would be sitting at the table in her school uniform doing her homework. The uniform at their school was much nicer than mine.' She pulled a face. 'Burgundy with an orange tie, it didn't flatter anyone. I hated it.'

'What were you saying about Mum?'

'Oh, just that she was more focussed than Kate.'

'What do you mean, "focussed"?'

'Well,' Maureen cradled her mug in her hands, thinking. 'Diana planned everything, and I mean everything. She was the sort of person who weighed everything when she cooked instead of just throwing things in. And she had so much patience, she loved embroidery.'

Rose thought fleetingly of the rose cushion, shoved in a dark corner of her understairs cupboard. 'But she couldn't bake cakes. One year, she made a Christmas cake that was so burnt she had to cut a layer off the top before she could ice it. After that she always bought the

Christmas cake and told Dad she'd made it.'

'Kate couldn't cook either. In fact, she was a regular Emma Woodhouse, surrounded by unfinished projects. She was happier watching TV than reading a book, which I thought odd for an actress, though I suppose she was watching actors act. And she had to read so much, learning lines and so on, that reading a book wasn't relaxing for her. She did love documentaries, travel programmes, I guess they allowed her to travel in her head. And she was so altruistic. World hunger, war, peace, it was the big things Kate worried about, not where her next pay cheque was coming from.'

'Didn't she have much money then?'

'Oh no, she earned a pittance, but it never seemed to bother her. She always managed to have a good time.'

This was her chance, her in, and Rose grabbed it. 'A good time with men? Lots of men?'

Maureen's eyes were filled with sympathy. 'Yes. I think there were lots of boyfriends, Rose, but I don't really know of anyone specific.' She rubbed her eyes wearily. 'She certainly never brought a man home to meet her parents, not to my knowledge anyway. She travelled so much that her visits were rare. I know Bizzie and Howard always worried about her driving all round the country in that beat-up old Mini. It didn't look capable of making it round the corner, let alone getting to Bath or Carlisle.'

'Kate had a Mini?' Rose held out her mug for a top-up and accepted a second piece of cake. It had whole cherries in it, her favourite. Bizzie must have made it. 'A Mini like mine?'

'I suppose so, the old sort. Tiny. It was orange, not black.'

'I'm amazed she could afford a car.'

'Well, she couldn't. But one summer we painted the outside of my mum's house. To make a bit of cash. Forest Fresh, the colour was called, pale green. Sounds like a toilet freshener, doesn't it?'

They both laughed.

'We didn't do it very well, but Mum was pleased. She was going to give us £10 each but she had a bit of a win on the premium bonds so she paid us from her winnings. £100 each. It was a fortune to us. I went to Torremolinos with Fred, we'd just started courting.' Maureen blushed slightly. 'Kate wanted a car. Diana put hers in the building society account she'd opened to save for her wedding to John.'

Rose remembered her mother's diary entries, planning the details of her wedding, and wondered how she would feel now to see her family so fractured. *Mum would know how to get Dad off the drink*, she thought. 'Have you seen Dad recently?'

Maureen nodded, chewing cake.

'How did he seem?'

Maureen swallowed and looked at her plate. She licked her finger and dotted it over the crumbs, catching each one. Then she licked her finger clean. 'Mmm. I thought he was okay, drinking too much but then he's always been prone to depression. He went through a very black period when you were tiny, it wasn't known then that husbands could get post-natal depression… well, you know what I mean.' She smiled apologetically. Could you get post-natal depression with an adopted baby? Rose wasn't sure, but she did recognise this dark picture of her father and instinctively reached beneath the table and tapped the leg for luck.

'I asked Fred to have a word with him about the drinking, not to let it get out of control.'

'I went to the allotment last week and he was too drunk to talk to. I'm worried about him. Mum would have known what to do.'

'Give him some time, love. He's just got a part-time job at EazySave, you know, and that'll help, give him a new routine, meet different people, people who didn't know Diana and have never heard of Woodbright Engineering. He's still mourning and his behaviour towards you is probably more to do with missing her than with your discovering the adoption.'

EazySave, thought Rose, *why don't I know about that? I have to talk to Dad again.*

'Yes, you could be right, I hadn't thought of it like that.'

The clock struck ten. Rose got up to leave and hugged Maureen tightly; it felt just like a hug from a mother should feel.

As they walked together towards the garden gate, Maureen patted Rose's shoulder. 'Don't you worry about your dad, Fred and I'll keep an eye on him. I'll get into the routine of inviting him round to dinner once a week. Get a decent meal inside him.'

Rose hugged Maureen again. She felt a bit better knowing her dad would get two square meals a week now, not just one. And Lily had done the honours last weekend. She really must invite her dad, Lily and William for lunch this coming Sunday.

I have to do my bit, I have to look after him. I won't just leave him, not like my birth parents abandoned me.

She was almost at her car, but turned back to Maureen. 'I know it would have been impossible for Kate to act and tour around the country, staying in bedsits with a baby in tow, but is that the only reason she didn't keep me?'

'I can't think why anyone would give away their baby, Rose. But the truth is that people do, every day. None of us can ever know the secrets inside other people's relationships, or the contents of their heads.'

31 ROSE

Rose was first into the office the next morning. The movement of something pink registered in her peripheral vision: A Post-it stuck to her phone fluttered in the breeze from the portable air conditioning unit. 'Maggie rang,' it read.

Maggie had been in Italy on a travel assignment so she didn't know about Nick, the kiss, about loads of things a girl's best friend should know. They always shared. The first time Maggie had sex, the first time Rose had sex, and the time Hallam Tye knocked Rose over when he careered round a corner on his bike and in recompense invited her to the premiere of *A Sunny Afternoon in the Snow* that turned into an exclusive interview for *Chill's* film column.

What if Susan and Kate had been best friends at school like Rose and Maggie? She logged onto Friends Reunited, clicked on the drop-down index, selected the school and the year. Kate went to school with a lot of Susans. She sent thirteen emails to the possibles. Each email was the same.

"I am trying to trace a girl called Susan who was at St Augustine's Primary and then Lady Grace's School for Girls, Richmond, Surrey, with my mother Kate Ingram during the 1950s and 1960s. You shared a

house together in Islington. If I've found the correct Susan, then I am delighted and I hope you will be too! If not, I'd be grateful if you could let me know so I can continue my search."

Now all she had to do was wait. This feeling of limbo was common to researching, waiting for someone else to do something, but Rose still hated it. The longest she'd ever waited for a reply was two months. The feature was for *Chill*, all the cutting-edge stuff she'd ever written had been for *Chill*. After almost giving up twice, she'd eventually broken into an animal research protestors' group. It was a nasty collection of people who made their point by leaving dead kittens and puppies on the doorsteps of scientists' homes, timed so their primary school-age children would find them as they stepped outside to go to school. That story had been *Chill*'s page one lead in a special issue about the ethics of protesting. The theme was, 'How far is too far?'

Rose looked at the advance features schedule pinned to her corkboard – rashes, burns & scalds, nipple discharge, sinus pain, and earache were next on her list – and sighed. How far is too far?

She checked her inbox. Nothing. Bored, she looked out of the window. Really she should finish the early menopause feature, but it was in hand and it was a sunny morning, the green of the verges, trees, and grass of the tiny park opposite the *Herald*'s building seemed brilliant, full of life, and she longed to be outdoors. That was it, that's what she would do. There was no reason she couldn't go to the squat. She sat up straight, excited. She'd go to Islington, to 12 Child Street. Ask around a bit. Be nosy. Check out the house. Perhaps take some photos for visual reference.

If she hadn't gone back for her camera, she would have got away with it.

'Miss Haldeen.' It was Sam, for some reason speaking with a fake cowboy accent. Rose stifled a giggle. 'I was beginning to think your contract had changed to home-worker. I sincerely hope you've got your handbag with you because you're nipping out to buy coffees for everyone, and not because you're intending to leave the office for the day, having just arrived. Remind me, when is your disciplinary review?'
Shit, thought Rose, shifting from foot to foot.

'Monday, Miss Holdeen. It's on Monday.' Sam's upper lip was damp with perspiration. Rose thought it made him look shifty. Her feet tried to escape, tapping heel and toe, heel and toe, but she was rooted to the spot by the anger in Sam's voice.

'What's that noise?' he snapped.

Rose pressed all her weight into the floor through the soles of her shoes and the tapping stopped. She so wanted to tell him her name was Rose Haldane.

I want that menopause feature on my desk, and the list of picture requests with Joan, by 4 p.m. Today.' Rose gasped. *Today?*

'And make mine a double espresso.' Sam clapped his hands. 'Listen up, everyone, Rosalie is going to Café Blanc for takeaway coffees. Her treat.'
Journalists only move quickly in two situations: if they smell an exclusive story, or have the chance of a free drink. The lack of alcohol content was academic. At this time of the morning, the priority was caffeine. As Rose was surrounded by hacks putting in their latte, cappuccino, and espresso requests, she watched a

satisfied grin spread over Sam's pouchy jowls. *Bastard*, she thought, *I've only got a fiver in my purse. Oh well, I'll have to put it on a card.* And then she had a moment of panic. Had she paid last month's bills? Which card had any credit left on it?

Five minutes later, with a list of thirteen assorted requests for coffee, three teas, and two hot chocolates, she hit the 'down' button on the lift.

'Want a hand?' It was Frank.

Thirty minutes later, they dished out the coffees round the office. Frank smiled at Rose and she smiled back, grateful for his knack of turning up at the right moment. Like Nick did. Oh God, Nick. The kiss.

'Fancy having a glass of vino at Pozzi's after work?' asked Frank, and Rose's head nodded without her telling it to. *Well, what the hell. He's helpful, and good-looking if arrogant.* The telesales girls always flocked to the coffee machine or the photocopier when he was nearby, giggling, sneaking glances at him from beneath their fringes, pretending they liked the crap coffee, standing with their feet in that V-shape that celebrities always pose in when they're on the red carpet and want to show off their dresses and breasts for the cameras. He was even nice to the work experience trainees who most people ignored. She'd seen him talking to that mousey new marketing girl in the canteen yesterday. Sometimes she thought Frank was a chameleon, presenting a different version of himself depending on whom he was with. Usually with her, he was Cheeky-Chirpy Frank who sometimes took the teasing too far. With Sam he was All-Lads-Together Frank, with May he was Keep-Your-Head-Down-And-Get-On-With-Your-Work Frank. She found herself wondering what Boyfriend Frank would be like. Would he kiss her back? There was only one way of finding out. So she smiled at him. It felt strange. It was a girlfriend smile, not a colleague smile. She stopped smiling. His sudden gratitude was rather unsettling, in fact, very un-Frank-like.

'Really?' He smiled. 'That's great. I'll… I'll see you there, shall I? No… that's stupid, I'll pick you up from your desk.'

As he walked away, Rose could hear him repeating one word.

'Great, great, great.'

Well, she thought, *it's just one drink. Not marriage.*

There was one quick call she had to make before concentrating on the menopause feature. Mrs Greenaway immediately agreed to call the Enfield Foster & Adoption Centre telling them to expect a phone call from Rose Haldane and authorising them to release to her any relevant archive records pertaining to Katherine Jane Ingram and Alanna Jane Ingram. Apparently Enfield Council was at the forefront of digitising its records and there was a good chance that 1968 was available online. Rose pottered around for ten minutes, tidying her desk drawer, re-arranging already tidy piles of notes, and cleaning her computer screen and keyboard with a disposable wipe.

Finally, Mrs Greenaway rang back. 'It's arranged for you, Rose. They've given you a user name and code, you've got access to their records on a one-off basis for today only until 5 p.m.'

Rose wrote down the website address and access codes. It seemed unbelievably simple.

'Good luck, my dear,' said Mrs Greenaway. 'Remember, you've only got access for today.'

Taking a deep breath, Rose logged into the Enfield Social Services database, clicked on 'Archive', and found '1968 Statement Books'. She clicked on August, then 29 August. And there it was. Five lines on a page full of writing, the digitised page clearly torn at the edges and mouldy in the bottom right corner.

Date of birth: 29 August 1968. 9.43 a.m.
Mother: Ingram, Katherine Jane (Room 4).
Child: female. 5lb 3oz. Name: Alanna Jane.
Father: not known
Address to which child released after birth: adoption confirmed to Mr& Mrs J Haldane, The Weavings, 14 Manor Drive, Richmond

Rose shivered.
She read the next entry.

Date of birth: 29 August 1968. 2.59 p.m.
Mother: Mellor, Joan Mary (Room 9).
Child: male. 5lb 6oz. Name: none.
Father: Mellor, Reginald James (uncle of the mother)
Address to which child released after birth: adoption tbc

Did Kate know Joan? Did they comfort each other in the maternity ward that same afternoon, both without their babies? This poor little boy, fathered by Joan's uncle, where was he now? Does he have any idea about his origins? Rose shivered again.

Date of birth: 31 August 1968. 3.15 a.m.

Mother: Fawcett, Cherry (Room 7).
Twins: two females 3lb 3oz and 3lb 10oz. Names: none.
Father: a serviceman, no name given.
Address to which child released after birth: adoption
tbc. Babies underweight, release delayed.

The list was endless. Names of babies and mothers separated at birth, conceived by mistake, by violence, in ignorance, in a desperate attempt to keep a man's interest, and given away in an effort to be a respectable single girl again.

Rose logged off and tossed the access code into her in-tray. The Statement Book was without doubt the coldest, hardest thing she had read yet. The last thing she wanted to do was write about fertility and childbirth, but Sam had walked past her desk twice while she was online. She pulled her menopause notes towards her; she didn't know how she was going to finish it by 4 p.m.

Three hours later, she surveyed the one remaining sushi roll in the lunch box balanced precariously atop the pile of medical textbooks on her desk and wondered whether the green bit was cucumber (which she tolerated) or avocado (which she hated). She doused the whole thing in soy sauce and balanced a huge slice of ginger on top. Every time she ate sushi she felt virtuous afterwards. It was a clean, raw meal.

She checked her inbox. There was one new email with an enticing subject: 'Contact from Friends Reunited'. At last.

Hello Rose,
I'm sorry, I'm not the Susan you're looking for. Good luck with your search.

Sue Reardon (nee Smith)

With a sigh, Rose turned back to her research, highlighter pen in hand. Whether you were or weren't menopausal all hung on the follicular stimulating hormone. As the ovaries started to fail, the brain sent out more FSH to stimulate them into working harder. So if your FSH level was high, it was a good bet that your menopause had started. Rose wondered if Lily's doctor had done a FSH test. Things could start to go awry ten years before menstruation stopped, usually in your fifties. But about 1% of all women suffered from premature menopause or 'premature ovarian failure'. A telephone interview with an early menopause sufferer from Cardiff, the same age as Lily but whose symptoms sounded completely different, made Rose wonder if Lily's problem was more to do with a fear of losing William than wanting a baby. Lily had confessed last night on the phone that her conservatory looked more like a potting shed. William was not amused, she said. The downstairs loo was full of seed catalogues and gardening magazines. Was Lily subconsciously trying to drive William away?

She typed a quick email to Lily, telling her to ask her doctor about the FSH test and scanned and attached the research clipping. She signed off her message with *Just do it, Lily. It's got to be beter to know. XX.* She clicked 'send'; no time to correct the spelling.

Next she wandered over to Candy, the paper's agony aunt, and ran Lily's situation by her as a possible anonymous sufferer's case study.

'Maybe deep down she's frightened of giving

birth. I was.' Candy didn't look at Rose but talked as she typed, her fingers flying across the keyboard, her eyes fixed on the screen. Rose recognised the symptoms of a rapidly approaching deadline. 'Or maybe she's afraid of being a bad mother, lots of women are. They look at the mistakes their mother made raising them and are afraid of repeating them.'

Well, Mum certainly made lots of mistakes, thought Rose, *but at my expense rather than Lily's.*

Then at three o'clock, Nick rang. He was driving back from Huddersfield, where he'd chaired an industry conference. He sounded cheerful, talked about his presentation and the guest speakers, but he didn't mention The Eagle, so Rose tried to pretend she hadn't kissed him. But the elephant danced down the phone line with such heavy steps that she twisted back and forth in her swivel chair while her heart thudded.

'Rose? Can you hear me all right?' He was shouting. 'It's a bad line, lots of squeaking. Can you hear it at your end?'

'No.' Rose stopped swivelling.

'Ah, that's better. Anyway, how are you, what are you doing?'

Feeling stupid for kissing you, she almost said. 'I'm trapped at my desk when I want to go to Islington to research Kate. That's where she lived, in a squat in Islington.'

'Why are you trapped?'

Rose hadn't admitted to Nick that she was on probation. 'Deadlines, and I can't sneak out while Sam is watching.'

'Look, if it'll help, I can go home via Islington and drive along the street where the squat was, have a look at the house. What do you think?'

Her mouth went dry.

But he pushed me away. 'I…'

'But if you'd rather wait and go yourself…' His voice suddenly had a polite tone to it, business-like.

'No. Yes. Can you go, please?' Slowly and calmly she told him about Susan No-Name. 'Interesting isn't it, that without a surname you can't trace someone. It's as if you don't exist. It's your family name. But when you know someone, you don't think about their surname. You know them by their first name, their given name. So does your identity rest in your first name, or your surname?'

'I don't know, love. Perhaps your identity is in your heart. Don't try to rationalise it so much.'

When Rose put down the phone, her face was split in two with a huge grin. Nick had called her 'love.'

'Remember I need those menopause photo requests in half an hour,' called Joan, the picture editor.

'I'm doing it, I'm doing it.' Rose did it.

She'd just sent the feature to Sam when her mobile rang again.

Nick was at Islington library now, checking the electoral roll. Rose didn't want to discourage him and so didn't tell him this information was available online. She got a buzz from hearing his voice.

'I didn't find anything, but what the hell,' he said, 'it was worth a go. No one at the squat address was registered for either 1967 or 1968. With hindsight that's pretty predictable; squatters aren't likely to pay rates or vote. So then I checked the current register for Child Street and surrounding addresses and there's one couple and one lady registered today who were on the 1967 list.

Maybe they remember the squat. What do you think?'
His voice was eager, just like Lily's when Rose had said
thanks for helping with the research.

'You're a genius, Nick, thanks. I'll go tonight.
What are the names and addresses?'

She scribbled them down and looked at her
watch. She couldn't leave until Joan gave her the okay
on the photos, there was just time for a quick check of
the list of internal vacancies on the *Herald*'s intranet.
Editorial Assistant on the travel desk (office-based,
booking flights and hotels for other people's travel
assignments); Online Editor, Asia Pacific region (office-
based computer drone, rewriting copy from foreign
correspondents who wrote English as their second
language); Copy Editor (correcting other people's
mistakes); Style Editor, Saturday supplement (Rose
didn't feel stylish enough).

At six o'clock, just as Rose was packing her bag,
her inbox pinged. Two new messages.

Rosie,
This menopause piece is good stuff. Keep it up. Next for
you is hormones and how they affect the unborn baby.
See attachments. Researchers have discovered that if
girl foetuses get more testosterone in the womb, they
grow up to be tomboys. 3,000 words. I want it in two
weeks.
Sam

Wow, no sexist joke. That had to be a first,
though he was still incapable of getting her name right.
She clicked on the second message.

Hello Rose Haldane,
I left Lady Grace's in the second year and moved to
Glasgow so I'm not the right Susan. I remember Kate
Ingram vaguely, she was in the year below me. Sorry I
can't help.
Susan Morris.

Rose didn't care about Friends Reunited now.
She had a better lead and Nick had found it for her.

32 ROSE

Child Street was in a grid of terraces built as
accommodation for workers at the Islington factories
that supplied bricks for the rebuilding of the City of
London after the Great Fire. Rose tried to imagine Kate
walking along this road carrying newspapers on a
Sunday morning, running to the tube station round the
corner, staggering home from the pub after one too many
lager and limes with the girls. She tried to see what Kate
saw every day. The monotony of red brick was broken in
a couple of places by pre-fab concrete cubes, legacy of
the post-war rush for housing. Not far away on the other
side of the road one house in particular shone; its bricks
and balustrade painted bright white, so bright in fact,
that Rose expected to smell new paint. The silvery grey
of the lime tree outside added to the overall bleached
effect. It was a style Rose liked. She hoped this was
Number 12, it was the sort of house she'd like to live in
if she could ever stretch to a bigger mortgage. She would
decorate it throughout with mocha walls, clotted cream
carpet, caramel leather sofas and dark wood furniture.
But the number on the ice-white door was 14.

The doorstep of Number 12 was clean and
simple. She wondered if the current inhabitants knew its
history as a squat. Rose knew Kate had left Westmead
Home for Ladies without Alanna, the day after the birth.

Alanna was taken home by Mrs Diana Haldane. That was the way things were done then.

Rose looked at the front door and knew in her heart that she had been conceived there. She pictured Kate, her long hair braided with thin yellow ribbons, her feet dusty in flat thong sandals, leaving a trail of patchouli scent and a jingle of bracelets in her wake. She imagined Kate climbing out of her orange Mini laughing with friends, their heads nodding in time to *Yellow Submarine*. She rang the bell, caressing the scratched brass button with her fingertip. It was the original, she was sure Kate had touched it, this was not a perfect shiny modern reproduction.

She fell forward slightly as the door opened leaving her finger suspended in mid-air. She smiled at the woman who stood on the doorstep. She looked about Rose's own age except for her eyes, which by right belonged to the face of a very tired seventy-year-old at the end of a long day.

'Hello. I'm Rose. Rose Haldane. My mother lived here, in the Sixties. I wondered if I could have a look around?'

'Well, I don't know…'

'It'll only take a minute. I never knew my mother you see, she died when I was a baby.' As Rose said it, she knew her request was weak. Would *she* let in a complete stranger? Er, no. She tried to look sad but quickly stopped, it felt more like a gurn.

The woman was frowning.

'I was adopted, you see, when I was a baby,' *Work it, Rose,* she thought, *work it,* 'so I never knew her. And now I've found out who she is, but she died.' She sniffed, then pulled Alanna's black-and-white baby

270

photograph out of her handbag.

'Oh no.' The woman's cheeks softened and her mouth relaxed, and suddenly Rose saw a thirty-year-old with tired eyes who was pretty in a fluffy kind of way.

'This is you?' Her hand stretched out to touch the small photo.

'Yes. I just want to get a sense of her, see if I can connect with her. I know she lived here, it's the only concrete thing I do know. It's so difficult... not knowing her...' She sniffed again, it sounded more like a flu-sniff than an upset-sniff.

'Oh, you poor thing, come in.'

Unable to believe her luck, Rose stepped into the narrow hallway and immediately understood the woman's hesitation. She could hear a baby crying angrily in another room and when she looked more closely at the woman, there was a large damp stain on her left shoulder. A huge glass vase, at least two feet tall, stood on a console table in the hall. 'Congratulations' said a small white card propped against it. The lilies were over-ripe, their waxy yellow leaves and sticky orange stamens scattered over the table, source of one of the two dominant smells Rose instantly identified. The other smell was synthetic lavender coming from a plug-in room freshener beside the skirting board, the kind that 'freshened' the room automatically every hour. Were babies that smelly?

'I'll make some tea. Come into the kitchen.'

The hall walls were lined to waist-height with original ceramic tiles, art-nouveau swirls of blue and green. Kate would have seen them every day as she walked out the front door. Rose reached out to touch them but snatched her hand back as the woman returned from a doorway off the hall, tying a baby to her chest in a papoose. She shooed Rose into the kitchen, chattering continuously as if demonstrating the house's good points to a prospective buyer, while she made tea.

'We decorated last year, we wanted everything to be perfect before I went into labour. We got it all from John Lewis. Their designs were wonderful, really captured the Victorian look. It was finished a week before little Chloe arrived, wasn't it, Chloe?' And she dropped a kiss on the baby's head.

Her words floated in and out of Rose's consciousness like dandelion clocks on a light breeze. She couldn't drag her eyes from the papoose. The only bit of the baby's head that was visible was the crown, wisps of fluffy dark hair. Rose could feel the beginnings of the howl on the escalator at Westminster tube station. Then she remembered Lily's advice and took one deep breath, then another and another. Better.

She followed Chloe's mum into the sitting room, being helpful, carrying the tea tray. Chloe's dad was reading the evening paper. He nodded, smiled, and reached out for the baby.

'Shall I take her, darling?'

'No, I've got her.' And the woman held Chloe closer.

He nodded, picked up his paper, and left.

John Lewis had got to this room too. Rose only needed one glance to know there was no sense of Kate here: new paint, new wallpaper, new carpet and curtains. As she balanced the cup of tea and plate of biscuits in her lap, Rose wondered what she should have expected. She didn't have time to be sociable. She looked at the woman cradling her baby. She'd made a family home here for her child, she was the opposite of Kate. *It's not fair*, thought Rose, *I want to hear my parents' voices in these rooms but there's no sense of Kate or the Sixties or the* squat.

'Your mother died when you were as tiny as Chloe? I can't imagine how that must feel. Your poor mummy. Poor you.' And she held her baby tighter.

'Yes,' said Rose vaguely as she looked around the room, its cushions plumped, the remote controls in a row on top of the DVD player. Was it the same upstairs?

'Is it John Lewis upstairs too?'

'Oh yes, but the colourways are different. Come and see.'

Rose put down her too-hot tea and followed her hostess upstairs, running her hand up the polished stair rail, enjoying the smoothness and warmth of the wood. It felt old. Walnut? Mahogany? Oak? Kate might have touched this rail each morning on her way downstairs to breakfast and each night on her way to bed. Upstairs, Rose looked into a new bathroom suite and three bedrooms so tidy they could be photos in a home furnishing catalogue. This was a Stepford house. She tried to look beyond the décor. One of these rooms must have been Kate's, but Rose couldn't sense which. It was a house of strangers making their own family history here, day by day. The woman led her downstairs and through the kitchen to the back doorstep where they looked out at the garden. The rectangular lawn was edged exactly as if cut by a sharp knife, the decking gleamed, the grass mowed to a precise number one crew cut. Next to a red-and-yellow plastic child's playhouse was a swing. It hung from a branch of the old oak, which cast shade over the shrubbery. Its wooden seat swung gently in the breeze, its rusty chain squawked like a magpie.

Chack-ack, ack, ack, ack.

Rose walked towards it.

'That's not our swing, awful old thing,' said the woman in a rush, 'it's been here for years. Unsafe, dirty. The landscaper arrives next week to re-design the garden and make it child-friendly. A new swing's on order and this one will go straight to the tip. Then everything outside will be ready for Chloe's playtimes.' And she kissed the baby's head again.

Rose looked at the woman and saw Lily, so eager with her newborn that she was practically buying her school uniform.

Chack-ack, ack, ack, ack went the swing.

Kate swung here, Rose was certain. She narrowed her eyes against the late afternoon shadows. There was something there now, she'd swear, swaying on the swing. A shadow? She screwed up her eyes to filter out the light and there was Kate, humming as she swung. Her bare toes scraped the ground and her cheesecloth skirt bunched around her knees as her brown legs ignored gravity to propel herself back and forth. Rose swayed back and forth too, her eyes rooted on Kate as she took a step forwards…

'Well, that's everything. Another cup of tea?'

A minute later, Rose stood on the pavement again, feeling hollow. Kate's spirit had been there and then gone. She closed her eyes and swayed back and forth, trying to recapture the essence of the girl on the swing but there was nothing, no matter how much she swayed. She opened her eyes and looked at what now seemed a very ordinary street that really could be anywhere.

She pulled Nick's list out of her pocket and checked the addresses.

Mr and Mrs Thomas Tyler, 14 Child Street. They lived at the white house? She tapped the cool steel knocker, and a thirty-something peered around the part-opened door, her foot with its red-painted toes in a fierce platform sandal braced against the bottom of the door to prevent unwelcome intruders.

The woman spoke through evenly capped white teeth. 'Mr and Mrs Tyler? They don't live here any more. Mrs Tyler died two years ago and we bought this when her husband moved to a flat. Sheltered accommodation, the kind with a warden. I've got the address somewhere, for forwarding post and such. Just a moment.'

She disappeared, shutting the door behind her. She left behind the floral scent of something Rose identified as expensive from the perfume advertisements in *Vogue,* the kind with the scented strip you rubbed against your skin. This was definitely not a plug-in air freshener sort of house.

As Rose rubbed at a brown mark on her linen trousers – squashed chocolate biscuit from Number 12 – the neatly ironed thirty-something re-appeared with a piece of paper.

It wasn't far. Cornwall Mansions was a tall red-brick mansion block with dusty dandelions growing out of cracks in the wide front steps. The front door was ajar. Rose stepped in, feeling as if she should ask permission. The reception desk through the hatch in the entrance hall was deserted.

Mr Tyler lived on the ground floor, Number 11.

His door stood part-open, one of a line of identical doors in the long corridor of cream-painted brick that reminded Rose of school. She knocked and an elderly man stuck his head through the gap, looked her up and down then beckoned her in with an impatient flick of his wrist. His eyes hardly left the television screen in the corner of the room where greyhounds wearing numbered jackets were getting ready to race. The voice of the commentator echoed off the sitting room's walls but Tommy showed no inclination to turn down the volume. Rose showed him Kate's photo, her NUJ press card as identification, and told him why she was there.

'Do I remember what, you say?' He cupped his hand to his ear.

She perched on the edge of the sofa, raised her voice and repeated her question. She knew that 130 decibels was the noise level of a Def Leppard concert. Normal human conversation measured forty decibels. This was in the leasehold deeds of her flat: 'Noise level not to exceed forty decibels between 10.30 p.m. and 7.00 a.m.' She'd checked it out two months ago when Michelle and Lewis's predecessor downstairs had played Michael Jackson at one hundred decibels seven days in a row until 2 a.m. and got an ASBO as a result.

'You'll have to speak up, lass, my hearing's not what it was.'

'Do you have a hearing aid?' Rose shouted each word with a slight pause between each one, and willed her mouth to curve into a smile.

Tommy fumbled beneath his green cable-knit jumper, producing a small grey box which he tapped on the arm of his chair. A high-pitched squeal echoed off the glass-fronted teak veneer cabinets and momentarily silenced the voice of the racing commentator.

'You'll have to talk a bit louder, young lady, I'm deaf you know.'

Rose wished for patience, then went back to the beginning.

'My name is Rose Haldane. I'm trying to find out about my birth mother, Kate Ingram, who lived at 12 Child Street. In the Sixties. I wondered if you might remember anything about her.'

She had to get him talking about something, anything. That was the secret to a tricky interview; first get someone talking, and then you could re-direct their conversation.

'Where is the greyhound racing coming from? Is it live?'

Tommy ignored this attempt at conversation. He continued to watch the dogs, his right ear tipped towards Rose. '12 Child Street?'

'Yes.'

'What do you want to know about that dirty place for? They never cleaned it, you know, rubbish piled up outside. I told my Eliza, "Don't you have nothing to do with them." I was afraid she'd get bitten by a rat and catch the plague.'

'The plague?' Positive affirmation showed interest and encouraged the person to continue talking, so Rose nodded and smiled.

'Aye, filthy people. It was just as bad in Queen Elizabeth's time. The first one. She drove to Islington one day for the fresh air… that was when it was in the country you know, not like now, no Tube, and her coach was surrounded by rogues. They arrested hundreds and sent them back where they came from, quite right too. I blame the brickworks. People coming from all over the country to get a job here.' He looked at Rose, waiting. 'Strangers.'

'Er.' Her mind went blank. He was one of those people who made statement after statement, stopping suddenly and expecting the listener to react as if they'd just explained the cure for cancer rather than the average inside leg measurement. Rose's news editor at *Medicine* magazine had been like that.

Tommy hissed. 'They don't teach history properly in schools these days. No, not now. In the 1800s it was.'

'Queen Elizabeth was…'

'Not her. Bricks. That brick company has a lot to answer for if you ask me. They say the bricks made here were used to build Victorian London. Ruined our gardens they did. Solid clay our soil is, that's why the brickworks were here of course.' He looked at her properly for the first time. 'You know how they make bricks, do you? You mix the clay with water and extrude it into a strip, then cut it into bricks with wires. Then you dry 'em.'

Rose didn't care about bricks.

'These days they make bricks in fancy colours and shapes, even bricks with holes that are supposed to keep the heat in. Sounds like nonsense to me. But we could never grow roses.'

Roses, she thought, *what have roses got to do with bricks? I've got to get him back on track.* 'Do you remember any of the people there?'

He looked at her as if she'd said Arsenal played rugby. 'No one lived at the brickworks.' He pulled out a pouch of loose tobacco and started to fill his pipe.

'No, at the squat.' Rose pressed her fingertips together so hard that the blood drained away from beneath her nails. She didn't know who was more confused, her or Tommy.

'All… long… haired… hippies.' His words issued between spittled sucks on his pipe. At last he inhaled smoke and leant forwards with a little sigh of satisfaction. 'You couldn't tell which were boys and which were girls. I wanted to take my scissors to the lot of them. Free love, that's what they called it. You know,' he turned his back on the dogs, his voice dropping to a conspiratorial whisper, ' they swapped around. It was in the paper last week. All hippies did it in the Sixties. Disgusting.'

Rose bit down a retort. *Just ask the questions,* she thought, *get the answers and go. I don't have to like him.*

'The council got them out in the end. Not soon enough for my liking. Not a job to rub between them but always enough money for booze and fags. Where's the sense in a welfare state paying people to do nowt? One girl hung a banner out of the top window, I remember. Peace.'

'Sorry?'

'That's what it said, the banner. "Peace". With an odd squiggle in the middle.'

'A squiggle?' Did he mean a symbol? The only peace symbol Rose could think of was CND. 'What did the girl look like, the one with the banner?'

'Damn,' he said, his eyes on the television screen as the race finished. He ripped up a slip of white paper before turning back to Rose. 'What? I can't remember that, it was years ago.'

The greyhounds for the next race were lining up and Tommy turned towards them.

Rose stood up. 'The girl with the banner, was she…'

'Aye, daft she was, stood on the windowsill once as well. Soft in the head if you ask me.'

Was it Kate? But why would she stand on a windowsill?

'She nearly fell out. I was all for calling the police. Stupid. Young girls these days aren't so daft, they have a baby so they can get a free flat.'

Rose was back on the pavement before the hooter started the next race. Outside it was a beautiful quiet summer evening. She referred to Nick's list again. A Phyllis Gladstone was next.

'Hey, miss. Miss!' Tommy was standing at the top of the mansion steps, holding her notebook out at arm's length.

'Oh, thanks.' Rose took it from him. She couldn't believe she'd been that desperate to get away from him that she'd left it behind. 'Thanks, Tommy.'

'All right, love.' He stared at her. 'Long, straggly hair, she had. The lass with the banner. Dark it was, a bit like yours.'

Did he mean Kate? She so wanted to believe Tommy, but the journalist's voice shouted in her head so righteously she couldn't ignore it. His description could fit half the hippies in the Sixties and Seventies. Was Tommy a reliable witness? No.

One interview done, one more to go.

She walked the few hundred yards to Mrs Gladstone's house, trying to forget Tommy, deeply inhaling the scent of plants, which spilled out of garden after garden. Jasmine. Buddleia. Lilies. But no roses, Tommy was right. The sky was like a Rothko canvas she'd seen in the Tate, the colours layered above one another like Eton Mess topped with mandarin segments and custard. She always found Rothko's paintings calming, the colours melting and merging together. She took a book from her handbag, the latest Frank Bale detective novel, ideal for the mode of stop-start reading demanded by commuting on public transport. She opened it to the current page and there was her bookmark: a postcard of Rothko's 'Light Red Over Black'. She breathed in the sweetness of the flowers, the glowing sky, and the layers of Rothko's paint, and let them soothe her.

Careful not to stand on the whitewashed doorstep that sparkled from daily scrubbing, Rose rang the doorbell of 17 Child Street. It was a tiny terraced house, immaculate, its postage-stamp garden packed with candy-coloured bedding plants. Not a single rose. The door was opened by an elderly lady who was wiping her hands on the sort of floral wrap-round pinny that Bizzie wore. Her eyes squinting in suspicion.

'Mrs Gladstone? My name's Rose Haldane.' She quickly explained her mission, showing her press card in response to a request for identification.

Mrs Gladstone examined the plastic rectangle, her eyes flitting from the photo to Rose's face, then smiled. 'Call me Phyllie, dear, like the cheese.'
Rose followed her down a dark narrow hall, swallowing the heavy oil scent of mothballs. The distinctive camphor smell took her straight back to her mother's wardrobe.

Phyllie wasn't deaf but she was able to speak without breathing. Rose sat for five minutes, nodding and smiling, as Phyllie talked while making tea. Rose wasn't sure she could face more tea.

'I had a bad night, gave up at five and made a cup of tea, tired all day, popping here and there, you know what it's like, tidying, so many things to do, so I thought I'd have a bit of early tea and put me feet up to watch *Win or Lose* and then you rang the bell just when it was the £500 question'.

'Sorry.'

'Oh, not to worry dear, someone else will win tomorrow.' She laid out two china cups and saucers, sugar bowl, delicate milk jug covered with strawberries, and a biscuit barrel decorated with a picture of the Queen Mother. 'Milk?'

Rose accepted the cup of tea which Phyllie poured with a slight wobble and spill.

'Now, what is it you want to know again, dear?'

'The squat?'

'Nice girls they were really, but they could have done with a regular bath and they were too thin. Didn't eat properly, you see. Eliza and me'd take them a cake now and then but we didn't tell our other halves. Eliza's Tommy would have gone mad if he'd known we was consorting with the enemy.'

'You knew Tommy and Eliza?'

'Oh yes, mmm. Lovely lady, was Eliza. Dead now you know.' She took a sip of tea and looked at the Queen Mother.

'Can you remember any of the girls, their names, what they looked like?'

'Well now, let me see.' Phyllie put on her

glasses as if to think. 'There was a lovely blonde girl, very pretty she was when she made an effort. She was always coming and going at odd times. Shift work, you see. Mmm. She always called hello and waved.'

Is this Susan?

'Lovely long strawberry-blonde hair. Sometimes she wore it in a French plait under a blue cap, a bit like a nurse or a bus conductress. Very neat.' She nodded to herself. 'I do like long hair, not these short cuts you have these days. Makes you look like men.'

Rose's hand ventured towards the curls at the nape of her neck. 'What about the other girls?'

'Well there were quite a few who lived there over the years.' Phyllie took off her glasses and wiped the lenses with the corner of her pinny. 'I only spoke to the nice ones who smiled at me; some were very sullen, didn't have time to say hello.' The glasses went back on her nose. 'Let me see, the other nice one had long hair too but she plaited it with beads, looked like it needed a wash, if you ask me. She wasn't always there, she'd disappear for long spells and then turn up again. Like a bad penny, my Bert said.'

Kate, it had to be. 'Did you see her boyfriend?'

'Humph. Never short of a man on her arm, that one. Used to wake us up at all hours, beeping their car horns, kissing and cuddling in the street. Tommy threatened to get his shotgun out once when she hung a banner out of the window. "Peace," it said. Quite right too, the world would be a better place if there was more of that around.' Phyllie humphed again. 'But he didn't.'

'Didn't what?'

'Get his gun out. Tommy didn't. Eliza talked him round, told him the bobby wouldn't do nothing about kids messing around. It was just a pretty girl with her boyfriends.'

Rose's stomach flipped like a pancake. Never mind the police, Phyllie had said 'boyfriends'. Plural.

33 ROSE

It was late when she got back home, but not too late to wash off the Islington grime with a long soak in the bath. She was squeezing Soothing Rose lotion onto her right leg when the phone rang.

'I think I've found Susan.' It was Maureen. 'I remembered an old scrapbook in the loft, with press cuttings of Kate's theatre appearances. There's a picture.'

Rose sat down on a hard dining chair. The blob of pale-pink cream resisted gravity for a second, and then started its slow downward drip towards her ankle. 'Has she got long blonde hair?'

'The girl in the picture has, yes. The caption says, 'Nurse Susan Abbott, friend of the cast, was presented with champagne last night by director Al Hall as thanks for administering life-saving first aid to a theatregoer taken ill at Friday's performance of *A Taste of Honey* at the Trinity Arts Centre, Wittinghurst.'

'How can you be sure her hair is blonde? Isn't the photo black and white?'

'Yes it is, but it's clearly fair hair, not brown.'

'Maureen, I could hug you. What date is it?'

'Erm, 1965. Why do you think she's blonde?'

'Because I've spent the evening talking to two elderly people who lived near the squat. The old lady,

Phyllie, was really sweet, she remembered two girls. One was dark, the other blonde.' Rose whooped inside, she'd corroborated Susan from two different sources. It had to be the same girl. Now she longed to look at the rest of the press cuttings.

'I didn't know you had a scrapbook about Kate.' She tried to keep the accusation out of her voice. There was the tiniest of pauses. 'Neither did I, I'd totally forgotten about it. Sorry Rose, I'm sure you'd like to see it, I'll drop it round. Is tomorrow soon enough?'

Rose instantly regretted her accusatory tone. The pink cream had reached the white scar above her ankle that she'd got climbing over the garden fence when was thirteen in a game of 'Diana the Huntress'. Rose had been the huntress, Lily had been a very slow and unwilling antelope.

'Tomorrow's fine.'

'Have you seen Lily today?' asked Maureen.

'No, I spoke to her yesterday.'

Yesterday. Suddenly it wasn't a sunny Tuesday evening in Wimbledon and Rose wasn't in her flat. It was yesterday again, at Westminster tube station and she was watching that newborn baby go up the escalator; it was yesterday and she was feeling again the stirrings of that howl. She recalled Lily's deep breathing exercise and felt a sudden fondness for her sister – her cousin – neither felt right. Lily would always be her... Sistercousin? What did it matter if she was hopeless at being an antelope?

'Is gardening a new thing? She seems... committed.'

Rose's shoulders sank. 'She did say something a couple of weeks ago about growing some plants from seed. I thought she meant a few lettuces.' But a memory nudged in Rose's brain, hadn't Lily said something about having forty seed trays?

Maureen laughed. 'More than a few, they've taken over the house since I was there last. They're on the windowsills, in the porch, even on the sideboard. I didn't know whether to ignore them or not. William looked distinctly fed up.'

'William was there? During the day?' He was the sort who was in the office by 7 a.m. and not home till 9 p.m., like it was a badge of honour.

'He muttered something about having to write an important report and needing peace and quiet. The only thing was, Lily was chattering away, you know how she does, following him around like a puppy.'

'Oh, that's not good.'

Only after she put the phone down did Rose realise she'd forgotten to thank Maureen for her detective work. Susan No-Name had become Susan Abbott.

Creamed and powdered, Rose curled up on the sofa in her favourite soft blue pyjamas. What was the quickest way to find Susan Abbott? She had been a nurse in the Sixties; perhaps she still was.

She picked up the phone and dialled. 'Mags, how do I find a nurse?'

'Royal College of Nursing, they keep a list of every registered nurse currently nursing. I know the PR there, I can give you her number.'

'A nurse from the Sixties.'

'A bit more difficult. Is this something to do with Kate?'

'Yep.' Rose precised the latest developments.

'But tomorrow I'm trapped in one of Sam's awaydays, brainstorming editorial ideas in a hotel, which you and I know means dry sandwiches, viscous coffee, and listening to some twit from marketing talk about a reader survey when we know our readers better than anyone else.' She stopped. 'Sorry, rant over.'

'S'okay. Do you want me to make the calls?'

'Would you?

'Of course I will, you idiot. But I thought you'd given up on Kate. How did you find these people to interview?'

'Nick Maddox.'

'The beauty guy? Does he know it was you who burped down his telephone?'

'He doesn't know, and I'd be grateful if you'd forget everything about that evening.'

Maggie laughed. 'Don't worry, I already have. So, spill.'

Rose filled Maggie in on the non-kiss and Maggie reciprocated with a story about a guy she'd met in a bar last night. They chatted for another half-hour, and when she put the phone down, Rose felt less isolated. She settled on the sofa with a pile of magazines and a cup of peppermint tea. As she flicked through the pages, a headline leapt out at her. 'I Was a Child Born of Hate.' Black inky words exploded off the page: adopted, struggle, disgust, rape. A footnote in red ink shouted at her from the end of the article: 'The names in this article have been changed to protect identities.' The picture caption warned: 'Photo posed by an actress'. Rose read:

Ginny had always wanted her parents to love her like they loved her sister, then one day she stumbled on the reason why they didn't – her mother had been raped.'

Her head spun. She stood up too quickly and felt dizzy, dropping the magazine onto the sofa. Is that what happened to Kate? Suddenly everything made sense. *Oh Kate, you didn't deserve this, no woman deserves this.* And in a flash Rose was back in the bedroom at the Rag Week party with that student with the odd goatee who started off being cute but ended up ugly, who hadn't known the meaning of 'no' or 'stop' or 'NO', who, if not for her tears and screams, if not for someone coming in and pulling him off her, would have …

She hadn't thought of that bedroom for years. *Please say that didn't happen to Kate.* She tried to focus on something positive and found herself thinking about the peaceful garden at the squat, the old oak tree and the swing, its rusty chain squawking like a magpie. Chack-ack, ack, ack, ack. Kate's spirit was there, swinging back and forth.

All sound dimmed, as if Rose was wearing the pink earplugs she kept for swimming, but there was something behind the chack-ack, ack, ack, ack. A single note, persistent, ringing. The doorbell at the communal door downstairs. Damn, was that it? Or was it the phone? The smoke alarm? The oven timer?
The noise stopped. Good.

Knock knock. There was definitely someone at her front door. She opened it a sliver and caught a glimpse of a pale blonde cropped head bending down, tying a shoelace.
'Hel–'
She slammed the door shut, and there was a yelp

from the other side. What was he doing here? How had he got upstairs? It was like a slap in the face. Not now, she didn't want to see him now, not like this. She wanted him to see her in control for once. She was supposed to be Strong Rose.

The knocking was constant now, fists hammering. 'Rose, let me in. Let me in, Rose.'

'Go away. How did you get upstairs anyway? No one knocks on my front door.'

'The woman in the downstairs flat let me in as she was going out. Come on…'

She didn't know how long she waited until, feeling tired, unable to fight any more, she freed the chain and opened the door.

'Ow, that really hurt. What did you shut the door on me like that?' Nick was nursing a bruised knuckle. He looked angry.

Because I like you and you don't like me, because you didn't kiss me back, because Kate, because Kate…

'K-K-Kate was… she was…'

And then his arms were around her and words were whispered in her ear and a hand pressed gently between her shoulder blades until she could breathe again.

'Kate, Kate was… I'm… I've just read this horrible article… I'm…'

'Shush, it's all right.'

Rose took a deep breath. It was important he listen to her. 'Kate was raped. It all makes sense now. That's why my father is unknown, that's why she was so ashamed of me. She gave me away because she was raped and she couldn't bear to look at me because I look like the rapist.'

Then he was holding her again, so close her ribs strained for breathing space, so close she could feel his heartbeat next to hers.

'Rose, you're you. Whatever happened to Kate, that has nothing to do with you.'

Then his grasp loosened and Rose heard a rustle of pages as he picked up the magazine and read the article. Then he was hugging her again, that reassuring clench around her ribs, her lungs, her heart. She took a proper breath and felt a little better.

'It's awful, what you've read.'

His voice was cool and calm and in charge, and Rose wanted to float in it. She sat up straighter and looked at him. He smiled. His teeth were almost perfect except for a slightly pointy canine. She was glad he wasn't perfect.

'Of course it's possible that Kate was raped. But you don't know that for sure, do you? And I know you, Rose. You interviewed me, remember. You gave me quite a grilling. I'm sure you want to know the truth. Don't you?'

She nodded.

'Well then, Ockham's Razor.'

'What?'

'Ockham's Razor: the principle that the simplest explanation is probably the correct one. Chances are it's the oldest story in the book, your father did a runner when Kate told him she was pregnant. Simple. Don't complicate it, Rose, don't look for things that aren't there.' He looked at her cold cup of peppermint tea and stood up. 'You need alcohol.' He walked into the kitchen and started banging cupboard doors.

Rose sat and waited for him to come back and hold her again, hoping he wouldn't pull away at the last minute like last time.

He put a glass of wine on the side table.

She didn't pick it up. 'I can't do this.'

'You'll feel fine tomorrow. You'll find Susan. You won't give in until it's well and truly over.'

'No, not Kate, not Susan. Us.'

'Is there an "us"?'

'You see,' she gesticulated vaguely towards the ceiling, 'that's what I mean. I don't know.' At last her words were coming out straight. 'I'd like there to be an "us" and sometimes I think you do too, but other times you act as if I'm an employee who never buys the coffees. I can't handle this on/off, will he/won't he, kiss thing.' That sounded more like Strong Rose and she instantly felt better.

For a moment there was silence. 'I didn't realise.'

'No.' She wondered for the first time if Nick actually liked Weak Rose. If he did, it was going to be a problem.

They sat quietly. Rose looked around the room, not seeing, wishing she could suck her words back in.

Finally Nick took her hand in his and brushed it with his lips. 'I owe you an explanation.'

It was simple, and such a cliché. He was married.

'I've separated from my wife, she had a thing with her boss. They live in Birmingham now. The divorce is due any day.' His smile was slightly stretched. Rose was furious with herself. Why hadn't it shown up in her research? Because being short of time she'd done company research, not the personal stuff. She'd been looking up Kate's death certificate, not searching the marriage records for Nick's name. *Stupid, stupid.*

'I thought it would complicate things... us. I thought you had enough to worry about, my far-off, most secret and inviolate Rose. And I do feel guilty about seeing you while I'm technically still married. But hey,' he smiled grimly, 'guilt is a man's thing, we have Adam to thank for that. It's one of the lessons men learn as they grow up, it's easier to get on with life if you accept your universal guilt as fact.'

'I'm sorry, Nick. I had no idea. You've been going through your own emotional turmoil while I've been wittering on about Kate. You make me feel like a brat.' A part of her felt thankful he had his own emotional baggage; maybe he had days of Strong Nick and Weak Nick.

'You're not a brat. No, we married too young and were both selfish. I like myself better when I'm with you.'

'I like you, too.' Strong Nick, Weak Nick, Whatever Nick; she liked him a lot.
They sat for a long while, quiet, just being together.

When, a little later, Nick led her by the hand towards the bedroom and sat down on the bed, she resisted the pull of gravity.

'Perhaps we should wait until your divorce is final.'

'No, it's too late, there's no going back now.'
They stood, nose-to-nose in the darkness.

'I like what you said, about me being your most secret and inviolate Rose.'

His face was in her hair now, breathing deep,

and she wondered briefly what shampoo she'd used that morning. He kissed each ear, then wrapped her hands in his, kissing each knuckle in turn.

'Unfortunately I can't claim the eloquence as my own. It's WB Yeats.'

She forgot all about shampoo.

34 LILY

Today was the first day of Lily's 'taking no notice' campaign. She had rejected the other option – relationship counselling – as a non-starter. If William wouldn't talk to her, he was hardly likely to talk to a stranger. She wasn't sure that ignoring him would help either, but was prepared to give it a go.

Since he'd stormed out of the kitchen on Sunday morning, they'd spoken politely to each other and eaten silent meals in front of the TV with trays on their laps. Lily had tried to talk to him, but her very presence in a room seemed to annoy him so she ignored him totally. William, presumably relieved that she wasn't making a scene, ignored her too. But it disturbed her that the more she ignored him, the less he talked to her, and the more she disliked him. Had he always been so horrible? Surely not, but this morning he'd thrown the newspaper back in the paperboy's face because he brought the *Telegraph* instead of *The Times*. And yesterday he'd actually shouted at Mr Bunn, who did the garden once a week, for putting the wrong sort of weeds on the compost heap. When had William ever cared about compost? Or known about good weeds and bad weeds? She was no longer automatically making him a cup of tea when she made one for herself, because he never said 'thank you' and never put his mug in the dishwasher. This felt so good she extended the 'taking no notice' campaign to not doing jobs for William too. It was oddly rewarding. She didn't collect his shirts from the cleaners; there were only two left before he got to the ones with missing buttons, and bought cheap own-brand lager instead of his favourite Japanese bottled beer. As she put up the ironing board, she pondered on whether it was worth carrying on, as he didn't seem to notice her efforts. Was not noticing enough proof of guilt? Not for Rose, who was always harping on about facts equalling truth, but possibly enough for her. Proof that William was up to something. She laughed at herself as she folded an ironed tea towel into a rectangle. 'Up to something' was Bizzie's euphemism for 'having an affair'. Lily wasn't sure what William was up to, but she couldn't see how he had the time for an affair. When he wasn't at home he was always at work, or rugby. Work; that was his love affair. She was a work widow.

No you're not, said a sharp little voice in her head. *No man loves his work that much. You may have no evidence that he's having an affair, but you have none that he's innocent either. Because you're not looking for clues, you coward!*

That sounded like something Rose would say. Halfway through ironing a pillowcase, Lily stopped. She was not a coward. Perhaps she should investigate. Researching, Rose called it. But researching your own husband, looking for clues, wasn't that snooping?

Not if he's acting suspiciously, said the sharp little voice again, *and boy is he. Start snooping, girl!*

Lily wasn't sure she should take advice from a voice inside her head, particularly one that sounded like Oprah, but she pulled out a pen and sucked the top for a while before writing 'Places to Search' on the back of her shopping list, which was the closest bit of paper to hand. His pockets. His computer. The desk drawers.

'Yes, yes. Just look everywhere. You don't need to write it! Just do it!

So Lily did. Glad her mother was not alive to see her, she went straight to the wardrobe to search his jacket pockets. Nothing. Neat William emptied his pockets every night and tipped the contents into a small silver bowl on his bedside table, decanting the lot back into his pockets the next morning.

His bedside drawer. This was a drawer she never opened out of respect for his privacy. She hoped he never looked in her bedside drawer either, from the same motivation, as that was where she kept her ovulation charts and thermometer. She was prepared to find a dirty magazine or two, that nude photo he'd taken of her on honeymoon, the 'his' vibrator that matched the 'hers' they were given as joke wedding presents, and lubricating jelly. Only the tube of jelly was there, the lid stuck with yellowing gum. She slammed the drawer shut and sat on the floor.

'You bastard!' she shouted. It was a swear word she never used and especially not now with Rose... Lily was furious with herself for swearing, and for finding out she cared about what William had done, was doing, with their vibrator.

'The bastard!' It was really quite liberating, so she said it again. Until now, she'd never understood Rose's fondness for a ripe swear word.

She turned towards the bathroom.

Not in there. You won't find anything there, said Oprah. *You know where you have to look.*

With leaden feet, Lily climbed the stairs to the room she should have started in, the room at the top of the house where William spent most of his time when he was home. The tiny attic room which she thought of as 'the playroom' and William called 'my study'. She logged onto their joint email account. There was one old message for her in the inbox, from Rose, recommending some test for early menopause. Lily couldn't think about that now. The rest was just spam, plus an email from William's Japanese teacher attaching a homework exercise. That was okay then.

No, it's not. The voice was getting shrill. *Rose wouldn't take things at face value*, thought Lily. She scrolled down the list again, stopping at the message from his Japanese teacher. Lily had never really understood why William had persisted with Japanese classes, two, sometimes three times a week. Whenever she'd asked him why, he said it would look good on his CV. Was he expecting to made a director and sent to the Tokyo office?

Like hell he is.

Lily was starting to dislike that voice but couldn't turn it off. Was that why he was working these horrendously long hours and learning Japanese? Were they going to move to Japan? She felt rather taken aback. It wasn't what she was expecting at all. But Tokyo. What an amazing place to live. What an opportunity. Lily, living in Tokyo. Rose had never been there, never would; Rose never went anywhere. Just think, geishas and jasmine tea and kimonos. Lily loved kimonos, beautiful bird designs on gloriously coloured silk fabrics. So graceful. She would get a kimono tomorrow. She read the message again.

To: William.Lodge@britishtelecom.co.uk

From: Midori2114@hotmail.com
cc. babycakes616@hotmail.com
Message: homework
Dear William,
Please find homework attached. Sorry, I must change the time of class on Friday. Can we meet at eight instead of six?
Midori

Lily tried to think back, where had William been last Friday? Out. She'd eaten beans on toast and watched two episodes of *Strictly Come Dancing* on Sky+. He'd come in at eleven, complaining that his train had been late and his lesson had overrun. She read the message again.

You do know what sort of person calls themselves Babycakes, don't you Lily, asked Oprah. 'Someone with a huge ego,' said Lily. 'It could be another student, except William's classes are one-to-one; that's why they cost a fortune. Maybe it's Midori's second email address?'

Or William's?

'Okay, okay.' She logged out, found the Hotmail home page, tapped in 'babycakes616@hotmail.com', then sat back and stared at the screen. If someone had nothing to hide, why would they have a second email address?

Come on, you're not that naive.

'Shut up,' said Lily, 'I'm thinking.' What was the password? She looked over her shoulder, almost expecting him to be standing there, asking what she thought she was doing, invading his privacy. He wouldn't be home for hours but she should hurry, she hated doing this. It felt dirty, as if she was reading his mind without him knowing.

Which is what you're trying to do, stupid!

'I am not stupid.'

She wondered how Rose would find a password. Should she ring her? No. Lily loved Rose, but she didn't want her sister to know how desperate she felt at this moment. Rose had never felt this desperate, she was always in control, she wouldn't understand.

You are not desperate. You are a woman empowered by wrong.

'Yeah, right,' and Lily giggled. 'I am a woman empowered by wrong.'

William's password for his normal email was 'Victor', the name of the cocker spaniel he'd got for his tenth birthday. Victor was long dead, but his memory lived on. She typed in 'Victor' and waited.

Rejected.

She tried 'Victor' again, adding a number at the end because a lot of websites wanted a password to include letters and numbers.

Rejected.

Again and again, she tried different combinations, including capital letters.

Rejected.

Her head started to ache. What other passwords did William use? He pretty much used 'Victor' all the time. There were quite a few variations, 'Victordog1' and 'Victorgooddoggie' were the most frequent. She tried both.

Rejected.

'Numberonevictor'.

'Numberonedog'.

'Victor4will'.

All rejected.

She kept trying long past the time when she knew it would never work. While she was victoring, her subconscious was working out another password, a hateful one.

She looked down at her notepad, where she had scribbled each password as she tried it.

You know this is it, you know I'm right.

'No,' she said aloud, rubbing her eyes. Only when her head was pounding and her right forearm throbbed with the strain of moving from the space bar to the keyboard to the mouse and back again did she stop.

Do it.

So she tapped it in and held her breath. Nothing happened, the website took an age deciding whether to admit her.

Accepted.

'Ohh myy Godd.'

35 LILY

The password was 'will4midori'.
Told you.

She was surprised at how quickly the emergency locksmith arrived, at how quickly he changed the locks, at how little he asked. She ran from window to window, turning the locks and hiding the tiny keys in vases and zipping them inside cushion covers. She locked the garage too, then took every other key she could find and put them in her oldest, rattiest suede handbag and shoved it behind the nearly new trainers in the bottom of her wardrobe.

Her anger fuelled the physical effort, enabling her to lift heavy loads, run up and down stairs like a mountain goat, masking her thoughts. She lugged the biggest black suitcases down from the loft and threw an assortment of William's clothes into them. His CDs and Xbox followed, boxes from the study stuffed with papers and books, then she dragged the lot into the front garden. All William's French wine in the kitchen was emptied down the drain. The empty cardboard wine cartons she stuffed with his dirty laundry. She passed through the house, leaving a trail of his clothing behind her, stepping on some of it and not caring.

She couldn't clear every single one of his

possessions from the house in an hour, but she had a pretty good try.

She watched the locksmith fold her cheque and crisp £50 note tip in his pocket and drive away. William would be horrified; he never tipped. The neighbour opposite, Maud-something, smiled and waved at Lily from her front window, so Lily smiled and waved back, trying to look normal, trying to behave as if it was usual behaviour to pile suitcases and boxes beside the front gate. And there was an unmistakeable smell she hadn't noticed earlier. She walked slowly around the pile. The Xbox had fallen off onto some fresh dog mess. William's belongings towered quite high, almost to Lily's shoulders, so he couldn't fail to see it when he came home, might even walk straight into it if he came home in the dark.

You read the email. What makes you think he's coming home at all?

'Because he doesn't know I know, and because he likes his comforts.'

She looked at her watch. If he caught the 7.05 from Waterloo, he'd arrive at Barnes station at 7.25. Five minutes to walk from the station. There was just enough time.

She ran upstairs to the attic and printed off the most incriminating email, slipped it into a clear plastic folder and carried it downstairs where she taped it to the box at the top of the heap. It fluttered in the light breeze like a flag. Then she went back into the house, locked the doors with the new keys, closed the curtains, poured herself a glass of whisky (leftover from a Christmas hamper) and put on *Strictly Come Dancing*. Very loud. After ten minutes, the whisky eased the knot in her stomach and the tears came.

She had done it. She had faced the demon, proved it existed and cut it out of her life.

She reached for the phone and dialled Rose's flat: the answerphone. Her mobile: no answer. Lily was disappointed; she wanted to hear Rose say she was proud of her.

I'm proud of you.

'Me too,' said Lily.

She allowed herself to check through the window once an hour to see if the pile was still there, otherwise she watched the noisiest, trashiest TV she could find. At eleven o'clock, she turned off the TV and looked out of the front window. The pile was still there but the email was gone.

A wail filled the air inside the house, like a fox rutting in the dead of night.

'What have I done?'

36 ROSE

'You are so precious to me.'

Rose could just make out his eyelashes in the green light of the bedside clock. It was 2.12 a.m. His eyes were smiling at her. She asked the question that had been nagging her all evening.

'Why did you come here tonight?'

Nick blinked again and the second stretched as she waited for him to speak. Not for the first time, Rose wished she could be so measured.

'When I was driving today I realised that I love you and, realising that, I had to tell you as soon as possible.'

'I love you too.'

She turned her back to him and tucked her bottom into the cushion of his stomach. He wrapped his arms around her, kissed the nape of her neck and then they fell asleep, fitted together like two perfect commas.

She felt so different the next day that she expected people to point and stare.

'Look at Rose Haldane, doesn't she look different?'

'What's happened to Rose?'

'Wow, Rose, you look really great today.'

Of course no one said anything of the sort. Her

mind drifted… her breathing fell in time with the swaying of the train on the rails… she tried to concentrate on the day's work ahead, but the thought of Nick's face, his voice, his touch pushed away her need to plan today's feature. Eczema.

The train stopped with a jerk at Limehouse. She closed her eyes again, remembering.

'When did you know?'

'That it was right, you mean?'

'Mmm.'

'Straight away.'

'You didn't, that's impossible.'

'Straight away, I'm telling you. As soon as you walked into my office.'

'Wow…'

Wow.

Somewhere, a mobile was ringing. Why didn't someone answer it? She opened her eyes. It was her mobile. Hurray, Nick. Bursting to tell him she'd known straight away too, she said, 'Hello.'

'Oh Rose.'

Lily never called this early.

'What's wrong?'

'It's over.'

Rose felt as if she'd turned on a film halfway through. 'What…'

'He's gone.'

'Gone where?'

'I don't know.' Another laugh; bitterness tinged with the sort of giggle induced by too much caffeine. But Lily never drank coffee. 'And I don't care.'

There was a moment's silence while Rose digested this. The train stopped and a man sat down on

Rose's left, the woman on her right turned a page of her newspaper and jabbed Rose in the ribs with her elbow.

'You love William.' There were many uncertainties in Rose's life, but she was sure of that. It was shock talking.

'He left. Last night.' And Lily started to sob.

'Oh Lily.' Rose was aware that everyone around her was listening now in that parasitic way passengers have on public transport when they sense the drama of someone else's private life unfolding before them.

'He'll be back, you'll see.' Rose thought this was unlikely, but she tried to keep her voice warm and supportive.

'No,' Lily sobbed, 'you don't understand. He didn't leave. I threw him out.'

'You... what?'

'He was... he was...'

And the train went into the tunnel at Canary Wharf station and the phone went dead.

'Having an affair.' Suddenly all Rose's suspicions clicked, the little acts or comments which meant nothing individually but which added up to a husband playing around. With shock, she realised she wasn't shocked.

Her mobile was without a single dot and the train stopped for an age at the platform underground. Just as she decided to get off and go to street level to get a signal, the doors swished shut. Oh how it dragged its wheels through the outbound tunnel, stretching out Rose's sorrow for Lily like a rubber band. She thought of Nick last night and how it would feel to lose him, this morning, now, and multiplied that by the years Lily and

309

William had been married and the time before that when they'd been together.

As soon as the train pulled into daylight, the phone rang.

'He's been having an affair with his Japanese teacher, Midori-Whatsit. Can you imagine it?'

Sadly, Rose could. William's Japanese obsession had always struck her as odd.

'How did you find out?'

'I researched him, like you do at work... '

Rose swallowed a chuckle at the thought of Lily doing research.

'… so I thought of what you'd do and I did it. This Midori emailed him at home to change the time of one of his lessons. But she made a big mistake. She cc'd the message to a Hotmail address. Babycakes.'

'What sort of person calls themselves Babycakes?'

'I know,' and Lily actually giggled. 'I logged into Hotmail, typed in "Babycakes". It took me over an hour to guess his password.'

Rose was impressed at Lily's tenacity. 'The odds must be huge.'

'Karma. It means I was meant to find out, doesn't it?'

Rose could hear the smile in her sister's voice. 'I'm proud of you, Lil. Well done.'

'Don't you want to know what the password is? Will4midori.'

'Ugh.' Rose worked hard at keeping her sadness out of her voice.

'I know, pretty sickly isn't it?'

'But Babycakes?'

'Baby's bottom. Bum. Buns. Cakes. Get it? There are loads of emails in the inbox. She goes on about loving his cute bottom and how she can't wait to stroke it.'

'You shouldn't have to read that rubbish, Lily. Don't look at it again.'

They were silent for a moment.

'What I don't get,' said Rose, 'is why she cc'd the Babycakes message to his home email. It's asking to get caught.'

'I have no idea and I don't care. Maybe she wanted me to find out.'

This calm voice didn't sound at all like Lily. 'So how do you feel now?'

'Pretty shitty, I didn't sleep much.' Lily stifled a yawn.

'You should have rung me.'

'I did, your phone was off.'

Instantly Rose felt guilty, then lucky as she remembered Nick again. Nick, the man she was meant to spend the rest of her life with. But… wasn't that what Lily had thought?

She coughed. 'Sorry… I… my…' She was about to mention Nick, then realised it was tactless.

'… my boss is being really naggy at the moment and I'm trying to avoid him. What are you doing today, are you at work?'

'Wednesday's my day off, remember? I'm sitting at the kitchen table, thinking about what to do. My head's going round in circles. Perhaps I should stand by my man, that seems to be what the wives of politicians and sportsmen do. Millie Smith had her photograph taken standing outside the front door with her husband. And he had an affair with a lingerie model. Everyone knows Millie Smith now, she's famous for it.' Who the hell was Millie Smith? 'I don't think you should make any decisions at the moment.'

'This time yesterday morning I so wanted William's baby. Now I don't know what I want, except that I don't want to touch him ever again.'

'Well, you'll have to talk to him at some point, to sort out the…' Rose couldn't say 'divorce', '…things.'

'Divorce,' said Lily. 'It's okay, you can say it.'

'It's a fresh start.'

'Yes. It'll be nice to be on my own and do what I want for a change.'

'You just said you don't know what you want.' *Lily has never known what she wants from one day to the next,* thought Rose. And suddenly she remembered Lily and the mustard.

'No, maybe I don't. But it'll be fun finding out. Will you help me?' Lily laughed that odd caffeinated laugh again.

With a pang, Rose wished Mum was there to help her, suggest what to say, tell her how to balance comforting with advising. 'Of course I will.'

But after they'd said their goodbyes she looked out of the train window without seeing, remembering Lily spitting Dijon mustard over their mother's immaculate kitchen floor and being sick three times.

37 ROSE

The Ena Harkness conference room was on the sixth floor of the Green Garden Hotel next door to Herald Tower. Rose slipped into her chair quietly. Her mobile was in her pocket and set on silent, just in case Lily called or Mags texted. She sat and scribbled down a few feature ideas; off-the-top-of-her-head ephemera but better than um-ing and ah-ing when Sam turned to her.

Dealing with stress: flight-or-fight, take a mental step back, Alexander Technique.
Anxiety, what is it and how to combat it: sense of dread, relaxation techniques, herbal therapies.
Depression: lack of energy, indecisive, antidepressants, talking treatments.

When she read her notes again, every single item applied to Lily. Poor Lily…

'Hey. Rose. That's the last time I offer to buy you a drink.'

What?

'Hey, Rose.'

She looked around. Frank was staring at her, thin-lipped. *Oh God. Pozzi's last night.* She sank lower into her seat as people turned to stare, alerted by the caustic note in his voice.

'I suppose you were off with Beauty Boy.'

Rose looked swiftly round the room. No sign of Sam yet, thank God. 'Sssh, Frank, I'm sorry.' Nick's business interview had been published in that morning's edition and when she got to her desk that morning, she found a giftbox of Biocare Beauty products couriered by Nick's PR company. Impersonal.

The personal touch had come in a text.

'Rub in the cream, wait for me naked. Tonight. My place.'

Now as she remembered Nick's words, she smiled.

'Sssh? Sssh?' A muscle flickered under Frank's right eye. 'Don't you sssh me.'

Rose focussed on him, her mind still with Nick. 'Something came up. I had to… do a late interview.' *That's plausible, isn't it?* She tried smiling at him.

'I'll bet something came up.'

Rose gasped. Heat crept into her cheeks.

'Yes, I thought so. Wouldn't Sam just love to know you're screwing the clients.'

'Contacts,' Rose corrected without thinking. 'They're contacts, not clients. We're journalists, not ad reps.' *Sam can't boss my private life*, she thought indignantly, *I'll go out with whoever I want.*

'I notice you're not denying it though.' More heads were turning to look at her. 'You've just broken Sam's number one rule.'

Rose poured herself a glass of water and added a drop of lime juice for something to do. *Don't react,* she told herself, *it'll make me look guilty.* She'd never seen Frank so angry. Usually he made a joke of things, it was a habit that usually irritated her but now she kind of

314

missed it. She should never have agreed to have a drink with him in the first place. She sipped, her head down. Sam didn't have a rule about shagging contacts, did he? She almost groaned aloud. If he found out about this before her disciplinary review, she'd be out the door.

'Think about it, Rose, it's one or the other. Your choice.'

What? What choice? Lose Nick or lose my job? Is that what lose/lose means? Why can't he offer me a win/win? Is Frank threatening to dob me in? Would Sam believe him?

She pushed the plate of biscuits along the table and softened her voice so it sounded contrite. 'Frank, I'm really sorry, okay? I didn't forget on purpose.' That at least was true. 'Biscuit?'

He scowled and turned away, beginning to talk to Emma, the young marketing trainee sitting on his left. At that precise point, Sam walked in and the meeting started.

Rose couldn't forget the bitterness in Frank's voice. What if he told Sam, or May, or HR? She'd be marched straight out to the street with no time to clear her desk. Was Nick worth that: losing her job, a black mark on her CV, not being able to pay next month's direct debits?

Yes, she wanted to shout, *yes he's worth it*.

She sounded like that shampoo advert, and she laughed.

She endured three hours of Sam's exhortations to define their readers, identify the *Herald*'s strengths and weaknesses, differentiate their editorial offerings, analyse their competition, and pin down the opportunities. Trays of sandwiches, already dry and curling at the edges, were wheeled in at lunchtime. Simply looking at the bottles of warm wine was enough to make her temples ache. And there were three more hours of brainstorming to come this afternoon. She glanced at the agenda: 'Autumn & Winter Feature Ideas' was next. She retreated to the street with the smokers, determined not to worry about Frank. The smokers' section was not her natural territory, but in addition to being Sam- and Frank-free, it was the best place to get a mobile signal.

Her mobile beeped. A text.

'Royal Coll Nursing has 3 Susan Abbotts on lists. 0 in Islington in 60s. Perhaps she married? More later. Mags.'

Great, and yet… the excitement bubbling inside her was tinged with envy. Rose wanted to find Susan herself. Then she chided herself, noting that Maggie was being helpful. Nick would tell her to be gracious and so that's what she resolved to be.

She rang Lily who insisted she was fine, absolutely fine, and that she was shopping.

'What for?'

'A new life.'

'That's fine, good, great. As long as you really are fine.'

'I am.'

Rose felt that familiar sense of foreboding, like the time Lily attempted a double twizzle on her roller skates and broke her arm in two places. *Please let this over-confidence not end in tears.*

Her phone beeped again.

'Checked marriage register. Susan Abbott

married Michael Hamilton, Islington May 68. Could be her. M.'

How was Maggie finding the time to do all this? *Xtra* must lack a managing editor like May Magdalene.

Back in the Ena Harkness, time crept by. At 3 p.m., Frank headed for the tea table with Emma. They were whispering, heads together, and then Emma looked over her shoulder towards Rose.

He's not telling that little girl that I stood him up last night, is he? Or am I being paranoid?

She ran through the revolving door to the tobacco-scented street. Dodging puddles, she headed for a large pine tree, which offered the only shelter from a steady drizzle. Her mobile beeped.

'Checked tel directory for address on marriage cert. Nothing yet. Mags.'

Rose tapped out a quick message.

'Am nearly finished here. I will check now. Thx for your help. R.'

Back inside, her feet slightly damp, Rose was the last to sit down. Surely it couldn't be that difficult to find a nurse called Susan Hamilton née Abbott?

'Miss Haldane.'

Rose started. Sam was scowling at her.

'As you clearly find something else more interesting than the ideas of your colleagues, perhaps you would share with us your inspirational six feature ideas.'

'Uh, yeah,' Rose mumbled. The feature on haemorrhoids was looming.

She picked up the notes she'd scribbled earlier, then hesitated. They were not inspirational. So she stood up tall, letting her hands relax on the table in front of

her, smiled – she knew she had a good smile because Nick told her so last night – and looked around the table, making eye contact with everyone in turn, confident, un-hurrying, not worried by the silence, just as she imagined Nick would behave in these circumstances. She didn't have a clue what to say, and then…
… the words appeared on her tongue.

'The family dynamic is changing and this is having an enormous impact on the notion of identity. Alienated kids, separated parents, non-biological parents: like it or not, the make-up of our society is changing. The family of the future is going to look very different from the kind of mummy-and-daddy-and-two-kids kind of home many of us here grew up with. Science is advancing and we need to catch up. It's a legal minefield. I'm thinking particularly of egg and sperm donation, IVF, surrogacy, cloning and identification of sperm donors, and the subsequent child support and parenting responsibilities. It's something that touches all our readers and I think it'd make a compelling series. Definitions of what's involved, responsibilities, psychological effects on everyone concerned, costs, legal implications, interviews with parents and children, grandparents, step-families, educationalists, behaviourists.'

When she sat down, she knew her proposal was a Tenner.

'Thank you, Rosalie,' said Sam, looking down at his agenda. 'Now I want to look at…'

But his words were drowned out by a round of applause.

'Great series of features,' said Caroline, the marketing director who sat facing Rose. 'Very challenging. Just the sort our readers want to see, according to our latest research.' And she waved a report in the air.

'I'd want to read about it,' added Emma. She smiled, and Rose noticed a gap between her two front teeth that cried out for dental attention. She also noticed Frank scowling at Emma. Emma's face fell.

'Yes, erm... Emma, I agree, I would too.' A voice floated in from the back of the room.

Rose jumped and sensed everyone else jumping too. She twisted in her seat, so did everyone else. Sam stood on tiptoe. They all watched May emerge from the shadows between two wobbly stacks of gold-framed conference chairs.

'Well done, Rose. I want a written proposal by Monday.' And then she disappeared as silently as she'd arrived.

Sam did that odd sucking-his-tongue thing he did when someone contradicted him; it pursed his lips like a Botoxed goldfish. He clapped his hands and frowned and the room was silent again.

'Okay folks, that's it. Today has proved to me you're not all a bunch of has-been hacks.' He was the only one who laughed.

At last. Rose ran for the street, rehearsing what she would say when she spoke to Susan Hamilton née Abbott.

'Hello, you don't know me but...'
'Hello, I'm Kate's daughter and...'

Her mobile beeped as soon as she got to street level.

'RCN has 3 Susan Hamiltons, 2 at Guy's + 1 at

St Thomas'. Still checking. M.'

Rose sat on a low wall next to a bus stop, a folded newspaper protecting her bottom from the damp, cursing her luck, wondering what unknown factor made Susan Hamilton such a common name amongst nurses in London. Her white silk top was speckled with dots of rain. She knew she shouldn't ring Susan out of the blue, she'd read somewhere that it was a bad idea to contact someone in an adoption search without preparation. So she sat while the bus queue lengthened and shortened, buses came and went, horns blared, brakes squealed, bells dinged, and aeroplanes whined overhead on the approach to London City Airport. The exhaust fumes made her sinuses fizz and bubble. She pressed her fingers around her eyes in an attempt to relieve the pressure, and then dialled ARAP's number. Thank goodness, Bella was there. Quickly she explained her situation.

'Mmm. Well, you need a storyline to explain your enquiries and be plausible, without containing any deliberate lies. Write it down and practise it. Perhaps you're researching your family tree and want to fill in some info about Kate. What her job was like in the Sixties, what her hobbies were, that sort of thing.'

'Why can't I just tell the truth?'

Bella paused before continuing. 'Rose, you'll probably only get one chance to talk to prospective birth relatives and the last thing you want to do is cause distress, fear, or embarrassment. Remember, you don't know the real story of your adoption. You may never know it. This Susan may have been a friend of Kate's, or she may have been involved in some other way with the adoption, in a way that she's now ashamed of, in a way that you can't imagine. Using your storyline means you won't arouse her suspicions at the first step. Believe me, it's worth taking a bit of time to work it out so you sound convincing. This way, no one gets upset.'

'I don't know, I don't like lying.'

'It's not lying, Rose. This is a tried and trusted procedure, recommended by all the adoption agencies. For it to work, though, you need to be able to think on your feet.'

'I'm a journalist, I make my living by thinking on my feet.'

'Yes, Rose, but this is personal. It's different.'

Rose sat on the wall. Bus after bus arrived and departed in front of her, too many. She got the number for Guy's from directory enquiries.

'We've got two Hamiltons. One's in paediatrics, the other is in geriatrics. Which do you want?' asked the switchboard operator with that end-of-shift weariness in her voice.

'I guess paediatrics first please.' Not that it mattered much. Rose waited as the operator transferred her.

'Bagpuss Ward,' said a brisk voice. 'Susie Hamilton? I think she's just left, hold on a mo.'

Rose tapped her fingers and shuffled her feet, looking from left to right in search of distraction. The wait was agony.

'Sorry, she's just gone. Can I take a message?'

'No, thanks. I'll call back.' Rose's stomach hit the pavement. The disappointment was immense, totally out of proportion for the one in three chance of it being the right Susan.

She asked to be put back to the switchboard,

then asked for the second Nurse Susan Hamilton.

'Hello. Guildhall Ward.'

Rose took a deep breath. 'Nurse Hamilton?'

'Speaking.'

'Susan Hamilton?'

'Yees.'

'Oh, hello. I'm sorry to call you at work but this was the only way I could find you. You see, we've never met but you were my aunt's best friend a long time ago. She was Kate Ingram.' She hesitated. 'Do you remember her?'

There was a pause. Rose kicked herself for rushing it.

'You'll have to run that by me again.'

Rose repeated her story.

'No, I'm sorry. This is my first week here, I'm newly qualified. I've never known anyone called Kate Ingram.'

'And your maiden name's not Abbott?'

'I'm not married.'

Rose hung up and was trying to psych herself up to call St Thomas' when the mobile rang.

It was Maggie.

'You're a star, Mags. Thanks for all your help today.' Silence. *Uh-oh.* 'What is it?'

'Oh Rose, I'm sorry. I think I've messed things up.'

Rose took a deep breath. 'Tell me what's happened.'

'I can't.' Maggie was whispering.

'Try.' Rose was trying to keep her voice soft, though it felt as sharp as shark's teeth.

'St Thomas'. For a start, the first switchboard

operator was a real job's worth. You know the type. Put me on hold. You would not believe how long I've spent today listening to Vivaldi. I finally got through to the ward but the sister answered, she didn't like me asking personal questions about her staff and banned me from ringing her ward again. Anyway, to cut a long story short, I'm afraid I rather lost it and rang the Press Office.'

Rose groaned before she could stop herself.

'I spoke to Alan Baring, he's…'

'Yes. I know him.' Boy, did she. There was a slight pause during which Rose felt the signs of a headache starting behind her left eye.

'Well, to get him to help me, I had to tell him rather a lot of the story. He only got interested when I mentioned your name.'

'I bet he did.' Rose groaned again. Alan Baring, assistant press officer, prize git. She pushed aside the memory of the sushi after that press reception, the one where St Thomas' unveiled the opening of its new Davenport Extension, the dancing after the sushi, the sake, the very brief unsatisfactory sex after the dancing, the morning after the very brief sex. Rose had never called the press office at St Thomas' since.

'How much of the story did you tell him?'

Silence.

'Maggie?'

More silence.

'You told him all of it, didn't you?'

'Not all of it, not the bit about Kate dying of an overdose. Something about his name was familiar, and then when he asked how you are these days I remembered you and he… err…'

Shit. 'So what did you say?'

'I told him I'd made a mistake, that I'd rung the wrong hospital. I don't think he believed me, but I hung up and he hasn't rung me back.'

'Well, it could be worse. At least you didn't tell him the name of the nurse you were looking for.'

Silence again.

'Oh Mags, you didn't.'

'I had to. He wouldn't talk to me at all until I gave him a name. I had to tell him it was for a piece in *Xtra* of course; that had him salivating.'

Shit, thought Rose.

Maggie was apologising again with a break in her voice.

Rose took a deep mental breath. Suddenly she felt the lack of sleep last night. 'It's okay, Mags.' Which of course it wasn't. 'I know you didn't do it on purpose.' As soon as Rose pressed the red button on her mobile, it beeped with an incoming text.

'Rosie darling. Understand the hospital can help you search for a long lost relative. Happy to help you anytime. Let's meet for tapas tonight to discuss. Mesón Don Jose. 7.30. Alan.'

She took great pleasure in choosing the delete option on her phone. His text disappeared. Rose was tired and didn't have a clue what to do next. So she continued to sit on the wall as a stream of Number 14s and 53s passed by, and tried to think. An ambulance passed, its siren screaming just as Rose's heart was screaming. Perhaps the best thing to do would be to go home. She could try again tomorrow. Now she felt empty.

She set off towards the DLR station, walking at

her own pace, her feet leaden, her bag heavy in her arms. In the quiet of the lawns and trees surrounding her, the ringing of her mobile sounded like another ambulance siren. The screen on her phone announced Maggie's name. Rose almost pressed 'reject', but couldn't. Maggie was trying to help.

'Mags, leave it, okay?'

'I've found her, Rose, I've found her. I swear I haven't messed it up.'

'How– ouch.' Rose stopped so suddenly, the man following had to swerve to avoid her but the sharp edge of his briefcase caught her knee. She staggered and dropped the phone.

'Watch where you're going. Silly cow.'
Rose retrieved the phone and sat on a nearby bench.

'Rose? Are you there?' Maggie sounded tired too.

'It's all right, someone just bumped into me. I'm fine.' She rubbed her throbbing knee.

'Remember the two nurses at Guy's? Well, I guessed if she worked at Guy's she'd live somewhere nearby. So I rang Directory Enquiries. There are twenty-three Hamiltons in Camberwell but no M's or S's. In Greenwich there are fifteen Hamiltons, no S's. But, two M's that could be Michael. So I phoned them both. The second one was her.'

Rose's heart sank. Maggie had given it all away, she'd done exactly what Bella said not to do. 'What did you say?' She felt rather sick.

'I haven't spoken to her. I know you want to do it. No, I said I was from a market research company researching over-the-counter remedies for the menopause, and wanted to ask the lady of the house a few questions. The man who answered said his wife was on her way home from work, so I asked for a few basic details and said I'd call back at a more convenient time.' Rose marvelled slightly at Maggie's inventiveness.

'She's called Susan, she's fifty-four and has two sons, sixteen and twelve. And she's a paediatric nurse at Guy's Hospital. Bagpuss Ward.'

Rose hardly dared believe it was the right woman. She wrote the phone number on the back of her hand in blue ballpoint pen. She rehearsed her storyline twice in her head, something she never had to do when interviewing someone, and dialled. So much thinking was bad for the nerves.

A woman answered the phone. Her voice sounded tired.

'Susan Hamilton? My name's Rose Haldane, I'm calling about a relation of mine, Kate Ingram.'

There was a silence. Somewhere in the City, a church clock chimed the quarter hour, another to the south followed suit seconds later, the peals in synch as if a conductor cued them in.

Susan took so long to reply, Rose thought she'd hear the next quarter hour chime too. 'Hello?'

'Kate? Of course I remember Kate. How could I forget her?' The voice was quiet now, it sounded younger.

Pure gold. Rose's next words came out in a rush. 'I never met her... I mean... I'm researching our family tree and I wondered... do you think... I could come and see you and talk to you about her?'

'Well, I don't know, this is all rather sudden. What did you say your name was?'

'Rose, Rose Haldane. My parents are John and

326

Diana Haldane.'

'Oh my goodness. Diana Haldane. I haven't heard that name for a long time. Kate's sister.'

'Yes.' Rose paused. 'So, can I meet you?' She felt awkward pushing. She did it every day for work but this was personal.

'I... sure, yes, I guess that's okay.'

'Tonight?' Tonight suddenly seemed soon.

'It's a bit short notice...'

Rose held her breath, trying to do the journalist thing, trying not to think of ways to convince Susan to say yes, trying to be measured and calm like Nick, trying to trust to silence.

'... but I don't see why not.'

Rose's stomach flipped like a pancake.

38 LILY

Lily sat at the kitchen table, surrounded by unopened shopping bags. In the four hours since she'd spoken to Rose, she'd surrendered to another post-William fuck-you flurry of activity. It had consumed her and she'd welcomed it, anything had to be better than the mind-numbing emptiness that had swamped her since she locked her front door with the new key last night. There was a world out there without William, she just had to find a place in it where she might fit.

Sitting on the bus on the way to Richmond to find her new niche in the world, she had found the energy to swear, to swear at William, at Midori-Whatsit, and William again, always at William. She even swore out loud, her mouth shaped in a snarl.

'Fuck you, William. Fuck you.'

But not too loud, because there were two elderly ladies sitting three rows in front of her.

'Fuck you, William,' she said again under her breath and no sooner were the words out of her mouth than the ladies were standing beside her, holding onto the rail, swaying with the motion of the bus, their handbags looped over their arms, waiting to get off at the next stop. She smiled at them, showing rather a lot of teeth.

They smiled back and said 'Good morning.'

She was glad they hadn't heard her say 'fuck'.

She spent up to the limit on the credit card William designated for household expenses. None of her purchases would fit the definition of 'household'. Lily decided her new niche in life was as a single woman, an independent woman like Rose, who would support herself, who would dress and behave appropriately. Single working women, Lily knew from her magazines, did not wear jeans every day like she did.

And I do have a job, she reminded herself firmly. *Nowhere does it say that a single working woman has to have a degree and letters after her name. Good Times may be a part-time job, but I am a single working woman.*

She walked into the first fashion shop she came to that wasn't aimed at people the size of large American fridges, teenagers who never covered up their knees or collarbones, or old people who wore such grey clothes they must be really depressed. She knew from *Stars* magazine that single working women had a specific outfit for each working day, with casual options for various weekend and special occasions. Each set of clothing would be tonally colour co-ordinated, featuring one expensive classic item (watch or handbag, for example) and only one fashion-forward splash (perhaps a brightly coloured top or scarf, a statement necklace, or a particularly aggressive style of heel), something affordable from a high street store. All should be age-appropriate, so no spaghetti straps or racerback tops. A correctly fitting bra should be worn at all times.

For the first hour, shopping proved effective distraction from the whirl of recurring thoughts. *This time yesterday I was doing...*

It's only twenty-three hours since I read Midori-Whatsit's email...
In an hour, it'll be a day since I found out...

Now she sat at the kitchen table looking at the carrier bags, waiting to feel different, waiting to feel like a single woman. The only trouble was, she wasn't single. She opened her purse and emptied out the credit cards. Her name was written along the bottom left of each. 'Mrs Lily Lodge'. Mistaken identity, now she was Lily... what? Certainly not Lily Lodge. Should she revert to Lily Haldane? But when she'd last been Lily Haldane, she was a girl; that would be like moving back in with Dad. She pressed her nail along the ridge of letters at the bottom of the card and a fleck of gold paint flaked off. Lily Babycakes? That made her laugh, though she didn't know why, marital separation wasn't at all funny. But Rose would be proud of her, and that thought made her smile more widely.

She looked at the carrier bags and knew she'd bought them for another person, not for herself. She wasn't a single working woman, chasing career goals, she was a woman with a part-time job who for the first time in her adult life had woken up in an empty bed, a cold uncreased sheet stretching out for yards to her right. Lily had never lived alone, never been without some kind of relationship with a man. These bags didn't belong to her. She picked them up and dumped them in the spare bedroom.

The largest bag fell open, spilling a rainbow of all-in-one suits, tiny socks and white cotton bonnets across the mulberry satin quilted bedspread until the colours spun together in her head into the worst case of colour run her washing machine had ever produced.

331

Slowly she stretched out a hand towards the nearest item. An aqua-and-yellow bib with an embroidered hippo on the front and a speech bubble that said, 'I Love Daddy'. Baby goods manufacturers seemed to be into aqua in a big way. She'd never liked aqua: It was a baby compromise colour like lemon, neither male nor female. With a single sweep of her arm, she pushed all the items back into the bag and added it to the reject pile. She would return it all tomorrow.

A small smile creased her lips at the thought of William opening the next statement, at the look on his face. If she delayed a few days before returning her purchases, with any luck the refunds wouldn't appear until the following month's statement.

She ambled round the empty, oh-so-quiet house. Finding herself in the kitchen, she searched the fridge for something to nibble on. She looked at the dozen eggs, the four-pint bottle of milk, the family-size bag of baking potatoes, the saver pack of Little Gems, the three different kinds of exotic mushrooms and the one kilogram Hereford Beef topside roasting joint she'd bought two days ago for tonight's tea. It'd take her two weeks to eat all that. How did you buy food for one person? William was always hungry, so she'd bought accordingly.

William.

She was still expecting him to call today. Slowly she got everything out of the fridge to make dinner. She had just taken the joint out of its wrapping and set it in a wide roasting tin before she stopped herself. She wouldn't cook a meal for William ever again. Blood oozed from the meat where her fingers had squeezed the flesh, making her feel queasy. She tipped the joint into the bin. She only ate meat because William liked it so much. Perhaps she should go vegetarian; he would hate that.

William.

She felt slightly cheated by his not ringing. She wanted her showdown, felt she deserved it. Rose was the only other soul to know of their split, unless William had told anyone. Midori-Whatsit must know, Lily thought, surely that's where William went last night. But suddenly Lily felt stupid. Midori-Whatsit might be married too. Perhaps her husband was sitting at his kitchen table surrounded by shopping bags, perhaps there was an uneaten beef joint in his fridge too. Or perhaps Mr Midori-Whatsit didn't know yet.

But Lily didn't think William would tell anyone, not yet, he would be ashamed. William didn't like failure. Lily didn't feel in the least bit ashamed, just empty.

Perhaps he'd emailed her. She went upstairs and logged on. There was only an email from Rose, dated yesterday, from the time before she read Midori-Whatsit's email, from the time when she thought she was married.

There were a couple of spelling mistakes in the email, which was not like Rose.

Hi Lil,
Just reading research for my menopause article and aprapently there is a test you can take. Ask your doctor for a Follicular Stimulating Hormone test. Just do it, Lily. It's got to be beter to know. XX

Lily closed the message, logged off and shut down the

computer. It didn't matter now, she didn't care.

Of course you care, you silly mare, said Oprah.

Lily had been hoping Oprah had left with William.

39 ROSE

Nick parked the car outside Number 122 in that irritating way every single one of Rose's boyfriends had of finding a parking space exactly when and where he wanted one. It never happened for her. While he fussed around – finding his mobile, putting his briefcase in the boot – she sat and looked at Susan's front door. Once the paint must have been glossy blue, fresh out of the tin, but now it was faded and peeling. Red geraniums spilled from a pot on the step. It was a welcoming door.

She took a deep breath and opened the car door, just as her phone beeped.

Rose. Got a great idea for your story. How about we reunite you and your relatives for the camera at the hospital? Ciao! Alan.

Ciao! What a git. She deleted the message.

'Ready?' Nick stood by the open car door, his hand held out towards her.

Susan, thought Rose, *I'm actually going to meet Susan.*

Nick's hand rested on her arm. 'Ready?'

Five minutes later, they were sitting on a sofa in a peach living room. Every surface was covered: wicker baskets, cushions, rugs, throws. The cushions looked homemade, all slightly imperfect squares with wobbly seams. Susan was warm and smiley with her blonde highlighted hair tied up in a Croydon facelift. Her husband Michael made a pot of tea and there were chocolate biscuits and homemade iced cherry buns, the like of which Rose had never seen outside Bizzie's kitchen.

Susan didn't seem to think it the slightest bit odd that the niece of the long-dead woman who had been her best friend had turned up out of the blue. 'It's just so lovely to see you,' she kept saying, 'lovely to see you.'

'Please, will you tell me about Kate, and what it was like to live in London in the Sixties? I've only ever seen the Sixties in films, I know it's not like *Austin Powers*.'

Susan smiled. 'It's an awful cliché, but they say if you can remember the Sixties, you weren't really there.'

Everyone laughed and Rose settled back against a cushion embroidered with the words, 'Follow your heart.'

'You know we shared a squat?'

Rose nodded.

'We had a great time in Child Street. We were young and wanted to try everything and we did try a lot of it. But mostly we hung out, got laid, smoked a few joints, drank a lot, and partied every weekend.'

Michael, who sat next to Nick, tutted and shook his head, a broad smile on his face. Rose smiled back. This was a warm house.

'I've never understood why you lived in a squat when you both had jobs.' It was difficult to ask family history-type questions when she wanted to blurt it all out. But a minute nod of Nick's head showed his approval of her tactics.

'Because we could. Because it annoyed our

parents. It was our way of being rebels while being safe, I guess.' She hesitated. 'Kate had some issues about her family. They were… controlling.'

Bizzie, controlling? No, thought Rose, *that can't be right.*

'Her father particularly, he was very… traditional, an upright citizen. Kate told them the squat was a dive to put them off, stop them turning up out of the blue.'

Rose was beginning to think the Ingrams of Kate's youth were just as divisive and dictatorial as the Haldanes of her own childhood. She turned to Nick, wanting to share the exhilaration of discovery with him. He was halfway through eating a cherry bun, a fleck of white icing stuck to the corner of his mouth. She smiled at him and licked her lip, pointing at his mouth, and he delicately whipped the icing away with a flick of his tongue. Rose watched it disappear, holding his gaze for a moment, her mind remembering how she had longed to escape her parents and go to university. Weren't all families like that?

'I get that, I wouldn't have wanted Mum and Dad turning up when I was a student. Embarrassing.' Susan was sitting back in her armchair, a cup of tea balanced on her knee, with that look on her face people get when trying to remember something from way back. She nodded.

'Yes, the squat was just like student digs. We liked it.'

'Tell me about Kate.' Rose leant forwards, the cushion now clasped on her lap. 'What did she like doing, what plays did she act in, who were her friends?' Rose wanted to soak up every tiny scrap of information about Kate, whose personality was coming more into focus with each new fact.

'Goodness, what a lot of questions. Kate was my best friend. For those few years we did everything together. We got into some scrapes, you know, we didn't have much money. I was newly qualified and Kate earned even less than me. But we had a good time.' She sighed. 'We were in London and we thought we were in the centre of the world.'

Rose nodded, remembering how it felt to grow up in the suburbs in sight of the bright lights, but they remained out of reach, so tempting, promising so much, and how she'd felt when she finally got a job in London and started commuting. It had been a rite of passage.

'What was Kate's work like?'

'The company went on tour a lot, but when she was acting here she'd get home from the theatre at about 11.30 after the evening performance. She liked to listen to music, she loved the Beatles. *With a Little Help from My Friends* was her favourite.' Susan hummed it tunelessly. 'We were all friends in the squat, everybody chipped in, helped each other. A bit like a commune I suppose. Kate made chili with a tin of baked beans, Donna was good at sewing, so she made us clothes. Mini-skirts, cotton dresses for the summer.'

'Did you sew too?' asked Nick.

Michael laughed out loud. 'Susie? Fat chance.'

Susan slapped him lightly on the thigh. 'Me? No, I grew potatoes in the back garden, lettuce in the summer. And tomatoes.'

Rose tried to imagine a vegetable patch beside the creaky swing. Chack-ack-ack. 'Do you remember any other people Kate knew at that time?' Really, she meant boyfriends, not people.

Susan described the other people in the squat during the two years she lived there. Some stayed only a few weeks, others were full-time residents. Straight-talking Donna from Barnsley, the dressmaker, lived on the top floor and called a spade a shovel. Millie, the Rolling Stones groupie who hung around Blaise's nightclub in Kensington.

'Why do I know that name?' Nick leant forwards on the sofa. 'Blaise's.'

'Blaise's is where Brian Jones was high on God knows what, and got mistaken for Mick,' said Michael. 'It was all over the papers. There was a court case. It was a big thing at the time.'

'Was Millie there when it happened?' Nick asked Susan.

Rose wished he'd shut up; she didn't want to hear about the Rolling Stones.

'Sure she was,' said Susan, 'but she was washing up in the kitchen so she didn't see anything. Then there was Kate's agent Charlie. He used to come round sometimes with a bottle. He was a maudlin drunk, the people from Kate's rep company were more fun. They'd come round for supper and do little cameos, you know Romeo and Juliet, Amanda and Elyot, Nora and Torvald. Girls played men, men played girls, even the most serious characters seemed funny. They could be quite wicked. Kate did a hilarious Katherine from *Taming of the Shrew*.'

'No one else?' *Perhaps my father was an actor.* Susan shook her head.

It seemed to Rose that Susan's lips tightened a little. *Don't push,* she told herself. *But I want to know*

now.

'Don't forget the neighbours,' Michael nudged his wife.

'Oh yes,' Susan said slowly. 'Yes, one lady was a sweetie. I think she thought we didn't eat properly, sometimes she'd leave us a homemade cake on the doorstep. I guess they didn't have any children of their own, so she sort of adopted us. Her husband was a real grump though.'

'Mrs Gladstone, and the Tylers.'

Susan looked at her with astonishment. 'How on earth do you know about them?'

Rose smiled reassuringly. 'Oh, there are records, archives… these days you can find information about almost anything.'

Susan looked long and hard at Rose. 'You seem to know a lot already.'

Here it was, the chance to come clean. 'I'm sorry. I haven't been entirely truthful with you.'

The smile dissolved from Susan's face. 'You lied.' Her mouth was a pencil-thin line. She stood up. 'I invited you into my home in good faith. What are you doing, getting your kicks out of someone who died a long time ago? Leave poor Kate alone.'

'Sit down, love, hear her out.' Her husband put a hand on her arm but Susan resisted it.

Nick put an arm around Rose's shoulder. 'Susan, please let Rose tell you her story.'

'Perhaps you'd better start by telling me exactly how you've lied to me.' Her voice was tight.

Rose took a very deep breath. 'Susan, did you know that Kate had a baby?'

Susan looked straight down at Rose then, as

340

silence fell over the room, she moved her head the tiniest bit, which Rose took as a nod.

'It's me. I'm Kate's daughter.'

Susan's hands flew to her mouth. 'You're Alanna?'

Rose nodded.

'But your name is Rose. You said – you said your parents were John and Diana Haldane, so I assumed you were their... natural child,' and she cried, 'oh my, oh my... but how... how...'

'How did I find out? You know that Kate's sister, Diana, adopted Alanna? Adopted me,' she corrected herself.

'Diana, yes, yes I knew.' Susan was speaking through her hands. Michael moved to her chair and gently pushed her down so she sat again, then he perched on the chair arm and stroked her hair.

Rose and Nick sat too. One look at him and she knew he really did believe in her, the Rose inside, the one she never showed to anyone else, and this gave her the strength to go on.

She spoke to Susan. 'The first thing they did was change my name.'

'I didn't know.' Susan blew her nose loudly in a white handkerchief. 'Alanna is such a pretty name.'

'After Mum, Diana, died earlier this year, Lily, my sister, and I found a diary. A diary! What a cliché!' She pulled a face at Susan. 'We never knew Mum kept diaries. She wrote in it that she'd adopted me because she couldn't get pregnant. Obviously, it was a shock. I went to see a counsellor who told me my birth mother's name. Katherine Ingram. My Aunt Kate.' She took a deep breath. 'So, I want to know everything about her.

Do I look like her? I've been told that I do, although my hair's short of course, but I think our eyes are similar and…'

'Rose, please. Slow down.' Susan was looking at her with wide eyes, her right arm reaching out towards Rose with her hand held vertical as if signalling 'halt'. But her eyes never left Rose's face. 'When I saw you on the doorstep, it took my breath away. People must have told you how much you look like Kate, you have her hair,' and her hand reached out towards Rose again. 'Oh this is so much to take in.' Michael squeezed her arm.

'Of course it is.' Rose took a deep breath, but her heart pounded hard against her ribcage. 'Take your time.'

Susan let her hand fall to her side. 'You could be Kate's twin sister. But of course I thought… on the doorstep… I thought you were Diana's daughter, Kate's niece, so of course you might look a bit like her.'

Rose smiled, encouraging, wanting more.

'How on earth did you find me?' Susan smiled at the look on her face. 'I mean, not that it's a problem. I'm pleased to see you. And I'll tell you what I can, though I suspect you're not really doing your family tree, are you?'

Rose shook her head guiltily.

'I've often wondered what happened to Alanna. I never saw you when you were born, Kate wasn't allowed to have visitors at the birth and of course you were taken away the next day. The way she described it, that place was Dickensian. But how… it all happened more than thirty years ago…'

'I know how to find people. I'm a journalist. Mum's friend Maureen remembered you first, she found

342

a photo in an old newspaper cutting that described you as a nurse. Then my friend, another journalist, traced you through the Royal College of Nursing.'

'Maureen? Yes, I remember her. She was good to Kate, but Diana... she was something else.' She paused. 'I'm sorry, Rose, of course Diana was your mother.'

Susan paused again and Rose realised she must have taken a sharp intake of breath. 'It's all right, Susan, go on. I want to hear what really happened, what it was like then.'

Rose waited as Susan leant forwards, hands on her knees, her eyes a little glassy, concentrating.

'The mother and baby home told Kate to forget that you existed. But she couldn't. Losing you tore her apart.'

Rose tried to fight back the tears and then, wondering why she was fighting, she gave in. Nick's hand pressed in the middle of her back, the warmth soothed her like a heating pad on a pulled muscle.

'Then Michael got promoted.' She glanced at her husband who smiled at her. 'He asked me to marry him and we moved to Coventry. It was the worst possible timing. I used to ring Kate, but she was never in. I hoped she was working again so I tried not to worry too much. I wrote but she didn't reply. When she died I felt so awful, I'd deserted her just when she needed me. I will always regret not being there for her.'

Michael took Susan's hand. 'I don't think anyone expected her to die, love. It's not your fault.' He looked at Rose.

'No, it isn't,' Rose rushed to agree. 'My family had no idea she was in such trouble either.'

'Where was Rose's father when all this was happening?' Nick asked, and Rose felt eternally grateful to him for saying the 'F' word. 'Why didn't he help? If he put Kate in the position of having to give her baby away he could at least have been there to pick up the pieces.'

'I never knew who the father was. Kate never talked about him. At the time I didn't understood why, but looking back, I'm not sure she knew who he was.' She pulled a face at Rose. 'There were a lot of boyfriends. A Scottish actor, one of her directors, the box office manager at the Royal in Sevenoaks. Quite a few one-night stands.'

'It's okay, go on.' Rose's tears continued to fall. Knowing was better than guessing.

Susan leant forwards and took Rose's hands in hers. Her fingernails were broad and bare of polish, slightly reddened and puckered as if soaked in bleach. 'I'm sorry, Rose. I did ask Kate but she refused to tell me.'

Rose swallowed. 'I understand.' She could hear her voice; it sounded small, disappointed, very young.

'But I can give you something.' Susan jumped up. 'Be back in a minute.' She walked out of the room. Michael followed, muttering something about more tea being needed.

'Michael,' Susan's voice came from the hallway, 'can you get a box out of the attic for me?'

Rose and Nick sat in silence, swaddled by the cushions with wonky seams, as the thumps and bangs of Michael climbing the loft ladder filtered downstairs.

'I will find him,' Rose said to Nick. 'Eventually.'

'If anyone can, you can,' he said, hugging her. Rose rubbed her cheek against the shoulder of his jacket and breathed in the scent of aftershave, London particulates, and warm flesh. Her man.

When Susan walked back into the room, they sprang apart. She was carrying a brown cardboard box. 'This is Kate's stuff. When Donna called me with the news about Kate, I got straight into Michael's car and drove down the M1. I cleared all her personal stuff from her room. I didn't think Diana should have it.' She frowned again. 'Maybe I shouldn't have done that, but I was angry. And anyway, there wasn't much to collect. Kate didn't believe in possessions.'

Rose dropped to her knees and ripped off the packing tape. First out of the box was a pile of purple paisley fabric. Rose grabbed it. 'That's the crinkly skirt she's wearing in my photo.' The bells around the hem tinkled just as she'd known they would.

'Take it,' said Susan. 'It suits you. All of this is yours anyway.'

All three bent over the box and rummaged inside. Next out were a dirty white crocheted blanket and a yellow knitted duck stained with mould.

Rose turned to Nick, her cheeks shiny with tears. She sat, stroking the blanket with a fierce look on her face. *Kate bought these for me.*

Nick laid his hand on her arm, and the weight brought more tears. Rose turned back to the box. There was a battered cardboard CND badge, two turquoise-and-silver rings, a wide blue Perspex bangle, and underneath everything, a black-and-white photograph.

'That's me.' Rose reached for the photo. It was the double of her photo, almost but not quite identical. In

345

Rose's photo, baby Alanna was looking clear-eyed at the camera as if considering the world with wonder. In this one, her eyes were crunched up, as if disapproving of what she saw.

Michael pushed open the door and appeared with a tea tray. 'We all need a sugar hit, I think. Biscuits for everyone,' and he poured the tea while Nick opened a packet of chocolate-chip cookies.

At the bottom of the box was a yellow notebook bound by a blue metal spiral. 'Here.' Susan held it out to Rose. 'This was Kate's diary. I gave her this notebook because I thought it might help her to write down how she was feeling. I read it after she died. I'm sorry, I know I shouldn't have done but I thought it might tell us something about how she died. But it just seemed like a lot of rambling.'

'I thought it was an overdose. Wasn't this police evidence?' asked Nick.

'No. The police had been and gone, the doctor signed the death certificate as 'death by misadventure', and no one else was the slightest bit interested in Kate's possessions. I took it all back to Coventry with me and put it in this box. We've moved house three times since then and the box has always come with us.'

She turned to look at Rose again. 'I found the diary upsetting. I'm not sure it has what you're looking for.'

Rose was still processing the thought that the police had been involved in Kate's death. In that case, there would be records somewhere, though reading a medical report of Kate's death by misadventure with a liver and heart heavily enlarged by drug and alcohol abuse was not something she wanted to do. She received the yellow notebook with palms outstretched as if handling a Ming vase, running her fingers over the cover, down the wire spine. She flicked through the pages and imagined Kate touching the paper, writing the words, trusting it with her secrets. She didn't want to read a single word, not now, not here.

She felt Nick and Susan watching her, waiting for her to say something, anything.

'This is great, Susan,' said Rose. 'Thanks. I'll read it when I get home.'

Susan asked Rose if she'd like her to wash the blanket and the duck, which looked as if they'd been buried at the bottom of an abandoned compost bin. Rose hesitated, wanting to touch what Kate's fingers had touched, then took one sniff and handed the duck to Susan.

She kept the diary on her lap while Nick and Michael drank more tea and talked football, later two teenage boys stuck their heads around the door to ask if they could go to the cinema. Life continued around the Hamiltons while Rose sorted through the box, idly turning the items over in her fingers, imagining Kate doing the same. Picking up one thing, examining it, being distracted by another object and then going back to the beginning and re-examining everything all over again. She pinned the CND badge to the lapel of her jacket. She just wanted to be alone in her thoughts, to read Kate's words. Someone put a Beatles album on softly in the background. She sensed Nick's eyes on her, concerned, and she tried to smile, her hands tightening round the diary as she refused another biscuit.

Susan clutched Rose's arm as she finally got up to leave an hour later. 'Don't think too badly of Kate. Please?'

'I won't, I promise.'

At the door, she handed Rose the cardboard box. Inside were the skirt and the bits and pieces. The blanket and duck, washed, were still warm and slightly damp from the tumble drier.

40 ROSE

They drove straight to Nick's place. It wasn't as they had planned. The giftbox of Biocare Beauty products was still on Rose's desk. Now she wanted to be in her pyjamas, snuggled up on her sofa at home with a mug of cocoa, Kate's diary, and Brad purring in her lap. But Nick's flat was nearer and she could start reading the diary quicker if they went there rather than all the way back to Wimbledon. *But ... Kate's words are The Past,* she told herself firmly as Nick drove over Battersea Bridge. *The diary will still say the same thing in the morning and I'll be the same too. I won't spontaneously change overnight. I'm here with Nick now, and Now is the most important thing.*

Nick pulled up outside the apartment block which Rose had only ever seen at night. This time, she entered through the front door. It was the most stylish bloke's flat she'd ever been in, the most stylish anyone's flat, for that matter. No one she knew lived somewhere like this.

'Can you open the terrace doors, let some air in? I'll have a quick shower, then we can order a takeaway.' Rose felt a sudden need for curry. She fiddled with the lock on the doors, then pulled them back in a concertina and let the warm night air flood in. She stood on the balcony, which seemed bigger than some people's back gardens, then switched her mobile on, hoping to hear from Lily. She leant forwards over the steel balcony rail and, with a sigh, let out the taut breath that she'd held deep inside every single night she'd jogged to the riverside path and looked up at the elegant glass and steel balconies. She couldn't see the black gate from here, nor the tall white wall.

Her phone beeped.

Rose. You're late. Remember you can't meet your birth mother without me. If Xtra doesn't take it, one of the weekly gossips will bite my hand off. More money for us. Think about it. Alan.'

She deleted the message. Another thing to deal with tomorrow. Now she wanted to be with Nick, eat a takeaway curry, just be.

She walked around the living room, stopping at the bookshelf that was crammed with everything from Stephen King, Ian Rankin, Elmore Leonard to, phew, some Hemingway, Beevor, and Greene. James had preferred magazines, the sort with soundbite articles that took thirty seconds to read and required no analysis. Rose preferred her men to be readers.

'I've run a bath for you.'

Rose jumped, her hand on a Cormac McCarthy. Nick stood in the doorway, a towel around his waist, the blond curly hair round his tummy button dark with damp. Rose's stomach fluttered.

'If I order curry now, it'll be here when you're done. What would you like?'

'Something with prawns please. Dupiaza, dhansak, anything.'

She hadn't come equipped to take a bath but found a clean towel folded on a small wooden stool tucked behind the bathroom door.

She swished a squirt of men's action shower gel

under the hot tap and watched as the bubbles foamed, then laid back in the blue water and gave her muscles permission to relax. The bath was a good idea after all. As her body floated, her mind did a triathlon. What was it with the Ingram sisters and diaries? Rose had never considered writing one, which, now she thought about it, was odd given her lifelong desire to be a writer.

She was just reaching for the towel when her mobile rang. Blue water slopped onto the floor as she stood up and extracted her phone from her bag.

'Midori-Whatsit.' It was Lily. 'Her name is Midori Mizuni, I've spoken to her.'

'Wow, Lily.' Rose sat back in the water. Lily seemed to have undergone some sort of character transformation since William's departure. Strong Lily. 'How did you find her?'

'I thought about what you'd do and looked her up online. She has a website about her Japanese lessons. I rang her business number. Well, first I thought I'd send her an email, after all I do have her email address, but it was much better speaking to her.'

'What did you say?'

'I told her he's a liar, a cheat and not to believe a word he's told her.'

'You didn't tell her to fuck off then?'

'No, I said she's welcome to him. Oh yes, and that she'll never really feel secure with him now we all know he's a leaver.'

'Wow, Lily.' Wow exactly. What a way to stitch up the adulterer, bond with his mistress and appeal to her secret fears. Maybe Lily would be fine after all. 'Well done, girl power!'

'I'm celebrating with a glass of wine. I emptied

all William's red wine down the drain, so I bought a wine box today. White wine. William would never let me get one before, he said it was bourgeois.' There was a moment's silence. 'I think I rather like white wine after all.'

Another pause, Rose assumed Lily was drinking.

'Anyway, Midori-Whatsit probably won't get pregnant,' Lily suddenly snickered. 'After all… no woman can get pregnant if their bloke only wants blow jobs.'

'What? He didn't –'

'Yep, he did. I mean, we did do it properly every now and then, but, well, the odds weren't very good were they?'

'Poor Midori-Whatsit,' laughed Rose. *Poor Lily*, she thought.

After they said goodbye, Rose stood up in the water and was towelling herself dry when there was a light knock and Nick put his head around the bathroom door.

'Did I hear your phone?'

Trying to cover herself up and at the same time feeling stupid for wanting to do that, she sat down in the water with a plop. The towel sank into the bath with her, instantly sodden, and water spilled onto the floor.

'Can I help?'

Nick leant forward and fished out the towel. Holding his hand out to her, like a gentleman helping a lady from a car, he paused expectantly. Rose, who hadn't been helped out of the bath since she was six, breathed deeply, and then stood up and took his hand, water running off her silky body like a nymph in a fountain. She didn't feel like a nymph.

'It was Lily.' She'd told Nick the Babycakes story on their way to Susan's earlier.

'Is she okay?' He held on to her hand until she was standing on the bathmat, then passed a warm towel from the radiator.

'I think so.' The towel wasn't really big enough, and she wondered fleetingly if he'd given her a small one on purpose.

'It's okay if you need to go and be with her. Do what you need to do. You're her family, whatever hurts you, hurts her and vice-versa. That's the way love works. If you hurt, I hurt.'

'She's okay, I think, but thanks.' And she wished suddenly she'd had a chance to tell Lily her news; that she'd got Kate's diary, that she was in Nick's bath. She wondered which of the two items was the biggest news. Then she looked at him and he smiled at her so warmly that thoughts of everything except Nick flew from her head.

He closed the door quietly behind him.

He hurts if I hurt. All right, 'hurt' used as a metaphor for love was a bit obtuse but still pretty wonderful. 'Love hurts'. As she stepped from the bath, the song started playing in her head. She remembered a happy trip to Brighton, Jim Capaldi on the radio singing about *Love Hurts,* Mum and Dad singing along, conducted by Rose and Lily from the backseat.
She started to hum.

She had never eaten a takeaway curry with such a view, sitting on the balcony above the Thames with London's lights spread before them. It felt as if they were at the centre of the universe.

'It's easy to forget, isn't it, that we're a small island? Insignificant, in the scheme of things.'

'Rose, my one perfect rose, you'll never be insignificant.'

'No, you've got it wrong, the quote is –'

'Ah yes, the actual line is something about wanting a practical limousine but getting an impractical rose instead. But,' Nick took Rose's hand in his, 'she was wrong.'

'You're a managing director. How come you can quote Dorothy Parker? Is there something about your past you're not telling me?'

'Only a degree in English. Nothing sinister.' He kissed her until her insides dissolved. 'I'll take this rose any day.'

Later in bed, they lay side by side, hands linked. 'Look. We're a perfect match.' Nick held out his outstretched palm. 'We fit exactly.'

She smiled slowly. 'How do you work that out?'
'Because your bottom fits into my hands perfectly. They are the same size. They are meant to be together. It's the 'bum equals hand' ratio. It's scientifically proven.'

'By whom?

'Me. And you.'

'Just think,' mused Rose, 'we could set up a new dating agency. Call it Bum in Hand or The Bottom Hand.'

'Yeah, it'll be really cheap to run, the only information we'll need is the diameter of the man's hand and the dimensions of the girl's bum.'

'We could make our fortunes.'

'Turn over, I just want to double-check our

suitability again.'

Later, Nick's hand was heavy, anchoring her to the bed and to him. She soaked up the new feeling. James had always wanted to sleep curled up together like spoons, every inch of flesh in contact, but it had made her feel claustrophobic and hot. As soon as he fell asleep she would disengage her limbs, roll away from him, and stretch out on the cool empty sheets. Now, though, her limbs felt like molten metal, her brain was wired. She gently lifted Nick's hand and placed it on the sheet, reached into her handbag on the floor at the side of the bed, and pulled out Kate's diary. She shifted her head on the pillow into a puddle of moonlight, and started to read.

Ten minutes later, Nick sat up. 'You can't read in the dark. Here.' He switched on the reading light beside her. 'I'll put the kettle on.' He dropped a kiss on her forehead and disappeared.

She flicked through the pages, reading snippets, hoping something would leap off the page.

'I've just read the bit when Kate finds out she's pregnant,' she said when he returned with two mugs of peppermint tea. 'She sounds so alone.'

Nick lay down and snuggled into her side, his head on her shoulder, his fingers stroking the crease of her groin left smooth by years of waxing. She tried to read but couldn't ignore the caresses. Mug and diary abandoned, she reached down with her left hand, her fingers at full stretch, and pinched Nick's bottom.

'*Pizzicato.*'

'Mmmm,' she nuzzled his collarbone.

'That pinch. It was a little one. *Pizzicato.*'

'I didn't know you spoke Italian.' *Or read poetry.*

'*Cara*, that's Italian for "darling" by the way, actually, my Rose, I had piano lessons until I was fifteen, which means I can speak six words of Italian plus what I've picked up ordering meals in Italian restaurants over the years.' He rolled her over until he was looking down at her, his legs pinning hers to the mattress. '*Pizzicato* is about bottoms, bottom-pinching to be specific.'

'Really?' She stretched out her tongue to lick his shoulder but it wouldn't reach. 'You are a mine of useless information.'

'There are three types of Italian bottom-pinching. Look.' He lightly pinched Rose's bottom. 'That's *pizzicato*. A quick tweak.'

He pinched her again and Rose yelped. 'That, my love, is *vivace*. A multi-fingered pinch. And this,' he pinched for a third time, harder, 'is *sostenuto*.'

With a cry of laughter Rose struggled to free herself but didn't succeed. She wasn't trying hard.

The mugs of tea on the bedside table grew cold.

Ten minutes later, Nick suddenly pushed her away from him. 'Shit.'

'Mmm?' Rose opened her eyes and surfaced with difficulty from the warmth of swirling suspended animation, waiting...

'The condom split. Sorry, love. I don't know how long they've been in that drawer. I should have checked the use-by date. I'm a stupid fuck.'

Rose rubbed her flushed cheeks, then wrapped her arms around him. 'Nick, it's okay. Don't worry. This happened to me once before, it's not a big deal. I'll get a morning-after pill on the way to work tomorrow.'

'Are you sure it's…'

'It's okay, baby. Just a duff one in the packet. Go to sleep.'

As she stroked his hair, Rose listened to his breathing grow slower and heavier. There was a pharmacy opposite the office, she'd go in there before she got her coffee at Café Blanc. Nick snuffled quietly as he dozed. Their lovemaking had been so fifty-fifty. Rose remembered sex with James: she'd felt like a tailor's dummy as he adjusted her legs to suit his objective. With Nick, she forgot her hair made mad by the steam-filled bathroom, her belly, her scar. She ran her finger from his parting down his forehead to the tip of his nose. In the dark of the bedroom the cleft below his nose looked deeper and blacker than ever, a veritable deep sea channel. As she brushed the cherry bow of his lips, he kissed her fingertip.

After thirty minutes of trying to sleep, she pressed her lips lightly to his shoulder, lifted his hand from her hipbone, picked up the diary, and tiptoed into the kitchen.

She started reading nine months before her birthday. The first thing she noticed was Kate's handwriting. Not the neat italic script of her sister, but a loopy style slanting to the left with extravagant tails on the y's and j's and g's, which flicked upwards. Just like Rose's y's and j's and g's.

23 February 1968
I'm definitely pregnant. Fuck knows where Jack is. It's like a scene out of Standing Room Only. *I wish that*

*London production had gone ahead, I'd love to work
with Alan Ayckbourn but no one's going to give me a job
now I'm preggers. It'd be easier to admit to murdering
someone than to say I'm unmarried and pregnant.*

'Jack?' Rose said to the empty kitchen. 'Who's
Jack?'

28 February 1968
*Wore that white dress, the one I got for the wrap party at
Theatre Royal Cardiff, and prayed for my period to
start. Prayed for red in my pants. Told Jack three days
ago and haven't heard a dicky bird from him since.*
1 March 1968
*It's well and truly fixed. The doctor's fingers mauled me
around inside while he put his other hand on the flat of
my stomach and stroked my skin. It gave me the creeps.
Can't face seeing another doctor after him and Susan
said I wouldn't qualify for a legal one anyway as I'm
past 24 weeks and healthy.*
7 March 1968
*Donna introduced me to a friend who used herbs. Day
six of taking dong quai, black cohosh, and vitamin C. I
feel so bad I've had to miss three nights of Titania. I'm
going tonight, no way is that snotty Amelia going to
stand in for me four nights in a row. My head aches as if
someone's hitting it with a hammer… my stomach is
bloated. Is that the baby or is it the herbs? Wish this was
over… it's an Ingram like me, so it's bound to be
stubborn.*

Stubborn, thought Rose. *Me?* And she smiled.

18 April 1968

*Yesterday was awful. Poor Daddy. Was terrified
someone would notice my big stomach but I got there a
bit late and stood at the back. I felt like there was a flag
waving over my head 'I've had sex'. Not appropriate for
a funeral. Thank God it was cold so I kept my coat
buttoned up. But D wasn't fooled. When I told her she
said 'poor Mummy and Daddy', not 'poor Kate'. She
wants it. I've got no choice.*

Oh God, thought Rose. The day of Granddad
Howard's funeral. It tallied with her mother's diary. And
no mention of Jack.

25 June 1968

*Tony Hancock's dead, fancy dying on your own and no
one knowing. That'll never happen to me, D is on the
doorstep practically every day. She even touches my
bump as if it's her own stomach. And the questions! Is it
kicking? Does it hurt? Are you drinking enough water?*

1 August 1968

Went to the Roxy last night to see Burton and Taylor in
Boom. *She was too young to play Sissy and he was too
old to be Angelo. Tennessee Williams must be turning in
his grave. Dreamt I was wearing a diamond ring as big
as the one Burton gave Taylor. Fat chance.*

12 August 1968

*I want my body to be mine again. Smoked a cigarette in
front of D today just to see the look on her face. Too
huge to move, too huge to think, too huge to do anything.*

13 August 1968

D made soup from her Cooking for a Healthy Baby
cookbook. I hate minestrone soup.

14 August 1968
Going to Enfield tomorrow.
15 August 1968
The best thing I can say about the Westmead Home for Naughty Ladies is that D's not here. The nurses are all enthusiastic Women's Institute members, Sunday School teachers every one of them. Not a touch of empathy. I suppose I symbolise everything they hate. The matron talks like Alastair Sim. I practise the accent, just to keep my hand in.
16 August 1968
Brown linoleum floor, beige walls, brown food. Found a library but there's only religious books. I guess magazines are deemed sinful. It's weird, no one speaks. The other two girls in my room spend all their time asleep or pretending to be. Their stomachs are much bigger than mine. Bought a yellow knitted duck and a blanket yesterday on the way here. The duck's in the bedside drawer now.

A loose piece of paper was tucked between the pages. Rose read:

Westmead Home for Ladies – Rules and Regulations
Patients are not allowed to arise before the morning bell at 6.30 a.m.
Lights out at 10 p.m. On no account should lights be turned on between 10 p.m. and 6.30 a.m.
All patients to be addressed by surname only.
Patients may walk to the village between 2 and 4 p.m. on Saturdays, with prior written permission of Matron.
The gardens are out of bounds to patients.
Patients are not allowed to receive incoming or make

outgoing telephone calls. In emergency, apply to
Matron.
No visitors. No exceptions.
Admittance 6 weeks prior to partum, departure 6 weeks
post-partum unless by prior arrangement.

It sounded like something out of *Jane Eyre*. Had she really been born in a place like that?

<u>*17 August 1968*</u>
We're never alone here. The nurses herd us everywhere like cows. To the communal bathroom, to the dining room, to the chapel for prayers. Prayers for forgiveness. Prayers for cleanliness. Isabella I am not; or perhaps I am. 'I had rather give my body than my soul.' What price my soul now? I know what Dad would say if he were alive: that I've let him down, let everyone down. Maybe I have.

<u>*28 August 1968*</u>
D gave a carrycot to Nurse Privet this morning. I'm not supposed to know but Cherry Fawcett in Room 7 saw her. She's going to take it home in a lemon carrycot and play happy families. Well I can play happy too. I'll be a happy, single, fulfilled virgin again. Ha ha. Virgin.

It…

Rose tried to push Kate's words to the back of her mind. *That was the day she gave birth, and she called me 'it'.*

It…

Think about the duck, she told herself, *Kate bought it for me.*

Rose took the duck from the cardboard box, held it close and sniffed, but it smelled of fabric conditioner.

She rubbed the yellow fluff against her cheek and tried hard to find it familiar. Had Alanna even seen the duck? Rose eventually closed the notebook at 4 a.m., poured a glass of water, and climbed into bed beside Nick, the duck clasped in her hand. The thought of Kate dosing herself with herbs made Rose's stomach ache. What must it be like to give up a child? How could a mother ever forget her baby? Surely no mother could. Once she'd acknowledged that truth, Rose knew with complete certainty that Kate never forgot her. She kept the duck, didn't she? And the blanket. She longed to meet Kate, to hold her and be held, to tell her about her life, her secrets, and about Nick. Never again would Rose dismiss her own birthday in her former cavalier fashion.

The light of dawn outlined the gap between blind and wall; the blur of furniture gave shape to the unfamiliar room. Nick stirred in his sleep and rolled over to face her, his cheek squashed into the down pillow. There was another name… Rose studied his face, his lips fluttering with the vaguest hint of a snore. With a wavering finger, she brushed the down on his cheekbone, which was underlined by the stubble below… and remembered her father hugging her, and his stubble scratching her cheek as he'd danced with her, waltzing around with her feet on top of his polished black leather lace-ups to The Temptations. Her dad had always been there for her. His name was hers. Rose felt like a Haldane, she hadn't known anything else.

'You're my little Rosie,' he'd sung, as he swung her around the sitting room, narrowly missing Mum's collection of porcelain shepherdesses, and they giggled together at their naughtiness.

41 ROSE

Nick inched his way into the stream of cars heading east towards Battersea Bridge.

'So, what does the diary say?' He pressed a switch and the roof folded back automatically, the warm morning sun enveloping them.

'She only mentions one boyfriend: Jack.'

Was Jack my father? Kate never wrote that he was, somehow I just assumed.

The weight of her Mulberry tote rested against her feet. Inside lay Kate's diary, half-read. The box of Kate's things was on the back seat. She wanted to read the diary now without distractions, read and not stop until the end, but there would be no chance today. Perhaps tonight, when Nick would be out until late. They'd fallen quickly into a routine where spending each night together seemed natural.

'Sounds like a good lead, honey.'

'Not really. We've been through this, a first name's not enough.'

'You found Susan, didn't you?'

Her mobile rang. It was Sam asking her to go to a press breakfast in Kensington. The reporter who was supposed to go had just rung in sick and it started in twenty minutes. Nick dropped her off and she stood at a crossroads, waiting for a cab. She stood with one hand held out like a flag while she used the other hand to check her mobile for messages.

Rose, The Sun *wants to interview Nurse Hamilton today. 2 p.m. Be there. Alan.*

Alan Baring really was a git! He'd got the wrong Nurse Hamilton. But before she could start formulating a caustic reply, a cab stopped in front of her. Rose sank against the backseat, debating how horrible to be to Alan. Really horrible, just a bit horrible, or business-like? She held her mobile at eye level as looking down to read in cars always made her feel sick, and awkwardly started tapping with her index finger.

Alan. Thx for yr texts. Wrong identity. Wrong hospital. Sorry for wasting your time. Rose.

Next she rang everyone to tell them about finding Kate's diary and ask them about Jack.

Lily almost screamed, 'Nick helped? Oh, Rose, that's great. What was his flat like?'

Her father had just come off the night shift at EazySave and between yawns was monosyllabic. 'Good… fine… fine…'

Maureen didn't know a Jack.

Bizzie thought she remembered Kate mentioning a Jack once or twice. 'Or perhaps it was Jake. He was a director, or an actor. Sorry, dear. That's not very helpful, is it?'

'Never mind, Gran.'

'So so.'

Rose made polite conversation at the press breakfast, which was for a cruise operator promoting a new route around the Barents Sea to observe the effects of global warming. She sat between an expert on sea ice who said nothing, and the hospitality manager for the cruise ship, who outlined to her in great detail his planned seminar programme for the ten-day cruise. Rose ate one croissant and drank three cups of coffee.

A voice startled her out of her reverie. 'Rose, it is Rose from the *Herald*, isn't it?'

Well, that's what it says on the iceberg-shaped name badge stuck to my chest, she wanted to say. 'Yes, that's me,' she said, forcing a friendly smile on to her face.

'Thank Christ you got here. I wasn't sure if Sam would be able to send anyone so I thought I'd better come too. Major advertiser, you know, Serendipity Cruises. Can't have them getting the huff. And there's always a good spread at these do's. Shall we have a Bucks Fizz?' Justin Clarke, the *Herald*'s travel editor, carried on talking, oblivious to the smear of marmalade on his chin.

Rose wondered whether to tell him. Thankful that she had no plans to work in his department, she excused herself. 'Deadline to meet, short-handed in the office, you know how it is,' she smiled.

He topped up her glass. 'Don't worry, I can give you a lift. We'll be back at the office before eleven, quicker than taking the tube. Sam can't be angry with you starting late when you've been helping out another department.'

Can't he?

Justin drove very fast. Rose felt nauseous the whole way and it didn't seem the sort of situation where she could produce peppermint oil. That, combined with the smell of custard creams from Butler's Biscuits which hit her as she opened the car door, forced her to bolt for the ladies' loo. She was, in fact, a little sick. She vowed never to get in a car with Justin Clarke again. She wanted to get upstairs, sit at her desk without being noticed, have a quiet moment or two to breathe deeply, sip water, gather her thoughts, be seen by Sam and hopefully May, and then nip out to the pharmacy.

'Rosalie. Here please.' Sam's voice came from nowhere. Did he have a system of CCTV cameras in reception and the lift so he could see who was coming and going?

'You met Justin didn't you, you clever girl. I suppose you're like all the rest, you want to write for the travel desk more than any other.'

When Sam was in a good mood, he liked to tease, as if bawling someone out then poking fun at them was funny. Rose stretched her mouth into a smile and amazingly, Sam smiled back. He might have CCTV, but he didn't have a sycophancy detector. She smiled wider and revealed her teeth.

'Well don't get your passport out yet, you're not writing anything about Arctic cruises for Justin until you've written 1,000 words about hay fever remedies.' He glanced at the back of an envelope he pulled out of his pocket. 'Non-addictive homeopathic tablets, nasal sprays, air cleansers which remove 99.97% of airborne pollutants in a room. You know the drill. Get on it.'

So Rose got on it. Twenty minutes later, when Sam had returned to his office and was arguing with the crime writer who was sporting a new black eye, she took her chance, grabbed her bag and headed for the loo. She could still smell custard creams, taste custard creams. She had stepped out into the corridor, trying to remember what normal felt like, when she heard

366

someone call her name.

She turned. Frank was mouthing the word, 'Coffee?' She nodded.

'Rose.' May was striding towards her from the opposite end of the corridor. 'A word, please. In here.' Rose's stomach sank. May needs me? Had Frank told her about Nick? Had Sam told her about the drooping penis insult? Was May doing the disciplinary review? She took a deep breath and followed May, who was holding open a door at the end of the corridor, leading into a room Rose had never been in before, a room used for project work and special supplements.

'You've proved that you have an eye for detail and that's what I need now. That, and someone who'll get the job done. Look.' May pointed at three harassed, grey-faced people who were hunched together, staring at a computer screen, shaking their heads, voices raised, hands gesticulating, pointing. 'This is Rob, no Bob... sorry, Bob... from IT, and what's left of the specials team. They're putting together a supplement for Tourism India and they've just managed to delete the entire "final page proof" folder. Everything's gone. Don't ask me how, but the computer bods say the auto backup didn't work as it should have done. And the supplement has to be finalised by 4 p.m. today so it can be printed overnight. We can't afford to miss tomorrow's issue. Tourism India is paying six figures. And the marketing department insists on being involved which, as you will appreciate, is a recipe for delay and disaster.'

Rose identified marketing trainee Emma's blonde head bent over a desk.

'Rose,' May said, nudging her towards the doorway and dropping her voice, 'while I go and murder the person in the IT department who's responsible for backing up files, I need you to go back to the raw copy and sub it all again to length so it'll fit this bog-standard page template. Bob will stick the copy in the page templates, the other two are trainees and don't know a widow from a standfirst. I wouldn't ask, but summer flu's run havoc through the specials team and we're down to a skeleton staff for the daily as it is. They can read and spell; at least, they have degrees, so I assume they can. Perhaps that's not a safe assumption.' She patted Rose's arm and smiled. 'I know you can do it.' Rose grinned back. She couldn't remember smiling at May before and feeling it would be welcomed.

'Oh and Rose, a word in your ear. Be careful of your boyfriend. I wouldn't want you to mess up your career now just for the sake of a nice bum.' With that, May turned and walked away.

Rose turned back to the specials team, who all looked at her expectantly. 'Okay, let's get started. Why don't you all tell me your names and what you're doing? We'll put this thing to bed by four.' While the team introduced themselves, Rose's head swam with implications. The ifs and buts and mights tossed and turned with her fears, twisting around her indignation like dolphins. How did May know about Nick? What did May know about Nick? What was worse, Sam knowing or May knowing?

They worked like Trojans. The words in Kate's diary throbbed inside Rose's bag, demanding to be read, but she turned the other way. A busy mind and a 4 p.m. deadline achieved what no amount of yoga ever could. At four exactly, she walked out of one door across the corridor and into another. The ladies' loo was empty. She breathed deep and tried to forget about India… the Lalitmahj Lake and its flamingos… tigers, elephants, buffalo… black tea, green tea, white tea… cardamom, cumin, cinnamon… Benitlimar Beach's Michelin-starred restaurant… prawn balchao …

She opened the diary. Was she at last going to find out about Jack?

30 August 1968
I couldn't wait to get out of that place, they wittered on so I just packed my bag and left. I'm not ill, just a bit sore, as if I've fallen down a cliff, torn and twisted. Nurse Privet actually tried to stop me at the front door, said I should be there for six weeks. I pushed past her and was standing at the bus stop when she came puffing up and gave me this leaflet.

I don't know if I can face writing anything but the leaflet says it will help, so I will try writing in my diary again. I have to write about how I feel so I can come to terms with what happened and 'move on'. Like I'm a broken-down bus. Susan said to treat it like writing a letter to a friend, a letter I'll never send. I used to be good at composition at school but that was making things up, that was easy. I'm good at imagining, becoming different people, but on these pages I have to be me. I have to write the truth.

I will always remember yesterday. I can feel every contraction, smell every smell, hear the time ticking by, every second, the chime of every quarter hour. When she's thirty and forty and fifty, every birthday I'll remember. I never want to forget.

The leaflet says to 'expel what happened' from my mind.

369

Expel. If I'd wanted to expel her I'd have had an abortion. But I could never do that to my Alanna, I never really meant the herbs to do that. The pain will come in useful, I suppose, if I get a role as a woman who gives her baby to a stranger or whose baby dies. Empathise. Identify. Improvise.

Where to start? She weighed 5lb 3oz and I called her Alanna. The nurse wrapped her up like a loaf of bread in a blanket and held up for me to see, just out of my reach. I could see her, smell her, like full cream milk and the richest honey. Eau de Baby. If I stretched my fingers… almost… I could reach her. That was the first and last time I saw her.

<u>*15 September 1968*</u>

A bad day. Got a letter today from Jack. Says he can't see me any more. As if I hadn't guessed. Donna found me in the kitchen, gave me something to calm me down and it worked for a while, sent me to sleep. Now I want vodka. It's the quickest way to feel nothing. Can't write any more tonight.

<u>*29 September 1968*</u>

Alanna is one month old today. I try to remember her smell, my beautiful Alanna. If I'd known how much this was going to hurt I'd have kept her and survived somehow. I'd have asked Mum for help or Maureen. Why didn't I ask for help? Who cares what people say? Some days I manage to forget for a while, if I don't look at my bedside clock where the yellow duck sits and stares at me. She'll be gurgling now and I'm not there to gurgle back at her. I wish she could hear my voice.

Suddenly Rose wanted the duck, but it was in the cardboard box in Nick's car. It was her only connection with Kate and it belonged with her all the time.

To make things worse, Susan moved to Coventry today. I know she has to be with Michael, but I need her too. Donna gave me some more stuff, stronger than the last lot. I dreamt Alanna was asleep in a cot at the foot of my bed, slept through the night, didn't cry once, my angel, my daughter, my baby. She's so good, so quiet. I listened to her breathing, touched her soft head... but I woke up and she was gone.

<u>10 October 1968</u>

Audition today for chorus in Kiss Me, Kate. *No callback. Charlie's not trying very hard to find me work, perhaps I should get a new agent. He says I'm too scruffy, unfocussed. Of course I'm unfocussed. I used to have a choice, used to have a life, but D's taken it away from me. 'If you really love your baby you'll give him to me' is what she said to me at Dad's funeral. What if I'd said no? I shouldn't have talked to her at all.*

<u>13 November 1968</u>

Last night I was in a dungeon, I could hear crying babies but couldn't find them. There was a long corridor with lots of doors locked with big padlocks, except one at the end which had my name on it in lots of colours swirled together like a raspberry ripple, pink and lavender and yellow and orange. Walked through it and was in my bedroom again cuddled up with Alanna's white blanket, listening to the Stones. But the music wasn't right, it sounded like a nail rattling in an empty tin can. Alanna's smell has gone from the blanket now, but still I wrap the soft crocheted wool around my neck like a scarf before I fall asleep.

<u>22 November 1968</u>
*Charlie's dumped me, the bastard, said he wouldn't put
me up for any more auditions unless I 'sorted myself
out'. Don't give a shit, don't need him, I just need
Alanna. The baby book I got from the library says at
three months old she'll be holding her head up now and
kicking and waving. She'll also be smiling at her
mummy. I'm her mummy, she should be smiling at me.*

Rose stopped reading to dig a tissue out of her
handbag.

15 <u>December 1968</u>
*Bedroom's getting smaller, four walls, trapping me. I
want to be free, want to fly away like the girl in the
Nimble advert 'cept it was my baby who was wrapped up
like a loaf of bread, high above the tangerine trees up to
the marmalade skies, with my head in the clouds...*
<u>19 December 1968</u>
Carol singers called. Donna told them to fuck off.
<u>21 December 1968</u>
*Want to make jammy oat slices for Alanna, like Mum did
for me. The tray's hot out of the oven, blow on it, don't
burn your tongue, it'll spoil your tea but never mind,
don't tell your dad. Cutting the squares in the tin, lifting
the slices out with a spatula and lining them up on the
cooling tray like soldiers saluting, pinching one and
rearranging the rest to hide the gap, except Mum knew,
Mum always knew. But no one knows my secrets now...*
<u>24 December 1968</u>
*It's raining outside, black dark. Horrible faces on the
telly, children not much bigger than Alanna in Biafra
with eyes as big as eggs and bellies as fat as footballs*

and legs like sticks. I can't go out, got no money, got no job, got no baby... Donna's lent me a fiver, said I can pay her back later. If I can't go out this Christmas I'm gonna get hii...

Alanna lay crying in her cot, her tummy like a football, but when I touched her my fingers went straight through her like smoke. I waited but she never came back.... I want to tell her I love her... I've never told her...

31 December 1968

I've let everyone down, I'm a bad mother. Tomorrow is a new year. 1969 will be better, I'll make sure it is. Going to party tonight with Donna. Tomorrow is another day. Scarlett O'Hara, I think. Vivien Leigh, beautiful woman, married Laurence Olivier.

That was the last entry. Kate died on New Year's Day 1969.

42 ROSE

The first thing she did when she surfaced from sleep on Friday morning was to reach for the yellow duck underneath her pillow. It was good to be back in her own bed. Not that the bed at Nick's flat wasn't comfortable, it just wasn't home. It was still early, so she curled on her side and cuddled the duck under her chin, trying to remember Kate's words. Kate died seven weeks before her twenty-second birthday. When Rose was twenty-two she dated junior lawyer Matthew and had her hair permed. If she'd got pregnant then and Matthew had left her, how would she have coped?

She slowly became aware of a heavy warmth next to her in bed, and a hand stroking her lightly along the line of her right thigh. She turned to face Nick, and smiled at the concerned look on his face. Was pain written across her face? It must be, because he hugged her without speaking. She'd sensed him creep into bed beside her at 1 a.m., late home from entertaining an important department store customer, glad she'd given him a spare key, thrilled at what that might mean.

They lay for a while, half-asleep, luxuriating in sharing space, before the alarm went off. Then while Nick went to the bathroom, Rose sat up with the duvet gathered under her chin and flicked through the diary. Poor Kate. She'd been so unlucky and one bad decision had cost her everything. Suddenly Rose was tired of chasing down the minutiae of Kate's life, tired of reading confessions not meant for anyone else's eyes. She closed the book and put it in her bedside drawer.

'I'm almost done here,' Nick called from around the bathroom door. 'I'll make breakfast while you hop in. What do you want?'

'I'm not hungry.' But faced with his scowl she added quietly, 'Muesli please.' She'd never been told off for skipping breakfast before and she wasn't sure she liked it. Being part of a couple could be hard work. She got out of bed and tucked the duck into her handbag. She went through to the kitchen, her kitchen, where a box of muesli stood next to a bowl on the table. Brad mewed to be fed.

'At least you don't tell me what to do,' she said to him as she opened a can of lamb Whiskas.

'It's a bad sign you know.' Nick's voice came from the doorway where he was wrapped in a towel.

Rose jumped. She hadn't heard his footsteps.

'Talking to yourself,' he grinned, '…it's a bad sign.'

He was dripping all over the carpet and in the instant she looked at the beige wool twist with the light grey fleck, the words shot out of her mouth.

'Er, Nick, I've decided to stop. I can't do it any more.'

'Can't…' He stopped towelling his hair. His eyes followed hers to the wet pathway from bathroom door to his feet. 'But we've made great progress over the last couple of days, really great. You're crying less, I'm trying to be less bossy.' And his eyes twinkled. 'Nothing is okay if you really don't fancy muesli.'

Ah, thought Rose, *at least we both recognise our failings even if we can't stop doing them.* But she wasn't going to be put off. She put the spoon down in the tin. Brad looked expectantly at his bowl and mewed.

Rose ignored him. 'I've decided to stop waiting, there's no point. I hate this limbo, this uncertainty.'

'No point? You won't have to wait long.'

'The emotions are too raw and I can't cope...' Brad was winding himself around her ankles now, nudging.

'What?'

She focussed on what she wanted to say, it was important that she said it so he understood. 'I made progress with Susan, but there's no way I'm ever going to find Jack. It's all here,' she picked up Kate's diary and waved it in the air. 'The Swinging Sixties weren't about liberation at all. People were trapped by archaic social expectations and forced into actions because of propriety, and Kate –'

Nick sat down heavily on the stool beside the fridge, breathing heavily, his face stripped of colour.

'What's wrong?' Rose panicked. He looked awful, almost panting in an effort to breathe. 'Are you ill?'

'Whoa, slow down.' He took two deep breaths. 'When you said you wanted to stop and "there's no point"', I thought you meant us. I thought you were dumping me.'

For the first time that morning, Rose looked at Nick properly. He looked stricken. She studied this tall, strong, authoritative managing director and marvelled for the thousandth time that he wanted her. She knelt beside him and took his hand.

'Stupid. I love you.'

'You do?'

She smiled at the wide grin spreading slowly across Nick's face like a ripple across a still pond. Colour was coming back to his cheeks now. It felt good saying it, so she said it again.

'Yes, I do. I love you. I've decided to stop searching for my father. There's nowhere else to look and I've put my life on hold for long enough. Perhaps Lily was right all along, it's not healthy re-living Kate's life like this. It's creepy. I've found out loads about her and it's enough, really, it is. I know my genetic inheritance now. Hey, Brad!'

The cat had jumped up onto the kitchen table and was eating from his half-filled bowl.

'No, Brad, not on the table.' She put his bowl and the half-empty tin on the floor.

Nick didn't speak until she looked up at him. 'What, so you think that we get all our genes from our mothers?'

Rose walked through the revolving doors into reception, breathing in the overly cleansed, highly perfumed air of the two-storey glass lobby. It was preferable to the smell outside: jammie shortbreads were coming off the conveyors at Butler's Biscuits today. It was Friday.

Rose nodded at the squat security man without a neck and headed for the lift, trying to drag her thoughts away from Nick's farewell kisses to today's feature: urinary control. Pelvic floor exercises for men and women. Pilates. Post-pregnancy and prostate cancer. Pads. Pads?

The lift stopped at the fourth floor. May got in with a man in a navy blue suit. She looked stern.

Rose felt a sudden panic. Was the suit from HR? Was he the one who sacked people? Her review wasn't today, was it? As she reached into her bag for her Filofax to check the date, May caught Rose's eye and... winked. May got out at the twelfth floor with the blue suit, leaving Rose wondering if she'd dreamt it. May, winking?

As the lift doors opened on the editorial floor, Sam was hovering in the lift lobby as if waiting for her to arrive. He must have CCTV.

'Rosalie. Can I see you please?'

Rose's stomach twisted. The review.

She dumped her bags beside her desk. The office was empty, it would be thirty minutes before the other journos drifted in. She flicked idly through her pile of post, scouting for interesting-looking invitations, knowing she should go straight to Sam's office, knowing delay would make it worse, but unable to make her feet move.

'Now please.' Sam was standing behind her so she followed him, her heart pounding, trying to rehearse what to say. *I strongly believe my future lies at the* Herald, *I'm an experienced feature writer and excel at challenging interviews.* Interviews: with a pop, a light bulb exploded in her head and she saw Nick's smiling face.

If it comes to a choice between Nick and the Herald, *if Sam issues me with an ultimatum, Nick wins.* Having decided this, she felt a little more confident. *I can succeed without either of them, I don't need either of them, but I do want Nick.*

There were two men already in Sam's office: a stranger, plus the blue-suited guy from the lift.

Oh. My. God. They're definitely from HR, just look at their suits: the sort that hire and fire, blue ties with tiny diamond patterns, safe patterns, more Next or M&S than D&G. Suits to wear when taking a conference call from the States or delivering a complicated presentation on marketing trends and strategies using PowerPoint and a whiteboard. Or sacking someone. But isn't this rather a lot of people for a review?

Sam cleared his throat and smoothed his bald head from back to front. He wasn't wearing a blue suit or tie. 'You know Andrew here, of course,' he said to Rose, waving towards the stranger.

Do I? Then light dawned, ah, Andrew Hollis the business editor who gave her the Nick interview.
Back to Nick again. She smiled at Andrew politely and hoped her face wasn't betraying her thoughts.
Why was Andrew Hollis at her review?

He didn't like the Nick feature. Her heart sank. She had it marked down as a Sevener, maybe an Eighter at a push.

'What you won't know is that Andrew is going to *The Guardian.* Paul, here,' a wave towards the blue-suited guy, who was sitting in the guest chair, 'has been promoted to business editor.'

'Yes, and I'd like you to join my team, Rose. You come very highly recommended.'

'Recommended?'

'I was impressed with that Biocare piece you did for me, Rose,' said Andrew, who perched on the edge of Sam's desk, his long legs stretched out in front of him. If Rose hadn't known otherwise, she'd have guessed this was his office, not Sam's.

'What will I be doing?' 'Would', she kicked herself, she should have said 'would' not 'will.' *Get your grammar right, Haldane.*

'As deputy business editor you'll be my number two,' said Paul.

Deputy, thought Rose. *Wow! Wow!*

'You'll run the business desk on a day-to-day basis, plan content with me, allocate assignments, manage the contributors' budget, brief the junior reporters, choose the lead story, approve headlines...'

'But I want to write,' she blurted, knowing at once that contradicting your new boss was guaranteed not to impress and realising just as quickly that she didn't care.

He nodded. 'Yes I agree. A business journalist who doesn't write can't be in touch with what's happening. You'll need to build up your own contact book. The high bar has just gone higher, Rose. Going forward, my objective is to give *The Times* a run for its money.'

'Great.' She smiled again. *Just do what they expect*, she counselled herself. *Say what they want to hear*. Rose couldn't negotiate her way out of a paper bag, but she knew she should ask about salary or seem weak. This sort of conversation demanded that a certain etiquette be followed or you were quickly labelled as a wuss.

'What's the... er, package?' *Package*, wow was that the wrong word. Pictures of Linford Christie at the Barcelona Olympics ran through her mind, knees lifting high, blue Lycra shorts, his package, er, swinging left and...

'HR will go through that with you,' said Paul.

HR, right. Rose nodded and Linford Christie disappeared.

'But I don't think you'll be disappointed. Sam and I have agreed you can transfer on Monday.'

Monday? This was happening too fast.

Paul stood up and moved to the door. 'Until Monday then, Rose.' He held out his hand.

Rose walked towards him, shook hands, and was back in the corridor five minutes after leaving it. She leant against the wall, feeling chilly, looking out of the window over the roof of Butler's Biscuits. That had been more coronation than interview.

'Don't be stuffy,' she said aloud to the window. 'It's a great opportunity. Don't mess it up.'

She wasn't even sure she'd actually accepted the job. And what about travel? She felt slightly sick.

She turned on her heels and bumped straight into Frank. If she'd seen him in time, she would have ducked into the loo. But he was smiling at her with his cheekie-chappie smile, not the 'come for a drink' sex-god smile, so she smiled back warily.

The door at the end of the corridor clicked shut and Rose caught a glimpse of marketing trainee Emma peeking through the small glass window in its centre. Then she was gone.

'What's the matter, Rose? You look like you've seen a ghost. Has Sam given you another bollocking?'

'I've been promoted to the business desk.'

He was silent for a split second, then he leaned down and kissed her chastely on the cheek. 'Well done. You deserve it. I'm serious. You work much harder than the rest of us. It's about time someone recognised it.'

There was a 'huh' from the other side of the door, and Emma's head re-appeared and disappeared. Rose stared at the place where her head had been, then looked at Frank. He was looking at the same spot.

'Ah, I'll just go and… erm…' He gestured towards the door.

'Sure.' Rose waited for him to disappear through the door, and then followed quietly and peered through the little window. Frank was standing in the cubby hole beside the fire extinguisher, talking to someone, gesticulating in that way he did when arguing a point he thought he was losing. Then Frank bent forwards, turned into the light, and kissed… Emma.

When Frank reappeared at his desk five minutes later, Rose's head was buried in today's edition of the *Herald*. He didn't say anything, and she didn't look up. But her mind was racing. So, Frank and Emma. How long had that been going on? Rose was glad she had never kissed him. But if he had something going with Emma, why did he ask her out for a drink?

She spoke quietly so only he could hear. 'Frank, why are you keeping your thing with Emma secret?' She smiled to soften the shock of her question, and waited patiently as the look of horror on his face finally faded. He stood up and walked round their desks to kneel at the side of her chair, his mouth to her ear. 'Does anyone else suspect?'

Rose looked around the office. No one was taking a blind bit of notice of them. 'I don't think so.'

'May… is Emma's mother.'

'May?' Rose hadn't thought about May's marital status. Only the secretaries talked about family, the journalists had deadlines. For a millisecond, Rose imagined unfolding her birth certificate and seeing May's name there instead of Kate's. Aaagh. She didn't realise she'd groaned aloud.

'Sssh, will you? Before Emma started working here, she got a thirty-minute lecture about not consorting with the bad types in the editorial and sales departments. Emma says her mother's a bit of a dragon.'

And this is news to us?

'So we daren't get caught, but oh, Rose, it's so difficult working in the same office as her and not being able to, to just be us. So I flirted with you as a diversionary tactic. Sorry.'

Rose tried to imagine how she'd cope if Nick worked at Frank's desk and they weren't allowed to speak to each other all day. Torture.

'It's okay. I'm seeing someone anyway, as you very well know.'

He grimaced. 'I'm sorry I was so foul, but I'm getting desperate.'

'Frank it's okay, I was pretty foul to you too. But you must know it's only a matter of time before someone works out about you two.'

'That's why I'm job hunting. Got an interview tomorrow, at *Bolt*.'

Bolt? 'Is that a magazine?'

'No, a website for men aged twenty-five to forty.'

'Is it a job with a salary? Most websites pay tiny fees to freelancers,' she pointed out, resisting the urge to say 'especially websites with names like *Bolt*.'

'I'll be editor. It gets 100,000 hits a day so the advertising is pretty strong. Toiletries, computer games, music, sports gear, online betting, snowboarding, cars.

It's a risk, but worth it if Emma and I can stop sneaking around.'

'Wow, Frank, that sounds great.'

Thirty minutes later, she received a letter and an email. The email was from Sam saying her disciplinary review was cancelled. The letter was signed by the HR manager, the ink was real and the letterhead was corporate. It was a job offer.

She rang Nick. 'They've offered me a ten-grand rise and private health insurance. I'll be in charge of two junior reporters.' *Why am I talking in the future tense rather than the conditional*, she thought. *I haven't accepted it yet, I'm nowhere near accepting it yet.*

'So they liked the way you interviewed me, did they? I have to say I agree with them.'

'No,' Rose laughed, 'it's not like that.'

'Well, I think the occasion demands a posh-frock dinner. Heels, stockings, much pinching later. What do you say, *cara*? Nobu.'

'Great.' She mentally assigned the aqua silk dress, which clung in all the right places, and her gold killer heels. She'd have to leave work early so there'd be time to iron the dress before Nick came round.

She wrote a quick to-do list, top of which was 'write proposal for May', then went back to flicking through today's edition of the *Herald*. Her early menopause article was centre spread. She hadn't expected that, it was her first. By the time she'd written it, she'd been sick to death of the subject but re-reading it now, she realised it was powerful stuff, one of the best things she'd written. And Joan hadn't taken the easy option and used the DNA graphic that 'would do'. She'd chosen a Jacob Maris painting, *A Young Woman Nursing a Baby*, thought to be his wife nursing their first child. Rose made a mental note to buy Joan an extra-large cappuccino with chocolate sprinkles.

She logged onto her email and found forty-three messages in her inbox.

One was from Maggie reminding her they were meeting for lunch later. The second was from *Mother & Baby* magazine commissioning a freelance article on early menopause. The Health Editor of *The Independent* wanted 2,000 words about early menopause. A producer of the BBC 4's weekly *Health Bites* programme was checking her availability to do a ten-minute package for their 'Working Women' slot. Mmm, what if?
And then there were the thirty-nine emails from early menopause sufferers.

Thank you for taking EM seriously. My GP thinks I'm being hysterical. You've convinced me to get a second opinion.

I've never written a thank you letter like this before. Great article. It's made a real difference to me.

I've been trying to get pregnant with no success and I have some of the symptoms you mention in the article. I've made an appointment to see my doctor tomorrow for a Follicular Stimulating Hormone test. Thank you so much.

I had EM but it was spotted in time and I now have a wonderful daughter. Please let your readers know that happy endings are possible.

For the first time, Rose understood what made a Tenner.

43 ROSE

'Here's to the future,' Nick raised his glass to Rose. 'To us.'

'And to escaping the *Herald.*' Rose sipped the champagne, not feeling quite herself. Telling Sam that she was resigning to go freelance had made her feel reckless and lightheaded. She couldn't believe she'd done it, but it felt good so it must be right.

Her aqua silk wrap-over dress was lightweight and seemed to be showing enough cleavage to keep Nick distracted. No one had ever looked at her breasts quite so fondly.

She leant across the table, moved the menus, bottle of soy sauce, and dish of wasabi aside, and took Nick's hand in hers. They were at Nobu. Finally.

'Thank you for all your help and support.' She smiled and hoped her love showed in her eyes.

'It's a big challenge, working for yourself. I know, I started my first business twenty years ago.'

'Doing what?'

'I went backpacking round India, found loads of great stuff. Imported ornate doors, inlaid with brass and mother-of-pearl, made them into coffee tables. I used to go from furniture shop to furniture shop on my motorbike, show them a portfolio, get them to buy a sample and put it in the shop window. I stored the tables in my bedroom, slept on the sofa, worked seven days a week, borrowed a friend's van at weekends to do deliveries. Then I set up a website, a mate did some PR, and a big department store started to stock them. That was the turning point. I sold the company three years later and went on to the next thing. By that time the market was flooded with cheap Indian tables, but I'd learned a lot.'

'Wow, that was really single-minded.'

'You have to be if you're going to work for yourself.'

They sat and smiled at each other, hands clasped between the carefully arranged glasses.

'Sir...madam...' The waiter was hovering.

Hurriedly they looked at their menus.

'We'll have the sashimi to start, and then the black cod,' said Nick.

It was now or never. She couldn't go through the rest of her life allowing him to order her food. 'I'm actually not keen on sashimi, darling.' She smiled at Nick then turned to the waiter. 'The edamame salad to start please, then the black cod.'

As Nick buried his head in the wine list, Rose's mobile rang. Nick grimaced but Rose saw the caller ID and mouthed 'It's Lily' to Nick, who turned back to the waiter.

'Lily, now's not a great time to –'

'Dad's had a heart attack.'

44 LILY

Lily sat in the waiting room next to the soft-drinks
dispenser, which erupted into an asthmatic hum every
ten minutes before shuddering back into silence. She'd
been there forty minutes before Rose arrived with a man.

'What happened, where is he? Is he… all right?'

'He's still alive. He's in surgery. They told me
to wait here.' She started to tell Rose what had
happened. That William had come back without warning
to collect some stuff he said she still had. If she'd known
he was coming she would have gone out, but of course
his key didn't fit any more.

'Perhaps Midori-Whatsit doesn't wash clothes,'
she said, and smiled weakly.

Rose smiled back at her. The man with her
looked puzzled.

'Did you let him in?'

'Of course I did, he's my husband, if only for a
little while longer.' She described how William had
thrown his remaining shirts and shoes into a bag. How
she ripped up her ovulation chart in front of him and he
actually laughed, laughed and said she didn't
understand, didn't know what he wanted, didn't know
what he liked. Then he threw open her scarf drawer,
pulled out armfuls and said he hated them. The hate rose
in Lily's heart as he scattered the scarves around the

room like confetti. She only wore the damned scarves because he bought them for her.

While he went up to the attic, presumably to get his collection of vinyl records, Lily picked scarf after scarf off the floor, carried them downstairs leaving a dripping trail behind her, and threw them on the bonnet of his car. On top she emptied the unopened bottles of exotic perfume he'd given her every birthday even though she only used Penhaligon's Bluebell. She mixed the concoction together, watching the perfume take the shine off the BMW's finish, and then marched down the road towards the bus stop. As soon as she turned the corner and couldn't see their house, she started to cry. She cried for the end of her marriage, in fear of what William might do to the house, and with shock that she had for even a moment been frightened of William, who may be a liar but was a gentle creature. She cried as she waited for the bus and was still crying when she walked up Dad's garden path thirty minutes later. And she cried harder when she found him stretched out on the kitchen floor, his face sweaty and grey, his eyes glazed and unseeing.

She'd managed to stop crying as the ambulance sped through the empty streets, siren blaring, unable to believe that she was sitting there holding her father's cold hand. He'd arrested again in the ambulance and she'd had to squeeze out of the way while they jolted him with a machine. At A&E they'd rushed him away on a trolley and she hadn't seen him since. The tears started again as she sat alone in the Family Room, opposite a tired-looking woman in a faded blue tracksuit who was holding a child's baseball cap and weeping silently.

Tears were catching, like yawns. Lily grasped Rose's left hand, so glad she was here. Tonight Lily hung onto her sister's hand as if it were a life-giving power source.

The waiting time on the A&E department's wall-mounted digital display said 'waiting time 72 minutes'. Nick, whom Rose had introduced as soon as Lily's words dried up, hadn't let go of Rose's right hand since they'd arrived. Perhaps Rose was tapping into his power source. Lily wished a man would hold her hand like that.

No one spoke. There was nothing to say.

It felt to Lily as if she'd been sitting there for days when a doctor came into the room and beckoned them.

'Mrs Lodge? Please come with me.' He was dressed top-to-toe in green; even his face had a green tinge.

Lily had been watching the swing doors where her father had disappeared and stiffened every time a nurse bustled through. Now, she couldn't move. She didn't want to hear, she couldn't hear; she knew what they were going to be told. Rose whispered something in her ear but Lily's ears were full of white noise. So it was just the two of them from now on. To lose Dad so soon after Mum wasn't fair; how could they both leave her? She was all alone now, no William, no baby. Through every argument with William she'd felt reassured that she could always go back home to Dad's. She could sit in the armchair there and smell her mum's perfume, eat her tea sitting in her old chair at the kitchen table, the chair where she'd always sat. But now Dad was gone. At that point, if William had asked if he could come home, she might have said yes. The room shrank, like a balloon with all the air sucked out.

She felt Rose take her firmly by the arm and haul her up out of the chair. They followed the doctor through the swing doors, down a corridor, and round a corner. Their father lay surrounded by machines. He looked insignificant in this high metal bed, his head small on the thin pillow. The sign on the door said 'Coronary High Dependency Unit'. His eyes were closed, his arms punctured by needles, their tubes leading to machines that blinked and beeped. The doctor turned to Lily, his mouth moving, but she heard nothing. He turned to Rose.

He's alive. Lily started to weep, her eyes never leaving the bed. *He's alive*.

'The next few hours are crucial. He must stay calm, it's best if he doesn't speak. If you need anything, I'll be over there.' The doctor disappeared.

A nurse gestured towards a desk in the corner of the room, ringed by computer monitors showing the same digital graphs and charts as the machines surrounding their father.

'Doctor will be around again later.'

Lily stood by the door. She didn't dare look at him. Rose walked towards him, bent over the bed, and then turned back to Lily and held out a hand. Every blink and beep of the machines made Lily's heart beat faster. She took Rose's hand and walked slowly to the foot of the bed. His hands lay at his side on top of the neatly folded sheet. Lily couldn't touch him, she didn't want to feel his skin, which looked ashen. She didn't know what to say to him, she didn't know if he could hear or what Rose expected her to say.

'Do you think he knows we're here?'

'Ssshh.' Rose was stroking her father's hand.

Lily edged closer. The black lines under her father's fingernails were evidence of the morning's trip to the allotment. The veins on the back of his hand were raised and crinkly like a tree trunk, his hands looked old and mortal.

Rose tapped the metal bedpost twice.

Lily looked at her sister. 'Should we do something?' Her hands gripped the metal rail at the foot of the bed so tightly her knuckles were white.

'Ssshh. Nothing. You heard what the doctor said. We just have to wait.'

They waited for what seemed like hours, arms folded, eyes closing occasionally to shut out the flashing lights of the machines, then getting up and prowling aimlessly, the flickering fluorescent tube highlighting the absolute stillness of their father. Lily remembered sitting by her mother's bedside. It had been so different at the end. They had known she was dying so, although there was despair, the shock, the disbelief at sudden death was absent. Lily had held Mum's hand and felt connected with her. Now she felt alone, cold and helpless, and knew Rose was feeling the same. So Lily walked up to her and wrapped her arms around her, hugging and squeezing her until she felt first Rose's muscles relax a little, then her own.

How Lily's head ached. She rested her cheek against the blue silk of Rose's shoulder and let the tears flow again, not knowing where all these tears were coming from. They stood there like one, supporting each other's weight, swaying slightly in the stillness of the room, their heartbeats united with the beeping machines.

'Hell…o.' A hoarse whisper.

Lily and Rose turned as one, still holding on. Their father's eyes opened into narrow slits, and then closed again.

'Oh, Dad,' said Rose. 'It's okay. We're here. You're going to be okay.' She rushed forward and took his hand.

'Lil…..' he whispered.

'Lily's here.'

He didn't open his eyes. Rose gestured to Lily to hold her father's other hand and Lily approached him slowly, unsure.

'My Rose.'

'Yes, Dad. I'm here.' Rose raised her eyebrows at Lily then turned back to her father and smiled widely. Lily thought the smile was a little overdone.

Rose spoke softly into their father's ear. 'The nurse says it's good for you to sleep. We'll be here when you wake up.'

'Rose… don't… Rose…' His whisper was hardly a breath, his words roughened by the oxygen mask he wore.

Rose bent closer. 'What, Dad?' She listened, then gasped, her face going whiter than Lily could have thought possible.

Then his eyes closed, his face relaxed.

'Dad?' Lily rushed to Rose's side, wanting to know, terrified he'd spoken his last words. 'Is he… is he dead? Dad. Dad!'

Rose was holding her father's hand and looking at him as if at a stranger, tears in her eyes now. The last time Lily had seen Rose cry was when she'd fallen out of a tree and broken her leg.

'Dad,' cried Lily.

'That's enough now, let him sleep.' A nurse appeared at Rose's side. 'The sedative has kicked in, he won't wake till morning. This is a critical time and he needs complete rest. You should go home and get some sleep. You can come back at any time tomorrow, normal visiting hours don't apply here.'

He's alive? He's going to be all right? What's happening? Lily's head spun, the room tipped and everything went black.

When she opened her eyes again, Rose was looking down at her. She touched her own face. It was cold, sweaty, she was going to be sick.

'Lily, it's okay, Dad's okay.'
Then Rose burst into tears and Lily cried too. They allowed themselves to be ushered from the room by the nurse. The heavy door closed behind them, the beeps and whines of the machines fell silent.

Lily turned to her sister. 'I thought he was... he was saying goodbye.'

Rose looked as if she was trapped in full-beam headlights. 'He... he said... he's Jack.'

45 ROSE

Nick poured them both a whisky. Rose didn't like whisky.

They were sitting side by side on the sofa. Lily was asleep in Rose's bed after throwing up in the car, Rose's flat was the nearest to the hospital and Nick's priority had been to get both sisters safe and warm. Rose felt numb. She tried to get things straight in her head but it had all happened so quickly. She sipped from the glass Nick gave her. The contents tasted sour and bile rose up her throat. She swallowed hard and pushed the glass away but he picked it up again and made her sip. She sighed, a long sigh that expelled all the stale air from the bottom of her lungs along with all the nagging doubts she'd bottled up since reading the first diary. And she started to sing as warm tears rolled silently down her cheeks.

'You are my little Rosie, Rosie....
And I am your Daddy-o....'

46 NICK

Rose's head fell back against the sofa cushion and she gave a tiny snore. Nick prised the empty glass from her fingers, and then added another inch of whisky to his tumbler. He sat back and looked at her, rolling the green recycled glass in his palm. In sleep her face was softer, the tight lines of the hospital's Family Room melted away. He loved her fierce independence, her self-confidence, her dissimilarity to every clingy girl he had ever known. He wanted to take care of her, to wrap her in his arms and protect her. But he also knew that Rose wanted to fight for herself, and he must let her if they were to have a future together.

There was one big thing about all this family stuff that for him didn't add up. He could understand the deal the sisters made: Kate not being able to support a baby, Diana desperate for one. All that was sad yet feasible. But he couldn't with the biggest stretch of his imagination see why Diana would treat Kate as she wouldn't treat a dog. Nick was an only child and well aware that he had no idea of how a sibling relationship functioned, but it sure as hell didn't function like Diana and Kate's. Had Diana guessed about the affair, was that it? Had she known all along that Rose was John's child? He stood up slowly so as not to disturb Rose, went to her desk and turned on her laptop. His search results ran into the hundreds.

Kate Ingram joined Finance Finders in 2001 as recruitment...

The innovative photographic memory box was designed by Kate Ingram and costs...

Nothing about Katherine Ingram. Daughter of Bizzie and Howard Ingram. Born 20 February 1947. Died 1 January 1969 aged 21. Nothing about a drugs overdose, nothing about the birth of a daughter.
Nick knew Rose had searched online for Kate that night after meeting the adoption advisor, with the same results. Kate had died too young to make it into the web archives. Nick swirled the amber liquid around the glass. It still didn't make sense. Kate existed, she'd been a public figure, an actress, successful, though admittedly not at the Old Vic.

He'd only ever heard her referred to as Kate. Were there other options? He tried again. 'Katherine Ingram' and 'Katie Ingram' yielded the same 128 wrong results. 'Katerina' didn't work either. He tapped in 'Kay Ingram'.

In the blink of an eye, the computer screen filled with a stream of entries including theatre reviews in newspaper archives in places like Burnley, Exeter, and Swansea. *The Importance of Being Earnest, A Taste of Honey, Twelfth Night, An Inspector Calls,* and *Jack and the Beanstalk.*

He clicked on the first result at the top of the list.

Obituary: Kay Ingram

_Richmond-born Kay Ingram, actress and committed
activist, has died at the age of 21._

Her performance as Ruth in Noel Coward's Blithe Spirit
_at the Southampton Mayflower received national critical
acclaim and promised much for the future. Her name
had recently been linked with the role of Ophelia at
Sheffield's Crucible Theatre, and with the lead role in
Georgia Mackay's so far untitled new play to be
directed by John Shawcross at Manchester's Royal
Court Theatre next spring. Kay died at home
unexpectedly last week._

_Born into a middle-class home in 1947, Katherine Jane
Ingram showed an early interest in the theatre by joining
her school drama group. Her first appearance was as
Mustardseed in_ A Midsummer Night's Dream _in 1956.
A project between Lady Grace's Secondary School for
Girls and Richmond Theatre in 1961 brought her to the
attention of writer-in-residence Wallace Costaroli who
wrote a part for her in his play_ Fields of Gold _which ran
for a record 32 weeks._

_Kay joined Surrey Players and was based at Guildford
playing Vladimir in an all-female cast of_ Waiting for
Godot, _Maggie in_ Cat on a Hot Tin Roof, _and Jeanie in_
Hair. _She adopted the stage name 'Kay Ingram' as the
names Kate, Katie, and Katherine Ingram were already
registered with Equity. She joined the actor-owned
cooperative repertory company Onward & Free, and
over the next few years toured the UK. Her free spirit
and candid characterisation made her the darling of up-_

and-coming writers.
After a short sabbatical last year, she was expected to
return to the stage this summer. 'She was our first
choice for Ophelia,' said the Crucible's Jonty Llewellyn.
'She was made for it. I am sorry not to see it.' Her agent
Charles Warren described her as 'luminous but
challenging.'
Richmond & Ham Reporter – 5 January 1969.

Nick scanned the other search results.

<u>*Local protestor Kay Ingram*</u>
Three Richmond demonstrators sit down…actress Kay
Ingram, 18, currently appearing…

<u>*Mayor defiant… Kay Ingram…*</u>
Troops Out march is stopped at first step… Mayor
subsequently refused permission …CND member and
actress Kay Ingram…

<u>*CND election: regional results … Kay Ingram…*</u>
Vote passed… successful actress Kay Ingram was
elected… local spokesperson and…

He started reading again from the top, slowly,
chewing over the sub-text.

'Hey baby. I sincerely hope you're not working.
It's 2 a.m. Time we were both in… Oh.'

Rose's hand grasped his shoulder. He could feel
the edge of her nails. She leant forwards and her hand
covered his on the mouse. He surrendered computer
control and his seat to her, kissed the top of her head,

and went to put on the kettle. Toast might be a good idea too.

47 ROSE

Kay Ingram, who joined CND at the age of 11 and was arrested more than 40 times throughout her years as a demonstrator, died earlier this week aged 21.

Kay, christened Katherine, was forbidden by her parents to join the Aldermaston march in 1959. So she caught a bus to Twickenham to take cakes to the demonstrators spending the night in a church hall. One marcher who tasted the child's lemon cake was EM Forster, author of Howards End *and* A Passage to India, *according to the memoir of Twickenham historian Angharad Beatty.*

Kay longed to join CND. 'I made myself a CND badge out of cardboard and a safety pin and I wore it on my coat every day,' she told The Worker's Bulletin, *many years later. 'The CND organisers in the church hall were very nice to me, they didn't tell me I was too young to understand, instead they made me an honorary member of CND and gave me a proper badge. I still have it today.'*

It was when establishing herself as a young actress that Kay adopted non-violence as the most effective form of protest. She was a regular figure at demonstrations in Surrey and London. She told The Worker's Bulletin *in 1967: 'I wish my family could understand that I'm not trying to upset them or to get myself into trouble, I just want to make the world a better place.'*

Joining a touring theatre company enabled Kay to attend demonstrations around the country, although her main base was in Islington. 'My family still hopes that one day I'll settle down. It's difficult being away from home, especially as my father hasn't been well,' she told Socialist Worker *magazine in 1966. Kay's father, Howard Ingram, was a key figure in Richmond & District Conservatives for 25 years. During her childhood, Kay and elder sister Diana accompanied their father around the streets of Richmond, canvassing for the Tories at local and general elections. Howard Ingram died on 12 April 1968 of a massive coronary, the same day Kay was found guilty of obstruction after a sit-in protest on Westminster Bridge. She was sentenced to five nights in prison. Nearly 200 mourners attended his funeral at St Agnes's, Kingston on 17 April 1968. Kay got out of prison on the morning of 17 April and went straight to the funeral.*

'I come from a suburban family of Tories. Imagine that, me a socialist!' she told Woman's Weekly *in a feature last year about opinionated women.*
The New Socialist – 5 January 1969.

Suddenly Rose had difficulty breathing. Why had no one told her about the stage name?

48 ROSE

They dozed fitfully together on the sofa, her head in his lap. At 7 a.m. Rose heard signs of movement from her bedroom, curtains being drawn, the shower running. Lily was up.

She carefully extracted her hand from Nick's, swung her feet onto the floor, and padded into the kitchen to make coffee for everyone, investigate the possibility of toast, perhaps scrambled eggs. She used the same ground coffee as usual but it smelled different. She went to the cupboard for the Portmeirion mug she used every day, 'Dog Rose', and examined the wings of the bumblebee, delicate like crêpe paper, the black spot on the wild rose's leaves, the brown-speckled delicacy of the butterfly. How could she have forgotten how beautiful the detail was? She'd stopped seeing things, focussing on the things straight in front of her rather than the ones in her peripheral vision. If she'd looked harder she'd have found Jack sooner. And now he was in hospital.

She reached for the telephone, but there was a light tap at her door. On the landing stood Michelle, a large brown paper parcel clutched to her chest.

'This is for you. I owe you a big apology, I've had it quite a few days, sorry about that. Your Auntie Maureen dropped it off, said it was too precious to put in the post. Well you weren't here and I didn't want to leave it on the hall table with the post so I put it in our sideboard out of Lewis's way. But first he had a toothache, then on Monday he started at a new nursery which was rather touch-and-go because they make him eat an apple at lunchtime, then my father got ill so we went to Cirencester to help Mum and… I forgot about it.' Her apologetic smile was stretched tight with anxiety. 'I hope it's not important.'

Rose looked at Michelle and saw a tired woman her own age with whom she'd rather like to become friends.

'Hey, don't worry. It's not urgent. Just a scrapbook with some old family photos. That's all.' And it didn't feel urgent. For the first time in weeks, Rose realised that the stab of urgency she'd got every time she thought of Kate was gone now. She made a quick call to the hospital: John had 'passed a peaceful night'. She poured herself coffee, took mugs to Lily and Nick, and then sat at the kitchen table, the Dog Rose mug and Maureen's package in front of her.
Inside the neatly tied brown paper and string parcel was a short note from Maureen.

Reading this brought Kate back to life for me. I hope you enjoy it too. Love from Maureen.

It was an old-fashioned sort of scrapbook, almost identical to the one Rose had used for a project on Princess Anne and horses which had won her first prize in the craft section of her school summer fete when she was probably ten or eleven, the kind with pages made of stiff multi-coloured card. Now Kate's face

410

shone up at Rose from each page. The newspaper cuttings were stuck in with photo corners and dated from 1956 (Mustardseed, school production, *A Midsummer Night's Dream*) to 1964 (Cariola, *The Duchess of Malfi*, Hounslow Arts Centre). Stuck between the pages were theatre programmes, and stapled to some pages were tickets.

Every single newspaper cutting referred to Kay Ingram.

49 ONE MONTH LATER, JOHN

John stood in the porch, sheltering from the autumnal August breeze, and watched Rose turn the sausages on the barbecue. It was the first time all the family had been to The Weavings since Diana's funeral, and now he wished he'd done something like this sooner. He felt closer to Rose since his heart attack but was scared to push the invisible boundary. Sometimes, when she angled her face like that, he could see Kate in her. He'd spent years denying it, avoiding it, not seeing, but it was obvious. Rose was a fair copy of her mother and the crinkly purple and lilac paisley skirt she was wearing today completed the effect. The tiny bells tinkled as Rose moved and in a flash of memory he knew for sure it was Kate's skirt.

Since his 'event', his heart attack, he'd thought long and hard about what to say to Rose. He'd got a book from the library called *A Little Blessing*. It was supposed to be for parents telling a small child it was adopted and he'd felt rather silly checking it out, but it gave him some useful pointers. He tried to remember them, but his mind was blank.

'Here, Dad, put this scarf over your shoulders. It's come over cloudy and the wind's got an edge to it.'

John allowed himself to be swaddled then took

her hand.

'Sit down, love. Nick'll look after the food. I want to talk to you...' he looked at her pale hand in his wide brown one, 'about, well about everything.'

'Mum?'

'Your mum, yes, and Kate. Oh...I know it probably doesn't seem like it now but we were all trying to do things for the best.'

Where to start? He'd thought about what he wanted to say in terms of the big picture, but hadn't decided on his first sentence. That was a mistake. He remembered the book. 'You were our little blessing. You were the one good thing that came out of the mess, and believe me, Rose, it was a mess.' He sighed, he'd been doing too much of that lately. He reached for the right words.

'We all felt we'd failed. Your mother didn't feel like a proper woman because she couldn't conceive. Kate would have been a pariah. And I let everyone down. But your mum and I, we lied to you. I cheated on her and she lied to me. It just made a bad situation worse.' He sighed and his eyes dropped to the grass.

'So did Mum hate Kate because of your affair? Is that why she wouldn't let Kate see me?' Rose's voice sounded very small, but John saw that the eyes fixed on him were clear and strong.

'No, your mum never knew about Kate and me. Our relationship... no, that's not the right word... our affair didn't last long, a few weeks.' He thought back, remembering the whirlwind when they were together.

'We lived in the now, being together now, we didn't think about next time because that meant admitting there was going to be a time in between when

414

we'd be apart. We never thought about tomorrow, about the outside world. We were each other's world.'

He scratched his ear. 'Huh, that was the trouble really. We never put it into context with the rest of our lives. She was... she... made me feel so alive, but she frightened me too. She was so intense, Rose. You never saw them together, but Kate and Diana were so alike in that.'

'Mum was intense?' Her nose wrinkled with incredulity.

'Oh yes,' John laughed, 'Diana could be intense. It's just that she and Kate were intense about different things. Diana never showed it, but Kate wore it on her face for all to see.'

'It started at *Jack and the Beanstalk,* didn't it?' There was a certainty in Rose's voice.

He gasped. How did she know that?

'Mum had a programme. I was sorting out her stuff again the other day and found it at the bottom of the same box where Lily and I found her diaries. It was ripped in two.'

John looked at her, horrified. Ripped in two? He'd given the programme to Diana when he'd got home, deciding it'd be more suspicious if he didn't mention seeing Kate.

'That's why Kate calls you Jack in her diary, isn't it? Because of *Jack and the Beanstalk.*'

John felt sick. Please let it not be true. He had never wanted Diana to know, had never wanted to hurt her, hurt any of them.

'Dad? You've gone very pale. Do you feel okay? Would you like a glass of water?'

If Diana were here now, he would ask her. He

hoped he would be brave enough to ask. He looked at his daughter. Rose made him feel brave.

'And then she got pregnant,' she prompted. Rose could be relentless, but he knew that. Kate had been too, and Diana.

'Yes.'

'How did you feel?'

How had he felt? John could remember now. Fear, like he'd never been really afraid before. Fear of having to stand by Kate, of having to be with her for the rest of his life. Fear of telling Diana, of losing Diana. He could remember the room they were standing in when Kate told him, her bedroom at the squat: a solid wooden bedstead, thick mattress, blue candlewick bedspread. He could remember what she'd said. 'I've got some news, Jack. I'm pregnant.' She'd started crying and asked him to help her.

But I didn't help, John thought now, *I ran away.* He looked at Rose, waiting patiently.

'Oh Rose, nothing could be worse. I was married. To her sister. It was the Sixties, you didn't have babies out of wedlock then. I was twenty-four, had a job with prospects, your mother and I hadn't been married long. I don't know what I was thinking... I could have lost everything.' *I nearly did lose everything.*

'So you ran away. From Kate, from the baby.'

Her voice was matter-of-fact rather than accusatory, and John was grateful she said 'the baby' and not 'me'. He didn't like to think that the baby was the same person, this wonderful daughter, sitting with him now. He didn't deserve her and she certainly deserved a better father than him.

'I didn't know what to do. That's not an excuse,

416

it's just the truth. I convinced myself she was better off without me. But then Diana said she'd found a baby to adopt.'

'Me.'

'Yes, you.'

Father and daughter exchanged a look full of pain.

'Anyway,' he continued, 'we had to make the best of it, for you. And we did, didn't we?'

'Yes, Dad, you did great.'

John recognised the implication. 'You were Diana's first child. She named you after her favourite flower. And she loved you.' John thought the last sentence sounded too much like an afterthought but it was out there now. 'I think it was more that you were so like Kate, you frightened her.'

'What, she thought I was going to go on demos and get arrested?'

John wondered if he could avoid telling her. But there were too many lies and secrets still lying between them like a brick wall and he had sworn to himself that he would be truthful.

'There's a lot you don't know, Rose. Your mum had two big problems with Kate. She didn't like her politics, and she didn't like the way that affected your Granddad Howard. He involved both girls with his politics when they were little, too little to understand party politics. He was a Tory you know.' He looked at Rose and she nodded. 'They went canvassing with him, knocking on doors, delivering leaflets, that sort of thing. I suppose their job was to look cute. We wouldn't approve of it today, but they enjoyed it when they were little. Your mum carried on helping him for years, she was still doing it when I met her. But Kate, well Kate decided quite young that she wasn't a Tory.'

'I already know about that. She joined CND when she was eleven and went on the Aldermaston marches.'

John looked at her in surprise.

'I read it on the Internet.'

Ah, the Internet. How Kate, who'd been dead for over thirty-five years, could be on the Internet was beyond him. Rose, the journalist, may think she knew all the facts, except she didn't, couldn't, know everything. So he told her. How Diana and Kate fought, physically hitting each other. Neither could remember afterwards who started the name-calling: Diana called Kate a communist; Kate said Diana was too stupid to understand what communism meant. Slapping and pinching followed, and hitting. Punching.

'They didn't speak for years.' John remembered the night, a week before their wedding, when Diana had confessed the real reason why he hadn't yet met his sister-in-law-to-be.

'They actually punched each other?' Rose's mouth was open. 'I can't imagine Mum punching anyone.' As soon as she said it, Rose remembered Mum hitting her legs when she'd been naughty or rude. Not fashionable now of course, but a slap on a child's legs by its mother in the Sixties was common.

'Well, she did.'

'When did they talk again?'

'At Howard's funeral. And then only a few words.'

'But Dad, I still don't understand why they hated each other so much. Why was Mum so horrible to Kate

418

when she was pregnant?' *I can't imagine hating Lily, hitting Lily,* she thought.

John knew the time had come at last to tell her the truth. He had hoped never to tell this story.
'The arguing had gone on for years, and believe me each gave as good as the other. But it all got worse when Howard died. The police arrived at his house one day looking for Kate. Diana was there for tea with her parents. They wanted to arrest Kate in connection with some demonstration on Westminster Bridge. Affray. Assaulting a police officer. They said she was evading arrest. They were threatening, very surly according to your mum. One officer put his foot in the doorway to stop Howard closing it, there was a lot of shouting and pushing and cursing. Well, Howard collapsed with a huge heart attack and was rushed to Kingston Hospital. I rang Kate, I thought she had a right to know about her father. She arrived after he died. Your mother rang the police straight away to tell them where she was. They arrested Kate in A&E, in front of everyone.'

Rose gasped. 'Mum dobbed her in?'

'Yes.' John felt uncomfortable as he always did when he remembered what Diana had done. It made him love her a little less. Diana blamed Kate's selfishness and her politics for their father's death. John had always felt sorry for Kate. In his mind, Howard's death was waiting to happen, such was the diseased state of his heart.

'Diana didn't think Kate was a fit person to have a baby. In her eyes, she was doing us a favour by getting us the baby we couldn't have ourselves, or so she thought,' he rubbed his eyes, 'and she was doing Kate a favour by removing a problem.'

'And what about me... did she think she was doing me a favour too?'

'Oh love, she just wanted to give a tiny baby a proper home. Not like the squat where Kate lived. There wasn't some big ugly plan to undermine her sister or kidnap you. She wanted to give you a life, a happy life.'

'So why was she so strict with me then? She was much stricter with me than with Lily. I suppose she was worried I'd become a teenage mum, or a communist or socialist like Kate?' Rose ran a finger along her eyebrow, he could see her thinking and wanted to stop her jumping to conclusions about Diana, or Kate, but knew she needed to work it out for herself. He would have to try and be patient. Looking at Rose now, waiting for her to spit out her angry words, felt a bit like talking to Kate again after all these years.

'But that was unfair. Mum should have treated me as me, and not pick on me because I reminded her of Kate.'

'Yes, she should, but when emotions run so high, sometimes it's difficult to say the right thing...' John picked at a loose seam on the hem of his shirt, pulling out the frayed ends of cotton and laying them across his knee. Telling the tale had tired him.

'And Mum never told you that I was Kate's daughter? Why not? Where did she say she'd got me from? I mean, obviously you guessed it was me, or did you?'

John sighed, this was where he really didn't want to go. He took a deep breath and prepared for his daughter to hate him.

'Yes, I knew you were Kate's baby, our baby.' He tried to remember how it had all unfolded, but the years of guilt cast a fog, which was difficult to penetrate. 'Love, we all lied to each other. Diana said she'd found you through a local agency who knew a single mother who would be prepared to make an… an arrangement.'

'An agency in Lewisham?' Rose looked him straight in the eyes. 'Grandma Bizzie said that's what Mum told her.'

John nodded, he hadn't known Bizzie knew that. 'Yes, Lewisham.' Even today, he didn't understand what had made Diana say Lewisham. But he'd long ago decided to accept that he would never understand either of the sisters he had loved. Both inspired him, both intimidated him. 'I was a coward. I didn't confront your mum about the holes in her story. And I didn't tell Kate that I couldn't see her any more. I couldn't face it, so I just stopped opening her letters.'

Rose gasped.

John nodded. 'It was a horrible thing to do.'

'But she was waiting for you to help her.'

He was starting to feel sick. This was all going wrong, he'd lost control of the conversation. 'To be honest, Rose, she was too much for me. At first it was exciting, she was so different to your mother. I even went on an anti-Vietnam march with her.'

Rose's eyebrows raised. 'You, married to a born-again Tory?'

'Yes, I know,' and he grinned at Rose who grinned back and the knot in his stomach eased a little. 'But I realised I liked a quiet life, so I ignored her. Let her down lightly, I thought. It was the coward's way out, I know that now. But the baby, you, had been born. Diana was over the moon and… I hoped Kate would get her life back on track. But she rang me at work, wrote letters. It got rather embarrassing, my manager had a word with me about it. So in the end I wrote her a letter saying it had to end.'

'You wrote to her?'

There was disgust in Rose's voice and it mirrored the disgust in his belly.

'I had to do something, there was gossip about it. She kept on writing and leaving messages at work, I'd been so horrible to her I couldn't understand why she still wanted me. And... and I was worried Diana would find out about the affair, so I wrote to Kate to finish it once and for all.'

Rose was staring at him, but he'd started now so he had to tell it all.

'If a man ever behaved like that to you, Rose, I would shoot him.' And suddenly the image of Kate's face in the morgue came back to him. He started to retch.

Rose was on her feet. She turned and walked towards the house.

That's the last I'll see of her, he thought. *She'll never come back now.* He put his head in his hands and rubbed his aching eyes.

A shadow fell over his feet.

Rose was standing there, holding out a book to him. 'How does 15 September sound?' She thrust the book at him. 'Read.'

Kate had sent him postcards at work, postcards from all the far-flung outposts of theatres and anti-whatever demonstrations. And she'd written letters asking for help, asking him to come to her, telling him she'd made an arrangement with Diana, and finally to tell him she'd named their daughter Alanna, that it meant 'beautiful' in Gaelic. He remembered being astonished

422

that Kate knew Gaelic.

He'd kept the letters all these years. When he'd been let go from Woodbright Engineering last month, he found them at the back of his desk drawer. He'd put them in a box and shoved them in the darkest corner of the loft space in a box with his old cricket gear. At the time he'd considered burning them, worried about the girls finding them after he'd gone, but he hadn't been able to make himself destroy something that Kate had touched.

As he read, her words gouged a chasm in his heart.

15 September 1968
A bad day. Got a letter today from Jack. Says he can't see me any more. As if I hadn't guessed. Donna found me in the kitchen, gave me something to calm me down and it worked for a while, sent me to sleep. Now I want vodka. It's the quickest way to feel nothing. Can't write any more tonight.

He didn't know what to say, he could only sob. 'Sorry, sorry, sorry…'

Rose stood in front of him, arms folded, looking just like Diana.

'Donna's the one who supplied Kate with the drugs that killed her, did you know that, Dad? She also bought her the vodka.'

'Oh God,' John rested his head in his hands. He didn't want to meet Rose's eyes, this was why he'd always avoided talking about Kate. 'Rose, I will never forgive myself. I was responsible for her death.' The sobs reared up inside him and he welcomed them, he welcomed the feeling of accepting the shame at last. The brick wall of lies tumbled around his feet.

He felt a soft hand creep into his clenched first, prising his fingers apart.

'Dad, it's okay.'

The warm fingers stroked his cold palm and the image of Kate's dead face started to fade.

'It wasn't your fault she died,' continued Rose. 'Poor Kate. Lots of people got it wrong for her, could have helped her, but she made bad decisions too. At the end of the day we're each responsible for our own life. She didn't have to start taking drugs. If she'd been living in a semi-detached house in Twickenham instead of a squat in Islington, she'd probably have got drunk, gone to a nightclub and shagged some unsuitable blokes, and then moved on.'

'Yes, but…'

'Dad, don't blame yourself. Mum and Kate are gone. It won't help either of them if you let it wreck your own life now. You've had a lucky escape,' she patted his chest, 'and you really need to start living again.'

'Oh love, I've blamed myself for years. A bit of shame now won't kill me. I'm pretty tough, you know.'

Rose smiled, her eyes pink.

John still felt sick. He surreptitiously monitored his pulse but all was normal. And then the smell of sausages blew in on the rising wind and his stomach rumbled.

'Hungry?' laughed Rose. 'Okay, I'll get you a plate.' She jumped to her feet. 'I've never been disappointed that you're my dad.'

'Go, lovely Rose!' said John under his breath as

he watched her retreating back. She looked so like Kate and his heart flipped, as it had flipped every time he'd looked at her as she grew from child to woman, as it flipped every time he'd heard someone say how much she resembled her aunt. Now, every time his heart flipped he thought he was having another heart attack. He had tried so hard to ignore the past, but now accepted he might as well try to ignore gravity.

'Go, lovely Rose –
Tell her that wastes her time and me,
That now she knows,
When I resemble her to thee,
How sweet and fair she seems to be.'

He whispered the Edmund Waller poem without hesitation, pleased he'd remembered it. He'd looked it up in 1968 when Diana chose Rose's name because it was her favourite flower. He loved the name, the child, and the poem.

She was back quickly with a loaded plate.

He took the plate and set it on the grass, then took both her hands in his.

'I messed up the lives of three women. Two of them are gone, but you're here. I'd like to thank you for being my daughter, and to belatedly welcome you to our family. There is a short blessing called the 'Thanksgiving for the Gift of a Child', which is said at the adoption of a child. You were a gift to us all those years ago, and you still are a gift.'

He looked down at their four hands entwined. 'I've talked to the vicar and he suggested it could be held beside Kate's grave. He thinks he met you in the graveyard one day.'

He couldn't read her expression. Her eyes looked far away.

'Here, pumpkin. The vicar gave me this leaflet.' He opened it and pointed at a page. 'This is the prayer I'll say for you.'

'Thanksgiving for the Gift of a Child'
God our creator,
We thank you for the gift of this child,
Entrusted to our care.
May we be patient and understanding,
Ready to guide and to forgive,
So that through our love
She may come to know your love;
Through Jesus Christ our Lord.

'Oh Dad.' Rose knelt and hugged him.

Slowly his muscles unclenched, and her tears spread across his shoulder like a cape.

50 THREE MONTHS LATER, LILY

Lily was watching *Sex and the City.* An advertisement for takeaway pizzas came on. She had an overwhelming craving for a Margherita with extra cheese. She phoned, ordered, paid, and waited for the delivery, all the time feeling naughty. William didn't approve of takeaways. *Why on earth do you feel guilty about pizza? He never felt guilty about cheating on you.* Oprah had taken up residence since the night William left.

The first thing Lily did at 7 a.m. the next morning was throw up. Bad cheese, she thought. To make herself feel better, she cut her hair short and dyed it pink. A new start. Three days later she was sick again. Vomiting virus; she blamed her boss. She was sick on the fourth day, and the fifth; norovirus. On the sixth day she took one sip of her morning cup of coffee and spat it out, it tasted metallic. She wrote 'coffee' on her shopping list, then took a bite of toast. Mmm, it tasted especially good this morning. What had she put…

Lily stared from the open jars to her toast. She'd eaten the holy trinity – honey, Marmite, and peanut butter – and liked it. She checked her diary, but she'd stopped noting her period codes after William left.

She couldn't be, could she?

Of course you are, stupid girl, said Oprah. *It only takes one fuck. It doesn't have to involve a red rose or mind-blowing sex.*

It had been ordinary sex. With William. A bonk-off bonk. Only the once, two months after she'd chucked him out. She hated herself for the weakness but the sex had been amazing, angry almost. She wandered the house, eating the second piece of toast.

'Please,' she said to the wan, pink-haired girl whose reflection in the aluminium-framed mirror in the hall looked like her but was as white as chalk. 'Please, not now. This is all wrong.'

She looked in the mirror again and this time Kate's pale pregnant face looked back. For the first time Lily started to understand the impossible dilemma her aunt had faced. She picked up the phone.

51 ROSE

Rose awoke in bed alone. Nick had made love to her this morning, so early it was still dark, then left for a 'Chemicals in Skincare: the Future is Now' industry conference. She reached for his pillow. It smelled of him, sweet sweat mingled with lavender soap. She breathed him in until her lungs were full of his scent, she closed her eyes and thought of his smiling mouth, the way his lips curved with a slight twist; she tried not to breathe out, not wanting to let him go. Her lungs bursting, she exhaled.

She felt the same today as at this time yesterday, and the day before, and the day before that, going back days and weeks and months to when she and Nick first got together. She did the calculation again and got the same answer: maximum sex, zero contraception, zero conception. She remembered the warmth in Nick's eyes last night when she'd told him of Lily's phone call about toast, and knew what he wanted. Only she didn't want a baby. But she did want Nick. *What was it Grandma Bizzie said, about Mum doing anything to keep Dad?*

Her fingers stretched towards her bedside table for the egg-shaped marbled pebble from the war memorial. It sat next to the double heart-shaped photo frame of her two mothers: Diana in the right-hand side, Kate in the left. It soothed her to stroke the pebble, the cool stone beneath her fingers, the slight sensation of crystal, the veins and wrinkles of grey and white.

She sat up, hugging Nick's pillow to her tummy, aching to tell Diana that she understood.

THE END

ABOUT THE AUTHOR

Born in East Yorkshire, Sandra Danby was a journalist for many years before writing fiction. This is her first novel. Although Rose Haldane in *Ignoring Gravity* is adopted, Sandra Danby isn't.

If you enjoyed reading *Ignoring Gravity* please leave a review at Amazon and Goodreads. Thank you!

To be one of the first to hear when *Connectedness*, the sequel to *Ignoring Gravity*, will be published, sign-up for Sandra Danby's e-newsletter at www.sandradanby.com.

WANT TO KNOW MORE ABOUT ROSE HALDANE?

To find out what makes Rose tick, see photographs of where she lives, read true life adoption stories, discover how 'Ignoring Gravity' was researched, visit www.sandradanby.com

Follow Sandra Danby at:-

Twitter: @SandraDanby

Facebook: www.facebook.com/sandradanbyauthor

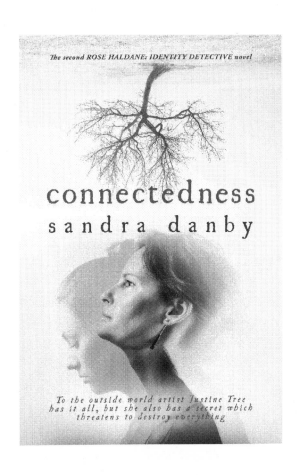

THE 'ROSE HALDANE: IDENTITY
DETECTIVE' SERIES CONTINUES...

Coming soon...

80748987R00264

Made in the USA
Columbia, SC
21 November 2017